SQUALOR, NEW MEXICO

LISETTE BRODEY

SABERLEE BOOKS

Published by
Saberlee Books
Los Angeles, CA
United States of America

saberleebooks@yahoo.com
www.lisettebrodey.com

Copyright: ©1997
First Edition: June 2009
Second Edition: August 2010
Third Edition: September 2013

Copy Editor: Laura Daly
Cover Designer: Lisa McCallum
Extended e-book distribution by Central Avenue Publishing
Book is set in Garamond Premier Pro 12pt. type

ISBN-13: 978-0-9815836-1-7
ISBN-10: 0-9815836-1-X

1. Coming-of-age—Fiction. 2. Family Secrets/Mystery—Fiction.

Printed in the United States of America

To Talatha

for all the gifts she has given me

Baby, you got to – sneak away
Somehow got to lose today.
Need to – elude the masses
Slow down, like sweet molasses and...

Avoid the angered world out there,
Breathe the – cool night air,
I swear, you got to go somewhere...

– Lisette Brodey

Acknowledgments

To Laura Daly, for your expert editing.

To Lisa McCallum, for designing my website (www.lisettebrodey.com) and for creating this fantastic new cover for *Squalor, New Mexico*.

To the following people for their ongoing support and kindness, in both the writing, publication, and promotion of my work: Talatha Allen, Diana Bayer, PattiAnn Cutter, Donna Foley, Michelle Halket, Henry A. Leighton, Jr., Lisa McCallum, Stuart Ross McCallum, Charles Roth, and Sheri A. Wilkinson.

To Charles Roth, without whom none of this would be possible. You are amazing.

To Jean Brodey, my mother, for your love and support. To Dara Brodey, my beautiful niece, just for being you.

There are several more people who have supported me in so many ways. I truly wish it were possible for me to personally thank each and every one of you. I hope you all know who you are. And last, but not least, thank you to all of my fellow authors for your support, advice, inspiration, and friendship.

Praise for Lisette Brodey's *Squalor, New Mexico*

I love this book. It's one of my top five books of all time. The characters were so believable and true to life that I wanted to meet them after I finished the book. I genuinely wanted to see how they were doing.

The reason this book is so powerful is because it offers so many lessons, very subtle lessons — the kind that offer tremendous growth to people of all ages. They are the kind of lessons that kids will learn without knowing there *are* any lessons.

While I wholeheartedly recommend this book for people of both sexes and all ages, I think it's an especially great book for kids and parents to read and discuss. I was particularly impressed by the way the author shows both sides of the parent/child conflict without taking sides. Lisette Brodey writes about a family. Without being preachy, she shows how good people can make bad decisions and stresses the importance of family unity in healing. But that's just the tip of the iceberg. There truly is so much more.

Ward Foley, *Author, "Thank My Lucky Scars"*

A great story of family being your biggest enemy and best friend as well as the gradual discovery of the humanity of parents and the depth of personal responsibility it takes to become an adult.

Christy Leigh Stewart, *Author, "Loath Letters"*

By turns gripping, poignant and wisely funny, author Lisette Brodey has created a narrative with *Squalor, New Mexico* that takes the reader on a ride that emotionally runs the gamut from a compelling coming-of-age story thru an unraveling of family secrets and disclosures that ultimately packs a real emotional wallop. It is a ride I would strongly encourage any reader to take. Be prepared to both laugh and cry as I did, with characters that are both unique and disarmingly real. I found myself in the very capable hands of a writer who imbues her characters with personality traits that feel authentic — namely her very winning heroine by the name of Darla McKendrick, a charismatic and at-times-fearless teen who is possibly the best argument for living a life of integrity that I can think of.

Ms. Brodey offers deep insight into the emotional inner life of Darla, capturing the intensity of a young girl's emergence into early womanhood through a series of circumstances that ultimately test her innocence and belief in what is real and what is lie. I found myself reading late into the night, drawn to the twists in the plot and rooting for Darla every step of the way in a manner that I haven't encountered often in recent fiction. A great read!

Mark Cote, *Singer/Songwriter*

SQUALOR, NEW MEXICO

CHAPTER 1

My aunt Rebecca lived in Squalor. I first heard my mother and my aunt Didi discussing this one day when I was nine. I was supposed to be in my bedroom doing homework, but I snuck down the back stairs into the kitchen for a McIntosh apple and an Oreo cookie. Mom and Aunt Didi were close by in the dining room, huddled together at the corner of the table, as they often were, and they were talking about Aunt Rebecca. To me, the most curious thing about Aunt Rebecca, whom I had never met, was that Mom and Aunt Didi only brought her up when they thought no one was listening.

"I'm sure she's still living in squalor," Aunt Didi told Mom authoritatively. "Unless she's screwed her way out!"

I had no idea what all that meant, but it seemed like such an odd thing to say that I was willing to take the risk of letting my presence be known and ask. "What's squalor, Mom?" I said, walking into the dining room.

"Goodness, Darla!" Mom said putting her hand to her throat. "How long have you been listening?"

"Not long. I just came down for an apple." (I thought it best not to mention the cookie.) "What's squalor, Mom?" I repeated.

Aunt Didi, knowing Mom would be loath to answer my question, took hold of the reins for her. "It's a town in New Mexico, Darla. It's an Indian name."

Mom looked at Aunt Didi in amazement. I figured she hadn't known what it meant, either.

"Oh," I said. And then I took a bite out of my apple.

"You have a book report due tomorrow," Mom said.

"I know," I said, taking another bite.

"Well, you're not going to get it done standing here, are you?"

"I guess not," I replied reluctantly. "All right, I'm going. Mom?"

"Yes, Darla?" she asked impatiently.

"What did Aunt Didi mean about—"

1

"Please dear," Mom pleaded softly. "Go upstairs and finish your—"

"But Mom, I really want to know what—"

"Darla!" Aunt Didi screamed. "Listen to your mother. Go upstairs, now, and finish your book report!"

"All right. Forget it!" I said indignantly. "How am I supposed to learn stuff if I don't ask?"

I walked back through the kitchen to make my way upstairs, mumbling about how I had been treated. I knew that Mom hated being angry and having to raise her voice, but from where I stood that was no reason to slink into passivity and to allow Aunt Didi to do her yelling for her—especially when it was directed at me.

But Mom wasn't the only passive one in the family. Dad very seldom got angry either, and even when he found himself in passionate discord with the rest of the world, he did little or nothing to argue his contrariety. Instead, he just seemed to "go with the flow"—always following someone else's footsteps rather than blazing his own trail. Naturally, he had plenty of opinions to express, but the things he griped about—like dishonest mechanics, rainy weekends, and bad restaurant service—never seemed to hold much importance. Once, I asked him why he didn't scream and yell like other fathers, and he told me that when you yell you lose control, and losing control is a very bad thing to do. Of course, the older I got, the more adept I became at recognizing his anger, as well as his oft-times Herculean efforts to keep it under wraps.

Dad had a penchant for speaking in clichés, which I suppose was a convenient way of acquiescing to "the flow." For him, quoting something that had been said before, meant that he didn't have to worry about holding unpopular or radical opinions. Clichés solved everything for my father. "Well, Darla, to coin an old phrase, you only go around once in life, you know," or "You never have a second chance to make a first impression," and "Well, that's the way the cookie crumbles." I found it strangely fascinating that you only go around once in life, yet what goes around comes around, and that absence makes the heart grow fonder, yet out of sight means out of mind.

Today, with my youth far behind me, I realize that my childhood perceptions, though surprisingly accurate at times, were also severely hampered by my limited time on earth. Observing my father's quintessentially dad-like behavior back then (because of the profound effect it had on me), I assumed that God had repeatedly pressed his dad mold into a giant slab of dough, thus creating an abundance of men just like my father and dispersing them at random throughout the world. Like a baker who has baked too many cookies, God had made too many dads just like mine. They were everywhere: my friends had them for fathers, they appeared on television sitcoms, and they modeled men's clothing in Spiegel catalogs.

My father was a complex man who hid behind a stereotype well into his forties. And even after that, he never really let go of it. For a long time, I was too young to understand the pain that he carried in his baggage. Deathly afraid of confronting his past, he clung tightly to society's perceived notions of fatherhood and husbandhood, obfuscating reality as if doing so would somehow ensure an error-free existence. He seemed content to exclude spontaneity and risk-taking from his life, thereby eliminating a great deal of the reward that can come from living each day like a new adventure. Don't misunderstand me: our home was not without mirth or joy, but most of it was like prescribed medicine, safe if taken in controlled doses. And sadly, my father's fears and regrets were echoed by my mother, only she had the added burden of trying to keep all of our lives free of malice and discontent: as if anyone, no matter how smart or skilled, could really accomplish that.

A real dilemma for Mom was when someone unwittingly asked her a question (especially when Dad was around) that required her to take a stand. No matter how Mom chose to handle the situation, her answers were always very calculated and clichéd, leaving little room for spontaneity or originality. Often afraid of expressing herself, or of discussing matters with me that Dad might not approve of, Mom would preface her remarks with "Between you, me, and the lamppost, Darla," a temporary absolution that would then allow her to proceed with whatever "secret" was on her mind.

Aunt Didi, on the other hand, didn't mind being outspoken or

3

controversial at all, but like Mom and Dad, she didn't reveal a lot about herself or the family.

One night, a few weeks after that day when I had heard Mom and Aunt Didi discussing Aunt Rebecca, my curiosity got the better of me, as it often did. It was a Saturday night, and Aunt Didi and Uncle George had come over for dinner with their three girls. Aunt Didi was in the kitchen helping Mom prepare dinner, and I sat in the living room with Dad, Uncle George, and my cousins. Suddenly, I just had to know, so I said to my father, "How far are we from Squalor, Dad?"

"Just a hop, skip, and a jump if we're not careful, Darla." He laughed. "What kind of thing is that to ask?"

"No really, Dad," I pressed. "How far are we from Squalor?"

"I really don't understand your question, sweetie," he replied in all sincerity.

I was getting frustrated. My voice got louder. "Come on, Dad. How far are we from Squalor? You know, where Aunt Rebecca lives?"

Dad and Uncle George turned quickly to look at each other. And as she seemed to do on so many occasions, Aunt Didi burst forth from the darkness, a virtual Johnny-on-the-trouble spot, to diffuse an unpleasant situation before it got out of control.

"I've explained this to you before, Darla," Aunt Didi said, wiping her hands on her apron. "Squalor is in New Mexico and that's very far away from here."

"Is that why Aunt Rebecca never visits?" I asked. "And how come we never visit her?"

"She lives very far away," she repeated, looking angry and uncomfortable. "Why don't you just forget about Rebecca?"

"But why?" I persisted. "And how come we never talk to her on the phone?"

"Darla," she said impatiently, "there are far more important things for you to concern yourself with than Rebecca."

"Like what?"

Aunt Didi looked despairingly at my father.

"Like...the tickle monster!" Dad shouted as he lurched toward me with his rapidly moving fingers. "The tickle monster is going to get you... and your cousins, too!"

The four of us reacted appropriately and ran screaming out of the room. Dad's quick thinking was an effective, albeit temporary, solution to the problem. But I've always been persistent when I want to know something. An hour later at the dinner table, I had not forgotten my original curiosity.

"I don't understand why Aunt Rebecca can't come visit us," I blurted out loudly.

Uncle George, who had been quiet on the matter up to this point, looked extremely agitated. He was a far less patient man than my father, and when the going got tough for Uncle George, the tickle monster never came to save the day.

"Darla, listen to me," Uncle George barked. "We don't see your aunt Rebecca because, well, as your aunt Didi says, she lives in Squalor, and knowing Rebecca, you can be damn sure there's no way she'll ever get out. That's it now!"

"She could screw her way out!" I said helpfully.

My cousins giggled and covered their mouths.

"Jesus! What's going on here, Maggs?" Dad asked my mother.

"What in the Sam Hill did you tell this kid?" Uncle George asked Aunt Didi.

"Darla, a lady doesn't use those words," Dad admonished me.

"But Aunt Didi—"

"I knew it," Uncle George said, nervously rattling the ice cubes in his glass. "I knew it!"

Aunt Didi remained uncharacteristically quiet.

"Jesus, Maggs," Dad said again.

"Won't everybody please calm down?" Mom asked sweetly.

Aunt Didi rolled her eyes and stuck her chin in the palm of her hand.

"Darla," Mom began, "we all feel very bad that Aunt Rebecca lives so far away—in New Mexico—and it's very upsetting to talk about it, for many reasons. So please, dear, let's forget about it until—"

"Until I'm older?"

"Well, yes," she said, breathing a little easier. "Until you're older."

"Much older," Uncle George mumbled under his breath.

"Okay," I said. "Could you pass the butter, Dad?"

For the next several years, Aunt Rebecca (to coin an old "Dad phrase") was "gone but not forgotten." I was intrigued by this mystery aunt who lived in a place called Squalor, New Mexico, and who nobody wanted to talk about. And she might have stayed "gone" for quite a while longer had it not been for a certain Friday in my seventh-grade American history class. My teacher, Miss Todd, was very excited, she told us, because a very special guest was going to speak to our class. He was a true Native American, and his name was Joe Running Horse. And no, we didn't have to call him Mr. Running Horse. He preferred Joe.

Though more years have now passed than I care to count, I can still feel the passion this man stirred in me, as he stood tall, bright with pride, and told the story of his people, diligently explaining how their land, their language, and their culture had been stolen from them so long ago. I was spellbound by his tales, as were all my classmates, and I remember thinking he must've magically materialized from one of our textbooks, because in "real life" no one could be that awe inspiring. When he was done speaking, Miss Todd announced that we were going to have a question-and-answer period, and that our homework assignment for that weekend was to write a report about what Joe had taught us in class that day.

As usual, Amy Ludwig (Lughead to me) was the first to raise her hand with a question. "Where do most of the Native Americans in this country live today?"

"Excellent question!" said Miss Todd, as she beamed at her prize pupil. "Excellent!" Amy smiled her smug "I'm-so-smart-and-everyone-knows-it" smile, and all eyes turned to Joe. I felt like throwing up. I hated her.

It was then that the inevitable happened. Within moments, a

discussion about New Mexico ensued. "Who can name a town or city in New Mexico?" Miss Todd asked, her eyes scanning the classroom for volunteers.

The Lughead's hand shot into the air like a rocket taking off. "I can, Miss Todd. There's Albuquerque, Santa Fe, and Gallup, to name three." It was just like the Lughead to give all the answers so no one else had a chance to look good for the teacher.

I raised my hand and glared at her.

"Yes, Darla." Miss Todd smiled. "Can you add to that?"

"I have an aunt who lives in Squalor!" I said proudly, looking right into the Lughead's eyes.

The Lughead broke into a broad grin and put her hand over her mouth. Someone giggled softly behind me and Miss Todd and Joe looked at each other, then briefly at the floor. I felt absolutely sick inside and had no idea why. I knew the mention of Aunt Rebecca had a strange effect on the adults in my family, but on the Lughead, Miss Todd, and Joe Running Horse? What could they possibly know about her? I half expected Aunt Didi to come barreling into the room and demand that the subject be changed. But instead, a loud hush fell over the room, one that was far more intimidating than anything my aunt had ever said or done to shut me up in the past.

"Thank you, Darla," Miss Todd finally said. "Now, who else has a question for Mr. Running Horse?" (Her sudden formality seemed to match the somber tone in the air.)

The subject quickly changed to Arizona, but the remaining ten minutes of class felt like an eternity. To this day, I thank God that it was the last class of the afternoon. I could not have endured another moment of school. I was humiliated, and even more so because I didn't understand what had happened. I was just desperate to get home and confront my mother. I practically tripped on my own two feet when the bell rang, trying to get out of class, but Miss Todd asked me to stay behind a moment. I was so upset that I could barely focus on what she was saying to me. I felt as if I were hopelessly caught in a nightmare, and I could hear the Lughead's laughter echoing in the hallways of my mind. The room

7

looked as if it were melting, like Aunt Didi's ugly "Candle of 100 Colors" from Greenwich Village (probably a fake place, too), and Miss Todd's voice sounded faint and far away. All I can remember was when she said, "You'll find 'squalor' in the dictionary, Darla, not on a map of the United States. I think it would be a good idea to go home and look it up."

I always took the bus home, but that day I ran home instead. I couldn't bear to be trapped on the bus (it might be melting, too), and even though running would take me longer, I would be free. I was filled with rage toward my weak mother and my take-charge aunt.

Mom was unpacking groceries when I came flying through the back door.

"Darla!" she said, hugging me with a box of Uncle Ben's converted rice still in her hands. "Are you all right? I was so worried about you when you didn't get off the bus with the others. You look sick."

"I am sick!" I screamed. "And it's all your fault, and Aunt Didi's too! Where's the damn dictionary?"

"Darla!"

"Never mind. I'll find it myself!" I screamed, and went running into the family room. I grabbed my father's dictionary off the shelf (I still had only a kid's dictionary with big, goofy pictures) and practically tore the pages until I got to S. And then I read: "Squalor: the act of being squalid." What the hell did that mean? "Squalid: foul and repulsive, as from lack of care or cleanliness; dirty from neglect; wretched, sordid." At that moment, I plunged into a self-deprecating hell. All my thoughts raced toward the Lughead. I thought about the way I had beamed with pride, when I looked right at her and said those dreaded words: "My aunt lives in Squalor." I couldn't stop beating myself up, pummeling my self-esteem with every admonishment my adolescent brain could summon. I was the worst kind of idiot. I should be excommunicated from the planet! From the universe! What a fool! I was finally going to show the Lughead up, once and for all, and it turned out to be the most embarrassing, humiliating, horrible day of my thirteen years on this earth. This horrible earth! Why was I born? Why had Aunt Didi and Mom been lying to me all these years? Why did Dad and Uncle George go along with it? Damn them! Why did they lie?

I threw Dad's dictionary on the floor, flung myself on the couch, buried my head in a throw pillow, and began sobbing. More deplorable thoughts squeezed their way into my head. By the ripe old age of thirteen, I had learned (without the aid of a dictionary) what "screw" meant, but until that moment, I hadn't thought about my comment that night at dinner, when I was nine: "She could screw her way out!" The pieces were all coming together and getting uglier all the time. What an idiot I was at nine. What an idiot I still was. Even my cousins had known what "screw" meant! I couldn't think anymore. My brain hurt. I sobbed uncontrollably. My mother sat next to me on the couch and put her arms around me. When I looked up, I saw she was crying. (I had asked her later how she could cry when she didn't know what was wrong, and she explained that when you see your child in such dreadful pain, the reason doesn't matter. You just want to cry too.)

It took Mom a long time to calm me down. I didn't want to calm down. I wanted to torture myself with tears forever. I deserved it. When I was finally able to tell Mom what had happened, she turned white as a sheet and put her right hand to her throat. Then she moved her hand to her forehead, closed her eyes momentarily, and heaved a heavy sigh. When she was finished doing that, she put her left hand to her throat and sighed again. Then she looked down at her lap, nodded her head slowly, and sighed again. Suddenly, in a surprise move, which I had never seen before, she hit herself on the forehead with her right hand and sighed the loudest sigh I'd ever heard. It was a beautiful bouquet of gestures, but I was growing impatient. Was she going to say something? Was she going to slap her forehead with her left hand now?

"Goodness, Darla," came the long-anticipated response. "Goodness gracious, my poor child. I'm so terribly sorry. I really truly sincerely am." When she had finished using every "ly" word in her vocabulary, she clasped her hands over mine. "What can I do to make it better?"

"Mom," I said frustrated, breaking her grip. "Why did everyone lie to me? Why did you let me exist on this planet for four whole years thinking Squalor was a town in New Mexico—and that Aunt Rebecca lived there? Why, Mom? Why did Aunt Didi tell me that? Why doesn't anyone see Rebecca, or talk about her?"

It was then, at that precise moment, that Mom began her most famous "lamppost" talk of all. And in typical Mom fashion, she kept glancing at the door for my father to come in, despite the fact that he wasn't due home for hours.

"Darla—" she began in a near whisper. "I know you've been wondering about your aunt Rebecca for a very long time now. I'm sorry that we've had to keep the truth from you, and even more sorry that the little white lie your aunt Didi told you so many years ago has come back to hurt you so deeply today."

I listened patiently, but I was wondering when she was going to tell me something that I didn't already know.

"We all love you and would never do anything intentionally to hurt you. Goodness, child, you know that, don't you?"

I was losing my patience. "Tell me about Aunt Rebecca, Mom. Now! I'm old enough to know." (I wanted to throw a "damn it" in there for good measure, but I'd already gotten away with saying "damn" and didn't want to press my luck.)

"All right, Darla," Mom said. "But it'll have to stay between you, me, and the lamppost. Okay?"

I knew the routine by heart. "Yes, Mom. I promise."

She paused for quite a while before continuing. "Your aunt Rebecca was always a problem child. Goodness knows why. She was raised the same way as Didi and I were. But although Rebecca is only four years younger than I am, and five years younger than Didi, it has always seemed as though she were raised in an entirely different generation—in a different place altogether. Different standards, different tastes in clothing, in friends, and even in music. And she never minded your grandparents the way Didi and I did. By the time she was eleven she had the filthiest vocabulary you ever heard."

I suddenly wasn't as proud of my "damn" as I had been five minutes ago, but I still didn't understand what made Rebecca so different from other eleven-year-olds.

10

"By the time Rebecca was thirteen," Mom choked, "things really got bad. She was smoking, drinking, and staying out until all hours. When she was seventeen, she dropped out of her senior year of high school and started doing drugs."

At that point in Mom's speech, despite the wretched pain we were both in, I was dying to burst out with a chorus of "When I Was Seventeen," just like Frank Sinatra sang it on Dad's record album, but for reasons too obvious and too numerous to mention, I didn't.

"Your grandparents were heartbroken, Darla. They did everything they could to help her. Even your grandpa's brother, my uncle Martin, who never did much for anyone, tried to help, but that only seemed to make things worse. One day he came over to talk to her, and Rebecca started cursing him and threatening to kill herself. It was horrid. She simply wanted nothing to do with any authority figure at all. Mom and Dad were frantic. They spoke to school counselors, police officers, psychiatrists—you name it. They even sent her to therapy, but she clammed up and wouldn't talk. Finally, when nothing worked, they put her in a detox unit, but after only a week and a half, Rebecca ran away. I was the one who found her. That very same day."

"Where was she?" I asked, mesmerized by Mom's strange tale.

"At her boyfriend's house. Or at least he was one of them!" Mom said in a surprisingly judgmental tone. "He was a college boy, but he was no good. He was as shady as that old oak tree in our backyard." (I hadn't heard that one before.) "Word had it around town that he sold drugs," Mom told me confidentially, surprising even herself. She looked cautiously toward the door. "Now, remember, Darla. This conversation is between you and me, and the lamppost."

"So what happened then?" I asked eagerly.

"Well, dear, Rebecca went back to the detox unit, but this time she stayed only a couple of days. She had no interest in being rehabilitated, and the director of the place told your grandfather that they were there to help people with drug problems, not to play prison guard, and that there was no point in bringing Rebecca back if she was just going to run away again."

11

Mom sighed, fluttered her eyelids, and looked toward the door. She looked at me and then looked at the door again. She checked her watch. I knew the "good stuff" must be coming, or at least the part of it that she would be willing to share.

"Goodness. This is so difficult," she said, looking around the room, as if doing so would help her to gather strength.

Suddenly, I saw a door slamming shut on the truth. "Don't you think I'm old enough to know all this? I was old enough to be publicly humiliated today!" I bravely reminded her.

"Yes, that's true. You're right. And you are old enough to hear this." She paused again, then blurted out, "Darla, shortly after Rebecca ran away for the second time, we found out that she had left town with a man."

"With that 'shady college boy'?" I asked enthusiastically, completely forgetting that I wasn't supposed to be enjoying this story.

"Yes," she said uncomfortably. She left with him and they went to another state."

"New Mexico?"

"No, dear. New York."

I suddenly felt like an idiot again.

"She ran away to New York City. But she didn't stay with the college boy for long. He came back here, and Rebecca moved into a horrible place with an awful man she had met God-knows-where and—this is very painful to talk about."

"I know, Mom," I said sympathetically. I prayed that she would continue with her story, even though I could see that telling it was taking a great toll on her.

"Darla, it was a wretched place. She lived in squalor." (After hearing the word used incorrectly for four years, the correct usage sounded so odd to me.) "It was a one-room tenement on the Lower East Side of Manhattan. The furniture, what little of it she had, was no doubt collected from the garbage—dirty, dusty, and downright dilapidated—oh, it was just plain hideous. The paint was peeling badly, and in some places, parts of the wall were missing altogether. The bathroom was unspeakable, and there was no kitchen. Only a hot plate, an old junky refrigerator barely larger than a bread box, and cold running water. The place was frightful—filled with rusted pipes, rotting food, and every kind of insect, vermin, and rodent known to mankind."

I was amazed by this revelation. "Eeewww. Gross! How disgusting! Were you there? Did you see it?"

"Yes. Your aunt Didi and I went to New York to try and bring her back."

"Alone?"

"Just us chickens. It was a dreadful experience."

"How did you know where to find her?"

"Rebecca told us. She called us with the address. Naturally, we were rather surprised at that, but we didn't think much of it because we were all just so happy to know where she was. In hindsight, we realized that she wanted us to follow her to New York and to see firsthand the filth she was living in."

"Why would she want you to see it?"

"She wanted to shock us, Darla. It's that simple. And shock us she did. In fact, she threw us out shortly after we arrived. It was all we could do to get out of that neighborhood alive and find a cab to take us back to the train station."

"How come Dad didn't go with you? You were married to him then, weren't you?"

"Yes," Mom said, disquieted by my question. "Yes, I was. But he had to work, and Didi and I thought it best if just Rebecca's sisters approached her."

"But I guess that didn't work, huh?"

"No, it didn't. So a week later, your uncle George went up there, hoping to succeed where we had failed."

"Did he have any luck?"

"Only the worst kind, Darla. George came home alone. And if all this weren't enough, your grandpa was in ill health at this point, and we simply couldn't bear to tell him about the ghastly place that his youngest daughter was living in. So, since Rebecca had turned eighteen by that point, and was legally of age, we told him that she lived in a modest apartment in Greenwich Village" (so it did exist!) "and had a job as a waitress, but, unfortunately, did not wish to be in contact with the family."

"But if you'd told Grandpa and Grandma the truth, maybe they would have been able to rescue her—and to bring her home!"

"Believe me, Darla, we considered it, but in the end, we felt that the truth would be too devastating to Mom and Dad, and that if anyone in the family were to seek out Rebecca, as Didi, George, and I had, she would rebel by placing herself in even greater danger. Rebecca had put your grandparents through enough pain already. So we told Dad the waitress story and left it at that. We had to. It made him very sad, your grandma too, but at least they never knew the truth. God rest their souls."

I started to feel really sad. I missed my grandparents. I was seven when my grandfather died, and eight and a half when my grandmother died. More than anything, I remember my grandfather as he was in the winter. He always wore a flannel shirt over a white undershirt and old faded jeans that Grandma regularly tried to throw out. He loved to snuggle with Grandma and me on the sofa. "Addie, you get to my right; Darla, you get to my left. We'll have a snugglefest!" Then, we'd sit down next to him, and he'd grin, squeezing us both as hard as he could. My grandmother would laugh and say something like, "Henry, you're going to squeeze the energy right out of me and Darla will have to cook dinner." Then, he'd turn to me, request some elaborate menu, and nonchalantly ask when dinner would be ready. I would laugh, protesting zealously that I didn't know how to cook, and Grandpa would keep the game going by insisting that I did. Grandma loved to play along too, but she was the one who usually ended it by telling him, "Henry, let's stop teasing this poor child."

My grandparents never felt the need to "set me straight" the way my parents did; they just enjoyed me. I didn't understand until much later that grandparents don't have the same responsibility and concerns that parents do, and as I grew up, I often resented my parents for not being able to just "enjoy" me too.

"Was that the last time you heard from Rebecca?" I asked, still reminiscing.

Mom sighed and looked at the door. "No, it wasn't. A few weeks later, she called to tell us she was pregnant."

"No way!" I gasped, reminding Mom that she was talking to a thirteen-year-old. "Get out of town!"

"The worst part of it all, Darla, was that we thought, once again, that Rebecca's call was a plea for help. But it wasn't. She just wanted to rub our noses in it. For some reason, she wanted us all to suffer. I will never understand why she hated us so. Never ever."

"So did she have the baby or what?"

"We don't know." Mom gulped. "We never heard from Rebecca again."

"Maybe she wasn't even pregnant!" I speculated.

"Maybe," Mom said, not wanting to discuss the possibilities with me. "Darla, I'm very sorry that your aunt and I deceived you."

She was about to close the door again. All the signs were there. "Didi only made up that silly lie on the spot because you were too young to know the truth, and, unfortunately, because it was the first thing that came to her mind. It was wrong of me to go along with it, but I just didn't know what else to do. I thought it would be forgotten that same day. As for Rebecca, well, she is our sister, and despite everything, we still love her and think about her. Goodness, we can't help but wonder what became of her. But she knows exactly where we are and obviously has chosen not to see us. And as for seeking her out, well, we can't endure the pain of being rejected again, and quite frankly, though I know it may sound cowardly, I don't think I could bear to see what terrible fate may have befallen her."

Finally, I was speechless. I just sat there, with my mouth open, looking at my mother.

"Darla, I hope now you'll understand, but I must ask you not to talk about this matter again. As your father says, 'It's best to let sleeping dogs lie.' If for some reason you must mention this again, please speak only to me." Mom checked the door and looked at her watch. "Whatever you do, Darla, never discuss this with anyone, especially people outside the family. We don't want a scandal, and stories like this can spread like wildfire. And the further they spread, the worse they get—and the more distorted they become. Okay, dear?"

I nodded. "I promise, Mom. I won't talk about it."

"Scandal could destroy this family," Mom warned, as if she had not heard me promise to keep quiet.

"Mom," I reiterated. "I promise I'll never say a word!"

"Good girl." She smiled nervously. "Now, go upstairs and wash your face. I'm going to finish putting the groceries away."

Obligingly, I scrambled up the stairs, momentarily too distracted (and exhausted) by what Mom had told me about Aunt Rebecca to wallow in a masochistic mire over what had happened at school. I collapsed on my bed and fell asleep. Mom, I assume, put Uncle Ben in the pantry, Sara Lee in the freezer, and went about her day. When I came down to dinner three hours later, life went on as though nothing had happened. At the table, I kept staring at my father, trying to figure out if Mom had told him anything, but his expression was pleasant and unreadable. It was my guess that she had not. After all, I remembered, it's best to let sleeping dogs lie.

CHAPTER 2

Sleeping dogs may lie, but they eventually wake up. And the following Monday morning when I woke up, I had to face the fact that school was waiting. I thought about pretending to have fallen sick over the weekend, but I knew that in the long run, feigning an illness would only make it that much harder to go back to school on Tuesday.

I got to Miss Todd's class early that afternoon, not because I wanted to be there, but because I didn't want to walk in late and be the center of attention. Miss Todd, noticing my reluctance to enter her classroom, pulled me aside before class and told me that I had no reason to be embarrassed about my "mistake," assuring me that it was unlikely that most of my classmates had even recognized it as such. Her kind words helped ease my pain, but there was still the Lughead to contend with, and I dreaded her arrival. To my dismay, she appeared just moments later, and right on cue, my stomach began to churn. The thought of having to endure her sniveling grins and mocking smiles made me shudder, so I quickly decided that my only recourse was to be strong and not act the victim. If she looked at me, I would look right back at her, with pride, as though nothing had happened. No, I would do better than that: I would look at her first.

I glanced in her direction, but to my great surprise she turned her head away. This made no sense to me. After all, I'd known this Lughead since the first grade, and she was not one to miss an opportunity to show off, or to throw something back in someone's face. (That's what made her a Lughead!) I looked at her again, only to discover that her head was buried in a book. What was going on?

Miss Todd called class to order, then asked the Lughead to come to the front of the classroom and read her homework assignment on Joe Running Horse aloud.

"Maybe someone else would like to go first today," the Lughead offered.

"Is there something wrong, Amy?" Miss Todd asked with a look of

17

concern on her face. "Aren't you prepared for class?"

"Of course!" the Lughead shot back, horrified that she had even been asked such a question. "Of course I am, Miss Todd. I'm always prepared for class."

Several of my classmates looked at each other. She made us all want to gag.

"Well, come on then. Let's hear what you have to say about our esteemed guest on Friday."

In a very un-Lughead-like fashion, she rose slowly from her chair, shuffled some papers (and her feet), and walked to the head of the class, keeping a steady eye on the floor. A few seconds later, I heard soft giggling coming from every direction in the room. It was music to my ears. I looked up from my own homework assignment and then at the Lughead, who stood before the class. Suddenly, it was a glorious day and all was right with the world. It seems that over the weekend, a giant, repulsive zit had grown on the end of the Lughead's very prominent nose, and lucky for me, it seemed to be thriving. My classmates may not have known much about squalor, but they knew a zit when they saw one.

And at that moment, as if by magic, my own humiliating experience of three days past seemed light-years away, while the Lughead's humiliation, burning so brightly at that moment, took its rightful place in my memory, where I felt sure it would continue to delight me for all the days of my life.

In the weeks that followed, although I never mentioned it again, everything Mom had told me about my aunt Rebecca replayed in my mind—over and over and over again. Every aspect of this mystery woman intrigued me. Even my own mother began to intrigue me. Why was she was so concerned about scandal? We were the McKendricks, not the Kennedys. What was there to know about us? As far as I could remember, the only family "scandal" I knew of concerned Didi's three daughters, April, May, and June. As legend had it, Aunt Didi had carefully planned her pregnancies, and the first daughter, April, was born on April 4, followed by May, a year later, who was born on May 11. But one year after that, to Aunt Didi's "horror," June was born late—in July. When I first heard this story, I was able to understand how Aunt Didi had planned when she would give birth, but I never quite understood how she had "arranged" to have girls. "Girls run in our family," Mom had explained, and being a girl myself, who was I to argue?

But that was silly stuff, I concluded. It was far more scandalous to have had a drug-addicted, pregnant, runaway aunt than a cousin named June who was born in July. But why would anyone care about that now, especially outsiders, some fifteen-plus years later?

I wondered if Aunt Didi had ever discussed Rebecca with her daughters, and I decided that she had not, unless it was in passing. My cousins all led such busy lives, and I was sure they had no time to obsess over an aunt they had never known.

A modern-day version of the Andrews Sisters, billed as "The Alexander Three," April, May, and June had been performing at talent shows, beauty pageants, private parties, community events, theatrical shows, and on local television commercials ever since I could remember. Yes, indeed, they were far too busy enjoying their glamorous life to think about Rebecca. I, on the other hand, had plenty of time for such an activity.

I don't know why she fascinated me so. But as I mulled over every aspect of Rebecca's life, I felt like Sherlock Holmes in search of an elusive mystery woman. A couple of times, when Mom and Dad were out of the house, I rummaged through the attic, in hopes of finding at least one photograph of Rebecca. My curiosity was killing me and if nothing else, I wanted to know what she looked like. Finally, on my second attempt, I discovered several family photos, wrapped in paper, that had been hidden under some clothes in Mom's old camp trunk. But all that the photos revealed was a beautiful little girl (the prettiest of the three), who only slightly resembled Mom and Aunt Didi. She was not a fire-breathing fiend, nor did she have the devil's twinkle in her eyes. Certain that I must've overlooked more telling evidence of Rebecca's true nature,

I continued to search for more photos, ones that might provide some real answers, but instead found only more likenesses of the same delightful child. Unfortunately, it appeared that no photographs had been taken of Rebecca after the age of twelve or thirteen. People who do drugs, I surmised, don't like posing for pictures.

My obsession continued. Day after day, I would imagine the poverty (it was still tough to say "squalor") that my mother had described. I wondered if Rebecca had really had rats in her apartment, if she had truly been pregnant, why she hadn't called home in all these years (or had she?), and how she could live in vermin-infested filth after growing up in such a comfortable home. And why were Dad and Uncle George even more unnerved talking about her than Mom and Aunt Didi were? She wasn't their "bad seed" sister! Perhaps men just didn't like talking about such things. I no longer had a clue; my questions were now just a jumble in my head, and I grew weary of groping for answers.

By the time I completed the ninth grade, my interest in Rebecca began to wane even more. Like any normal teenage girl, I was interested in boys, shopping malls, music, makeup, and hanging out with my friends. And since I had actually kept my promise to my mother and had never discussed Rebecca with anyone, I had only a residual interest in playing Watson to my own ineffectual Holmes.

But once again, just as the mystery of Rebecca was fading from my mind, something happened to renew my interest. Mom's uncle Martin, yet another "runaway relative" whom I had never met, came to town with his new wife, Maudie.

Martin was my grandpa's brother, fifteen years his junior, and even I knew that he was a loser. I remembered his name had come up once at the dinner table, and that Dad had referred to him as "the black sheep of the Connor family" and as "a lazy-good-for-nothing slob." But unlike with Rebecca, no one gave him a second thought, and no one ever asked me not to discuss him. What was there to discuss? I guessed that he was such a dud that no one, myself included, gave a damn.

Right before Martin's visit, however, my curious nature got the better of me, and I went to Dad for some background information. From what he told me, Martin had barely finished high school when he went to work as a clerk for F.W. Woolworth Co. Apparently, the family was pleased because they didn't think he'd get a high school diploma, much less a job. After a year, Martin surprised everyone by getting promoted to assistant manager on the evening shift. He must've done a great job in that position, Dad told me, shaking his head, because he stayed in that very same job until he was forty-two years old, when F.W. Woolworth closed the store.

After his severance package had expired, Martin eventually found another position selling auto parts, which was something he knew nothing about. "That lasted only a few weeks," Dad told me, "before he entered the exciting world of ice cream. Well, scooping cones didn't seem to tickle his fancy, either, and within a month's time, he left for Toronto. Said he had a friend who'd offered him a good job up there. Except for an occasional Christmas card, that was all we ever heard from Martin."

"Wasn't Grandpa upset that he just left the country like that?"

"Relieved," Dad assured me. "Your grandpa Henry had far more important things to worry about than his socially inept, good-for-nothing brother."

I knew that Dad was referring to Rebecca, but I didn't dare ask.

"So why's he coming to town now, after all these years?"

"Who knows?" Dad said, shrugging his shoulders. "Seems the poor slob finally got married, at sixty-something years old, and he's passing through town on his honeymoon. According to Martin, his new wife wants to live in Florida and enjoy 'the good life.' Canada is too cold for her. Wants to have fun in the sun."

Dad rolled his eyes. It was obvious that he didn't have an ounce of respect for this man, or for his new wife, whom he hadn't even met. "I've told you all that I know," he said sincerely. "You'll just have to meet him and judge for yourself."

Mom agreed to make dinner for Martin and his new wife at our house. She had, however, first offered Aunt Didi the opportunity to play hostess, since Aunt Didi was the oldest Connor sister.

"Sure, I'll cook for Martin," Aunt Didi had told Mom, "when hell freezes over!"

At first, Aunt Didi and Uncle George didn't even want to see Martin, but then Aunt Didi decided that it was an evening she couldn't pass up. (It would fuel the conversational fires for months.)

It was a warm July night. My cousins were on Cape Cod, visiting their cousins on Uncle George's side of the family, so it was just the five of us. We sat in the living room and waited. Mom had made a beautiful plate of hors d'oeuvres, which sat untouched on the coffee table, in anticipation of the guests of honor. My parents kept exchanging weird looks with my aunt and uncle, and no one looked at me, not until I uttered the dreaded words, "I think they're here."

And so they were. I had never met anyone like them in my entire life.

Martin, who appeared in the doorway first, was a sleazy-looking old man with a bad toupee and bad teeth—and the ugliest plaid jacket I'd ever seen. It was orange, black, brown, and green, and it looked just like the old couch in my best friend Melanie's basement. He reminded me of this creepy used car salesman I'd recently seen in an episode of "The Twilight Zone," and he had a grin that made me want to gag. I looked at my mother in horror.

"Ted, you old son of a gun!" Martin practically shouted. "Good to see you, buddy." He grabbed Dad's hand and began shaking it vigorously.

Then he looked at Mom and Aunt Didi. "My dear nieces, Margaret and Deirdre! As I live and breathe—"

"Unfortunately," I heard Uncle George mutter under his breath.

"You gorgeous gals, you. Who's gonna be the first to give your old uncle Martin a great big bear hug?"

Naturally, it was Mom who consented to hug him first, trying her best to touch him as little as possible. Mom had this thing about vermin, and from looking at her face, I could tell that she feared that some noxious creatures might be gestating in his plaid jacket.

"Welcome, Martin," she said unconvincingly. "It's so nice to see you again after so many years."

Before Uncle Martin could even attempt to smother Aunt Didi, Uncle George diverted his attention with an enthusiastic handshake, while Aunt Didi offered a minimal greeting from across the room. Martin explained to us that his bride would be along momentarily.

"She's out in the car, puttin' on the last touches of her rouge. You know how women are. Gotta look their best to meet the family."

Then he noticed me. "Who is this beautiful girl?"

"This is our daughter, Darla," Dad said, looking at me apologetically, as though he had wanted to spare me the introduction.

"Darla. Now, that's a beautiful name. Come give your uncle Martin a big bear hug!"

He stood there, his arms outstretched, with a big come-hither grin on his face. I couldn't go through with it.

"Nice to meet you," I said. "I have a cold." (And you have disgusting fingernails, I thought.)

Martin laughed loudly. "You're a shy one, aren't you? Don't worry, we'll be old friends by the time the evening is through. I can tell just from looking at you that you're a one-in-a-million girl."

And then, at that moment, she came through the front door.

"Hello, everybody! I'm your aunt Maudie."

I honestly thought that Aunt Didi's eyes were going to pop right out of her head and dangle from her eye sockets, and that my mother was going to lose consciousness and wake up at the heels of Maudie's faux leopard pumps. This woman was a sight! I guessed her to be in her late fifties, though with the mask of dime-store makeup on her face, it was hard to tell. She was fairly slender but revealed far more skin than human dignity allowed. Hugging her hips was a fire-engine red satin dress that accentuated all her negatives, including, but not limited to, her sagging cleavage, knobby knees, and bulging stomach—right down to a big mole (with a hair growing out of it) that was situated just due north of her right breast. The loose flesh on her upper arms swayed to and fro as she sashayed into our home. To complete this vision of loveliness, she wore long, pearly white press-on fingernails and had false eyelashes so long one

23

might think she had pet spiders snoozing on her eyelids.

Her dyed strawberry blond hair was done up in what Uncle George referred to later as a "beehive do," and it looked as though it had been forced into place with some type of industrial varnish. On her ears, she sported hoop earrings large enough for Uncle Martin to jump through, and her excessive costume jewelry clanged so loudly when she walked that she sounded like a one-woman marching band that was seriously out of tune.

As if the visual impact of this woman were not enough, the scent of her was enough to disencumber the most clogged of nasal passages. I knew she had to be wearing some bargain brand of cologne, but her particular scent reminded me of something that had been in storage in the attic, like Rebecca's baby pictures. The best I can say is that it smelled like a mixture of camphor and jasmine musk.

Not in the movies, not in the city, not on television, and not in my most grotesque nightmares had I ever seen anyone like Maudie. Shortly after she arrived, I excused myself for a moment and ran upstairs to call Melanie. Normally, my parents would have considered it rude to leave when we had company, but in this case, I knew they wouldn't even notice, or care. Besides, there was no way I could wait until later to call my best friend and describe this mutant piece of modern art on loan to the McKendrick gallery for the evening. And naturally, I couldn't wait to rub it in that the companion piece to this monstrosity, entitled "Uncle Martin," was wearing not only a terrible rug but a jacket that looked identical to Melanie's parent's old couch.

After Melanie's twenty-fifth "Omigod," I hung up the phone and returned to the party. Everyone was seated in the living room and Maudie had the plate of hors d'oeuvres resting on her lap.

"These are scrump-dilly-icious, Margaret," she said to Mom. "No pigs in the blanket, huh?"

"No. Sorry. No pigs in the blanket. And please, it's Maggie."

"Ah well, maybe next time. Don't worry none, though. These are absolutely dee-lish. Really, hon. What are these little things?"

"They're miniature quiches with bacon and green onion."

"They look like little pies to me!" Maudie said, popping one whole in her mouth. And as she chewed, she carefully surveyed the room. "Hey, ya know, you got a lotta nice stuff in this house." She put the hors d'oeuvres tray back on the table and proceeded to pick up a candy dish, which she promptly turned over, dumping the butterscotch candy all over the coffee table. "Wow, Wedgwood. Nice. Take a look, Marty."

"Real nice, babe," Martin said, as he eyed the dish, then handed it back to her.

Maudie continued to look around, as if she'd lost something. "Oh well," she announced, "this'll do." She opened up her bag and pulled out a cigarette. From where he was sitting, Martin lurched forward with a cheap black lighter and lit it for her. Using the candy dish as an ashtray, Maudie began puffing away, completely oblivious to the obvious objections around her.

I saw Dad start to ask her not to smoke, but then his famous "Why bother?" look crossed his face and I figured we would just fumigate in the morning.

"So what does a pretty girl like Darla McKendrick study in school?" Martin asked me.

"I don't know. History, algebra, English. Whatever."

"I'll bet you and your friends spend most of your time studying boys!" Maudie said assuredly. "Aunt Maudie remembers when she was a teenager."

"Exactly when was that?" Uncle George asked. "That you were Darla's age?"

"Well, it's not as long ago as you might think," Maudie replied. I could tell she was annoyed by the question, but she was still aiming for the impossible—to be charming. "I can tell you this, though. I remember my girlhood days as if they were yesterday."

"You sure are pretty," Martin repeated, staring at me. "A one-in-a-million girl. That's what you are."

And you're a one-in-a-million asshole, I thought, wondering what my parents would do if I said it aloud. It was hard to imagine that this man was my grandpa's brother. They were nothing alike.

25

"Thank you," I muttered because I thought I should.

I glanced over at my uncle George, who appeared to be seething with contempt. I knew his patience was wearing thin and that meant his manners couldn't be far behind.

"That's some beehive do, Maudie," Uncle George said, trying his best to insult her.

"Glad you like it, Georgie. You know, men come straight to my beehive when they want some honey." She pointed to her lips. "But here's where they come to get sugar."

Aunt Didi put her hand over her mouth as if she were going to get sick, then rose to join Mom, who had already slipped off to the kitchen.

The conversation continued to deteriorate for another fifteen minutes until dinner was served. Then it got really bad. And then it got even worse.

"Tell me, Martin," said Mom, still determined to take her role as hostess seriously. "What have you been doing for the last seventeen years?"

"Well," Martin began, "I've been in women's shoes, Margaret. Oh—but don't take me too literally. I just sell them."

Maudie laughed. "He uses that line all the time. He's a real joker."

"Hey," Martin said, encouraged by her praise, "did you hear the one about the Jew radio operator who gave up being a ham 'cause it wasn't kosher?"

"No, we didn't hear that one!" Aunt Didi said sharply. "And I can guarantee you that nobody in this room wants to hear 'that one.'"

"I think she's a little touchy, hon," Maudie told her husband through a mouth full of food. "Probably a Democrat or some other kind of liberal."

Aunt Didi looked at her as if she had two heads. (In a way, she did.)

"So, you've been selling women's shoes, have you?" Dad said, trying to turn the conversation around.

"Sure have," Martin answered. "And had a successful career of it too. I'm no loafer!"

Maudie and Martin roared hysterically. The five of us stared at him. I wanted to laugh because he was so weird, but not because he was the least bit funny.

"Seriously, though," Martin went on, "I found my niche when I found shoes. Worked as a salesman for a chain in Toronto, and ten years ago, I made manager. Increase in salary, health bennies, the whole nine yards! But you wanna know the best part about working in shoes?"

"What?" asked an agitated Aunt Didi. "You don't step on rusty nails?"

Maudie laughed. "Oh, that's a riot, Deirdre! I can see what family member you get your sense of humor from!"

Aunt Didi grimaced at the unintentional insult.

"Nope!" said Martin to Aunt Didi. "The best part of the job was meeting people. And the best day on the job was the day I met my Maudie."

"Don't tell me," Uncle George said, feigning interest. "She came in for a pair of platforms."

"How did ya know?" Maudie asked, as a huge glob of marinara sauce took a nosedive into her sagging breasts.

"It must've been love at first sight," Aunt Didi groaned. She looked at Maudie with utter disgust. "You've got marinara between your boobs."

Mom looked as if she were going to burst out laughing. It was the first time I'd seen her crack a smile that evening.

"Well, so I do!" Maudie said, looking down at her dress. Without missing a beat, she dipped her napkin in her water glass and wiped the sauce off, leaving a huge water stain on the material. "Actually, it was love at first sight, but when we started dating, I wasn't so sure this romance was going to get off the ground."

"Gosh, why not?" Aunt Didi encouraged her.

I, by the way, was having a marvelous time, despite the fact that I was dining with what I then referred to as "lost art treasures from the planet Way Weird."

"Well—" Maudie said. She looked right at me, and then at my parents. "We're all adults here, right? We're family, right?"

Nobody answered her. Suddenly, Mom looked at me as if she wanted me to leave the room. I pretended not to notice.

Maudie took a huge gulp of wine. "Marty, if you will, had a little trouble raising the flag at first."

"Oh God!" Aunt Didi and Uncle George moaned simultaneously.

"Maudie!" Mom said angrily. "Please!" I had never seen my mother react so negatively to anything in front of company before. This was a true milestone. I wondered if perhaps her wholesome façade was starting to splinter. Maybe I would be lucky enough to get a glimpse of the real woman behind the enduring smile.

Dad looked extremely uncomfortable and then glared at me to gauge my reaction. Actually, at first I hadn't been one hundred percent sure what Maudie meant, but when my family reacted as they did, it didn't take me long to figure it out. I looked at Martin. Amazingly, he didn't seem to be the least bit embarrassed by this disclosure of his sexual dysfunction.

"Before I met Maudie," he began, "I was a lonely bachelor. The darn thing stayed at half-mast for so long, I didn't know how to—"

"Really Martin!" Mom scolded him. "That's quite enough. Stop it now!"

"You heard Maggie," Uncle George cautioned, glaring at him.

"Aw, he's kidding," Maudie assured everyone. "It was just a medical problem. Happens to men in their golden years, you know. Could even happen to a virile man like yourself, George."

Uncle George looked as if he wanted to strangle her.

"Anyway," Maudie continued, "the doc fixed my honey up just fine, and I've been pledgin' allegiance ever since!"

Martin and Maudie broke out into raucous laughter.

"Don't ya just love her?" Martin asked, beaming with pride.

My family was too appalled to speak. I couldn't wait to repeat all this to Melanie. Nothing like this had ever happened at my house before; I was anxious to report every detail.

"Could ya pour me some more of that cabbernetslowvineyone, Teddy?" Maudie asked Dad, holding her wine glass in her outstretched right hand.

"I'd be happy to," Dad lied, as he poured her another drink. "Anyone else?"

"Don't mind if I do," Martin replied.

"I'm fine for now," Aunt Didi said.

"How 'bout yourself, there?" Maudie asked Dad. "Why aren't you having any wine? Geez, you're not a recovering alcoholic or nothing, are you? I find that's usually the case when someone don't drink. 'Course, half the time those people will tell ya they ain't drinkin' 'cause they're taking their 'Auntie's Biotics' or something."

Dad looked livid. "I'm just not a drinker. Is that okay with you?"

"You don't know what you're missing," Maudie said, taking another gulp of wine. "This sure is good stuff."

"We usually buy it by the jug, though," Martin offered. "More bang for the buck that way. And it's sweeter, too."

"I think it's time to clear," Mom announced cheerfully, as she got up and began collecting our dinner plates. Any perceptible cracks in her resolve had apparently repaired themselves. False alarm; she was Mom again. I was disappointed. "Hope everyone has saved room for dessert!"

"Oh sure, hon," Maudie told her.

Martin shifted nervously in his seat and then looked at his wife. She winked at him curiously, as if she were giving him the green light to do something.

"Ted," Martin began officiously, leaning back comfortably in his chair. "I think you and George here will be very interested to hear about some red-hot business opportunities in Florida that I've recently come upon. Lucky for you, these men I know are real smart operators and they're looking for a few savvy investors, like yourselves. These guys have the know-how to turn pennies into profit with the snap of a finger. I can promise you this, fellas, these deals aren't for just anyone. But if you're willing to take a risk—"

"I don't think—" Uncle George began, "that we're—"

"Like I said," Martin continued, ignoring Uncle George completely, "I wouldn't give just anyone the inside track on this. Now, repeat after

29

me. Shopping centers, golf resorts, retirement communities, you name it. The whole nine yards. And to think, I came upon all this by accident. Why, I was just lookin' for a place for me and Maudie when I met these developers. Boy, they sure do know the lay of the land down there. And these are one-in-a-million deals."

"Uh-huh. And did you buy yourself a home?" Dad asked, trying to change the subject.

"Not yet, Ted boy," Martin said patronizingly. "No use buyin' a trailer home seeings that Maudie and I'll be rich by year's end, is there? Now, because you're family, and smart businessmen too, I'd like to give you both a chance to climb aboard the golden ship of opportunity."

"Not interested, Martin. It'll have to sail without us."

"We're not in the market for swampland this year," Uncle George threw in.

"Now wait, boys," Maudie said. "Hear Martin out. He's checked into this here thing, and it's on the level. There's some big bucks to be made."

"Just how many pennies are you investing?" Uncle George asked with a sneer.

Martin looked at the tablecloth, then exchanged looks with Maudie. Even at the age of fifteen, I could tell that they wanted money from Dad and Uncle George. That was the real reason for their visit, as Dad later confirmed.

"This isn't the appropriate place to discuss business," Dad said, doing his best not to let the situation get out of hand.

"He's right, Marty," Maudie condescended. "Wait'll after dinner, hon, when the kid's gone upstairs."

I found it interesting that she didn't think about "the kid" going upstairs when she was discussing their sex life.

Martin looked extremely disappointed, but he changed the subject.

About ten minutes later, Mom entered the dining room carrying a tray of desserts.

"Yum-yum," Martin said, taking a bowl from the proffered tray.

"Homemade rice pudding. Just like your mother used to make."

Mom smiled tolerably as she walked around the table to serve the rest of us.

"Gee," Martin continued, "we've been having a wonderful time here tonight. I'm just sorry that little Rebecca couldn't join us. What's she's doing these days, anyway?"

Mom laid the tray on the nearby sideboard and took her seat. I knew she was giving this one to Dad. My ears perked up and my eyes grew wide. I looked like an alien preparing for a transmission from the home planet. Mom looked right at me. She could see that I was excited about this turn in the conversation, and she didn't like it one bit. Knitting her brow, she silently warned me not to open my mouth.

"Rebecca lives in another town," Dad said matter-of-factly. "I'm sure she's just fine."

"Get to see her much?"

"No, we don't see her. Martin, I think this conversation—"

"Ran away from home when she was seventeen, didn't she?" Martin plodded on. "And just how old was she when she returned?"

"She didn't," George said contentiously. "Why don't we table this discussion? Now!"

Martin ignored him. "Poor kid; she was a one-in-a-million girl. Hated to see her turn to drugs and drinkin' like that. I tried to help her. I sure did. Tried to be a friend. I guess she just saw me as another adult tellin' her what to do. Ever find out why she went bad?"

"Martin," Mom said, determined to stay calm. "Please drop the subject."

"I'd guess she was just about Darla-here's age when she started turning rotten. Wouldn't you say that, Margaret?"

"For God's sake, shut up!" Aunt Didi screamed. "And don't talk about her like she's a piece of fruit. Drop it, will you?"

"I sure would like to see Rebecca," he persisted. "Where does she live?"

Squalor, New Mexico, I thought, looking at my aunt Didi. A part of me was still very angry.

31

"We don't have her address," Dad said irritably.

"Too bad. Sure would like to see that pretty gal. You know, she might have a man who's interested in this deal I've got going. Really, fellas, you gotta let me tell you about it. It's a one-in-a-million opportunity."

"Saved by the bell!" Aunt Didi proclaimed as the doorbell rang. "Excuse me, everyone." Aunt Didi got up and rushed out of the room, returning a minute later with my friend Melanie at her side.

"Hello, dear," Mom said to Melanie. "What are you doing here at this hour?"

Melanie could barely answer. Her mouth had dropped open and she was staring incredulously at Maudie and Martin. I guessed that my description over the phone had not quite done them justice. My best friend was going into shock. We might have to call the paramedics.

"Melanie," Mom repeated. "Is there a special reason for your visit tonight?"

"Uh," Melanie mumbled as if she had fallen into a trance.

"Melanie. Are you okay, dear?"

"Uh, yeah," Melanie finally managed to say. "Darla told me that she wanted to read this book. So I brought it by."

Mom took one look at the book, *American Indians*, which we had read in the seventh grade, and instantly recognized Melanie's visit as the setup that it was. She shook her head and smiled. After all, how could she blame us? How could we not want to share this incredible experience?

"This is Melanie Davenport," Mom said politely to Martin and Maudie. "Melanie is Darla's very best friend."

"She's also a very talented artist," Dad told them, smiling at Melanie.

Melanie looked embarrassed.

"You've got the most gorgeous long red hair!" Maudie gushed enviously. "You can't buy that color, you know. Lord knows, I've tried. Listen, kid, if you ever feel like getting a short cut, I'd be real innerrested in buyin' that hair from you. I could make a piece out of it and dye the rest best as I could to match."

"Omigod!" Melanie whispered. I feared she was falling back into the trance.

"I'm as serious as a heart attack!" Maudie told her before taking a rather obscene swig of wine.

"She sure is a pretty girl," Martin said as he leered at her. "Melody. Just like a song."

"Melanie," she corrected him, then looked as if she wished she hadn't.

"That's a pretty name too. You're a one-in-a-million girl." He grinned, showing off his bad teeth.

Melanie turned and looked at me wide-eyed, just the same way my family had been looking at each other all night.

"Melanie," Dad said jovially, "why don't you pull up a chair and have some of Mrs. McKendrick's famous rice pudding with us?"

"Thank you, Mr. McKendrick. That would be nice."

Mom got up and headed to the kitchen to get another bowl of pudding. Melanie started to pull up a chair to the table when Maudie stopped her.

"Before you sit down, hon, be a love and get my ciggies from the living room."

I didn't like the authoritative tone in Maudie's voice, and I could tell Melanie didn't either, but she complied with Maudie's request out of respect for my parents.

Melanie retrieved the cigarettes, then handed them to Maudie. I saw her look oddly at Maudie's pearly white press-on nails, and I could tell from the way she scrunched up her freckled nose that she smelled Maudie's "cologne" too. I started to get an uneasy feeling.

"Thanks, hon. Oh, while you're still up, could ya bring me that Wedgwood ashtray from the coffee table?"

Melanie glared at her defiantly. She was getting angry.

"Ah, never mind," Maudie said, understanding the look. "I'll just use the rice pudding bowl. Wouldn't want to make an ash of myself!"

Martin exploded with laughter. Mom, who had just re-entered the dining room with some more pudding, looked positively sick. She put the bowl in front of Melanie, then took her seat.

"We'd rather you didn't smoke at all," Aunt Didi said. She turned to Melanie. "Please, honey, sit down and have some pudding."

"Don't worry your pretty little head about it, Deirdre," Maudie snapped rudely. "They're light cigarettes. They won't bother anyone."

I could see Aunt Didi tighten up. Uncle George looked menacingly at Maudie's pack of cigarettes, as if he wanted to confiscate it on the spot, but my aunt put her hand on his arm to stop him.

Melanie sat down next to me and whispered "Skieve me out!" in my ear. Maudie lit up a cigarette, and I knew, at precisely that moment, that my family would no longer tolerate the eccentric characters who sat among us. Maudie had barely inhaled her first drag of nicotine, when Dad suggested that Melanie and I take our desserts up to my room, where we wouldn't be bored by adult conversation. I was just as happy to comply. Earlier, they had just been weird people, who for various reasons, made my uptight family squirm. Now I was beginning to see that they were mean people, and rather than delight in the wake of their conduct, I just wanted to get away from them. I felt frightened and protective of those I loved. Besides, it would be much more enjoyable observing them from a distance, where Melanie and I, hidden from view, could snicker to our heart's content.

Soon after we retreated upstairs, the party returned to the living room. Melanie and I assumed our usual listening posts at the top of the stairs. After about ten minutes, things started to get really ugly.

"That was a meal fit for a king!" Martin said. "Gotta say, a man needs a full stomach to talk business. Speakin' of business, you girls'll excuse us men for a bit, won't ya? I'm sure you've got some dirty dishes or recipe swappin' to tend to in the kitchen, huh now? This is whatcha call a man's conversation."

"The women aren't going any damn place!" George told him harshly. "And 'us men' aren't doing any damn business. Now, how many ways to Sunday do you want me to spell it out for you, Martin?"

"Way to go, Mr. Alexander! Kick his slimy ass!" Melanie whispered gleefully.

"I think you could show your uncle a bit of respect and listen to what he has to say," Maudie scolded Uncle George, as we heard the click of a cigarette lighter.

"He's not my damn uncle," Uncle George snorted, "and put out the goddamn cigarette! We don't smoke in this family."

"Right on!" Melanie exclaimed quietly as her arm rose victoriously in the air. "All right!"

"They're not innerrested, hon," Maudie said to Martin. "I guess some people just don't wanna be millionaires. Seems like we wasted our time comin' here."

"Looks like we did!" Martin said indignantly.

"I thought you came here to see your family!" Aunt Didi challenged him. "Isn't that what you said when you called? 'Missed us terribly over the years.' 'Couldn't wait to be reunited.' 'Nothing more important than family.' Isn't that what you said?"

Suddenly, Martin didn't sound so sure of himself. "Well yeah, I said that, but there's nothing wrong with throwin' a little business proposition into the mix, is there now?"

"Business my rear end!" Aunt Didi cried out.

"He's your father's brother!" Maudie jumped in angrily. "Your father, may he rest in peace, would want to see his only brother get some respect in this house!"

"You came here for money, Martin," Aunt Didi bellowed. "It's as plain as that haystack on her head!"

"Now we're getting nasty," Maudie roared.

"Let's face it," Uncle George roared back. "You two don't have a plug nickel to invest. And furthermore, no developer worth his salt would deal with the likes of you."

"How dare you speak to my husband in such a way!" Maudie screamed.

"I think it's time we all said good night!" Dad intervened in a Dad-like way. "Let's end this now before we all say things we're sorry for." I couldn't imagine why he didn't just tell them to get the hell out of our house. But then I remembered: "it's a bad thing to lose control," and cursing at your dinner guests, I surmised, is a definite sign of control gone astray.

"I think it's too late for that!" Martin said huffily. "Maudie and I've been dealt a raw deal here tonight. There's no denying that."

"You've been dealt a raw deal?" Aunt Didi howled at him. "You came here with no other intention than to get money from us for some phony baloney land scheme in Florida. And she's been puffing away like a chimney despite numerous requests to stop. Is that showing respect for us?"

"The gloves are gonna come off if you don't stop, hon," Maudie warned Aunt Didi.

"Omigod!" Melanie gasped. "I hope no one gets hurt!"

I was going to tell her not to be ridiculous, but I suddenly shared her apprehension.

"We can settle this right now," Uncle George challenged.

"Let's go, Maudie," Martin said. "I think we've overstayed our welcome. What a shame! And after so many years apart. Who would've thought it would end like this? My beloved brother would've been very disappointed in all of you."

"Your beloved brother would've been the first to haul your sorry behind out of here!" Uncle George bellowed.

"Thank you for a lovely dinner, Margaret," Maudie said. "You went to a lot of trouble for us and we appreciate it." Then she said, presumably to Aunt Didi, "Don't let it be said that Maudie Ferguson Connor has no class!"

"Get lost!" Aunt Didi said in disgust.

"Goodnight now," Mom said cheerfully. "Thank you for coming."

Melanie turned to me. "'Thank you for coming'? Darla, I really love your mom, but sometimes she acts so unreal, you know, with her glued-on smile and sparkly eyes. I mean, even Betty Crocker isn't that nice!"

I agreed with her but couldn't bear to discuss it. "It's just Mom's way of handling an unpleasant situation and avoiding confrontation," I explained. "What do you know about Betty Crocker, anyway?" I desperately wanted to change the subject. "She isn't even a real person."

"Duh. Do I care?" Melanie said. "The point is, Darla, that your aunt and uncle have much more interesting ways of handling 'unpleasant situations' than your parents do!"

The next thing I heard was the front door slamming and Uncle George announcing that he needed a drink. Within moments, the phone rang and it was Mrs. Davenport asking Mom to send Melanie home.

✳ ✳ ✳

When I woke up the next morning, Dad was sitting beside me on my bed, smiling at me.

"Dad?" I said sleepily. "What are you doing here?"

"I just want you to know how much I love you, Darla. And I'm very sorry that you had to bear witness to the excitement here last night. Believe me, had your mother and I known what to expect, it never would've happened."

"It's okay, Dad," I said yawning. I couldn't bear to tell him that in some perverse way I'd enjoyed myself, despite the fact I was rather shaken by the way it had all ended.

"No, it's clearly not okay," Dad corrected me. "I'm certainly not in the habit of subjecting my daughter to the company of unsavory people, especially those who are drinking and smoking. I told you before the visit that Martin was no prize, but I never expected him to come here for the sole purpose of emptying our bank accounts. Absolutely not."

"He's gross," I said, rubbing my eyes.

"I suppose he is. Well, I'm off to work now. I love you, sweetie." Dad bent down and kissed me. "It's a beautiful summer day, Darla. Get outside and enjoy yourself."

Although I was half asleep, I was very touched by Dad's impromptu visit. And although I loved feeling like "Daddy's little girl," I hoped that when the new school year began, I would be treated more like the mature adult that I was quickly becoming.

CHAPTER 3

September appeared way before I was ready. I wasn't prepared for the change in weather, the change in schools, or the many changes in my life that were to follow. My desire to be perceived and treated as a grownup depended entirely on the situation at hand. Though I hated to admit it, being a kid still had its perks, especially when it came to avoiding certain adult responsibilities that were tiresome and boring. But mostly, I was at that age when hormonal activity dictates that one must demand recognition of one's maturity, especially when one's social life is threatened in any way. My parents, unfortunately, had their own agenda, and just when I had hoped they would become more lenient and grant me greater privileges, they suddenly seemed suspicious and fearful, trusting my good judgment far less than they had in the past.

Two weeks into the tenth grade, Brenda Davenport, Melanie's older sister, invited me to her twenty-first birthday party. My biggest problem, or so I thought, would be choosing an appropriate gift while staying within my meager budget. At the dinner table one night, in an attempt to make conversation, I presented this matter to my parents, hoping that they would either offer a brilliant solution or, better yet, substantially raise my allowance for that week.

"Where's this birthday shindig going to be held?" Dad asked. To my dismay, it was obvious that he couldn't care less about my gift predicament.

"At The Captain's Table," I told him. "In one of their banquet rooms."

"The Captain's Table. Isn't that the restaurant down by the waterfront?"

"Yeah. So?"

"Hear that place is a bit on the wild side," Dad said, cutting into his glazed pork chop. "Especially on the weekends. Is this shindig going to be on the weekend?"

"Well, yeah, Dad," I groaned. "It's next Saturday night."

Dad shook his head in a way that meant trouble. I looked at Mom for support, but she quickly averted her glance.

"Dad, it's a seafood restaurant. What's wrong with that?"

He thought for a moment. "I suppose nothing. But I'm not happy about your being in a place where people are drinking heavily and acting promiscuous."

I was stunned. I had been invited to a birthday party, not a bacchanal. Suddenly, anyone with a yen for lobster or fish was an alcoholic, prone to deviant behavior, with perhaps a penchant for indulging in aberrant sex acts between bites of shrimp scampi. Had my father suddenly gone bonkers? Were we even talking about the same subject?

"Dad!" I said loudly. "Earth to Dad! I'm talking about going to Brenda's birthday party, you know, the one her parents are giving—in a perfectly normal restaurant."

"I understand," Dad said. "Please lower your voice, Darla." He took a bite of his food, then paused for several seconds while he chewed. "Well, I suppose it will be okay, as long as you come and go with the Davenports, or better yet, if I pick you up. I'm sure I sound like a worrisome old man to you, but that waterfront area is known to be a haven for some pretty wild things, and I wouldn't want you involved in any of them."

"Really?" I asked enthusiastically. "Like what?"

My sudden enthusiasm for the seamier side of life was about as welcome as the atomic bomb, or even worse, a question about Aunt Rebecca.

"We'll talk after dinner. Meantime, let's enjoy this 'scrump-dilly-icious' dinner your mother has fixed."

We all laughed. I figured that if Dad could make a Maudie joke, his apparent flight from reality must've crash-landed back to earth, and once again, all would be right with the world.

After dinner was over, I jumped at the opportunity to help Mom with the dishes. I decided that spending some time away from Dad would help him to forget about this "after-dinner talk" that loomed so ominously in my immediate future. I hoped that Mom would be capable of providing me with some insight into Dad's strange behavior at dinner, but all I could get from her was the repetitive exegesis that my father had some very legitimate concerns about my welfare, as naturally, did she. I don't know what possessed me to even try and break her down, especially when my father was in the very next room, for as usual, "mum" was the word with Mom.

I was drying the salad bowls when Dad stuck his head in the kitchen doorway. "Darla?"

"Is it lecture time already?" I whined. "I didn't even do anything! I just got an invitation to a birthday party! Lock me up and throw away the key!"

"You're absolutely right, Darla. You didn't do anything. And I have no intention of lecturing you. I just want to have a father-daughter chat. Now, what's wrong with that?"

"Nothing," I moaned.

It was hopeless. He was going to take me prisoner and I had no recourse but to go willingly into ye good family room. I saw Mom crack a smile and then turn her back to Dad so he wouldn't notice. Once in the family room, Dad continued to explain what he had started at dinner. "Darla, I'm sure that my reaction to your party invitation sounded a bit irrational to you."

"Sorta more than a bit, Dad."

"Well, that's because I'm a dad. And dads worry." (If that wasn't a prelude to a lecture, I didn't know what was!)

"Dad—"

"You know, I've been remiss. I should have spoken to you about this several years ago." And so it began. And for the hour that followed, it continued. Dad made up for lost time, talking about the myriad perils of drinking, and how they would lead to drugs and eventually ruin my life. When I asked about the waterfront in particular, he explained that it had a reputation for inviting trouble, and that although The Captain's Table was a respectable four-star restaurant, it was situated in an area that at times could be anything but respectable.

Even at fifteen, I had the good sense to know that his points were valid, but I was not about to become a nun or shut myself off from the world at large. I had no intention of becoming an alcoholic or a drug addict (who ever does?), but I was also looking forward to discovering life outside the family room, and perhaps, becoming a responsible social drinker. My father spoke as if taking even one sip of alcohol would destroy me forever. And, of course, I couldn't help wondering why he didn't drink. But beyond all that, there was one question that really stood out, and although I had to break a family taboo to broach the subject, I was willing to take the risk.

"Dad," I said matter-of-factly, "do you think I'm going to turn into Aunt Rebecca?"

Dad looked absolutely stunned, his eyes fixated on me in a way that I had never seen before. Instantly it dawned on me: my mother had never told him about my humiliating experience in Miss Todd's class, nor had she explained how it had led her to divulge the story of Aunt Rebecca to me.

"What do you know about Rebecca?" he panicked. "Darla, why would you even think of asking me such a question?"

I was in a real bind. I couldn't tell him that Mom had confessed the awful truth to me. Her worst fears, whatever they were, would be realized if I did so. I had to ease Dad's mind and protect my mother.

"Don't you remember, Dad?" I asked nonchalantly. "That scuzzy Martin was rambling on about Aunt Rebecca last summer. He said she was just about my age when she started 'going rotten' and Aunt Didi yelled at him and said Rebecca wasn't a piece of fruit."

"Oh yes. I remember," Dad said, looking relieved. "I'd forgotten about that. The whole evening was just a disaster, a spectacle of the absurd. I'm sure that's why I didn't remember. It's best to let sleeping dogs lie, Darla. Especially rabid ones."

"Dad," I began cautiously, "I know you don't like talking about that evening, but do you remember when Maudie asked you why you didn't drink, and you got really angry?"

"If I looked angry, Darla, it's because her question was inappropriate and rude."

Dad, like Mom, had a talent for answering questions by telling you nothing you didn't already know. I decided to resort to psychological trickery to get Dad to come clean.

"You know, Dad," I began, "lots of my friends' parents lecture them on drinking and stuff, but it's really hard to take them seriously 'cause a lot of them are pretty serious drinkers. I really admire you because at least you practice what you preach and you don't drink. Would it be rude or inappropriate for me to ask you how you found the willpower not to drink at all? And also, what's wrong with social drinking, like Aunt Didi and Uncle George do?" (I thought it best not to mention the fact that my mother enjoyed a glass of wine from time to time.)

"Well!" Dad said, impressed. "You're quite an insightful young woman." He paused and puffed up his chest. I could feel another lecture coming. Perhaps I was not as clever as I'd given myself credit for. "Darla, it's all about losing control. Now, I've told you before that when people yell and scream they lose control. If you add alcohol to that equation, you've got a royal mess on your hands. Quite simply, I'm a man who likes to be in control of himself and his behavior. Even with the best of intentions, one social drink too many can lead to disaster. In order to ensure that doesn't happen, I find it best to stay off the stuff completely. And in case you're wondering, because I know you have a very curious nature, no, I am not a recovering alcoholic as that trollop suggested."

I didn't know what "trollop" meant, but I made a mental note to look it up later. "Dad, did you ever drink?"

"Well," he answered avoiding my gaze, "like most college students, I did indulge, but I eventually learned that it just wasn't for me."

"I guess it's good that you found out before anything bad happened," I said.

Dad gave me a fatherly smile and nodded. I had a hundred questions in my head, but I knew that no matter how cleverly I phrased them, he wasn't going to divulge any more than he wanted to be made known. Whatever kept him locked into this paternal stereotype was not likely to reveal itself anytime soon. It was useless. I waited for him to wrap up the lecture, which ended with "So take a lesson from your old man," and then I went upstairs to call Melanie.

✳ ✳ ✳

Commiserating with Melanie on overprotective parents turned out to be a huge mistake. After our phone conversation, Melanie innocently shared my woes with Brenda, who in turn told her parents. The very next day, Mom got a call from Mrs. Davenport, inviting my parents to Brenda's birthday party.

I was furious. This invitation had been a milestone of sorts in my life. It was the first party I'd been invited to that wasn't at someone's house, not at the local pizza parlor or in the school gymnasium, and it was to be the first party where the boys, for the most part, would be older. But suddenly, because of alleged promiscuity on the waterfront, or maybe because of my mysterious aunt Rebecca's past, my parents were going to this party with me. I could understand why the Davenports felt obliged to invite them, but I didn't understand why they had to accept. Not only were they invading my privacy by doing so, they were degrading and humiliating me at the same time.

I tried explaining this to Dad. (I didn't even bother with Mom, because I knew she had no power to change any of it.) Dad would not break down, assuring me that we'd just be like "ships that pass in the night." There was no reason that his and Mom's presence had to interfere with my good time—not unless I let it.

As Melanie and I sat on my bed lamenting the situation, she apologized profusely for inadvertently getting my parents invited. "I'm really sorry, Dar," she said, vigorously chewing her gum. "I guess I'll have to watch what I say to Brenda from now on. Sometimes she has the biggest mouth!"

"It's not your fault," I said, rearranging my stuffed animals. "You didn't know what would happen."

"Cheer up, Dar. My parents are going to be there too, you know."

"Yeah, but they're giving the party," I moaned, holding my stuffed Tigger for moral support. "It's their daughter that's turning twenty-one."

"Darla," Melanie said as she popped her gum loudly, "I was with

43

Mom when she booked the room, and trust me, it's humongoid. I mean, it's not like your parents are going to be on top of you or anything. There will be plenty of older people for them to shoot the breeze with. Chill out, it'll be fine."

"I guess you're right," I said. But I was still angry.

The Captain's Table exceeded my expectations. From the moment the white-gloved doorman ushered us inside, my romantic imagination took flight. Before Dad could order me to stand at attention, I was two feet inside The Galley, the restaurant's cocktail lounge, feasting my eyes on everything and everybody. The walls, which were tastefully adorned with various nautical memorabilia, featured a portrait gallery of famous ship captains. Each man's face, I mused, looked crustier and saltier than the next. To me, there was something mysterious about the sullen, stained faces of these seafaring souls. Something romantic, I imagined, about the way their skin peeled like driftwood and their tears rusted in the rain. Of course, I personally wasn't in the market to meet such a rugged specimen of manliness, but I found it terribly romantic all the same.

As I surveyed the room, I couldn't help but feel envious as I looked at all the couples, who appeared, to my inexperienced eyes, to be madly in love as they gazed into each other's eyes through the amber glow of the softy lit room.

A million things crossed my mind. For one, The Captain's Table was certainly the classiest restaurant I'd ever been in, and I just couldn't fathom my father's absurd objections. But more than that, I imagined how it might feel to be in love—to sip exotic cocktails dressed with paper umbrellas, to dine on gourmet dishes with unpronounceable names, then to follow it up with a glorious night—one filled with dancing and resplendent in romance. Certainly, this was the place to be. Just maybe, that evening, I would meet the special guy who would help make my romantic fantasies come true.

As I continued to soak up the ambience, drifting further into my dreamy-eyed trance, I heard my father say to someone, "We're looking for the Davenport party."

"Starboard Room, sir. To your right and down the hall."

"Darla," Dad called loudly to me. "This way."

I resented my father so much at that moment. In fact, I felt a pang of sheer hatred toward him, and I wasn't feeling much kindlier toward my feeble mother, who had sat idly by and allowed all of this to happen. They were invited to this party because of me, not the other way around. But instead, I felt like a ten-year-old kid being dragged to some dreadful family party—the kind of party where strangers tell you they "know all about you" and how you were "this high" when they last saw you, and "my, how you've grown" and "you look just like so-and-so." Whatever the reality of the situation, I didn't want to be anywhere near my parents. I just couldn't figure out whether to lag behind them or sprint quickly down the hall in an effort to enter the Starboard Room before them. I opted for lagging.

"Don't dawdle, Darla," Dad alliterated as he turned to look at me.

Dawdle? That's something you say to a toddler! He was regressing me even further. I hate you! I thought. Why are you doing this to me?

I gave my father the dirtiest look I could, and just as he was about to censure me for it, I saw Mom touch his arm gently, whisper a few words, and nod toward the banquet room. Finally, at least in some small way, she had come through for me. They walked on ahead without giving me another glance. I fell several more paces behind them and made my grand entrance alone.

The room was huge, and there appeared to be at least two hundred people present. To the left was a long banquet table, stocked with fruit, cheese, shrimp, tea sandwiches, and a host of "scrump-dilly-icious" cold hors d'oeuvres, while hot hors d'oeuvres were offered to the mingling crowd by waiters dressed like sea captains. Toward the back of the room was a well-stocked bar, and to the right of the bar, on the stage, was a six-piece band dressed in black tie playing "Eleanor Rigby."

There were far more adults present than I had imagined, and I felt relieved that my parents would not stand out like the proverbial sore thumb I had feared. Rather, they would blend into the crowd and disappear. I scanned the room for Melanie. Despite my desire to enter the party alone, I did feel rather awkward and out of place.

"What's a nice girl like you doin' in a place like this?" I heard a male voice say.

"Huh?" I said, turning around to find the most adorable guy I'd ever seen.

He burst out laughing. "I'm sorry. I know that's a ridiculous line. It's just that I've always wanted to say that to a girl, and this is the first place I've been that seemed appropriate. I swear, I've never said it before and I'll never say it again!"

I couldn't stop looking at him. He was about five feet eleven, with sandy brown hair and the most gorgeous blue eyes and the sexiest smile I'd ever seen. He was wearing brown corduroy pants, a white shirt with navy blue suspenders, and a dark red bow tie. If someone had described his outfit to me, I would've bet he had to be the biggest geek in the world. But he was far from geekiness and I was falling in love.

"I'm Ryan Mullavey," he said, holding out his right hand.

His eyes were so blue. "Oh," I said, weakened by his touch. "Hi, I'm Darla McKendrick. I'm Melanie's best friend."

"Cool. I'm a friend of Ben's. We work together at the supermarket after school, in the produce department."

"You work with lettuce...and fruits, I guess?"

I wouldn't call them fruits." Ryan laughed. "But some of my coworkers are pretty weird! Especially Ben."

"Sheesh!" I laughed nervously. "I can't believe I said that."

"But you did," he said with a grin. "So, who did you come with tonight, Darla?"

I couldn't tell him. It would be too humiliating.

" I came alone," I told him, just as I saw Dad waving at me from across the room.

"Did you drive here?"

"No," I muttered uncomfortably. "I got a ride."

"Maybe I'll be able to take you home."

"Maybe," I said, frustrated by the implausibility of that scenario.

Dad, who had no clue that I saw him just fine the first time, began waving at me a second time. I diverted my glance once again, this time looking straight into Ryan's blue eyes, as if he were the only other person in the room. Suddenly, my legs began to shake, registering God-knows-what on the Richter scale, and every clever line I'd ever rehearsed flew right out of my head. I was a mess. Luckily, Ryan was not as awestruck by this magical first encounter as I was and had no trouble making conversation.

"I've been scoping out this room for the last half hour, Darla, and all I can say is, the Davenports sure know some strange people. Present company excluded and all that."

"Really?" I asked, perpetually fascinated by oddities. "Like who?"

"Come with me and I'll show you," Ryan said, taking my hand, and before I knew it, he was walking me through the crowd. I prayed my parents were no longer lurking nearby, and I got angry all over again as I thought about how much more fun this would have been had they remained home in their natural habitat.

"Check it out, Darla." Ryan laughed as he nodded his head to the left. "Get a load of that!"

"Wow!" I exclaimed, noticing a seventy-something-year-old blond lady dressed in a gold gown with a jeweled crown on her head. "Who's she?"

"The Queen of Rich, I guess. Dig those fake jewels on her shoes. Is she a trip or what? And see that guy in the brown jacket over there? The one with the red hair? Every time he raises his Heineken bottle with his right hand, he picks at his pimples or something with the left."

"Oh yeah," I said, feeling more comfortable. "What's the 'or something'"?

"I'm not sure," Ryan teased. "But if you really wanna know, I'm sure I can arrange an introduction. Maybe even a show-and-tell. 'Excuse me, sir. Are those blackheads or boils you're hacking away at there? This young lady would like to examine one. She's doing a science project on the many faces of acne.'"

"Eeewwww gross!" I screeched, as thoughts of the Lughead's nose embellished the mental picture I was painting. "No way! No thanks! Sheesh, Ryan, did you have to go into such disgusting detail?"

"Sorry," he said, straightfaced. "Guess you didn't appreciate my suggestion, huh? Well, Darla, there's no need to zitpick!"

Ryan and I stood there for several minutes, roaring hysterically, as we bonded over the hilarity of facial blemishes.

"Wow," I finally said, wiping the tears of laughter from my eyes, "who's that woman in the tacky black dress? See her? The one with the dyed black hair?"

"The groper," Ryan said authoritatively. "I've been watchin' that broad since I came in. Miss Touchy Feely with a hundred pounds of makeup. Look at those dark circles under her eyes, Darla. She's Uncle Fester—with hair. She gropes and paws every man she talks to. Check her out now. She's going over to that good-looking guy in the navy blazer. Man, he's about to find out how a melon feels."

We watched with stunned amusement as this hideous woman caressed the stranger's face, obviously whispering something of a sexual nature in his ear. The man instantly stepped back from her in blatant disgust, but unfazed, she moved closer. Then, without missing a beat, she put her hand on his shoulder and slowly worked her way down his back until she got to his butt. He stood there frozen, like a statue, his eyes fixated on her while his nostrils flared, and his left upper lip curled upward in revulsion.

"Can you believe this, Ryan? Who is that woman? I didn't think the Davenports even knew people like that! Why doesn't that guy just push her away?"

"Beats me," he said, mesmerized by the action.

Suddenly, a beautiful young blonde in a jade-colored dress (obviously the man's wife) walked over and yanked the woman away from her husband. Then, in what appeared to be a carefully orchestrated move, she took her brandy alexander and poured it, like an ice cream topping, over the woman's jet black hair. Soaking wet, and looking just like a hot fudge sundae minus the cherry, the groper hissed and snarled, then raised her hand to the blonde. Just as all hell was about to break loose, Mr. Davenport intervened and separated the women. He muttered a few words to the black-haired woman through the dripping drink, then, taking her sternly by the elbow through a crowd of amazed onlookers, he led her quickly and forcefully out of the room.

"Omigod!" I heard Melanie say from somewhere in the crowd.

"Melanie!" I said, turning around. "Did you see that or what?"

"Your parents sure know some strange people," Ryan told her.

"Gee, Ryan," Melanie said. "They don't know her at all. She crashed the party. My dad just escorted that hussy outta here. Skieve me out. Did you get a close look at her? She had hickeys on her neck!"

"Eeewww, gross!"

"They oughta arrest whoever put 'em there," Ryan said.

"Like, can you even imagine the guy who would suck her neck? Must've been some degenerate vampire or something. Skieve me out!" Melanie said.

Suddenly, Melanie noticed that Ryan and I were "together" and quickly lost interest in the hickeys. "Well, when did you two meet?"

"Just a while ago," Ryan told her. "Over by the front door."

"Darla is my very best friend," Melanie warned playfully. "Better be nice to her."

"No problem." Ryan smiled and winked at me.

At that moment, Melanie's brother Ben came rushing toward us. "Hey, Darla. What's up?" He turned to Ryan. "Did you see my old man throw that hooker out of here? Did you get a look at that broad? Man, that was too funny when that lady creamed her. Come on, we're waitin' for you."

"I'll see you later," Ryan said as Ben eagerly pulled him away. "I'll be over there, by the band."

"A hooker?" Melanie gasped. "Omigod!"

My heart sank. As I turned to see which direction Ryan had gone, I couldn't help but notice my father standing nearby, looking my way and shaking his head in a revolting, I-told-you-so nod.

"Forget about your dad!" Melanie said, noticing him too. "C'mon, let's check out this feast. We'd better. My parents only paid a small fortune for it!"

"Really?" I asked. "How much?"

The next two hours were great. Melanie and I gorged ourselves on the food, including a piece of Brenda's birthday cake, then went over to join Ryan and Ben. My nervousness finally dissipated, and I got to know Ryan better, learning that he was a drummer and planned a career as a professional musician. When he asked me if I'd like to hear him play some evening, I fell into a heavenly delirium, completely forgetting that my parents were even within miles of us. After talking for a good hour, Ryan and I danced about five dances, until Ben Davenport cut in, and later Ryan and I found a seat and talked some more. Melanie, who spent most of her time with Brenda and her friends, kept giving me the "thumbs up" sign from across the stage. My spirits were soaring and it was the first time in my life that I really felt like a grown woman.

Around eleven o'clock, the band came back from break for their final set and announced they were going to "slow down the tempo." Ryan smiled, took my hand, and led me onto the dance floor. The evening was getting better all the time. The disco light above our heads turned slowly, illuminating a shower of stars that floated gloriously around us. I imagined we were dancing in a galaxy of our own, and when we were too tired to dance anymore, we would drift slowly downward, to rest on a nearby cloud and gaze at each other through the pure white mist. Halfway through the second song, Ryan pulled me closer to him. I could feel his breath on my neck. I squeezed his hand in response and he squeezed back. I was positively euphoric.

I was so caught up in the enchantment of it all that I barely felt the tap on my shoulder. Suddenly, Ryan pulled away from me and stared at the person behind me.

"May I cut in?" the voice said.

I turned around to find my father standing there, grinning, holding out his hand to me.

"Dad," I said flatly as the color drained from my face.

"You won't mind, young man," he said to Ryan, "if I have this dance with my daughter."

"Oh," Ryan said, quickly assessing the situation. "Sure, Mr. McKendrick."

Dad took my hand and began to dance with me. I felt like my old Raggedy Ann doll, dull and spiritless, as if the life blood had been siphoned from my body. I started to breathe heavily as I felt my eyes well up with tears. As he spun me around the dance floor, I caught a glimpse of Melanie, who stood there gaping, obviously feeling every bit of my pain, as best friends will do.

When the song ended, Dad stood there and beamed proudly at me. He had absolutely no idea of the devastation and anguish that he had just caused. Here was a man who had just ruined my entire life, and he was unquestionably clueless.

"Thank you for that lovely dance. Well, say good night to your friends, Darla. It's getting late and we'd best hit the road."

I hated every insensitive bone in his body. I turned and walked over to Ryan.

"I've got to go," I said, praying that the tears would stay inside my eyes. "It was great meeting you."

"I'll call you, Darla," he said sincerely. "We'll go out some night."

"Sure," I said, convinced that I'd never see him again. "I'll look forward to it."

I walked over to Melanie, who greeted me with an anguished "Omigod, Darla."

"Call me tomorrow," I said (as if it were even necessary), and I rushed, in complete and utter humiliation, out of the room.

"That was some shindig!" Dad said outside the banquet room, as we were walking toward the exit. "Mike and Grace Davenport sure know how to do it up!"

I ignored him completely.

"Did you have a good time, honey? Sure looked to me and your mom like you did."

I stopped and turned slowly toward my father. "I hate you."

Dad looked crestfallen. He stared at me in disbelief and then looked at

51

my mother, as if to ask for help. Naturally, Mom could do nothing but offer a weary sigh. I could tell that he was completely bewildered. Not in my angriest moments had I ever said anything like that to him, and now, just after what he had perceived to be a special father-daughter moment, I was expressing hatred for him. Now he looked as if he were going to cry, and on top of the mortifying embarrassment that I had just suffered on the dance floor, there was the added burden of having totally destroyed my father's image of his loving little girl. Dad just stood there, helpless, staring at me, as if he were waiting for me to explain or confess that I'd made a horrible mistake. I didn't know what to do, so I stood there and looked right back at him, then at the floor. Finally, he just turned and walked toward the front door. Mom and I followed quietly behind him.

Dad never said another word that evening, except to describe his car to the parking valet, and the three of us rode home in agonized silence.

CHAPTER 4

I fell into bed some time after midnight, drained from the life-shaping events that had suddenly rocked my neat little world. I could not sleep. Like a leaky faucet, my brain went drip, drip, drip, filling my head with a bucketful of misery. Finally, sheer exhaustion knocked me out around one-thirty, but internal chaos woke me up at two-thirty, continuing repeatedly every hour, like a demented cuckoo clock bent on revenge. Nothing made any sense at all, least of all my dreams, and I prayed that when the darkness passed into light, my troubles would pass along with it.

My parents were sitting at the kitchen table when I came downstairs the next morning. I'd been hoping to avoid them, at least until I'd had time to formulate a plan of action.

"Good morning, Darla." Mom smiled cheerfully. "You're just in time. Here, I've squeezed some fresh orange juice for you."

"Thanks, Mom," I said, taking the glass of juice that sat waiting.

Dad, who was reading the business section, lowered the paper momentarily and looked at me. His eyes seemed hollow, as if his soul were missing.

"Good morning," he said coolly. "I trust you slept well."

"Yeah, fine," I lied, unwilling to give him the satisfaction of knowing what my guilty conscience was doing to me.

"Sit down, Darla," Mom said, as if she were talking to company. "I'll make you some pancakes. How does that sound?"

Why was she being so nice to me? "Don't go to any trouble, Mom," I said, taking my seat.

"No trouble at all. I still have plenty of fixings left from your father's breakfast. Batter up."

Dad looked glumly down at the stack of pancakes on the table. "My eyes weren't as big as my stomach," he said. "Just don't seem to have much of an appetite today."

So now he was rubbing it in. He was twisting the knife, ever so

53

gently, taking a sick pleasure in torturing me. It was my fault he lost his appetite. My guilty conscience took a walk. I started to feel angry all over again. He went back to reading his paper and I waited, for what seemed an eternity, until my mother put my breakfast on the table.

"Well, I'm off for a day of shopping with Didi!" Mom announced brightly, unfastening her apron. "Are you and Melanie going to do anything special today?"

"I dunno," I mumbled through a mouth full of food. "Maybe."

Mom smiled and kissed me on the forehead. She walked over to my father, who obligingly lowered his paper again, kissed him, and left.

Mom had only been gone for seconds when Dad put the paper down for good. "Darla," he said emphatically. "We need to talk."

"Okay," I said begrudgingly, resting my fork on the plate.

"I didn't sleep well last night," he confessed. "In fact, I'd say I didn't get much shuteye at all. Last night my daughter told me that she hated me. Can you imagine that? And just at a moment when I was feeling so proud—proud that she had grown into such a beautiful young lady and that the two of us shared such a special relationship."

Dad often spoke to me in the third person when he was hurt or angry. I suppose it expunged any discernible intimacy from the conversation, thus enabling him to detach long enough to make the proper points.

"I didn't mean it," I mumbled awkwardly.

"Well then," he asserted. "I can't imagine why in the world you'd say it."

"You embarrassed me in front of everyone!" I retorted, looking directly at my pancakes, as if they were the object of my scorn.

"Exactly how did I do that?" he challenged, pushing his plate out of the way.

"You know," I said giving him an evil squint of the eyes, then looking away.

"If I knew, Darla," he said sternly, "I wouldn't have to ask."

"You cut in on me when I was dancing with Ryan! I really liked him, Dad. And now he'll never call me. Ever! And it's all because of you!"

He rolled his eyes, as if to discount every word I'd spoken. "Darla, if that young man decides not to call you, based simply on the fact that you had a dance with your father, then he isn't the kind of young man you'd want to be associated with anyhow."

I hated the way he spoke so calmly and authoritatively, as if he knew everything and there was no room for debate.

"You just don't understand," I said despairingly.

"I understand that after less than three hours in that boy's company, you told your father you hated him. That much I understand. Which leads me to believe that he may not be the best influence on you."

I resented the fact that he was now referring to Ryan as a boy. "Ryan is a great guy," I rebutted. "And it wasn't him that made me angry; it was you. You and Mom shouldn't even have come to the party."

"The Davenports invited us, Darla. Apparently, they wanted us to be there."

Even in my state of fury, I didn't want to tell him how the invitation had come about. "Why didn't you just stay with the adults then? Why did you have to break in on my dance?" I was growing more and more agitated with his passive-aggressive posturing.

"I must have inadvertently crossed the line," he said sarcastically. "Where was it, Darla? Was it a chalk line? A red line? A yellow line? Did it go down the center of the room, or was it just around the dance floor? And just how was I to inform you that it was time to go home? Would you have preferred that I used the public address system?"

"I really liked him, Dad," I repeated, thinking about Ryan and ignoring his sarcastic rhetoric. "I was having the best time at that party until you humiliated and embarrassed me."

"Perhaps I shouldn't have cut in on your dance," he admitted, "but if doing so 'humiliated and embarrassed' you, then perhaps you're not old enough to participate in social situations of this nature or to date boys like Ryan."

Now I was seething mad. He was downright insulting me—and

Ryan. I was going to tell him the ugly truth: "The Davenports only invited you because Brenda went and blabbed to her parents that you were worried about the waterfront. And I am too old enough to go to parties and date guys. I'm older now than I've ever been in my life!"

I saw him suppress a smile. I wished I could take back that last sentence. What a foolish thing to say! No doubt he would later share my stupidity with Mom, giving them both a good story to swap with their friends who also had bumbling teenagers for children.

Dad quickly straightened his face. "First of all, Darla," he said bluntly, "your mother and I are well aware of why we were invited to the Davenport party. Second, you're almost sixteen and I believe you are old enough to date boys and attend various social functions, but that doesn't mean that you have carte blanche to go anywhere with anyone. Oh no. Far from it. Now, I'm sure that this Ryan boy is a fine, young man" (now he was a boy and a man) "but if he does call to ask you out on a date, I'd like to know something about him and his family before you accept."

"Oh God!" I moaned. "I hope his résumé is up to date. Do you want to interview him or what? Or maybe have the FBI or the CIA run a background check on him. How embarrassing!"

"Don't be ridiculous, Darla!" he snapped, annoyed by my sarcasm. "If you want to go anywhere, young lady, you'd better watch your mouth. If fraternization with the opposite sex is going to wreak this kind of havoc on your personality, then all bets are off. If you plan to test your wings, you'd better learn to straighten up and fly right. Now, I'm well aware that you're anxious to partake in activities that other kids your age are enjoying. But you've got to understand that I'm going to do everything I can to provide for your welfare, whether you like it or not!"

If that wasn't a speech straight out of the Dad handbook, I didn't know what was. He paused and looked at me, as if to determine how well his message was being received. I waited for him to tell me that I'd thank him for all this some day. That was always a key point in his most profound lectures.

"I know it's tough being a teenager, honey," he softened, "but you know what? It's also tough being a parent, being legally and morally responsible for another human being. It's not always easy to make popular decisions. But as a parent, you do the best you can. Some day, Darla, you may even thank me for some of the unpopular decisions I make today. Now, do we understand each other?"

"Yeah, I guess," I muttered lazily, biting my bottom lip in defiance.

Dad folded his paper neatly, tucked it under his arm, and rose from the table. "I'll leave you to finish your breakfast. If you need me, I'll be in my study working." He kissed me on the forehead, in exactly the same place Mom had, and walked out of the room.

I was emotionally depleted and my pancakes were cold. My entree into young adulthood was everything it was not supposed to be. The changes in my life, for the most part, were not the changes I had happily anticipated the previous summer. Without wanting to, I had disappointed my father and made him suspicious of me. The trust he had in me was tarnished, and all the polishing in the world would never make it shine the way it once had. As for my mother, her chipper demeanor that morning had verified her usual intent of leaving the whole mess in my father's "capable hands." It angered me to know that her true feelings would be revealed to Aunt Didi over lunch, but with me, she would continue to play what Melanie had dubbed "Betty Crocker."

As I tossed the uneaten pancakes in the garbage, I cautioned myself to be more careful in the future. I could no longer use my innocence or lack of experience to justify my mistakes. I was not the dumb kid who once announced helpfully at the dinner table that Aunt Rebecca might screw her way out of squalor. Now I was responsible for everything that I said and did. Every action had a price, and in the future, I would have to consider the price tag before I bought anything. If I didn't, Dad would probably condemn me to a life of solitary confinement and send me to school with an armed guard. It was all so awful, and to make everything worse, I still had the nagging suspicion that my aunt Rebecca's teenage misfortunes were directly connected to my father's apparent lack of faith in me.

I grabbed an onion bagel from the bread box, buttered it, and went upstairs to the telephone, where I spent the next several hours philosophizing with Melanie.

When the next couple of weeks passed without word from Ryan, I blamed it all on my father. No guy worth having, I surmised, would want to date someone with such an overprotective and meddling dad. In my mind, there was no question as to why he hadn't called. But as time wore on, I realized that my anger was concocting an unfair and unrealistic description of my loving and well-intentioned father, and that the problem lay with me: I was awkward and ugly and had nothing to offer a good-looking guy like Ryan. My father was right. After all, if cutting in on our dance were all it took to turn Ryan off, then it was doubtful he had ever been turned on at all.

Since Ben Davenport was Ryan's best buddy, Melanie tried nonchalantly to pump him for information, but after one failed attempt, she quickly dismissed her brother as a potential news source. Guys, though they denied it, talked just as much as girls did, and we both agreed that I would probably suffer untold humiliation if word ever got back to Ryan that I was sitting around waiting to hear from him. But, despite the painful revelation that this relationship was not to be, I hoped against all logic and reason that he would still call. Surprising even myself, I decided to start praying at night. Maybe God could get him to call.

I didn't know a lot about praying. It felt awkward to me, as though I were begging God to help me when he had more important things to tend to—like famine, war, poverty, racial intolerance, environmental disasters, a cure for cancer, and things like that. Asking God to have Ryan call me seemed absolutely ludicrous in a way, but then again, a small favor like that wouldn't take up much of God's time and I had never asked Him for very much in the past.

I sat up in my bed with the lights off and put my hands together in a praying position. "Hi, God," I said fervently. "It's me, Darla McKendrick. It's about midnight, Eastern Daylight Time, on October the second. If you have a moment, I'd like to ask you for, or pray for, a quick favor."

I decided that I wasn't going about this in the right way. Having no idea how to pray to God, and being too embarrassed to even ask Melanie, this was something I'd have to figure out for myself. One thing was for sure: I didn't have to identify myself to God and time stamp my prayer. And not only that, I should ask God for something more substantial than a phone call from Ryan. If I didn't, He would just see me as a shallow, selfish teenager and refuse to help me at all.

"Sorry for the interruption, God," I continued. "I'm not very good at this, but I hope you'll listen anyway. You see, things have been really tough for me with my parents, especially with my father. I made one little mistake and now everything has changed. He doesn't trust me anymore. I'm really a good person, God. I haven't done anything to be ashamed of. I swear to God, I mean to You. My father still talks to me and stuff, but it's so different than before. It's like he's always mad at me. And as for my mother, could you get her to open up more and stop being afraid of my father, and of her own shadow? It would really help the both of us. And one more thing, God: if you could get Ryan to call me, that would make me really happy. (I was pleased at how smoothly I'd slipped that in.) Oh, and please tell Grandpa Henry and Grandma Adelaide that I miss them a whole bunch. Well, I've taken up enough of your time. Thank you and amen."

Pleased with my second attempt at prayer, I continued this ritual several times a week, hoping desperately that this cold war with my father would end and that Ryan would call. I was miserable, but I kept telling myself that God would answer my prayers in His own good time, certainly not in mine. I just had to be patient.

Not all of the changes in my early sophomore year of high school were bad. The best thing that happened was that my cousins, April, May, and June, had finally convinced their parents to let them finish out high school in public school. They were sick of the stuffy private academy they attended, which was a good hour away, and I suppose my uncle was also sick of paying for it. Besides, the girls were still busy with their performing careers, and being nearby in public school afforded them far more time and flexibility to pursue fame and glory.

I honestly believed that April, May, and June were destined for stardom. But aside from their myriad talents, they were also terrific people, especially May, who was my age and also my favorite. She was the sweetest sister, the kind of person who took the time to care about everyone, even strangers. I remember one Christmas when Uncle George had arranged for the girls to entertain at a local nursing home where a colleague's mother lived. Graciously, and with bright, beautiful smiles on their faces, the girls delighted the residents for over an hour with their amazing repertoire of songs. But long after that afternoon had ended, it was May who went back to the home, time and time again, to cheer the residents with her love of life. Being so sweet, she was also extremely sensitive, which was a trait I shared with her. The only difference was that I was more inclined to let my feelings show, and May was the type to hold her pain inside, so she wouldn't hurt people by letting them know how much they had hurt her.

April, although she was the oldest, was frequently mistaken for the youngest of the three sisters, probably because she giggled a lot when she was embarrassed or at a loss for words. For a long while, I was baffled by April's nervous, or shall I say inappropriate, giggling. After all, as a professional entertainer, she had so much experience being in front of people. But being in front of crowds was the easy part. Aunt Didi, in her haste to prepare my cousins for stardom, forgot somewhere along the way that they were human beings first. She didn't realize that before they could be "three," they needed to be at one with themselves.

As a child, I was often envious, even downright jealous, of them for having each other. I was surprised in later years when May confided to me that she had always been envious of me for having an identity all to myself. At first, I was stunned by her statement.

"I'll bet no one ever walked up to you, looked you right in the face, and said, 'Which sister are you?' " May challenged me.

She went on to explain that if she, or any of her sisters, went anywhere by themselves or with friends, they were frequently approached by some meddlesome acquaintance who wanted to know where the other two sisters were—as though the law demanded that they exist in triplicate, like some official government form.

"I love being with April and June, most of the time," May confessed, "but the older I get, the more I need my own identity." She smiled. "Any reason I can't just be May Lynne Alexander, human being extraordiniare?"

"None at all," I had told her. "You already are." She had the neatest way, I thought, of often ending a conversation on a positive note. It was a trait I sometimes wished I had but tried desperately not to pick up.

And then there was June, the youngest, whom strangers often mistook for being the oldest. I suppose one of the reasons had to be that she was much more endowed than April or May (probably because she stayed in the womb until July). But aside from having a large chest that made her look older, publicly, June was the most outgoing of the three, which is why she often served as the group's unofficial spokesperson. Unlike April, who giggled a lot, or May, who tread softly, June had a warm, inviting presence that simply commanded attention. Her greatest fear, that of being left behind by her two older sisters, was so well masked by her exuberance and verve, that it was easy to forget.

One incident in particular, which was probably the only bright spot of those first two dreary weeks in October, really illustrates June's grace and poise, as well as her ability to think quickly on the spot. My cousins had agreed to perform at a charity benefit called "Salute to Broadway," which was held annually at a local university. The emcee, a college senior, was also an aspiring Broadway performer, who opened the show by advising the audience to "remember his name," because he was headed for the Great White Way—destined for some sort of thespian sainthood. Unfortunately, this misguided candidate for canonization was laboring under the misconception that the audience had gathered en masse to worship his golden talents, rather than those of the show's featured performers.

After introducing my cousins as "The Alexander Three," he praised them for their many accomplishments, then asked the girls to introduce themselves individually. April went first, as she always did, and June finished by quoting June Havoc from Gypsy: "Hi, everybody, my name's June. What's yours?"

The audience, largely comprised of Broadway show enthusiasts, appreciated June's humor and laughed out loud. The girls took their marks and prepared to sing their first number, "Matchmaker, Matchmaker," from Fiddler on the Roof.

"Before we begin, ladies and germs," the emcee suddenly blurted out like a rowdy vaudevillian, "I have something to say." He looked at the piano player (whom Uncle George found out later had been bribed in advance) and said, "Hit it, Maestro!"

Then, as the music began, he turned to June with some dramatic sweeping hand gesture and sang a rousing, yet barely on-key version of "June Is Bustin' Out All Over." Mom and Dad were quietly astounded; Aunt Didi went ballistic in her seat; Uncle George looked as if he were going to rush to the stage waving a loaded gun; and I, of course, had a delightful time surveying the chaos. Some members of the audience, at first not realizing that the emcee's performance (and that's being kind) was not in the script, laughed politely, but most just sat there—in stunned, embarrassed silence.

Up on stage, April giggled nervously, and May, though she retained her composure, looked (to me) as if she wanted to cry (not for herself, but for what she perceived as June's humiliation). June, with a genuine-looking smile on her face, waited patiently for this insect to finish.

When the very minimal applause had subsided, June walked pleasantly up to the microphone, scratched her head in mock confusion, then said to the audience: "Don't they spray for cockroaches in this place?"

The auditorium came alive as the room filled with cheers, whistles, and applause. Even Aunt Didi's and Uncle George's faces resumed their normal color. Without missing a beat, June turned to the piano player and, using the emcee's very same words, said, "Hit it, Maestro!" My cousins performed their number beautifully as the emcee slunk gloomily off the stage. When their second number was over, the girls received a unanimous standing ovation, and when it was time for the emcee to introduce the next act, the show's director appeared in his place, gaily marveling to the audience about the miracle of theatrical makeup, and how it can change a person's appearance drastically in just a matter of minutes.

I went home that evening, thanked God for the comical diversion, and prayed that my life would get better soon.

CHAPTER 5

Ryan called me on the third Tuesday of that October, at eight thirty-five in the evening, just as I was suffering through the last algebra problem on my homework assignment. My father had always told me that "good things happen when you least expect them" and that "good things come to those who wait," so even though we weren't on the best of terms, I gave him credit for being right about something. I certainly wasn't expecting Ryan's call, but at the same time, I had done nothing but mope, pray, and wait for his call.

It was Mom who yelled up the back stairs that "Ryan Mullavey was on the phone." I was so ecstatic that I couldn't think straight. The glorious moment I had imagined for weeks was now a reality. I picked up the receiver and waited impatiently for Mom to hang up the kitchen phone.

"Hello, Ryan," I said, trying to sound confident and relaxed. "How are you?"

"Fine, Darla. How are you?"

"Oh, I'm fine. And you?" I said, suddenly afflicted with etymological redundanitis.

"I'm doing great. Glad to hear you are too."

"Oh, yeah, I'm fine," I said, feeling worse by the moment. "What have you been up to?"

"Well, my dad's been really sick. He had pneumonia for a couple of weeks and was in the hospital."

"I'm so sorry to hear that. Is he all right?"

"Yeah, he's doing fine. But that's why I didn't call you sooner. I was really busy going back and forth to the hospital and helping my mom with stuff, and in the little free time I had left, I had to work and practice with my band."

I was thrilled—not that his father was recovering from pneumonia, but that he had such a valid reason for not calling me. Silently, I began to calculate the date of our anniversary, trying to determine if we should celebrate from the night of Brenda's party or from our official first date, which I assumed he was about to ask me out on.

"Oh, that's okay," I assured him. "I'm just glad to hear from you. Is your dad all better now?"

"Yeah. He just went back to the firm yesterday."

"Is he a lawyer?"

"Nah, he's just an investment banker," Ryan replied, as if it were a disappointing alternative.

"Get out of here!" I shrieked. "So is my dad!"

"Hey...no kidding!"

I couldn't wait to tell Dad that Ryan's father was an investment banker too. He would have to approve of my dating Ryan now. Darla Mullavey, I thought. I won't even have to change my monogram. Remembering that I didn't own anything that was monogrammed, my thoughts returned to the conversation at hand.

"What's the name of your dad's firm?" I asked, figuring it best to get the background check over and done with.

"Mullavey, Hartman, and Richardson."

The name didn't mean a thing to me, but I figured that if his dad's name was first, it was all I needed to impress my dad.

"Listen, Darla, I was wondering if you'd like to go to a Halloween party with me."

"Cool. Where and when?" I asked, trying to hide my excitement as I danced victoriously around the phone.

"Uh, in the city, on the Saturday before Halloween. At my cousin's condo. He's just a law student, but my aunt and uncle have wads of cash, so he gets to live in this really dynamite place with this, like, totally incredible view. Anyway, I just talked to Ben and he said that Melanie is coming with her new boyfriend, Jesse, so I was hoping you'd like to go with me."

"Cool," I repeated, as the disease progressed. "What should I do about a costume?"

"Do whatever you want," he said, sounding uninterested. I was a bit disappointed. I had hoped he'd say, "Let's go as Romeo and Juliet," or something equally as improbable.

"Okay," I said, trying to suppress my ebullience. "That sounds great. I'll look forward to it."

"I will too," Ryan said. "I'm really glad you can make it."

Miraculously, the conversation not only continued, but managed to sustain itself for a grand total of sixteen and a half minutes, as we discussed such intriguing topics as algebra versus geometry, Ben Davenport's recently pierced ear, the high cost of drums, and the hooker who got brandy-alexandered at Brenda's party.

There was no doubt about it. Ryan was the guy for me.

* * *

"Omigod!" Melanie screamed in my ear, when I phoned to tell her about Ryan's call. "Gee, Darla, I'm so happy for you. I knew he would call you. I mean, the way he looked at you on the dance floor and all—it was totally obvious that he liked you. Have you thought about a costume?"

"I'm kinda lost in that department," I told her.

"Jesse is totally psyched about going as Tarzan, but I told him, 'I don't do Jane!' And I mean it, Dar. There is no way I'm going anywhere wearing a wraparound jungle dress and bare feet, especially in October. No way, José! Hey, maybe you and I should do something together."

"Like what?" I asked, intrigued by the possibility.

"I don't know—wait—Omigod! I've got it!"

"What?" I pleaded with her. "Tell me!"

"Are you ready for this?"

"Yeah! I'm ready already. What is it?"

"Whattya say we go dressed as your skievoid uncle Martin and his wife? Is that a scream or what? Omigod! I love it!"

"Don't we have to go as people everyone knows?"

"Duh, when did you last go out for Halloween, Darla? In the second grade? We don't have to dress up like famous people. We'll just go as a geeky couple. That's all anyone needs to know. C'mon. Think about it. Every Halloween you see someone dressed up as a witch, a hooker, or some kind of gypsy. Do you think they all have names, like 'The Happy Hooker' or 'The Wicked Witch of the West' or 'Grizelda the Gypsy'? No, Darla, they're just hookers and witches and gypsies. And we'll just go as geeks, something you come by naturally. Really, Dar, you can be such a bozo head at times."

"Thanks!" I replied, amused by the insult. "So which one of us is going to go as Martin? It give me the creeps to think about dressing up like him and staining my teeth and stuff."

"I'll go as Martin," Melanie offered. "I don't mind skieving myself out. You can go as Maudie. We'll have to take, like, a hundred rolls of film. This is so totally awesome."

Melanie and I rambled on for another hour, going over every aspect of our plans, including how we would record the event for posterity, how our dates would be impressed with our creative genius, and mostly, how much fun we would have. I wondered why it was so easy to talk to Melanie, and why it was like pulling teeth to talk to Ryan. I figured that you couldn't have an easy conversation if romance was involved; it just wasn't part of the deal. I suppose I didn't want to consider the possibility that Ryan and I simply didn't have the right chemistry. A wise, but not yet matured, part of my brain knew that I was far from "the real thing," but at fifteen and a half, when a gorgeous guy pays attention to you, holds you close and dances with you, then calls you and asks you out, it's only polite, and only right, to fall madly and deeply in love with him.

The writing was on the wall. I shouldn't have expected the euphoria to last. But in the excitement of the moment, it simply never occurred to me that anything could ruin my good mood.

He was sitting in the living room reading the evening paper when I approached him. She was in the armchair next to him, wearing Grandma Adelaide's apron and darning his sock, looking as if she had just popped out of a Norman Rockwell painting to say hello. At any moment,

I expected to hear a timer go off and then to see her react, like Pavlov's dog, and run into the kitchen, where she would remove a freshly baked apple pie from the oven. The aroma would fill the house and he would momentarily lower his paper and say, "Gee, what smells so good?"

"Good evening, Darla." Dad smiled as I stood before him. "Is there something special you wanted to talk to me about?"

"Well, yeah—if you have a minute."

"For you, certainly. I think the closing stock prices can wait," he said, folding the paper and resting it on his lap.

"Why don't you have a seat, dear?" Mom said without missing a stitch.

I sat down and looked nervously at my father. "Dad, I guess Mom told you that Ryan called me the other night."

"I was here when the call came in," Dad said matter-of-factly. "What about it?"

"Well, he asked me out to a Halloween party. It's on Halloween. At his cousin's place," I told him, fearing the dreaded "And where does his cousin live?" question about to pop.

"I suppose that will be okay, provided I know where you're going to be and at what hour you'll be returning. I'd also like to know more about this boy."

He reminded me of some TV sitcom dad. Like Ward Cleaver. Didn't he ever tire of being such a stereotypical dad and asking such dadlike questions? Wasn't there a real person underneath the cardigan sweater?

"Ryan is a junior at Wellington High. His father is the Mullavey from Mullavey, Something, and Richardson. He has the same job as you."

"He must be Pete Mullavey's boy!" Dad exclaimed, as if this were the best news he'd heard in years. "What a small world this is!"

I hadn't expected approval without a fight.

"Now, where's this shindig going to be held?"

I hated how he called every social function a shindig. He had even called my friend Rachel's bat mitzvah a shindig. He could be such a geek.

"At his cousin's," I said, trying to slide by with minimal information.

"Does his cousin live nearby?"

"He lives in the city, Dad. Ryan said he's got a really nice place. And I'll be going with Melanie and Ben and their dates. C'mon, Dad. There'll be six of us."

"Well," he said hesitantly, "I see no reason why you can't go, providing you follow the rules."

"Thanks, Dad," I beamed. I turned to my mother. "Mom, it's gonna be so cool. Melanie and I are going as Martin and Maudie. She agreed to be Martin. Isn't that hysterical?"

Dad looked appalled, and Mom, who was on the verge of laughing, shut her mouth in the nick of time.

"Did I hear you right, Darla? You're going to dress up like your mother's uncle's trollop wife and go gallivanting into the city? Over my dead body!"

"Dad! It's Halloween! You're supposed to dress up! And I won't be 'gallivanting.' Whatever that is!"

"Absolutely not! I won't have my daughter seen dressed like that woman and risk her being mistaken for a prostitute. Not in this lifetime!"

I was outraged. What was wrong with him? Why was he trying to ruin my life? "Well," I snapped, "maybe I should just go dressed as your faith in me, and then I'll be completely invisible!"

Dad picked up his paper and slammed it angrily on the arm of his recliner. "Call the Mullavey boy and tell him there's been a change of plans. You're staying home!"

"Ted, please!" Mom begged, surprising all three of us. "This means so much to Darla. She's been waiting for Ryan to call her for weeks now. I'm sure she's not going to be walking around the city dressed in that costume. She'll be with a group of six people, who are also in costume, and I'm certain they'll go from the car directly to the party. I don't think anyone would mistake her for a prostitute, certainly not in the ridiculous getup she plans to wear, and of all evenings, on Halloween night!"

Dad was clearly uncomfortable with Mom's show of strength, but he wasn't about to argue with her in front of me, or allow himself to get out of control. Besides, she made a lot of sense, even though, admittedly, I cringed at the part where she called my intended costume "a ridiculous getup." "I'll think about it," he muttered and went back to the financial section.

Mom smiled and winked at me. She had really stood up for me, and that meant even more to me than the permission I knew Dad would eventually grant me to go to the party.

Ryan, dressed as a nerd, plastic pocket protector and all, came to pick me up at eight-fifteen. Mom and Dad greeted Ryan at the door.

"Welcome to our home, Ryan," Mom said. "That's a wonderful costume. I just love those glasses. Did you buy them especially for this occasion?"

"Nah, I just used junk we had lying around the house. I'm not great at this costume stuff."

"Well, son, you look exactly like a guy I went to college with, Ned Forthright." Dad laughed, patting Ryan on the back. "What a brain. There wasn't anything that Ned couldn't take apart and put back together again. Even the professors had a tough time keeping up with him. A technological wizard that boy was. 'Ned the Head.' That's what we called him."

Dad was embarrassing me to death. Ned Forthright? Technological wizard? Couldn't he just say, "Have a nice time," and be done with it?

"Ryan," he continued, "how's your father doing? Darla tells me he was in the hospital for a spell."

"A spell"? Things were getting worse. He had gone from sounding like Ward Cleaver to sounding like Jed Clampett in a matter of seconds. I looked helplessly at my mother, who smiled at me sympathetically.

"He's doing fine, Mr. McKendrick, thank you. He went back to work a week or so ago."

"Pete and I go back a long way," he said. "I'll bet your dad must've gotten a real kick when you told him you were taking Ted McKendrick's daughter to this shindig."

"Oh, yeah," Ryan said blankly. He looked at me. I looked at my mother.

"Well, you kids have a great evening!" Mom blurted out. "You'd better get going, though. Don't leave the others waiting in the car too long. They might leave without you!"

As Dad shook Ryan's hand, grinning broadly at him, I quietly thanked my mother for the intervention, and we left.

"God, I'm so embarrassed!" I said to Ryan once we were outside.

"No sweat," he said. "You should meet my dad!"

✳ ✳ ✳

Ryan wasn't lying when he said his cousin lived in a beautiful place. It was on the eleventh floor of a sleek black high-rise, and once inside, the view through the sliding glass doors off the balcony was spectacular. Though the spacious living room and adjoining dining area were minimally furnished, they were done in tasteful, muted colors, which were complemented by the lush tropical-looking plants in the corners of the room.

As Ryan had explained to me before we arrived, most of the people at the party would be older, and a good many of them would probably be his cousin Keith's fellow law school students.

"Check out these costumes!" Ryan said to me as we came in. "Are we tripping, or what?"

He was right. There was almost too much to take in with only one set of eyes—the assortment of colors, shapes, objects, and people implied the result of a play date with drugs, not just a mere coterie of costumed partygoers. First, there was a woman dressed like Marie Antoinette cozying up to her date, who was dressed like a giant sunflower. He was

71

smoking a cigarette through the center of the flower. Another woman next to him, dressed as a hospital patient, kept waving the smoke away with her hands.

The hospital patient was a sight. Her costume consisted of little more than an open-back hospital gown, and when she turned around, she revealed a set of enormous plastic buttocks. On her feet were a pair of pink bunny slippers, and in her hand was an old white, chipped porcelain bedpan.

"Omigod," Melanie shrieked quietly. "Skieve me out! She's drinking from that thing." Sure enough, just at that moment, we saw a hideous green-faced witch (Ryan's cousin) pour a shot of Johnnie Walker Red into the bedpan.

"Bottoms up!" the woman shouted, as everyone within earshot laughed.

One of the oddest couples I spotted had to be a freckled-faced Mona Lisa and a husky green turtle wearing a red fez and black hiking boots, carrying a Gucci handbag. I didn't even bother to try to figure the significance of his bizarre accessorizing, as I was far more intrigued by the gorilla behind them, decked out in a pink bowtie and having a hell of a time trying to stuff popcorn through the tiny mouth hole in his suit. At first, he tried to stick his hand under his neck and gain access to his mouth that way, but that was a total disaster. His hand got momentarily stuck inside his head, and the popcorn dribbled down his hairy chest and onto the carpet. Eventually, he gave up on the popcorn altogether and took to drinking a can of soda through a straw.

I was having a great time with Ryan, moving through the room and surveying the guests. The fascinating mix of people provided us with more than enough to talk about, and I was no longer haunted by our first, bungling phone conversation, which, naturally, I had decided was entirely due to my social ineptitude. I had a flash of concern when Keith offered me a real drink, which I declined, and I wondered what Dad would think if he knew Ryan had accepted a beer. But I wasn't fazed at all, despite my father's dire warnings about the nasty effects of alcohol. After all, Ryan was seventeen years old, and I thought it was pretty cool being with a guy who drank beer, especially since he was nothing like the out-of-control drinker that my father had so eloquently described.

Just as I was wondering where we would go on our second date, a bag of groceries with very shapely legs tramped in the front door and immediately began waving at Ryan. He excused himself and made his way over to this faceless bag, hugging her on arrival. I felt an immediate twinge of envy but told myself that I had no reason to worry. Even in my state of hormonal bedlam, I had the good sense to know that insecurity was not only an ineffective aphrodisiac, but poison to a budding relationship. But when ten minutes passed and Ryan was still chatting up this bag, who now had her arm around his waist, my jealousy became as obvious as the nose on Maudie's face.

"She's his ex," a voice said.

I turned to my right to find the gorilla standing next to me. "Hi, I'm Sam," he said. "I'm Ryan's other cousin. Keith's brother. The one who doesn't live here. That's Lisa. Ryan dated her a year ago. He broke up with her after ten months because she was really possessive."

"Oh," I said. "Well, it doesn't look like she's changed, does it?"

" 'Fraid not," he said sweetly, "but I can guarantee you Ryan won't be going back to her. What's your name?"

"Darla," I said, barely looking into his gorilla eyes.

"Great costume! I just rented mine. Yours shows a lot of creativity. It's really fantastic."

"My friend Melanie made it. She's the creative genius, not me. That's her over there in the plaid jacket. The pretty girl with the long red hair."

"I see the plaid jacket, but nobody with long red hair."

"Oh, right," I said halfheartedly. "That's because she rolled her hair into a nylon stocking cap and put that ugly toupee on her head."

"Gee, I'd love to see what you and your friend really look like! I'm sure you're both gorgeous. Especially you."

Sam was a sweetheart, but he was getting on my nerves.

"Thanks," I said.

"There must be a hundred people in this place. It feels like a mini-

Mardi Gras in here, condo style!" Sam laughed. "Have you ever been to Mardi Gras, way down yonder in New Orleans?"

"No, I haven't," I said flatly. I didn't care how many people had stuffed themselves into Keith's apartment: Ryan was the face in the crowd that mattered.

"It's really getting hot in this costume," Sam continued. "I think I'm gonna have to take my head off pretty soon."

"Right," I muttered, distractedly. My good mood was rapidly deteriorating as I watched Ryan continue his animated conversation with this Lisa person.

"I think I made a mistake drinking so much soda," Sam said.

"Oh?"

"Well, Darla, if you'll excuse me, I've got to go shed my fur. They oughta make these things with some kind of trapdoors, if you know what I mean."

"Nice talking to you," I said, grateful that nature had called him away.

Ryan had now been with Lisa for fifteen minutes, the music was growing louder, people were dancing and carrying on, and I was feeling very out of place. Melanie, noticing my predicament, excused herself from Jesse and came over to console me.

"Gee, Darla. Don't you just hate girls like that?"

"He's talked to her long enough," I whined. "Is he just going to leave me here forever or what?"

"I'm sure he'll be back in a few minutes," Melanie said, casting an evil eye in Lisa's direction. "You know, if I were going to dress up like a bag of groceries, I sure wouldn't have a box of Kotex sticking out the top of my head. Maybe a box of corn flakes, or even some toilet paper, but Kotex? How personal!"

"Really?" I asked, trying to focus in on Lisa from where I was standing. "I can't see anything."

"You have to stand next to her to see."

"Yeah," I said dejectedly. "Just like Ryan's doing."

"Red alert, Darla, he's coming back over. See ya later."

Melanie made a quick exit as Ryan wended his way back over to me.

"I'm sorry, Darla. It wasn't what you think. That girl was just talking to me about our band. She knows someone who may be able to get us a gig at Pier 23, the club down by the waterfront."

"Oh, it's okay," I said cheerfully. "No problem."

But it was a problem when twenty minutes later, Ryan excused himself again. This time, however, he profusely apologized, put his arm around me, and gave me a loving squeeze upon his return. I was a teenage sucker. It took me only a matter of seconds to feel special all over again, just like that night on the dance floor when we met. Even dressed like Maudie, I felt beautiful.

Suddenly, everything changed. I didn't know what hit me. All I saw was the hospital patient moving quickly in our direction to get away from this unshaven pirate, who was determined to talk to her. They were both visibly intoxicated.

"I'm not gonna let you get away with that crap!" the pirate shouted. "Just because you dress like an ass doesn't mean you have to act like one!"

"Leave me alone, you bastard! Get off my case!"

"We're gonna talk about this, Elise. Now!"

"The hell we are, pirate breath!" she shouted as she plunged into me, forcing the devil behind me to spill his drink down the back of my slinky red dress. "Oh, crap, I'm sorry!" she said to me as she spilled the contents of her bedpan down the front of my dress, before dropping the entire thing on my foot. "I hope you weren't planning to wear this costume again."

But I was the least of her worries. She had no sooner bent over to pick up the bedpan when the pirate grabbed her forcefully by the arm and pulled her away. The last thing I remember were her large plastic buttocks disappearing into the carnival-like atmosphere of the room.

✳ ✳ ✳

75

I was thrilled when Melanie told me that she and Ben, and their respective dates, would be getting a ride home with "someone who lived in the neighborhood." This meant that, finally, Ryan and I would be alone together. I was very grateful to Melanie for arranging it all for me.

Ryan and I laughed most of the way back to my house. There was so much to talk about, that I almost forgot I was soaking wet.

"Well, at least no one poured a drink on your head," Ryan said, laughing.

"Really!" I joked back. "But I draw the line when it comes to brandy alexanders—oh, and red wine. Personally, if someone's gonna spill a drink on me, I prefer that it be vodka. It's nice and clear looking. And relatively odorless. Like water."

"Is that what your father drinks? You seem to know a lot about the stuff."

"My dad despises alcohol. I've never seen him take a sip—ever. He acts like alcohol is the scourge of the earth. Like the Black Plague or something. But he does keep it in the house."

"He does? How come?"

"I dunno. I guess 'cause he and Mom have a lot of company over, you know, for business and stuff. It would be pretty weird for my dad to just tell these people that because he hates drinking they've gotta drink milk or something."

"Yeah, and imagine your mom serving cookies with it. Could you see these investment banker guys going out for drinks after work—to a milk bar? Man, that's too funny. You know, my dad would be pretty pissed if he knew I had a beer at the party," Ryan admitted. "But I only had one. No big deal."

"Does your dad drink?"

"Sure. But not a lot or anything. Besides, my dad doesn't need booze to make him do embarrassing things. He comes by his weirdness naturally."

"Really? Like what kind of stuff?"

"Well, once when I was in the eighth grade, I really liked this girl named Jennifer Anne Rush and I asked her out for her birthday. I was totally jazzed when she said yes and I really wanted to make a good impression on her. Anyway, she calls me about an hour before our date to say she'll be a bit late, 'cause her grandparents stopped by with her present, and the next thing I know my dad is singing 'Happy Birthday' to her on the phone. Then, like that's not enough, he starts singing a chorus of 'How old are you now? How old are you now?'"

"You're kidding!" I interjected. "No way! I would've died!"

"Yeah way. So listen, Darla, the next time your dad says something corny, think about my dad and I promise you'll feel better."

I was on top of the world. Aside from having an almost perfect time at the party, Ryan and I were really getting to know each other. We had moved past the raillery of others to the sharing of our own secrets. Ryan was starting to really feel like my boyfriend.

He pulled into the driveway behind Dad's dark blue Chrysler sedan. My stomach began to rumble as I sensed "the moment" fast approaching. As the rumbling progressed toward full-fledged queasiness, I considered how ironic it was that I was about to get my first real kiss dressed like someone else, and of all people, "that trollop" Maudie.

I could tell he was going to do it. He turned off the ignition and then shifted in his seat to face me. He made the move quite smoothly, I thought, considering that the bulky steering wheel was clearly handicapping his agility. I wondered if he'd say something first or just go right into it. I tried my best to pretend I didn't know what was coming. It felt really weird to just sit there and wait for someone to kiss you. At that moment, I thought of Dad's older sister, Aunt Louisa, and how she always pointed to her cheek and told you to "plant one here." Then, I had a flashback of Maudie, pointing to her lips as she said to Uncle George: "Here's where men go to get sugar." And I was dressed like her too.

"I had a really nice time with you tonight," Ryan said in his kiss prelude. "You're really a lot of fun to be with. And you're really pretty, even with that weird orange wig you're wearing."

He leaned over and kissed me. He had such soft, tender lips. I certainly had no expertise in the kissing department, but I knew instinctively that Ryan was doing it right. About five seconds into the kiss, he put his left arm around me and pulled me closer, kissing me for another fifteen to twenty seconds. Slowly, he pulled away from me, smiling sweetly as he gently touched the right side of my face.

And then, although I was clearly focused on Ryan's blue eyes, I could not help but notice that the front door of my house was wide open. I could not help but see the silhouette of my father standing in the brightly lit foyer and looking in our direction.

"My dad's watching us," I said gritting my teeth. "Wanna trade fathers? I think I'd rather have one who sings to my friends on the phone."

"Don't let him bug you," Ryan said, coming toward my lips again. "Just pretend he's not there."

"It's kind of hard," I said, feeling my entire body tense up.

"Yeah, I know what you mean," he said, pulling away. "Listen, Darla, I really enjoyed myself. But under the circumstances, I guess I better get going. Let me walk you to the door."

"No, don't bother," I told him, afraid of what my father might do. "I'll talk to you soon. Good night, Ryan. And thanks for a really great time."

I got out of the car, stood in the driveway for a moment, and waved to Ryan as he backed out and drove past me down the street. Then, with tears welling up in my eyes, I made my way toward the front door where my intrusive father waited.

"Good evening, Darla," Dad greeted me as I stepped inside the house.

"Hi," I grunted, feeling resentment for him yet one more time.

"That's not much of a greeting, young lady."

It was more than I had wanted to give him at all.

"I trust you had a good time," he said, inspecting me with his eyes.

"Yeah. I had a good time." I walked toward the stairs, barely looking at him.

"Darla!" he said sharply.

"What?"

"I'd like to talk to you for a moment. In the living room."

"All right," I groaned, as I felt history about to repeat itself. I followed him into the living room, wondering why he had to ruin every good time I had.

"Ryan seems like a fine young man," Dad began, settling into his chair, "but it troubles me that you can barely stand the sight of your father after spending an evening with him. When you left here a little after eight, you were acting like my daughter. Now you're an insolent young woman with an attitude. Frankly, I'd like an explanation."

Well, frankly, Dad, I thought, I don't give a damn.

I plopped myself down on the sofa. "I don't know what you want me to say," I muttered, challenging him.

I could see Dad's face turning red with anger. I knew he was fighting to stay in control. "I'll repeat it one more time, Darla. I want to know what it is about that boy that turns you against me every time you're with him."

"It's not him! It's you, okay? Last time you broke in on our dance, and tonight—oh, forget it!" Hard as I tried, I couldn't come up with a way to tell him he had interrupted a probable second kiss, and that he had ruined the aftermath of the first one. That would be like throwing a raw egg into a burning hot frying pan and expecting it not to sizzle and fry. "Just forget it, Dad."

"I've been accused," he averred. "And I have every right to know what the charges are. What did I do tonight to incur such wrath from you?"

I wanted to ask him the same question. But I traced the floral design in the upholstery with my finger instead.

"I'm waiting, Darla."

Finally, I found my nerve. "Why did you have to stand in the doorway and stare at Ryan's car?"

Dad just looked at me. He seemed almost baffled. "Who's questioning whom here?"

"You asked!"

"Well, Darla, it was almost midnight and I was concerned about

79

you. I heard a car pull up and I opened the door to see if it was you. Is that any reason to take my head off?"

"Why couldn't you just look out the window?" I asked, still not wanting to bring up the kissing thing. "How long did you have to stare at the car to make sure it was us?"

Finally, a light seemed to go on in Dad's head. "Darla, I could not see inside that car, and if I had, I certainly wouldn't have expected anything untoward to be going on. But most importantly here, I do not like your attitude one darn bit!"

I was speechless. I had no idea how to respond. He got up, walked over to me, then sat down next to me on the couch. I thought he was going to say something else, but then his nose started twitching and it looked as if he were going to sneeze.

"Is that alcohol I smell on you?" he said, staring incredulously at me. His paternal proboscis started sniffing in my direction. He reminded me of a pig I'd seen at the 4-H Club when I was ten that did nothing but sniff frantically around the pen in search of food.

"Some woman crashed into me at the party and spilled her drink on me, and that made the guy behind me spill his drink too. That's why I smell like alcohol. That's the only reason!"

He sat there with a somber look on his face. "You've been drinking," he said. Pausing for a moment and looking almost helpless, he continued, "First the mean words at the Davenport party, now the alcohol. What's next?"

I didn't know what he was talking about. "Dad!" I said, desperately trying to convince him. "I swear. I wasn't drinking!"

"Why were you even at a party with so much alcohol? With any alcohol?"

"Dad—Ryan's cousin is twenty-six years old. His fruit punch days are over."

Dad was not in the mood for jokes. "You smell like a distillery."

"Because two people spilled their drinks on me!" I repeated in frustration. "Why don't you believe me?"

"Darla, someone's personality doesn't change merely because a drink was spilled on her. Alcohol has to be consumed, drunk, ingested, to have such an effect on a person, and the change in your attitude clearly indicates to me that such an action has taken place!"

I turned to see my mother, sleepy-eyed in her woolly blue bathrobe, standing at the entrance to the living room.

"Mom!" I said running over to her. "Dad's accusing me of drinking just because these people at the party spilled their drinks all over me. I can't help it that I smell like alcohol. I wasn't drinking, Mom. I swear! You know I don't do that!"

Mom didn't know what to do. She put her arms around me and gave me a hug, then looked at Dad for further explanation.

"Her attitude was terrible when she walked in here tonight, Maggie. She was definitely under the influence of something and would barely give me the time of day."

"Because he had the front door open and just stood there staring at me and Ryan in the car!" I said in my own defense, hoping that Mom would understand.

"I see," she said, knowing exactly why I was upset but not wanting to oppose my father in front of me. "Why don't you go up to bed, honey? You and your father can talk tomorrow when you're both a bit calmer."

That was good enough for me. Without looking at him again, I raced up the stairs. In the interest of knowing what I was up against, I slammed my bedroom door shut so my parents would think I'd gone inside, then tiptoed back to the head of the stairs to listen.

"Ted, I honestly don't think Darla was drinking. I believe her story. I think I know my daughter pretty well, and I say she's innocent."

"Maggie, you didn't see what I saw. There was no other logical reason for her impertinence."

"Maybe not logical to you, Ted, but that's another issue entirely. Don't you remember when we were sixteen? Remember that night, on the porch, when you kissed me just as Dad was peeking at us through the curtains? I could barely bring myself to speak to him for weeks. You embarrassed her, honey, and she didn't know how to explain that to you. Ted, she's not even sixteen yet! Think about me when I was her age."

"Maggie, she doesn't remind me of you at that age. I wish she did. I hate to say it and I hate to think it, but she's beginning to remind me of her. You know how much I love Darla. Do you have any idea what this is doing to me?"

"She's nothing like her! And I want you to remember that! Like the rest of us, Darla isn't perfect, but she's never given us a reason not to trust her. Have some faith, Ted. Let the demons go. Goodness knows, I'm trying to!"

"To hell with faith!" Dad said. "Look what faith did for your parents. Faith wasn't enough to save that baby sister of yours, was it? Who knows what's become of her! Faith! Jesus Christ, Maggie, I've taken the real me and stuffed him so far down inside that I don't think I could retrieve him if I wanted to. I've pushed all of me aside, just to be a good father, to make up for all that I did… and I'll be damned if I'm going to screw it up now by letting 'faith' guide my way."

"Damn it, Ted!" Mom said angrily. Faith is half of what being a good father is all about. If you don't have faith in Darla, she won't have any in herself. Can't you see that?"

I was riveted. I was finally getting an earful of the real Ted and Maggie McKendrick, and didn't want to miss a word. I grabbed the railing, afraid that in my eagerness to eavesdrop I might tumble headfirst down the stairs. I was so transfixed by my mother's anger and by my father's reference to the "real me," that only a bowl of popcorn could have enhanced the entertainment experience. I couldn't imagine what he could've ever done that he now needed to atone for, much less suppress his true self. And of course, I was always fascinated by any and all references to Rebecca.

"All I see is all hell breaking loose if I don't take control," Dad said harshly. "You just keep coddling that kid, Maggie. Coddle away. See where it gets you."

"Really, Ted! Be quiet! You're so wrapped up in your precious need to control that you can't even see you're losing it now! I don't want to discuss this anymore. I'm too upset. I'm going upstairs."

Hearing that, I ran back to my bedroom, remembering to open

and close the door quietly since I was already supposed to be inside the room. It was so ironic. I wasn't supposed to talk about her, I had never met her, and yet she was playing such a significant role in my life. Mom had told me all the bad things Rebecca had done, but those things happened before I was even born. Why was my father comparing my behavior to hers? Why was he expecting the worst from me all the time? I had chastised myself once, for fixating on this mystery relative, but it seemed that my family's obsession with her was just as great as, if not far greater than, mine.

The fun was over and I was angry. This development wasn't in the game plan. I was supposed to come into the house, wash off all remaining traces of Maudie, and get in bed, where I would think only about Ryan as I replayed my first kiss over and over again. Instead, Ryan was the last thing on my mind, and as I lay awake until the wee hours of the morning, I was haunted, once again, by my aunt Rebecca.

CHAPTER 6

The dream began very normally. I was sitting in the living room with Dad's dictionary on my lap, and I was thinking about Ryan. Before I knew it, my father was standing in front of me, clad in a judge's robe.

"Darla!" he demanded. "Take off your head!"

"What?" I said, sure that I had misheard him.

"I said, take off your head! Now! Give it to me! I want it!"

"No, you can't have it!" I screamed, clutching my head with both hands.

Very calmly, and with great authority, Dad walked over to me and removed my head. I must've had a second set of eyes somewhere, because I could see my very animated face protesting vehemently as he carried my head away.

Dad, now in surgical attire, laid my head on an operating table, which had appeared in the living room. The light above was harsh and bright, and I could see my eyes squinting from it. "Nurse!" he barked. "Gavel, please!"

It was then that Mom, dressed in a nurse's uniform, handed him an oversize gavel. As soon as she did so, she smiled, revealing Uncle Martin's ugly teeth. Then, as she bent over the table to kiss my forehead, I noticed she had a set of large, plastic buttocks where the back of her nurse's uniform should be. Suddenly, her right buttock sprouted a big green eye and started winking at me.

"Lights! Camera! Action!" Dad shouted, as he took the gavel and banged me on the head. My head split open like the parting of the Red Sea, and Dad, with a look of arrogant gratification on his face, announced, "I knew it! I was right all long!" He reached into my head and pulled out a bottle of Johnnie Walker Red. Putting it on the table, he put his hand inside my head for a second time and pulled out a beer.

"Now that I've removed the tumors, it's time to have a party! Let's get this shindig rolling!"

At that moment, the room filled up with people. First I saw Ryan, dressed like Romeo, with the Lughead on his arm as Juliet. Standing behind them stood the devil, who was smiling and holding a bouquet of three balloons. Only they weren't ordinary balloons, they all had the animated face of someone I knew.

There was Melanie's face saying, "Omigod, Darla! I'm a balloon head! Help me!" Next to Melanie was Maudie's face, puffing frantically on a cigarette, and next to her was Uncle Martin's grinning face. I then saw Uncle George walk over, grab the cigarette from Maudie, smash it in her face, and then smash it in Martin's face. Popping them into rubbery oblivion, he sang "Pop Goes the Weasels" and walked away.

Out of nowhere appeared Grandpa Henry and Grandma Adelaide. I felt so happy to see them, as if a longing in my heart had finally been healed. I desperately tried calling to them, but they could not see or hear me.

"I hope Rebecca isn't here," Grandpa Henry said. "She's been a bad girl and needs to stay in the detox home. I have no time for her insolence, or for that one-in-a-million-good-for-nothing brother of mine. And I'm tired of being sick. I don't want to die. I want to have some fun. Can't an old man have any fun?"

"Sure, Henry!" Dad said, now dressed as a baseball player. "Let's play catch!"

Dad grabbed my head off the table, which was crying uncontrollably, and tossed it to Grandpa Henry, who threw it to the most insidious-looking creature I'd ever seen. It called itself "Ned the Head" Forthright and had a television monitor in place of a human head. As I turned to look, its "face" began to replay a scene from The Wizard of Oz, the one that had always scared me silliest as a child. Dorothy, trapped in the witch's tower, was looking into a giant crystal ball. First, a vision of Auntie Em appeared, calling for her, only to be replaced seconds later by a vision of the cackling, threatening Wicked Witch of the West. As this scene replayed on Ned Forthright's monitor face, a slimy black swamp creature burst through the side of the monitor, wagged its bright red tongue in the air, and thrust forward its fist, punching the monitor face into emerald green smithereens. This creature compilation, which was still holding my head, tossed it to Grandma Adelaide, who accidentally dropped it into a bag of groceries.

"Oh, butterfingers!" Grandma Adelaide giggled.

"For God's sake, Mother!" Aunt Didi screamed, coming out of nowhere. "Can't you do anything right? Will someone please get that head out of the grocery bag? Oh, never mind! I'll do it myself!" And with that, she pulled out what was supposed to be my head, but rather, looked more like a moldy, withering piece of fruit.

"Why bother?" Dad said with disdain. "It's already gone rotten."

I found it eerie and almost incomprehensible to think that my brain could conjure up such a perverse and peculiar group of symbols and people, then weave them together into some twisted tale of terror, only to play encore performances in my mind's theater—a grim playhouse with only one seat. How could the trials and tribulations of my young teenage life translate into such a macabre collection of images? Perhaps it wasn't Rebecca's past promiscuity and substance abuse that Dad feared might repeat itself with me. Maybe Rebecca had been mentally ill with some dreaded disease known to manifest itself in fifteen-and-a-half-year-old, green-eyed, brown-haired blood relatives. Maybe I was diagnosed the day I was born, and for all these years, Mom and Dad had just been waiting for the illness to strike. It had to be something like that. Normal people, I decided, do not invite garishly grotesque creatures to cavort and carry on with the dead; most have visions like those of the sugarplums, which danced in the children's heads.

When I finally woke for good at quarter of eleven the next morning, my body was weak and my thoughts were so muddled that I didn't immediately remember the night before. I sat up in bed, feeling like a zombie with a hangover, and stared blankly at the inviting posters of Paris and Rome on my wall. I did so for almost a half hour, until I felt steady enough to walk to the bathroom and take a shower.

Mom was sitting on my bed waiting for me when I came back

into my bedroom. I was wearing my gray sweats and had a large yellow towel wrapped around my head.

"Hello, Darla," she said with a look of sweet sadness in her eyes. "Are you okay, honey?"

My brain began to resume its normal function, and my father's actions and accusations from the night before came flooding back to me. I sat down on the bed and looked at her. She took my hands in hers and held them as she often did, and smiled sympathetically at me.

"I've been so worried about you, honey. What can I do to make it better?"

That was all the encouragement I needed. I burst into tears and put my head on her shoulder. The towel fell off my head onto the floor, and between my sopping wet hair and the avalanche of tears that poured out, Mom's shoulder didn't have a chance to stay dry.

"Cry it out, Darla," Mom said, rubbing my back. "Everything will be okay."

I lifted my head off her shoulder and looked at her. "I'm getting you all wet."

"I'll dry."

"Mom—"

"Yes, dear?"

Sniffling, I dried my tears on the right sleeve of my sweatshirt, while Mom reached over to my night table and grabbed a handful of Kleenex. "Here, blow your nose, honey." I complied. "Now, tell me what's on your mind."

"Remember when we had that talk about Aunt Rebecca a few years ago, and you told me that if I absolutely had to talk about her again, that I should come to you?"

"I remember."

"Well, I'm coming to you now."

"What do you want to know?" she asked cautiously.

"I know it's real painful for you to talk about," I went on, prefacing my remarks, "but I'm going to go crazy if I don't ask you some questions."

"Okay. Ask away."

"Well, first, I don't understand what's going on with Dad. He's changed so much. I mean, why does he hate me now? Why does—"

"He doesn't hate you, Darla," Mom interrupted. "Oh no! Far from it, honey."

"But ever since I began the tenth grade, my whole life has changed so drastically. I mean, he expects the absolute worst from me. I don't care what you say, I know he's expecting me to end up just like Aunt Rebecca! It's not fair. I'm nothing like her. What's the point in being so good if he's always going to think I'm bad?"

"Okay, okay," Mom said, trying to calm me down. "Let me answer one question at a time. First of all, Darla, you should be 'good' for yourself, above and beyond anyone else, including your father and me. You should always be the kind of person that you want to be. You can't live your life for anyone else. And the main reason you shouldn't be 'bad' is because you're not the kind of person who would enjoy living her life in that fashion. Of course, it is important to please the people you love, but first, to thine own self be true."

It was quite obvious to me that Mom was speaking from her own painful experience, and at that point in our conversation, I wasn't quite sure if she was talking about her situation or mine. I had noticed, however, that as my problems with Dad had developed over the past few months, there had also been a gradual change in the way my mother handled herself. Slowly, she had started to come out of her shell and speak up to my father. The changes were subtle in one way, but so remarkably dramatic in another that I began to see her in an entirely different light.

For years, she had given my father control, letting him make all the family decisions, and play Lord, Master, and Protector of us all. But when she started to question his methods, and when she felt he wasn't doing his job (especially where I was concerned), she jumped in where she would previously have feared to tread. She skillfully managed to play the lioness protecting her cub, while at the same time, allowing my father to retain his "control."

"Of course I don't want to be a bad person. I just want to know why Dad doesn't trust me anymore."

"Darla, I think you've both been a victim of an unfortunate set of circumstances. Your father just wasn't thinking when he cut into your dance with Ryan that night, but you also weren't thinking when you told him you hated him. And I can certainly understand why seeing him at the front door last night might have bothered you, but perhaps you overreacted to that as well, maybe just a bit."

"Did I overreact when he accused me of drinking? How about that?"

Mom looked at my bedroom door and then down at the floor, as if she were reluctant to say what was on her mind. "Between you, me, and the lamppost, Darla, I think he was wrong to accuse you of drinking. He was just worried. Very, very worried."

"Because of her!" I said angrily. "Because of Aunt Rebecca!"

Mom just looked at me. She heaved a few sighs and looked again at my bedroom door. "I suppose so," she whispered.

I felt as if I were finally making real progress. I had gotten her to admit the obvious truth, and now perhaps I could get her to explain the not-so-obvious truth to me. That would be the real challenge.

"I've never even met Aunt Rebecca," I stressed, as if I were telling her something new. "How come I'm being judged by stuff that she did before I was even born? And why is Dad so obsessed with her? She's not his sister!"

"Darla, as you know, your father and I were high school sweethearts. We met when we were sixteen and married some five years later. When I was sixteen, Rebecca was twelve, and it was during those five years of our courtship that my family had to endure all those problems with her. Hearing about them now may sound like ancient history to you, but living through them was an entirely different matter. Some things you get over, and other things, well, they can scar you for life. However, that doesn't mean that because you have scars, you should allow them to rule your life or color your otherwise good judgment, but the healing process works differently with different people. Your father saw firsthand how Rebecca's actions took their toll on Grandma and Grandpa. He spent many a night comforting your grandma as she sat and cried over Rebecca, while your grandpa was out trying to help her, or in many instances, simply locate her."

"Yeah, Mom, but I still don't—"

"Please let me finish, honey."

"Sorry," I said, blowing my nose again.

"As I told you a few years ago, we really don't know where Rebecca is today, or quite honestly, if she's even still alive."

Mom took a deep breath to contemplate the painful words she had just spoken. "I suppose there's never been any closure, which is what makes this situation that much more difficult."

"So if that's the case, how come nobody even tries to find her?"

"Hurts too much," Mom said softly, as if she were shutting down. "Honey, you're absolutely right. It isn't fair of your father to make comparisons. He knows that too. But you're his only child and he worries. Can't you just give him a little leeway?"

"Like he gave me?"

Mom gave me one of her "you know better than that" looks.

"Yeah, okay, Mom," I said, feeling cheated out of my emotions.

Mom picked the yellow towel off the floor. "I'll throw this in the wash for you. Now, dry your hair before you catch cold. I'll see you downstairs."

As Mom walked out of my bedroom, I got the feeling that I was a package, one that she had just wrapped up neatly with a big red bow and could now put aside without worry. I had been too busy admiring the positive changes in her to realize that once again, she hadn't revealed a thing I didn't already know.

Except for a few bright spots, it was a long, lonely, and cold November. As the leaves on the trees started to change color and fall to the ground, I began to think of myself as a tree, once brimming with life, but now growing stark and empty as it prepared to stand alone in the coldness of winter.

Ryan called a couple of times, and gradually, I got to know him a bit better (though never well), but between his part-time job at the supermarket and playing with his band most weekend nights, there was little time left for me. We did get together once in early November for a football game, when his school's team played mine, and we even shared a common (and very unpopular) belief that our respective schools' rivalry was bordering on the absurd. But despite that common ground, the raucous laughter, and the hilarious popcorn fights we enjoyed that Saturday, a part of me knew we were as close as we'd ever get.

I suppose that's easy for me to say now, in hindsight, but it was quite a different story back then. Aside from the normal teenage longings, I desperately needed Ryan to fill an empty space in my heart that my father, my mother, or maybe even Aunt Rebecca had created. I told myself that lifelong romances take time to grow, and that "Rome wasn't built in a day" (as my father often liked to remind me when I was impatient about something). So I persevered, waiting for our budding romance to blossom into something that only happens in old black-and-white movies.

At home, things were calm on the surface, but there was an underlying tension that never left. Dad had even apologized to me for the "drinking accusation," but I could still feel his watchful eyes fixated on me at all times. He was sad and serious now, and even though he tried his weary best, he could barely bring himself to laugh or to make even the tiniest of jokes at the dinner table. Mom continued her role as the keeper of peace, but the house was becoming less and less of a home with each passing day. The November chill had taken refuge inside our home, and though we all fought it in our own way, we were powerless to change it.

Melanie, though still my very best friend, didn't have quite as much time for me as her relationship with Jesse continued to progress. Like me, she was also traveling the rocky road to womanhood, only her journey seemed a lot smoother than mine. Perhaps it was because her mother, a business executive and former model, had the aplomb and self-confidence to pass on to her daughter, whereas mine left me relatively alone to navigate the real world. Melanie also had an amazing capacity for humor, and she didn't let pain cleave to her indefinitely, the way it did to me. She was also a far more spontaneous individual (which could be as dangerous as it could be fun), but together we balanced each other out. I've always thought that no one should go through life, especially childhood, without a friend like Melanie.

I couldn't blame her for wanting to be with Jesse, though I did wish she had waited another few weeks to "fall so deeply in love." My cousins, to whom I had grown much closer, also had little time for me. Aunt Didi was becoming increasingly more frantic about their futures, and had filled their days and nights with singing engagements, as well as every kind of lesson imaginable. It was a wonder they had time for homework.

There was one weekend, however, when I did get to spend some precious time with my cousins, and to make, what I then perceived to be, a complete fool of myself with Ryan.

The whole thing started because of Miss Joanna Lund. She was the girls' voice teacher, an extremely well-connected and prestigious woman who took only a few privileged and gifted students under her wing. Aunt Didi never missed an opportunity to impress her, so when Miss Lund turned sixty years old, although there were many parties given in her honor, Aunt Didi insisted that the girls throw yet another party and invite past and present students. She had initially wanted to have it catered and avoid the bother, but Uncle George had maintained that spending all that money would make Aunt Didi look like she was "kissing up to her" (which she was), and that it would look much better if the girls prepared the food and did everything themselves. So April, who had no culinary skills at all, was put in charge of the shopping and setting up, while May and June (who fancied herself a gourmet) were put in charge of preparing the "scrump-dilly-icious" birthday banquet.

April, who knew I was having a rough time at home, begged me to go shopping with her and help with the party. At first, I felt like a real outsider, not knowing the prestigious Miss Lund and all, but April reminded me that I was a "very important" part of their family and convinced me that I was wanted and needed.

***

The whole escapade began innocently enough, when I suggested to my cousins that April and I do the food shopping at the supermarket where Ryan worked. I explained that doing so would give me a legitimate excuse to see him at work, as up until that point, I had no reason whatsoever to be shopping for groceries.

"Sure," April agreed. "We'll go wherever you want. Listen, Cuz, I'm just so happy that I don't have to do this alone. I'll shop on the moon if you'll come with me."

"Darla," May said, looking rather serious, "you don't think Ryan will know that you only came in there to see him, do you?"

"I dunno," I said, suddenly feeling worried. "How could he think that if April and I are filling up this huge cart with groceries? I mean, he's gotta think it's legit or we wouldn't be spending all that money, right?"

"May could be right," June said. "What if he asks you why you came to that supermarket, when it's not in your neighborhood or ours. What will you say?"

"I dunno. That I was in the area? That Melanie asked me deliver a message to her brother, Ben? Ben and Ryan work together, you know."

"Nah, that sounds real weak to me," June said. "I'd hate to see this backfire. If you're bummed out now about barely seeing him, what's he going to think if you go chasing after him at work? Men like challenges, remember?"

"So I should play hard to get?"

"Not 'hard to get' necessarily," June told me, "but I don't know how turned on he'll be if you stand there and watch him unpacking peppers and onions. It's not exactly glamorous work, especially when the guy'll be wearing his supermarket duds, apron and all."

"Yeah, Cuz," April agreed. "It's not like he's got some macho job and works with a jackhammer, or has a big manly tool belt strapped to his waist."

May, June, and I looked at April incredulously.

"You're a ditz, Sis!" June finally said. "You really are."

"So, what's the game plan going to be?" May asked. "Are you guys going, or not?"

"I dunno," I muttered, feeling like a much bigger ditz than April. "I just know I really wanna see him. I miss his face! Someone tell me what to do!"

"I got it!" April said excitedly. "I've got the most fantastic idea ever!"

"Batten down the hatches!" June shouted teasingly. "Warn the masses! April's got an idea!"

"Okay," said April, as if she were an international spy, "here's what we do. We go, but we go in disguise. We see him, but he doesn't see us. Whattya think?"

"Will your shopping cart self-destruct if you get caught? Will headquarters disavow all knowledge of you?" June asked.

"I'm serious," April said, looking intently at me for a reaction. "Whattya think, Cuz?"

"I say, 'Go for it!' " May encouraged. "Sounds good to me!"

"All right!" I chimed in. "Let's go for it!"

✳ ✳ ✳

Melanie, an avid fan of harebrained schemes, thought this was a brilliant idea and checked Ben's work schedule to make sure that Ryan was working that Saturday. Really, the only obstacle that lay in our path would be having May and June distract Aunt Didi and Uncle George long enough for April and me to get out of the house in our disguises. That, we knew, would be a piece of cake.

Because the girls had been professional entertainers all their lives, they had an extensive knowledge of stage makeup and plenty of costumes up in their attic. But even with their expertise, it was hard to turn two teenage girls into eccentric old women, especially under the scrutiny of bright supermarket lights.

April, who was tall, blond, and slender, sported a short gray wig and a wine-colored velvet hat (with plastic garden flowers) on her head. She wore a once-smart, way-too-big, slightly tattered green suit with three big black buttons in the front. Using the techniques for "stuffing Maudie" that Melanie had taught me on Halloween, I helped April fill herself out in all the appropriate places. On her feet she wore an ugly pair of "practical shoes" and carried a square, black vinyl purse that snapped shut.

I, on the other hand, looked rather "Norma Desmondish," as May so aptly put it. With my face swathed in heavy makeup, a fake beauty mark applied strategically to my chin, a large black turban hunkered on my head, and an indescribably ugly crushed velvet dress enveloping my body, I was ready for action. I had wanted to carry a cigarette holder in my right hand for effect, but June reminded me that these disguises were supposed to be believable, and that Halloween had been over for two weeks. The four of us must've been existing in some teenage Twilight Zone to have even considered, for one solitary second, that anyone, and I mean anyone, would believe the absurd camouflage that April and I had shrouded ourselves in.

We arrived at the supermarket at ten o'clock on a crisp fall morning. April fought the chill with a withered old brown cloth coat, while I stood comically warmed in one of Aunt Didi's old fake furs. The first dilemma we encountered, while still loitering outside the market, was what to do with our coats once we got inside. Would we leave them on or take them off? Just as we agreed that it would be easier to keep them on, April reminded me of all the trouble that May and June had gone to in dressing us for the occasion. Concluding that it would be unfair not to display the proof of their fashion acumen, we reversed our decision. Throwing our coats on the cart, and feeling excited yet cautious of what lay ahead, we walked gingerly into the market.

We were in the store for a matter of seconds, when we found ourselves standing smack in the middle of Produce. Melanie had obviously failed to mention (or maybe I had forgotten) the fact that Produce was the department nearest the store's entrance. I panicked and told April that I needed time to warm up and get used to my new appearance, and that we'd best start our shopping at the opposite end of the market, as Melanie had suggested, in Frozen Foods.

"Don't make a lot of eye contact with people," I warned her. "Just be cool and no one will notice us."

I could not have been more wrong. The curious looks began a mere five paces out of Produce. Fifteen paces away, in the Meat Department, I started hearing remarks.

"They're just kids; must be doing it on some kind of dare."

"Look at those old ladies. Geez, Lou, they remind me of your mother and that wacko sister of hers."

"What's wrong with those ladies, Mom?" ("They're just old and poor, dear.")

Amazingly, April had managed to refrain from giggling, a small but very significant fact I was extremely grateful for. Her giggling could be contagious, and I knew that once she started, I might not be far behind and that would ruin our entire plan.

I had everything worked out in my head. We would walk parallel to the long meat case, which was in the very back of the market, until we got to Frozen Foods at the far end of the store. After getting what we needed there, we would then make our way back, going up and down each aisle, until we ended up in Produce, where we would complete our shopping. I was just about to share this strategy with April, when I saw Ben Davenport approaching us, pushing a large metal cart piled high with boxes of Washington apples.

At first, I thought we were safe when he merely glanced oddly at us. But then, as he passed us, something must've registered in his brain, because he craned his neck at an almost unnatural angle as he gaped suspiciously in our direction.

"Wasn't that Melanie's brother?" April whispered, stopping dead in her tracks.

"Yes," I said under my breath. "But don't look back at him."

"I think he recognized us!" April panicked.

"Maybe not. Maybe he just looked at us like that 'cause we look so weird!"

"Gosh, I hope he doesn't tell Ryan what he saw!"

"April! Do you wanna give me a heart attack or what?"

By now, every shopper and every employee in our line of vision were looking at us. Some were giggling softly, some were laughing out loud, and some were simply staring in various stages of incredulity.

"Pretend you don't notice them," I instructed April, "and start moving."

Not wanting to look directly in the eyes of the shoppers walking toward me, I decided to avert my glance and look down the aisles as I passed the people coming in my direction. No sooner had we gotten to the back end of the Canned Meats and Vegetables aisle than I saw Ben standing at the front end with Ryan, and he was pointing in our direction.

"Holy cow, Darla!" April whispered. "They see us."

"Keep cool," I told her, as I felt my stomach churn. "Remember, keep moving."

When we got to the next aisle, Juices and Cereals, Ryan and Ben were once again at the opposite end, and even from a distance, I could see them doubling over in laughter, as a crowd gathered around them. One more aisle over, in Baking Goods and Picnic Supplies, they were there again—following us, taunting us, torturing us.

"Oh no, Darla!" April whispered again. "How are we going to get out of this?"

I was starting to panic. Suddenly, nothing felt real. My whole life flashed before me, and I started trembling. The churning in my stomach grew louder, in taunting synchronism with the pounding of my head. I knew it could only be a matter of minutes before I would come face to face with Ryan, a meeting that would undoubtedly be the most humiliating, embarrassing, mortifying confrontation of my pathetic life.

"Let's go back the other way," I told her. "Toward Produce."

We retraced our steps back one aisle to Juices and Cereals, but Ben and Ryan were on to us and moved backward in the same direction. I saw Ben slap his knee as he howled with laughter.

"Darla!" April screamed. "I'm so freaked out! What are we going to do?"

I took a deep breath. There was no time to lose my mind and go crazy. I could do that later. "All right," I told her, reversing direction yet again. "Change directions again and walk calmly with me toward Frozen Foods. Stand right here, in front of this cookie display, between the two aisles, so they can't see us when they look down the aisle. Wait, like, fifteen seconds and then I'll count to three. We'll grab the coats, ditch the cart, run back toward Produce, and get the hell out of here. Are you with me?"

"Oh Cuz, I hope this works!" April said despairingly.

"It has to," I told her. "One, two, three, go!"

We began to run through the market, our plan going smoothly enough, when April collided head-on with a dairy clerk, who had his arms loaded up with several cartons of large white eggs.

"What the hell!" he shouted, as the eggs fell and cracked around him. "What's going on here? Hey, stop, lady!"

"I'm going to throw up!" April warned him in an old lady voice. "So clear a path and move out of my way, sonny. Now!"

It turned out to be a brilliant move on her part. No way did this guy want to detain her any further and take the chance that she might be telling him the truth.

Unfortunately, however, in the excitement, April dropped her old brown coat into the pool of broken eggs, and there was no time to stop and retrieve it. But despite the gawking and guffawing around us, we made it safely out of the store and back to Aunt Didi's car, where we immediately locked the doors and hightailed it out of the parking lot.

Miss Lund's party went off the next day without a hitch. April and I, once having gotten out of the supermarket alive, shed our costumes and completed the necessary grocery shopping at a supermarket closer to her home. Later that day, May and June, as master chefs (and April and I as sous chefs) turned the groceries into a magnificent celebratory feast, and

Aunt Didi gushed with pride at what her four girls had accomplished.

Aside from the fun and frolicking, I was entirely consumed with worry over the supermarket incident, wondering, with every waking thought, if Ryan and Ben had known it was us. I was sure they had recognized us, but maybe it was true what I'd told April in the store—maybe they were simply laughing because we looked so totally weird. After all, Ryan never did see us up close, the way Ben had, and how could Ben be totally sure who we were? He'd only seen us for a matter of seconds. I called Melanie that Saturday afternoon, shortly after we returned from shopping, to fill her in on the caper and to see what she could find out for me.

The following morning, Melanie called me at my cousins' to say that Ben hadn't mentioned one word about anything when he got home from work. Surely, if he had recognized one of the "old ladies" as his sister's very best friend, he not only would've said something, he would've "made every joke in the book" and tortured Melanie unmercifully (obviously, a Davenport family trait). According to Melanie, Ben wasn't "mature enough" to let something like that drop, so his silence could only mean that he was completely ignorant of the facts. That made me feel better, but it still didn't stop me from worrying.

Despite everything, I cherished the memory of that weekend, from the supermarket caper to the all-day cooking marathon and subsequent sleepover party with April, May, and June. I could've lived without the party itself (and the snotty divas), but it was wonderful being included in my cousins' lives. Being with them, I felt whole, while going back to my own home that Sunday night left me cold, fragmented, and frightened.

✳ ✳ ✳

Uncle George dropped me off at home a few minutes before eight o'clock, just as Dad had finished watching "60 Minutes." He greeted me with a smile, told me that Mom had called to say that the "shindig" was successful, and said he hoped I'd had a good weekend with my cousins. Mom, who had also been at the party, was still there, working the cleanup

99

detail. She was Aunt Didi's "partner in grime," as she so eloquently put it, and couldn't leave until everything "shone like sunshine." She had insisted, however, that I go home and get ready for school the next morning, so that I might shine as well.

Under normal circumstances, Dad would've invited me to sit down and tell him "everything that happened." Now, although he was managing a smile and courteous small talk, he still had a vacant air about him.

I stood before him for a few seconds, hoping he'd say something like, "Oh, honey, this is ridiculous. I miss my little girl. Give your old man a hug and let's start all over again." But he didn't. He just gave me that "anything else?" smile and reached for his copy of U.S. News and World Report that lay on the table next to him. I desperately wanted to end this misery and tell him I was sorry, but I didn't know how to do it and I still didn't believe I'd done anything wrong. A part of me had surmised that his chilliness toward me was his way of manipulating me into taking the blame for everything—or into feeling guilty. Naturally, that made me angry. But for the most part, my anger toward him had dissipated, and following McKendrick family tradition, it had found a home deep inside my soul, where it could thrive and subsequently manifest itself into a dysfunctional form of my choice—in this case, depression.

Thanksgiving was now just a week away, and I was really looking forward to having fun with my cousins again. Ryan hadn't called in the four days since "the caper," and though a part of me was grateful for that, I missed him terribly and continued to torture myself about what had happened.

Mom, on the surface, said and did all the right things where I was concerned, but I felt as if she were pushing me away, fearful that I might continue to pursue my interest in ancient family history.

As if that weren't enough, I noticed a new wrinkle in the family fabric, one that made me feel even more helpless. Mom and Dad had changed toward each other, and although there was no outward fighting or bickering, they seemed to me like strangers on a train. They engaged in necessary and polite conversation but went their separate ways when the conversation ended. Mom had stopped telling Dad all about her day, and Dad, for the most part, had stopped giving Mom a nightly rundown of his activities at the office. After dinner, it was different too. In the past, they had always sat side by side in the living room, even if she was clipping coupons and he was reading the paper. But now, Dad would read in his study, leaving Mom alone in the living room. And if he did stay in the living room, she would often go into the kitchen or upstairs to her sewing room. Once, I found her alone in their bedroom, reading a novel. She looked as if she had been crying.

It was all my fault. I was responsible for leading my family to this cold and lonely place. I cried myself to sleep at night, when I could muster the energy to do so, and I continued to have nightmares.

When I could think straight, I prayed to God to help our family (and especially me) through this awful time. To start with, I asked for a wonderful, joyous Thanksgiving, one that would bring the entire family together in love and laughter, just as it had for all the previous years of my life.

CHAPTER 7

Thanksgiving as I had wished it was not to be. Two unforeseen twists of fate saw to that. First, Uncle George's sister Nancy (the one who lived on Cape Cod) took ill with her lupus condition, so, at the last minute, Uncle George, Aunt Didi, and the girls packed their bags and drove north to Massachusetts to spend Thanksgiving weekend with Nancy and her family.

For about a day, it seemed as if it would be just the three of us for Thanksgiving dinner. But then Dad's sister, Louisa, called, to say that her "darling daughter Nadine" was coming down from school up north, and wouldn't it be "lovely" if she, Uncle Everett, and "darling" Nadine came to visit sometime over the holiday weekend. Mom, being Mom, insisted they come for Thanksgiving, assuring Aunt Louisa that it would be a "very special treat" for all of us.

The Hoover family lived about five hours away from us and usually spent their holidays with Uncle Everett's family, who lived in the same town as they did. It had been about three years since I'd seen any of them, and I was in no hurry to make up for lost time. For one thing, I didn't care for any of them, especially my self-absorbed cousin Nadine. If and when Nadine took the time to talk about someone other than herself, it was usually only for the purpose of making some sort of comparison so that she could feel superior to that person. If she asked me how I was doing in school, it was only so she could brag about having done better. If she asked to see my bedroom, it was only so she could tell me how much bigger and prettier hers was. This was all especially ridiculous since Nadine was a good eight years my senior.

Aunt Louisa, a ninth-grade English teacher, had met and married Everett when she was thirty and he was forty-nine. He was a fellow high school teacher at the time, who later became principal, and had since retired. Everett, who fancied himself a walking beacon of light and an icon of inspiration, often boasted about his unique ability to reach troubled teens. His braggadocio revealed not only his ability to educate and motivate these wayward souls, but his God-given talent to turn them into future world leaders who would, in turn, guide their successors down the same golden road. Everett would spout this babble to any compliant ear, though after a while, few could abide the pretentious discourse of such a pompous ass.

It was a terrible visit from the start. Aunt Louisa, being true to form, smiled "auntily" at me as she stuck out her right cheek, tapped it five times in rapid succession, and waited for me to "plant one" on her. It was a vulgar, unnatural ritual that she had been forcing me to perform since I was three years old.

Nadine, all preppy and proper in her navy blue suit, kept touching her overpermed hair as if she needed the assurance that it was still on her head. At regular intervals, I caught her admiring the enormous diamond on her ring finger, and I got the notion she was more impressed by what it represented than in love with the man who had given it to her. At less frequent intervals, she would casually lift the cuff of her suit jacket to see the diamond tennis bracelet on her wrist, and she would smile, almost imperceptibly, as if to commend herself for obtaining it.

Uncle Everett, in his tweed jacket with brown suede elbow patches, was quite the academic as he puffed heartily on an old carved pipe. He had this way of nodding knowingly through his black frame glasses when something was said, to indicate that he had a sharper, more intuitive take on the subject than anyone else in the room.

When we sat down to dinner, I was fully prepared to "grin and bear it," as Dad liked to say, but I had no idea that the party would turn into a heated debacle and that, naturally, I would be the one held responsible.

"So what do you think of my little girl, Ted?" Uncle Everett crowed. "All grown up, in her second year at Harvard Business School, and engaged to a doctor. Pretty impressive, wouldn't you say?"

I didn't think it was impressive at all. Nadine had been spoiled rotten since the day she was born, and most likely, Uncle Everett knew someone who knew someone who got her into Harvard. Now she was engaged to a rich society doctor and would live the rest of her life on Easy Street.

"I'm very proud of my niece," Dad said. He smiled and turned to Nadine. "We'll have to compare economic theories after dinner. Meantime, let's hear about this lucky fella you're engaged to marry."

"What can I tell you?" Nadine said, as she twirled a piece of hair lazily around her forefinger. "His name is Ethan Charles Montgomery. Isn't that a beautiful name? I can't wait to become Nadine Montgomery. I just love the sound of that. Nadine Montgomery. It's almost as pretty as Aunt Maggie's name, Margaret Connor McKendrick."

I wondered if she was going to keep the Hoover name in there, just to remind people of her innate ability to suck up to them. When I was younger, I used to call her "vacuum head," but it wasn't until seeing her that night that I thought of the sucking analogy.

"You're too kind," Mom said. I could tell she really didn't know what to say to Nadine. "So you're going to marry a doctor!"

"Oh yes, Aunt Maggie, and he's a wonderful one at that. He's in the Army, you know, and right now he's stationed in Germany, which, of course, is why I'm here with you and not somewhere celebrating the holiday with him."

"When will you be getting married then?" Mom asked, ignoring the unintentional insult.

"Nadine's going to be a June bride," Aunt Louisa cut in. "That's when Ethan finishes his post in Germany. Isn't that lovely?"

Oh, lovely, I thought. A June bride named Nadine Montgomery. What could be lovelier?

"It's going to be a huge wedding!" Nadine exclaimed. "Three hundred people, at least, wouldn't you say, Mom? Of course, you'll all be there too. Ethan has such a large family, and an even larger group of friends. His mother is a daughter of fine lineage, you know. Anyway, we're doing the deed in Newport; that's where Ethan is from."

I looked at her in amazement while trying to chew a mouthful of turkey.

"That's Newport, Rhode Island, Darla. And it's very chic! Ethan and I know practically everyone in town. Everyone worth knowing, that is."

I wanted to let her know I was quite aware of where Newport was, but I didn't want to be gauche and talk with my mouth full.

"Our daughter is quite the social butterfly," Aunt Louisa said proudly.

"Always has been," Uncle Everett added. "I believe Nadine learned the fine art of socialization starting from a mere two years of age. Wouldn't you say, Louisa?"

Aunt Louisa nodded obligingly as she put a dainty spoonful of sweet potato pudding in her mouth.

"Personally," Everett continued, "I would attribute it to the motley crew of learned folk that often visited our home. At any given party, you'd find at least one scientist, one physician, one mathematician, one artist, and God knows how many educators and such. I believe that it was this exposure to intellectual society that made Nadine the charming, well-rounded young woman that she is today. I've always believed that it is extremely important for young people to be exposed to mentors and positive role models from an early age. Whoever said that children should be seen and not heard was dead wrong. All children have a voice—black or white, rich or poor—and that voice needs to be heard from a very young age. Gives them confidence, self-esteem. People who've got self-esteem can go anywhere, do anything. It's a powerful tool, but the key is—start 'em young!"

"So, Darla," Nadine interrupted, as bored by her father as we were. "Tell me, have you started dating yet? Got a special boy in your life?"

I hated her condescending tone. "Yes. He's a musician and his name is Ryan."

"A musician?" She laughed. "Not a real musician? You mean he plays some instrument in the school band, right?"

"No! He plays in a band. A real band. He's a drummer."

"Hope the boy's got a career to fall back on," Everett advised, climbing back up on his soapbox. "It's a tough row to hoe out there for the musically minded. But enough about him. He's just a stranger to me. Darla, it's time we got around to you. Now, you're in the tenth grade, isn't that right?"

"Yeah," I said, tensing up inside at the thought of another long-winded speech.

"Got any career plans?" he said, squinting his eyes and biting his bottom lip, as if his brain were in the process of giving birth to some extraordinary concept. "Have you thought about a career at all, Darla?"

"I might want to be an investigative reporter."

I saw Mom and Dad smile proudly at me. For a moment, I forgot about our family problems and felt grateful that they, and not Louisa and Everett, were my parents.

"Hmmm," Everett said, as he took another helping of chestnut stuffing. "An investigative reporter. Do you know what investigative reporters do?"

"Well, yeah," I said, my voice hinting at the anger I felt. "They investigate something and then they report on it."

Nadine laughed out loud, as if I were just a dumb, clueless kid.

"That's a good guess," Everett said, "but there's a lot more to it, you know. Darla, if you're really serious about this, because I don't want to embarrass myself, I want you to call me next week and I'll give you the names of my personal contacts, some investigative reporters who can speak to you personally. They can teach you the ins and outs of the business, and you'll soon know if you've got what it takes to survive in the fast-paced, dog-eat-dog world of journalism. It all may sound glamorous to you, but a career like that involves a lot more than trench coats and crazy deadlines. You're just a kid, but in no time you'll be on your own. It was no picnic in the park for my Nadine, but with hard work and persistence, she got into Harvard University and went on to be at the top of her class in the business school."

I couldn't imagine how that vacuous female could be at the top of anything, but I no longer cared. I thought of my wonderful cousins, April, May, and June, who had so many things to brag about, but who were the most lovely, down-to-earth girls you'd ever want to meet. But Uncle Everett was relentless in his pursuit to make a positive difference in my life. For another hour, he droned on and on with his bombastic drivel about the ways of the world, how to be an achiever and then how to be a mentor. Dad tried to interrupt him countless times, but he just rambled on and on, ignoring any attempt Dad made to terminate his incessant preaching.

I had tuned him out the best I could, but I hated him so much I started to tremble. I felt as if my head were going to implode with all the garbage that had been filtered through it. The Hoovers were a pretentious, despicable lot and I wanted them gone.

"Darla," Nadine said wickedly (she was the only one who could successfully interrupt her father), "after dinner we'll have to have a little tête-à-tête, and I'll show you how to snare a real man. Not the little drummer boy, no pun intended, but a man with a real future—like my Ethan."

I don't know where it came from, and I certainly didn't plan it, but I couldn't help myself any longer. "Shut the hell up, you vacuum head! You make me sick!"

"How dare you!" Nadine shrieked, grabbing her chemically saturated hair in horror. "You've got some nerve, little girl!"

"Really!" Aunt Louisa said, slamming down her fork.

"Nadine was trying to be a mentor to you!" Everett defended her. "You had no business speaking to her like that. None at all!"

I looked him squarely in the eyes. "Why not? She insulted my boyfriend! And you speak to me like I'm some idiot who can't even tie her own shoelaces. I hate the way you talk down to me, like I'm some stupid kid who needs some big smart man like you to teach her right from wrong. And for your information, I know two investigative reporters that I met through the career guidance program at my school. One works for Newsweek and the other for Merriman Newspapers. Next year, I might even do an after-school internship at the Pennwater Post. So thanks but no thanks for your stupid, useless connections. I'm not impressed. Now, leave me alone!"

I rose abruptly from the table, trying not to notice my parents' stunned reactions, threw my linen napkin on the table, and stormed upstairs. I heard my parents offer confused apologies, while Aunt Louisa suggested immediate therapy, and Nadine and her father ranted and raved in anger. I ran into my bedroom and closed the door. I began sobbing and shaking as I grabbed Pierre the Bear and held onto him for dear life. About ten minutes later, after the muffled voices subsided, I heard the front door slam shut and all was quiet.

✳ ✳ ✳

It was a good half hour before Dad made his way up to my bedroom. For some reason, my parents always took turns when it came to situations like these. It was always one of them or the other, depending on who was better equipped to deal with the problem at hand.

Dad was surprisingly calm when he entered my room. "Mind if I sit down?" he asked.

"I don't care," I said, trying not to look at him as he sat down on the bed next to me. (I hated to make eye contact when I knew I was wrong.)

"Well now. That's the second disastrous dinner party we've had in this house. Of course, I certainly can't hold you responsible for the first one."

"I'd rather have dinner with Martin and Maudie than those creepy Hoovers any day! They make me sick!"

"And so you told them, Darla. It was quite embarrassing, to say the least."

"Well, tough!" I snapped. "They deserved it."

"I won't argue with you there. Maybe they did deserve it. I didn't care for the way Everett or Nadine spoke to you either. But that's not the point. They were our guests and did not deserve to be insulted like that."

"No..." I snarled at him. "But they can insult me all they want. Right?"

Dad gave me a dirty look and continued talking. "Louisa is my older sister. She took good care of me when our mother died, and she's the only sibling I've got. Now, I may not be gung ho about the man she married, and I'm certainly not wild about his endless sermonizing, but I also don't want to part company with my sister. I see her little enough as it stands now. After tonight, I'm not sure if I'll ever see her again."

"Who cares?" I mumbled.

"I care! I care very much, young lady. This isn't up to you, do you understand that?"

" 'Plant one here, Darla.' Gross! I hate kissing her stupid cheek."

"She is my sister!" he said, pounding his fist on the bed and looking embarrassed because it made no sound. "Do you understand me, Darla?"

"Oh yeah, I understand."

"Then first thing tomorrow, you'll either write or call the Hoovers with an apology."

"When hell freezes over! No way!"

"Darla!"

"Uh-uh, Dad. Sorry. They owe me an apology. Not the other way around. I'm not apologizing to that pompous ass and his snotty daughter. No way!"

"You will apologize, damn it!" Dad shouted, rising from the bed and momentarily losing his precious self-control. "And that's an order!"

I was afraid to say any more, so I just sat there and shook my head defiantly.

"I've had enough of this, Rebecca!" he screamed. "I've taken all the crap from you that I'm going to take!"

I looked at him in horror. He was still huffing and puffing so hard that he didn't realize that he had called me Rebecca.

"My name is Darla," I told him.

He looked at me blankly for a moment. "Oh, Jesus!" he finally said, flustered. He sat down on the bed, shaking, and desperately tried to compose himself. I had never seen him tremble like that before. It frightened me. Finally, he looked at me, shook his head despairingly, got up, and walked quickly out of the room.

The temperature in our house dropped even lower with the advent of December. I steadfastly refused to apologize to the Hoovers, for whom I now had developed an obsessive loathing, and my father made it clear by his silence that he had nothing much to say to me until I did. Mom, in her eternal quest to keep the peace, suggested repeatedly that I write a "painless little apology note" and "get it over with." She seemed committed to resolving Dad's "uncomfortable position" with Aunt Louisa and was visibly distressed when I flatly refused to help her. In some odd way, the Thanksgiving debacle had brought Mom and Dad closer together again, but sadly and predictably, that only made me feel more alone than ever.

With each passing day, my depression grew worse. Ryan hadn't called in over two weeks, and I was convinced that I not only had made a complete fool of myself in the supermarket, but had lost him forever as well. Melanie, sweetheart that she was, kept insisting that "the guys" didn't know a thing.

And once again, right smack dab in the middle of my problems, was the invisible, yet ever-so-present Aunt Rebecca from Squalor, New Mexico. I considered discussing Dad's Freudian (or Rebeccian) slip with Mom, but I was certain Dad had already confessed it to her, and even more certain that if I asked for an explanation, I'd get nothing more than another dose of her dubious double-talk.

I was sick of Mom's pretense, tired of her counterfeit sympathy. "Oh yes, dear; of course, dear. You deserve to know the truth, dear. I feel so bad for you. Of course I'll tell you what happened." But then, when she thought I wasn't looking, she'd pull the same old storybook off the shelf, replace its words with new ones, and present it in the form of a fresh, new revelation. But I was wising up and had finally figured out that Mom had told me all that she would ever tell me about Rebecca in that very first conversation.

Now she was playing a similar game with the Hoover debacle. Being oh so sweet, she had come to me expressing great empathy for what had happened, reiterating that Nadine's condescending attitude toward me had "gotten her goat," and that Everett's inflated sense of himself was "simply too much to bear." But when all was said and done, all Mom really wanted was for me to write that stupid apology note. She didn't want to deal with my reality or my pain. It didn't matter to her that I was vehemently opposed to doing so for what I considered a very good reason. The bottom line was that apologizing to the Hoovers would make Dad feel better, and that would inevitably make her feel better.

I was furious with both of them. The tension between us got so bad that I started taking dinner up to my room, and although it was at my insistence, I was hurt and angry that my parents barely raised an objection. Eating alone at my desk, night after night, spilling food on my homework assignments, I felt like a prisoner, banished to solitary confinement to mull over my pernicious behavior until I was sufficiently remorseful and would agree to mend my evil ways. And to make it all worse, as I stared solemnly out my bedroom window each evening, I couldn't help but notice the growing display of Christmas lights and decorations at my neighbors' homes. As the bright lights sparkled and shone in the distance, reflecting the joy of their holiday spirit, I felt consumed by my own deep sense of holiday sadness that was slowly destroying me. By the middle of December, I barely ate my dinner each evening, made little effort to do well in school, and for the most part didn't really care if Ryan, or anyone else, called me. In fact, I couldn't think of anything that really mattered anymore, not even unlocking the mystery of Aunt Rebecca.

I just kept wondering how things had gone rotten so quickly. A mere couple of months before, we were a happy, well-adjusted family (or so I thought), who dined together, laughed together, and lovingly shared their lives together. Now we were bitter, sad people, alienated from one another with no idea of what really stood between us. Dad had frequently indicated that my "behavioral problems" started the day I met "that Mullavey boy," but I never could figure out exactly how Ryan had been a negative influence on me. The truth was, as much as I liked Ryan (or thought that I "loved" him), I really didn't know him that well, nor did I see him very often. To complicate matters, a few days after Thanksgiving, I overheard Dad tell Mom that although Ryan seemed to be a "decent young man," he somehow had served as the catalyst in my current and ongoing state of self-destruction. At the time, I didn't really understand precisely what that meant, but it infuriated me just the same. I, on the other hand, blamed everyone but Ryan—Aunt Rebecca, Mom, Dad, the Hoovers, and even Aunt Didi.

CHAPTER 8

My emotional malaise took a much-needed hiatus on the second Saturday of December when Melanie came charging over to my house, insisting that I get out of my "blue funk" and go Christmas shopping with her. I certainly hadn't thought about gifts, much less about buying them for my parents, but I desperately needed a change of scenery. I also needed to extricate myself from the pain, and that meant telling my best friend "everything," including the taboo tale of Aunt Rebecca. It also meant breaking my promise to Mom. But I needed to talk, and at that point, I trusted Melanie a lot more than my own mother. Perhaps it was merely guilt-induced rationalization, but I truly believed that Mom would understand my betrayal, and maybe even be grateful that there was someone to help me.

Melanie was wonderful. Between her frequent "omigods," she was incredibly supportive and perceptive. She explained how some of her sister Brenda's high school antics had influenced the way her parents currently treated (and trusted) her, and she related firsthand to how frustrating and unfair that could be. I had the feeling, though, that her best-friend sensibilities might have been slightly bruised by my failure to "tell all" earlier.

As it turns out, it was Melanie who convinced me to break my promise, yet one more time, and to let my cousins in on the mystery. Melanie had faith that we might be able to pool our familial resources, no matter how minimal, and solve the mystery once and for all.

"But most of all, Dar," she said, looking into my eyes, "it'll bring you even closer to your cousins, and that's what you really need right now. So cheer up, forget about this whole mess for a minute, and start thinking about what you're going to buy me for Christmas!"

Melanie's intervention had come just in time. She was just what the doctor had ordered to bring me back to life. The very next day, as soon as Mom and Aunt Didi left for the mall, I called April (the only one of us with a driver's license) and asked her to come over and pick me up. I explained that there was a family mystery that needed solving, and that she and her sisters were just the ones to help. Intrigued by the prospect, April appeared on my doorstep within the half hour, and in no time, I found myself sitting on April's bed, knee-deep in conference with my colluding cousins.

In my excited state of catharsis, I kept forgetting pertinent details and had to jump around the narrative a bit, but eventually, I managed to relate the story in its entirety.

"You know, I remember that night at your house," April said. "You were asking about Aunt Rebecca and then you said 'screw' and everyone freaked out — I'd forgotten all about that. We were so young then."

"How come you guys knew what that word meant and I didn't?" I asked, still feeling embarrassed.

"Probably 'cause Dad used the word all the time," June said. "And he still does."

"Yeah," April agreed, "and that wasn't the only four-letter word us Alexander girls knew back then!"

We all looked at April. " 'Screw' has five letters in it," May said, laughing. "Shall I count them for you?"

"Oh, yeah," April said, then giggled.

"But 'ditz' is a four-letter word." June said.

"So tell me, you guys, has your mom ever told you anything about Aunt Rebecca? I've only been dying to ask you this for years, you know."

"Then what took you so long?" April questioned, stretching her arms over her head.

" 'Cause she promised Aunt Maggie she wouldn't say anything!" May told her. "That's pretty simple to figure out."

"Mom told us about Aunt Rebecca a couple years ago," June explained, "and it was probably right around the time that your mom first said something to you."

"Knowing the way our mothers talk," May said, "they probably thought it would be safer if we all knew relatively the same amount of information. Don't you think?"

"Makes sense to me," June replied, putting a pillow behind her back and leaning up against the headboard.

"Why would that matter?" April asked May.

"So," May explained, "if Darla blabbed to us, we wouldn't go running to Mom asking questions because we'd think we already knew the answers."

"Yeah, I guess," April said, squirming restlessly.

Being able to release years of pent-up emotions and nagging questions felt wonderful, but I wasn't feeling overly optimistic that my cousins had anything new to share. However, I wasn't the least bit regretful for having spilled my guts and was enjoying our conference immensely.

"There's got to be more to this story than they're letting on," May theorized.

"Yeah, Darla, there's no way your dad would be so obsessed over the things Rebecca did if there weren't," June added. "I mean, really, that was a lifetime ago. And to call you 'Rebecca' now! Wow, that's heavy!"

"Wait a minute!" April said in her secret agent voice. "I think I remember something!"

"What?" the three of us asked in unison.

"Well, one night about a year ago, Mom and Dad came back late from this party at the Reillys' house. You know Mrs. Reilly, the bleached blond babe who wears short skirts and practically lives at the tanning salon?"

"Yeah, we know her," May said. "What's the point?"

"Well," April said, lowering her voice, "this particular night, I got up to go to the bathroom, and I heard Dad telling Mom that Phyllis Reilly was nothing more than a tease, and that it was disgusting that she acted the way she did, especially in front of her husband's friends, and that she reminded him of the tease Rebecca used to be and probably still was."

"Go on," May encouraged her.

"Anyway," April said, delighted to be imparting such juicy gossip, "then Mom got all weird and said something about it's too bad that being a tease wasn't all that Rebecca was! Then Dad got all quiet and Mom told him that she bet he was sorry he even brought up the subject. Then Dad said, 'Get off my case, Didi,' and that was it."

"Heav-vee!" June exclaimed. "I wonder what that meant."

"I dunno," I said, "but it's really interesting."

"Do you think we'll ever figure all this out?" May asked.

"I've actually thought about trying to find Rebecca some day," I said, "but even though part of me wants to do that, another part of me gets the chills just thinking about it."

"I get the chills just hearing you say it!" April agreed.

"Besides," I continued, "from what my mother has told me, not that I trust her completely, no one's even sure she's still alive, due to all the drugs and stuff she took."

"And the 'shady' company she kept!" June said teasingly. "Right?"

"I guess so," I said, thinking about how ridiculously puritanical my mother sounded.

"Well, if she's dead," April concluded, "you're not going to find out very much from her."

"You're wacko," June said to April, rolling her eyes.

Suddenly, a strange look crossed April's face, one that I had never seen before.

"What's wrong, April?" May asked, concerned. "You look like you've seen a ghost."

April just sat there, as serious as I'd ever seen her, and stared into space. May, June, and I just looked at each other. We didn't know what to make of it.

"Maybe I have," April said in a dire tone. "Oh—my—God. She's not dead. I'm sure of it. At least she wasn't when—"

A chill shot up my spine. "What! Tell us! What?!"

"Oh—my—God! I can't believe it!"

"What already!" June shouted. "Out with it, girl!"

"It's her," April said, almost talking to herself. "Oh my God. It's her. Rebecca."

"What's her?" May asked impatiently. "Who's her?"

"I saw her once," April said, clutching a pillow for support. "I saw her a really long time ago." She turned quickly around to face May. "Don't you remember? I was eight and you were seven and we were playing in the backyard. June was inside 'cause she was really sick, and Mom was freaking out worrying about her."

May shook her head. April's sudden recollection was not registering with her at all.

"I remember," April continued. "We were outside by that wooden sandbox we used to have, making castles or something, when all of a sudden this strange lady with dark sunglasses and a scarf over her head appeared. She was smiling this creepy smile at us and then she said, 'You two must be Didi's daughters. You're both very pretty.' Then she looked up at the house, and I guess she saw Mom in the window or something, because she got real spooked and ran away."

A weird look began to cross May's face too. "I remember that now," she said softly. "Gosh, it's amazing what's tucked away in your brain. I never would've remembered that on my own in a million years. April is absolutely right."

"So what happened then?" I asked, feeling as if the mystery were finally starting to unravel.

"Mom came out of the house acting totally ballistic. She started asking where 'that woman' went and ran around the house looking for her. I'd never seen her like that—ever—which is probably why I remember it so well. I think she probably asked us a million questions, and she got really upset when we couldn't answer them all."

"And then Mom got so nuts that I got scared and started to cry," May remembered. "Mom apologized for scaring me and gave me this big hug, but she was still acting kind of crazy."

"Later I heard her talking to your mom about it," April continued, "on the phone in the kitchen. She kept saying, 'Maggie, she was here! She was here!' And I remember Dad getting all freaked too, when she told him."

"Wow," June said. "This is really heavy!"

"If it was Rebecca," I conjectured, "I wonder why she came back to town?"

"I have no idea," April said.

Something suddenly clicked in my brain. "Wait a minute, April. Didn't you say that you were eight and May was seven?"

"Yeah, I remember because it was in the early summer, and I was playing with these dolls I had gotten for my eighth birthday. May got the same dolls for her seventh birthday, and we were building a home for them."

"Well, if you were eight, then I would've been seven, like May, and I was seven when Grandpa Henry died. Do you think it could've been around that—"

"Oh God!" April screamed, jumping up and running like a banshee around the room. "That's it! Mom wasn't just upset about June being sick. Grandpa Henry had just died! I remember now! Darla — Rebecca must've come back for the funeral or something!"

"Then why didn't she stay?" May wondered aloud.

"Who knows?" April told her. "But I'll bet you anything that woman was our aunt Rebecca!"

"And I'll bet you something else too!" June said, jumping on the bandwagon.

"What?" April, May, and I screamed at a feverish pitch. The excitement was more than we could bear. It was better than the ghost stories we used to tell.

"I think she's the one who used to call here," June speculated, with a wide-eyed look on her face.

"Yeah!" April agreed. "The person who calls here and then is never on the phone."

The three of us looked at April—again.

"I mean, the person who calls here but doesn't say anything," April said, correcting herself.

"That's right!" June said. "I remember when those calls started coming regularly, just several years ago. I thought it was really weird that Mom would always run to another room to answer the phone. Probably so she could scream stuff in her ear or something and we wouldn't hear."

"Yeah," April concurred. "Like, 'Stop calling here, you bad girl,' or 'I know that's you, Rebecca. George has put a tap on the line and we're going to get you! And your little dog too!' "

"Yeah, or 'Why don't you call your sister Margaret's house instead!' " May added. " 'Why don't you bug the McKendricks for a change and leave us the hell alone!' "

We all burst out laughing, which led to a severe case of the giggles and the sillies, which lasted a good hour, ending with a bed-hopping, knock-down, drag-out pillow fight, and four very worn-out teenagers.

✳✳✳

Although the stalemate with my parents had not changed, there was great improvement in some other areas of my life. For one, the simple pleasure of spending a Sunday afternoon with my cousins had lifted my spirits immensely. And although I was by no means close to solving the Rebecca mystery, I finally had unearthed some new and exciting information—a welcome change from years of Mom's recycled, rehearsed, and "spontaneous" disclosures.

The best news, however, was that Ryan called the following Tuesday to invite me to a Christmas party that his parents were giving on Friday night.

"You'll get to meet my corny dad." Ryan laughed. "But don't worry, he won't try to sing to you unless it's your birthday or something."

"My birthday's in April," I told him. "I should be safe."

"Yeah, probably," Ryan agreed. "But he might sing a Christmas carol or two, you know, if the urge to belt one out should arise. Listen, Darla, I'm really sorry that I can't call you all that much, or get together. I really do like you a lot, but my music is sort of my priority right now, and I just can't get that involved. But I don't want to break up or anything. I just sorta wanna be straight with you."

"That's okay," I assured him. I had a sick feeling in the pit of my stomach that he probably thought I was desperate and would agree to anything.

"Well," he said uneasily, "most of my friends, and probably yours too, usually get together a lot more with the people they're seeing, and I was thinking that you probably wanted the same kind of relationship with me."

Naturally, I wanted much more from him, but in another sense, I didn't want a boyfriend to consume all of my free time the way Jesse was consuming all of Melanie's time (much to my dismay). At least now I had a plausible explanation for our somewhat limited relationship, and I no longer had that nagging feeling that I was being somehow duped or played for a fool. I didn't really know how to express myself to Ryan so that he'd believe I felt okay about it, so I decided to just tell him the almost truth.

"Well, I would like to see you more, Ryan; I'm not going to lie. But there's a lot of other stuff I like to do too, and I'm really not looking for a boyfriend who's attached at the hip or whatever."

There was an awkward silence on the phone.

"Ryan, I'm serious."

"Good. I'm really happy to hear that."

With that matter settled, we talked for almost an hour. I filled him in on the trouble I was having at home, and though he had no sage advice to offer, he was as supportive and interested as a seventeen-year-old guy could be. By the end of the conversation, I was finally convinced that he had no knowledge of my participation in the supermarket caper, and it felt as if the weight of the world had been lifted off my shoulders. Ryan ended the conversation by telling me that he was really looking forward to seeing me on Friday, but that he also wanted to stop by my house the following Wednesday, Christmas Day, because he had some special gifts for me.

I was ecstatic. I knew that Melanie was home alone that evening, and I couldn't wait to call her for some expert advice on my newest dilemma—what to buy Ryan for Christmas!

The party at Ryan's house passed without incident. Dad, via Mom, had given me permission to go, and there were no words of contention or post-event battles. But Dad was still barely speaking to me, and I figured he had only said yes to the party because he knew Ryan's dad and, mostly, because he was simply too tired to fight with me anymore.

Christmas was now a mere three days away, and I still hadn't bought anything for my parents. It seemed as if all they wanted from me was that stupid apology note for the Hoovers, and that was one gift I just couldn't give. I started to sink back into my depression, but this time, it lasted only until Sunday morning, when I woke to find May, standing in my bedroom.

"I want you to go somewhere with me today," she said as she sat on my bed and put Pierre the Bear on her lap. "We can take the bus there, and I'll ask April to pick us up later. We can talk on the way—and you can tell me all about Ryan's party—and anything else that might be on your mind."

May was amazingly intuitive. Even more so than her sisters, she knew when I was having a hard time or when I was feeling depressed.

"Where are we going?" I asked suspiciously. I was sure she had some plan to cheer me up, and then drag me off to the mall, where she would force me to buy gifts for Mom and Dad. May was so sweet and sensitive (and much more mature than I was), and it seemed exactly like something she would do.

"You'll see. Please come with me, Darla. It's really important."

"Does this have something to do with Christmas gifts?"

"Yes. But I promise, it's not what you think."

I looked at her doubtfully.

"I swear, Darla. It isn't! Now get your rear end out of bed and let's go."

＊ ＊ ＊

The nursing home was large and austere. The last thing I wanted to do was go inside. I stood in the cold and stared at the old, gray building. It looked more like a haunted castle than a nursing home, and if the people who lived inside were as ghoulish and gray as the building itself, then I

121

had no desire to go inside and collect more nightmare material for my twisted subconscious to torture me with in the black of night.

"This is where you go to visit people?" I asked May incredulously. I knew she often visited nursing home residents, but I'd never really given it any more thought than that.

"This is the place." May smiled cheerfully. "Let's go inside. I'm freezing my you-know-what off out here!"

"Wait!" I said, grabbing her by the arm. "Not yet."

"Are you afraid?"

"Well, I dunno, well sorta, well yeah! I am!"

"I can understand that. April and June don't like to come here either, unless it's to sing, but even then, I can tell they're uncomfortable. Especially April."

"Does that bother you?"

"No, not at all. I understand. Besides, Darla, I kinda like doing something without them and being just me for a change."

"Oh," I said, shivering. "Then you don't think they're cowards for not wanting to do this?"

"No way! But June and April do go to the Children's Hospital and dress up like clowns. April comes by that quite naturally, as you know." She laughed. "And this is what I like to do. Maybe you'll like it too."

"Nah, I don't think so. I'd rather be a clown."

"You already are. C'mon. Just try it once," she said, playfully pushing me forward, "and I won't bug you again. I swear!"

"And what if I won't go?"

May thought for a moment. "I don't know," she said. "I guess the tickle monster will just have to make you go!"

We giggled like kids as May chased me to the front door. I said a quick prayer, and entered the building behind her.

Inside, the home was bright and cheerful. The walls were freshly painted in light colors, and there were lots of artwork hanging on them, mostly of landscapes and seascapes—of all the pretty places more preferable to be. Christmas and Hanukkah decorations hung everywhere, and many of them appeared to be craft projects done by some of the more artistic residents. The nursing home was not as dismal as I'd feared, and I was beginning to enjoy this unusual outing that May had planned.

As we entered the residents' lounge, a chubby nurse with big green glasses waved exuberantly at May just as a handsome young orderly walked by and winked at us. May was about to brief me on the place, when a piercing scream came from the end of the hall and a flurry of people in white went running to investigate. Everyone else stood still, unsure of what to do or what to say next. From that moment on, I lost track of May. I was too consumed by watching the sea of startled faces, shipwrecked in the lounge. One by one, as the seconds ticked away, their collective calm began to crack, as it became painfully clear to all of us that the death toll had just risen by one.

There was one wintry old man in particular who caught my eye; he did not react like the rest. He just sat in his wheelchair, pale and motionless with his head hung sorrowfully, as if he were waiting to die. I noticed that he had only one leg, and that there was a beautiful handmade afghan of many colors draped over his lap. I imagined it must've been one of his few remaining treasures, though I doubted he even knew it was there. The man had no reaction to the ensuing panic that surrounded him—just the hollow, sad stare of a being long gone, whose body was waiting to die, and whose mind already had.

As I glanced around the room, I noticed a beautiful older woman sitting on the sofa. Her lovely demeanor and sweet half smile reminded me of Grandma Adelaide, though physically, she bore no resemblance. Well groomed and delightfully "proper," she wore a neatly pressed blue dress with matching jewelry. Unlike the others, she seemed determined to hold steady, but when the second scream came, her resolve disappeared. Clutching the skirt of her dress, she looked frantically around for a nurse, but they were all at the end of the hall. Even though she looked too healthy to live in a nursing home, I knew that probably wasn't the case, and that she was probably scared of being the next to die.

The moment the first tear fell from her eyes, a tear fell from mine, and without even debating it, I rushed over to her side and sat down next to her. I took her right hand in mine and held it tightly. The relief that

123

swept her face was like nothing I could've imagined. She smiled at me with a look of gratitude and love, so deep and so real, as if I had literally saved her life. It was uncanny. It was exactly the way my grandma had looked at me when I last saw her in the hospital before she died.

I smiled back at the woman as I continued to hold her hand. I had never felt anything so wonderful in my life. I was loved and needed, and for a brief moment, I almost missed the melancholy that filled her eyes.

"God bless you, sweet girl," she said to me. "Are you here to see someone special?"

I wasn't sure what to say. "You're special. I guess I'm here to see you."

"What's your name?" she said, trying to smile through her tears. "My name is Victoria Emmaline Ashbury."

"I'm Darla McKendrick. That's my cousin May over there."

"You're May's cousin!" She brightened. "You're every bit as lovely. May I call you Darla?"

"Of course!" I said, surprised she had even asked.

"Well, then you'll call me Victoria. No point in being formal, now, is there?"

"I guess not."

"Do you sing too?"

"Oh, no. Only in the shower. There was only so much singing talent to go around in my family, and I think my three cousins got it all."

She laughed. I saw a look of serenity slowly return to her face. By this time I noticed that some of the nurses had resumed their stations. The cheerful chubby one had a tissue and was dabbing her eyes.

"Why did she have to die today!" came the wail of a well-dressed woman, who was walking down the hall, comforted by her husband and son on either side. "I knit her a red sweater for Christmas. She picked out the pattern herself. She was so excited about it. Why did she have to die now? Oh, Mom—come back, Mom, please. Don't leave me now. I finished your sweater. I was going to embroider your initials on it, to surprise you. Oh, Mom, not now—it's Christmastime—please come back—Mom!"

As her crying intensified, her knees wobbled beneath her, and the men, who were every bit as stung by the loss as she, struggled to keep her standing. When they approached the front doors, the woman cried louder. "No, wait, I can't leave her here. Go back: I have to see her again! Mom!" The woman's son held the door open while her husband gently guided her through it. I listened to her screams as they diminished with distance, trailing off into morbid silence. When everything was quiet, I looked into Victoria's eyes. She looked back as if she were begging me for answers to questions I couldn't possibly know.

"It'll be okay," I told her, still holding her hand. "Really it will."

With all that had happened, I hadn't given a moment of thought to May. When I finally saw her again, she was making the rounds, stopping to speak to each resident. About fifteen minutes later, she got to Victoria.

"Hello, Victoria," she said, flashing a beautiful smile. "I see you've met my cousin, Darla."

"I told her," Victoria said, "that she's as lovely as you are."

"Thank you. You're very kind. How are you feeling?"

"Oh, I've had a pretty good week." Victoria smiled. "My son called, and he and his wife will be in from Oregon on Christmas. I'll be spending the entire day with them. Christmas Eve, too. I'm looking forward to it. But today, well, it's been a little rough for us, as you know. And yesterday, we lost Daisy Mulford."

"Mr. Selak told me." May smiled sympathetically. "It's very sad. But I'm so happy to hear your son will be coming in. That's wonderful news. Listen, Victoria, I'll be back to see you real soon, but Darla and I have to be going now. I hope you understand."

"Oh certainly," she said, putting on a brave front. "I'm just so grateful that you were able to come at all. Goodbye. And have a very merry Christmas. And Darla, thank you, my dear."

"Goodbye, Victoria," I said, as the tears rolled down my cheeks. "And a very merry Christmas to you too."

* * *

April was waiting outside for us in Uncle George's car. She was parked in the side lot, reading a copy of Weekly Variety. I said hello to her as I climbed into the backseat, then turned my head to look back at the somber gray building that May and I had just left.

On the ride home, April and May engaged in quiet small talk, while I sat silently, thinking about the people and events that had shaped the past few months of my life. The best of it and the worst of it had started the night of Brenda Davenport's party. That was the wonderful night when I met Ryan, and also the terrible night that had marked the beginning of my declining relationship with Dad. And then there was the Halloween party, when a woman with a plastic rear end had drunk from a bedpan and shouted "Bottoms up!" as her friends chuckled at her cleverness. In the place where I had just left, bedpans were a way of life and no one was laughing at them. I remembered my first kiss with Ryan and thought of the old man waiting to take his last breath. Surely, I was too young to think about these things. I had to be.

I saw April glimpse in the rearview mirror to see if I was okay. I turned my head so she couldn't see my tears and stared pensively out the window. I could still feel Victoria's fear in me. It had permeated every inch of my body and was festering in the pit of my stomach. I ached for her. And although I knew that I had touched her heart for a brief moment, I felt ashamed and guilty knowing that she was destined to live out her life with many more such frightened moments, and that I would be somewhere else. Maybe I'd even be laughing and having fun. I hoped that her son was good to her, and I felt sad that he lived so far away. I wondered if she had any other children, or people who came to visit her. I prayed that she did.

My somber train of thought inevitably led me back to my own parents. I thought of the woman at the nursing home, who had just lost her mother, and wondered, without wanting to know, how it might feel.

I just couldn't understand how it had come to this. Here it was, a precious few days before Christmas, and I had nothing but bitterness in my heart for my parents. What could I have been thinking? Would I open their gifts on Christmas morning and have nothing but empty thank-yous to give in return? How could I spend my hard-earned babysitting money to buy something for Ryan and Melanie, not to mention the Alexander family, when I had nothing for Mom and Dad? It would destroy them. It would destroy me! When was I going to wake up and smell the insanity?

For the first time in months, I couldn't wait to get home. When April pulled into the driveway, I thanked her for the ride, and I thanked May for taking me with her. My reluctant journey to the nursing home had served its purpose, and I understood clearly why May had chosen this particular time to include me in her good-deed doing.

When I opened the front door, Dad was coming down the stairs with a large box of Christmas ornaments in his arms. Mom was standing by the bare Christmas tree that had obviously been bought during my absence that day. When he saw me, Dad put the box down on the sofa, and the corners of his mouth turned slowly upward, as if he desperately wanted to smile at me, but were afraid to.

Mom's eyes sparkled, like they always did at Christmastime, and I stood there looking at them both, feeling the warmth of their love, as I felt Victoria's fear and the loneliness that now was her life.

I burst into tears and ran into my mother's arms.

"It's okay, Darla," Mom said, caressing my hair.

I lifted my head from her shoulder and glanced over at my dad. He looked at me like an eager puppy dog, who wondered if there was a treat in store for him as well. I pulled away from Mom and ran to him. As he held me, I had the sense that he was desperately clutching something that had been lost, and something he'd never hoped to find again.

The three of us spent a wonderful evening trimming the tree and making plans for Christmas morning. To my surprise, while I was debating how to broach the very touchy subject of apologizing to the Hoovers (which I still refused to do), Mom and Dad brought the subject up first. Mom told me that they had decided it would be wrong to force me to write an apology letter. Dad awkwardly added that "time heals all wounds," and that he felt confident that our relationship with Louisa and her family would eventually mend. But he also seemed extremely uncomfortable discussing the subject any further, as did I, so it was happily dropped.

For the first time in months, I felt like my old self. I ate my dinner in the dining room, laughed with my parents, and, to my great relief, slept peacefully through the night.

CHAPTER 9

I woke up Christmas morning feeling wonderful. I sensed that the day would be everything that Thanksgiving was not. First, I had reconciled with my parents and was no longer expected to write an apology note to those dreadful Hoovers. Second, my cousins were coming over for our traditional Christmas dinner, and we'd just heard that Uncle George's sister Nancy was improving tremendously. Melanie (whose family had celebrated the night before) was going to join my family for dinner, and to make my day complete, I was going to see Ryan. Just that past weekend, he had introduced me to his family, and we'd had a blast together at his parent's party. Now he was coming over after dinner with not one, but two Christmas gifts for me. It was all so amazing. Things had gone from bad to worse to wonderful—all in such a short period of time.

Ryan called at the end of dinner to say that he'd be arriving in about a half hour and was bringing Ben Davenport with him. The excuse was that they'd been together at a mutual friend's house and that it was out of Ryan's way to drop Ben off at home. I didn't care if he brought Godzilla with him: I just wanted to see him, and I was dying to see what gifts he'd bought for me. I asked to be excused from the table, so that the five of us girls could go up to my bedroom and prepare for the visit. I was hoping that Melanie could reverse my bad hair day while June performed some quick makeup magic on my face.

"Listen up, girls!" Melanie said as soon as my bedroom door was shut. "I didn't want to say this in front of your parents, but I know the real reason Ben is coming over here."

"What do you mean, the real reason?" I asked naively. "Ryan said it would take too much time to drop Ben off at home. Isn't that the reason?"

"How dense are you, Darla?" Melanie scolded me cheerfully. "We only live a few blocks away. Duh! Wake up, little Snoozy! My big brother has got an ulterior motive for wanting to be here, and I'm looking right at her." She smiled devilishly at April. "You're in my brother's English class at school, right?"

"Yeah...so?" April said, making herself comfortable on my bed.

"Well, haven't you noticed him ogling you all the time?"

"Me?" April giggled. "I don't think so. Maybe in your warped brain he is."

"How would you know what your brother's doing?" I asked Melanie. "You're not in their class! You're not even in their grade!"

Melanie plopped down on the bed next to April; the rest of us sat cross-legged on the floor. "Listen, dumb Darla, I know. First of all, when my brother sees a girl he likes, he doesn't just look at her, he ogles her. Just like your uncle Martin from the Planet Skievoid." She turned to my cousins. "You don't know what you missed not meeting that creature."

"We heard it was ug-lee," June said. "I'm just glad we were on Cape Cod at the time so the old geezer couldn't ogle us too!"

"Well, I'm not glad we weren't here," April moaned. "It sounded really interesting. Especially to hear Mom tell it."

"Melanie," June said, "get back to the dirt you were dishing on Ben. How can you be so sure that he has a crush on the ditzy one?"

April shot June a dirty look, then turned to Melanie with rapt attention.

"I found out on Christmas Eve. I was in Ben's bedroom, by myself, and I was wrapping the gifts he'd bought our mom and dad. He'd asked me to, 'cause his wrapping is the absolute pits. Anyway, I saw these two pieces of crumpled up paper under his desk and being the good sister I am, I went to pick them up. But then, just for the heck of it, I decided to uncrumple one of them, and lo and behold—"

"What?" we all asked.

"Don't rush me," Melanie said, soaking up the attention. "Now, where was I?"

"At 'lo and behold,' " May reminded her.

"Yeah. So lo and behold, I uncrumple the paper, and what's written on it?"

"Well?" June asked. "What?"

" 'April Alexander, April Alexander, April Alexander, April

130

Alexander, April Alexander, April Alexander, April Alexander, April Alexander, April Alexander!' " Melanie laughed. "My brother's in love!"

April started giggling with embarrassment. "You're making this up!"

"No, I'm not!" Melanie assured her. "And wait, there's more!"

"She hasn't gotten to the second piece of paper yet," June told April. "The one that says 'Ditz Alexander, Ditz Alexander, Ditz Alexander.' "

"You mean the one with your name on it!" April said, giggling and throwing a pillow at June. She turned to Melanie. "I'm afraid to ask, but what did the second piece of paper say?"

"It's too funny!" Melanie said, laughing hysterically.

"Are you going to tell us?" May asked.

"She loves to torture people!" I explained to May. "It's in her genes."

June turned to April and smiled. "That's 'genes,' as in chromosomes. Not blue jeans, you know."

April got up from the bed and gave June a whack with my other pillow. "Give it up, you bozo brain." She turned to Melanie. "Ignore this alien reptile and spill your beans, will you?"

"That's *the* beans," June corrected her.

"Who cares whose beans they are?" April replied, resuming her seat. "Just a long as she spills them."

"Well," Melanie began, amused by the repartee, "at the top of the paper, in big block letters, it said, are you ready for this, it said 'April in Paris.' Isn't that a riot? Then, underneath that it said 'Ben in Paris.' Then, underneath that, it said 'April and Ben in Paris,' and then there was a little drawing of the Eiffel Tower with these two stick figures holding hands! Omigod, is that funny or what?"

The five of us burst into hysterics, and when Mom came upstairs to tell me that "the boys had arrived," I had forgotten completely about my beauty makeover.

✳ ✳ ✳

It didn't take us long to get downstairs, but by the time we arrived,

Dad had already engaged Ryan and Ben in corny conversation.

"Ben Davenport! I don't think I've seen you since you were ten. I must've missed you at your sister Brenda's shindig. What would you say, about two hundred and fifty folks there?"

"Yeah, just about, Mr. McKendrick," Ben said as he looked dreamy-eyed at April. "My parents have a lot of friends."

"It's no wonder! Mike and Grace are great people. Did you know that Ryan's dad and I know each other?"

"No, I didn't," Ben said, looking right at Dad as he realized he been staring at April. "You know Mr. Mullavey, huh?"

"We worked at the same firm, years ago, when we were just starting out in the investment banking business."

I couldn't bear it. This was humiliating. I was just thankful that Dad hadn't referred to himself and Mr. Mullavey as "young whippersnappers" back then.

"Have you fellas met my sister- and brother-in-law yet, Didi and George Alexander?"

"Uh, no," Ben and Ryan said as everyone shook hands.

Uncle George was smiling. He was quite amused by Ben's obvious adoration of his eldest daughter. He looked at April, tilted his head in Ben's direction, and winked at her. April started giggling and June elbowed her to stop, which, naturally, only made April giggle more, much to her father's delight.

"Ben," Uncle George asked innocently, "what year of school are you in?"

"I'm a junior."

"April's a junior too. Do you know my daughter April?"

"Uh, yeah. We're in a class together."

"I'll bet my daughter is the prettiest girl in that class. Am I right?"

"Dad!" April pleaded softly.

"Uh, yeah," Ben told him, turning red. "As a matter of fact, she is."

I looked over at Melanie. She was holding her stomach and doing everything in her power not to laugh. Seeing her brother being tortured by Dad and Uncle George was simply too delicious. Ryan smiled and rolled his eyes at me, and I knew he was hoping that he wouldn't be next. Ultimately, Aunt Didi rescued Ben from the clutches of her sadistic husband, by calling everyone into the dining room for dessert, but Uncle George got in one last jab by insisting that Ben sit next to April at the table.

After we had all stuffed ourselves with everything fattening, it was time to return to the living room and exchange gifts. Not only was I dying to know what was in the two large boxes that Ryan had brought, I was scared to death that he wouldn't like the denim shirt and suspenders (his trademark) that I'd gotten for him.

Luckily, my fears were unwarranted. I could tell by the look on Ryan's face that he genuinely liked my gift. He thanked me profusely and then it was my turn.

Ryan insisted that I start with the smaller of the two boxes, which I opened to find a gorgeous hunter green, V-neck sweater.

"Who said that men don't have good taste in clothing?" Mom said as I held up the sweater. "That's lovely, Ryan."

"Yeah, thanks so much!" I gushed. "I really love it, Ryan."

"Looks like there's one more gift for you," Aunt Didi said, curiously eyeing the larger box. "Is that also from you, Ryan?"

"Yes, it is." Ryan grinned, looking at Ben. "Actually, it's for Darla and April. From me and Ben."

"Oh, really!" Uncle George chuckled. "For April too?"

"Dad!" April said under her breath.

Melanie looked at me, puzzled, and shrugged her shoulders. I could tell she had no idea what they were up to.

Ryan and Ben grinned from ear to ear as April and I began to open the package. Melanie, June, and May had formed a circle around us, each of us more curious than the next.

It was April who screamed first as she saw "the gift."

"We had it dry cleaned for you!" Ben told her, as he and Ryan slapped five. "I'm just hoping they got all the egg off."

"Yeah," Ryan said, barely able to keep from splitting his sides. "Raw eggs are a bitch to get off!"

"Omigod! Is that what I think it is?"

The five of us took turns screaming, much to the complete bafflement of the adults, none of whom could see the contents of the box from where they were sitting.

"Well, I'm curious!" Aunt Didi said, walking over to look at the box. "What in the world! Well, I'll be damned. Look, Maggie. It's Mom's old brown coat!"

"What's that?" Mom asked, getting up from her chair.

"Look!" Aunt Didi said, grabbing the coat out of the box. "This is Mom's old coat. Remember it? This ratty old thing she wore for years and refused to get rid of? The last time I looked it was in my attic. How the hell did you boys get ahold of it?"

They were too far gone with laughter to answer her, and we weren't far behind them. Ryan and Ben had outdone themselves. It was truly a brilliant scheme, and April and I deserved it. Never, in my wildest dreams, did I think that being found out in that ridiculous supermarket caper would be the topping on the most wonderful Christmas I'd ever had.

Whoever coined yet another of Dad's favorite clichés, "What goes up must come down," had to be talking about my life at that time, which had more ups and downs than an elevator. It was inevitable, after experiencing the "up" of an extraordinary Christmas, that I would be doomed for another major "down" in the not-too-distant future.

The five days that followed Christmas were almost idyllic. I was still on a high from Ryan and Ben's hilarious Christmas "revenge," and I was also feeling very content about my relationship with Mom and Dad. I was confident that they finally understood that I was not the only one at fault in the Hoover debacle, and that time, and not an apology note from me, would heal the Hoovers' wounds. Of course, I personally didn't care if the Hoovers bled themselves dry from those wounds (they deserved it), but Aunt Louisa was Dad's sister and although I couldn't stand her, I had to, as my father said, respect the fact that he loved her very much.

For me, the best thing about Christmas was that Mom and Dad got to know Ryan better and were able to see for themselves what a great guy he was. I truly believed that my father no longer thought of him as "that Mullavey boy who seemed like a fine young man but who was really a bad influence on my daughter." So, when Ryan asked me out for New Year's Eve, even though Dad had several reservations, he gave me his permission, albeit with a few conditions.

The party was to be held at Melanie's boyfriend Jesse's house, about fifteen minutes from our home, and was to be chaperoned by his parents. Before I could go anywhere, Dad wanted Jesse's address and phone number, and I had to promise to abide by his one o'clock curfew. But above all else, I had to swear that I wouldn't touch any alcohol, and that Ryan wouldn't either. If these conditions were met, Dad said he could rest "as easy as any parent could ever rest" and would allow me to go.

I was in love with the burgundy-colored dress that my mother had bought me for New Year's Eve. Not only was the dress itself beautiful, but my all-day shopping trip with her from where it came attested to a clear show of support for my relationship with Ryan. Aunt Didi, who thought Ryan was "adorable," had come over that afternoon to do my hair for me. Being the perennial stage mother that she was, hairstyling came as naturally to Aunt Didi as getting up in the morning. My own mother, though not untalented in the hair department, had a very limited, and extremely antiquated, idea of what was hot and what was not.

Dad said that I looked more beautiful than he'd ever seen me. I was so excited about the evening that I wasn't even embarrassed when he insisted on taking "just a couple of shots" of Ryan and me in our New Year's Eve finery. In fact, I was secretly thrilled, knowing that I would now have photos of the two of us to cherish forever. My mind was working so fast that I found myself already planning to blow the best picture up into an eight-by-ten for my bedroom, and maybe even a poster size for my wall. But, of course, once Ryan and I got out the front door, I would bemoan the fact to Ryan that my shutterbug dad was a perpetual source of embarrassment (which most of the time he was).

I quickly forgot all about the photos, when once outside I noticed that Ryan's green Mustang was not waiting for us in the driveway as I had expected it to be. Instead, there was a souped-up yellow Chevy Malibu with black racing stripes, and the motor was running loudly. Although it was difficult to see in the dark, I could tell there was a guy in the driver's seat and a wild-haired woman in the front seat next to him.

My heart sank. Ryan had not told me that we would be riding with anyone else, and I instinctively felt that these people were trouble. But what was I to do? Turn tail and run back into the house to my parents? Reject his friends without even meeting them first? Embarrass him by showcasing my pubescent fears, right there in the driveway? Surely not unless I wanted to kiss Ryan goodbye forever. I crossed my fingers and prayed that I had misjudged the situation. Perhaps I harbored an unfair prejudice toward Chevy Malibu owners without ever having realized it. I was being silly. What could go wrong? After all, we were only going to Jesse's house, and if this mystery driver had plans to secretly drink at the party, I could easily get a ride home with someone else.

Ryan looked at me uncomfortably. "Listen, Darla, I'm really sorry I didn't tell you we were going with another couple. I only found out myself a few hours ago."

"Who are they?" I asked skeptically.

"Greg Cheyney and his girlfriend, Corky. He's the guitar player I told you about. He's played with our band a couple of times. Believe me, Darla, he's not my favorite person in the world, but he knows everyone in town and may be able to get us a gig at Pier 23. I sorta have to stay on his good side for the band's sake, even though I'm not really sure he has one."

That's reassuring, I thought.

"I sort of mentioned him to you at the Halloween party. Remember that girl Lisa I was talking to, who was dressed up like a bag of groceries?" (How could I forget?) "Well, she introduced us. Anyway, when he stopped by my house earlier to bring me some music, he happened to ask what I was doing tonight. I told him we were going to Jesse's party and, unfortunately, the guy just sorta invited himself along. I didn't really know how to say no—guess I'm a wimp, huh? I feel kinda weird about bringing these people to Jesse's house. But most of all, I'm really sorry to do this to you."

"Oh, I understand," I lied. By the time we got to the car, I had developed a seething dislike for these people, especially since Ryan's trampy ex-girlfriend had introduced them. And, of course, Ryan had never admitted to me that Lisa was his ex-girlfriend, which made me all the more furious.

"This is Darla," Ryan told them as we hopped into the cramped backseat area. "Darla, this is Greg and Corky."

"Hey, Happy New Year, baby!" Greg said as he took a macho drag from a cigarette and passed it to Corky. "Ready to party hearty?"

"Nice to meet you," I said, refusing to answer his question.

"Hi, there!" Corky said, blowing smoke in my face as she turned around to greet me.

They both appeared to be in their early twenties. He looked like an Elvis impersonator with a skin condition, and she looked like Morticia Addams with a perm. She had some kind of gold paint sprayed in her wild black hair, and her red nails were so long that they curved ghoulishly at the end. I could barely see her overly made-up face through the cloud of smoke in the car, and although I didn't drink beer, I had no trouble detecting the strong odor of it on both of them.

"Step on it, baby!" Corky said to Greg, as he backed hastily out of the driveway. "I'm ready to have some fun! To the party, James!"

She turned up the radio and moved her body to the rhythm of the hard rock music that blared through Greg's elaborate sound system. I was already feeling claustrophobic and was on the verge of tears. The car raced down the quiet street, and as Greg abruptly spun the wheel to make a right-hand turn, he narrowly missed hitting my neighbor's Ford station wagon as it was turning up the street.

"Whoa! Move over, asshole! You don't own the freakin' road! I do! Heh! Heh!" Greg turned around to Ryan and me. "That asshole's probably rushing home to watch the ball drop. Is that shit lame, or what?"

Ryan managed to laugh politely, but I could tell he was as uncomfortable as I was. I looked at Ryan nervously. By this time, I no longer felt obligated to pretend that I was okay with the situation.

"I'm really sorry, Darla," he told me over the music.

Corky, at this point, had turned up the music even louder and was now singing at the top of her lungs to some abhorrent song. "Baby, baby, you're in my danger zone, stroke it, touch it good, babe, just like it was your own—oh yeah, feels so good, babe, please, now do it again. I'll just close my eyes, babe, touch it on the count of ten. Whoa, feels good, babe…"

By now, Greg had turned off in the opposite direction of Jesse's house, weaving and winding his way at warp speed through several neighborhoods. About fifteen minutes later, he revved up the motor as he sped dangerously onto a two-lane limited-access highway.

I turned to Ryan. "I don't like this at all. Where is he going?"

"I don't know. I'll ask him." He leaned forward to speak to Greg. "Hey, man, the party's in the other direction. Darla and I are really anxious to get there. Where are you going?"

"Don't sweat it, Mullavey! We'll get there. Gotta make a pit stop first. Gotta get some more brewskis! Down to my last one."

Greg reached between his legs and pulled out an open bottle of beer. He took a huge swig and handed the bottle to Corky. She took an equally large swig and handed it back. Greg then finished off the bottle and threw it under the seat. I could easily tell by the rattling sound it made that there were already several empty bottles there.

"Yeah, brewskis!" Corky repeated, her body still moving to the music. "Gotta get some more brewskis! Whoa, feels good, babe—touch it in a special way!"

Ryan looked upset enough for the two of us. Not only was he nervous about Greg's driving, I knew he didn't know how to tell him that "brewskis" weren't allowed at Jesse's house, and most likely, that creeps like Greg and Corky weren't either.

Ryan wiped his brow and muttered "shit" to himself. I could tell he was in a tough position, not wanting Greg to think he was a kid, but at the same time, not willing to let the situation get any further out of control. "Listen, man, I don't think beer is allowed at the place where we're going."

"Excuse me!" Corky said loudly through the din of the music. "I thought I heard you say that brewskis weren't allowed. I know I didn't hear you say THAT!"

"That's what I said," Ryan repeated nervously. "This guy Jesse's only eighteen and this party is at his parent's house."

"Oh shit!" Greg said. "Man, why didn't you tell me this was a goddamn party for teenyboppers? We gonna play 'ring-around-the-fuckin'-rosy' or what?"

Ryan shrugged his shoulders and didn't respond. "I should've said something to him earlier," he said softly to me. "I'm such a jerk."

"Shit! I ain't spendin' my New Year's Eve at no kindy garden party, pinnin' tails on some donkey's ass. Hell, Corky and me got some serious partyin' planned. Grownup shit, if you know what I mean."

I felt greatly relieved that Ryan had successfully dissuaded Greg from wanting to join the party, but by now we were over thirty minutes away from Jesse's house and I didn't know how we were going to get away from these people, much less to the party.

"So whatta we do now?" Corky asked Greg.

"Don't sweat it, baby. We'll go to Eddie's. There's always something happening there."

"Would you mind dropping us off first?" Ryan asked reluctantly.

Corky turned around and looked at Ryan as if he were crazy.

"What!" Greg shouted. "I look like a frickin' taxi cab to you?"

Your car is yellow, I thought to myself in all the absurdity.

"Man, I'm not drivin' all that way just to 'drop you off.' Fuck that! You can come with us."

By this time, I was afraid that I would pass out. Ryan and I had been riding for over a half hour in this speeding car, in an uncomfortable, smoky claustrophobic backseat space, and neither of us could even stretch our legs, not to mention breathe properly. I started to think about my father, and didn't even want to imagine how he'd feel if he knew where I was. Suddenly, his corny talk about "shindigs" and such seemed actually welcoming. Greg was drunk and I was frightened.

He continued to speed down the highway, narrowly missing the median rail a few times, until finally, he pulled the car into the parking lot of a beer distributor and got out. Ryan and I briefly discussed "jumping ship" at that point, but we were concerned about the dangers of being stranded on a dark highway, in the middle of nowhere. I was so frightened that I even thought about calling Mom and Dad and throwing myself to the parental wolves, but I feared it simply wouldn't be worth the price I'd then have to pay. I looked despairingly at Ryan for answers.

He grabbed my hand and held on to it tightly. Somehow, in the middle of all the chaos, I felt momentarily at peace. "I'll work it out," Ryan whispered reassuringly to me as he squeezed my hand. "I'm so sorry, Darla. You have no idea."

It seemed like forever until Greg came back to the car with the beer. He took a few bottles and threw them under his seat, then put the remainder of the carton in the trunk. Corky was still smoking and singing, and had completely ignored us the entire time he was gone, a small fact I was very grateful for.

"Listen, man," Ryan said to Greg as he climbed back into the car, "how much did you pay for that beer?"

"Twenty-something bucks," Greg told him. "What's it to you, dry guy?"

"Why don't I give you the money to pay for the beer, if you'll just drop us off at my place so I can pick up my own car."

"Shit, I don't know—" Greg moaned, as he popped the cap on a fresh bottle of beer.

"C'mon! That's worth it! Give us a break, please."

"Yeah, all right," Greg agreed. "You do play a mean set of drums."

I didn't know what Ryan's musical talent had to do with any of it, but I wasn't going to question Greg's logic. It had been well over an hour since we left my house, and I knew it would be at least eleven o'clock at best if and when we got to Jesse's party. I hoped that Melanie was too busy having fun to notice my absence, but somehow, I doubted that.

The wheels of Greg's Malibu screeched loudly as he sped out of the parking lot. Unfortunately, we had to go two miles in the wrong direction before Greg could change direction at the light. Once we were headed in the right direction, I could feel the car picking up even more speed. Ryan and I exchanged looks, but there was little either of us could do. Greg must've heard the sirens before I did, because I saw him look in the rearview mirror and spew out a rash of expletives before I even had a clue that the police were chasing us.

"You better pull over," Ryan told him, leaning forward to be heard. "They're practically right behind you."

"Not for long they're not!" Greg vowed, and stepped on the gas pedal.

"Please stop!" I screamed, uttering my first words to him since "Nice to meet you" way back in the driveway. "Please!"

I was sure we'd all be killed. Bursting into tears, I put my head on Ryan's chest. I just couldn't bear to look. I couldn't believe my life was going to end like this. I would never see my family again, and I would never learn the mystery of Aunt Rebecca. How ironic that would be! Everyone would think I had turned out just like her too. Poor, tragic Darla. Hanging out with shady characters, drinking alcohol, talking back to her parents, and now dead, at the hands of a drunk driver, a mere three and a half months before her sixteenth birthday. Pitiful. Serves her right. I hoped they would bury me with my Pierre, and I prayed that the Lughead and the Hoovers wouldn't attend my funeral.

"Maybe you'd better pull over, Greg," I heard Corky say nervously. "Really, I think you should." That frightened me even more. If she was scared, we were doomed for sure.

"No way, baby! I'm losin' these pigs!" Greg roared. "Hold on to your hats! It's pedal-to-the-metal time. I'm floorin' this ride!"

My head was still buried in Ryan's jacket when the car crashed into the median rail. There was a moment of deadly silence afterwards. Trembling, I lifted my head slowly to see what had happened. A multitude of sirens had now surrounded us, and Ryan's warm hand had gone limp in mine.

"Oh God, help me!" I prayed, fearing the worst. "Please let Ryan be all right."

I slowly moved my head to look at Ryan. I couldn't see his face, which was turned away from me, but I could see that he wasn't moving.

"Ryan?" I cried. "Can you hear me?"

He didn't answer. I sat there. Frozen. Sick. Terrified.

"Are you okay, Darla?" Ryan's dazed voice finally said softly.

I looked up. Ryan's forehead was cut and was bleeding profusely, but he appeared to be okay. There was no movement or sound in the front seat at all. The next thing I saw was a brilliant flash of light in my eyes, and then I heard the excited voices of several people outside the car window.

"Are you all right in there?" an officer asked, as he opened the back door for us, shining the way with his flashlight. "Can you make it out of the car?"

"Yeah, I think," Ryan said, as he tried to get out of the car. He was very weak and had trouble just stretching out his legs, which had been cramped in the small space for such a long time. Finally, he just barely managed to stand up.

"You need an ambulance, son," the officer told him, grabbing him by the elbow to hold him steady. "Come over here and sit down."

The officer helped Ryan into the police car, while another one helped me. "Are you all right, young lady? Can you get out of the car?"

I had an easier time of it than Ryan, but my legs were wobbly and sore and my neck hurt. As the officer helped me out of the car, I couldn't help but look in the front seat, although my good sense told me it was a bad idea.

Greg and Corky were both unconscious. The windshield had shattered into a million pieces, and I shrank in horror as I saw how still and bloodied they both were. I didn't want to know any more. I heard the officer ask Ryan if we'd been drinking, and I heard Ryan try to explain what had happened.

Within moments, a female officer came over to talk to me, but in the confusion, I could not concentrate on or understand what she was saying to me. The last thing I remember was seeing the ambulance pull up and the team of medics jump out. My next memory after that was of the police officer bringing me home to my frantic parents.

* * *

I stood behind the young (and very serious) police officer as he knocked on our door at exactly midnight. It took Mom and Dad only seconds to answer. Their faces were pale and panic stricken, and I could see they'd been sick with worry.

In my dazed perception, everything, even my own home, seemed strange and surrealistic. The loud celebratory noises in our usually quiet neighborhood (horns, noisemakers, and cheers) directly contrasted with the somber faces of my parents.

Not having seen myself in a full-length mirror since leaving the house earlier, I had no idea how the events of the past several hours had drastically altered my festive appearance. My hair looked as if it had been styled in a windstorm, not by Aunt Didi, and my face looked like a palette of black, blue, and purple smudges. My eyes, from the tears and smoke, were red and scratchy, and there was blood on my coat from Ryan's injuries. My stockings were torn to shreds, and my shoes were covered with mud from standing on the side of the highway. Other than that, I suppose, I looked just fine.

"Darla!" Mom screamed, seconds after Dad had opened the door. "Are you all right? We've been so worried!"

"Thank God you're alive!" Dad sighed in relief.

I ran past the officer and into my mother's arms. Dad turned to look at me, to see for himself that I was in one piece, then invited the officer into the house.

"I'm Officer Martinelli. I can see by the worried looks on your faces that you were already aware there was a problem."

"Well, yes!" Dad said aggressively. "We've known there was a problem for quite a while. My daughter's best friend, Melanie Davenport, called us hours ago to say that Darla never arrived at the party she was going to, which was fifteen minutes from here, at best. Naturally, we've been frantically calling every place we could think of since that time, with no luck. The Mullavey boy's parents are frantic too. What the hell happened here?"

"Your daughter was involved in a car accident, Mr. McKendrick. Out on Route 44 by Jaegerstown."

"What! That's nowhere near here!" He turned to look at me. "Darla, what in the world were you two doing out there?"

"Was it a bad accident?" Mom asked.

"I'm afraid so, ma'am," Officer Martinelli explained. "The driver crashed head on into the median strip. He was highly intoxicated and was not wearing his seat belt. He was killed on impact."

My knees went weak and I collapsed onto the couch. I couldn't believe that Greg was actually dead. As much as I disliked him, I could not fathom the fact that he was really gone, and that he had almost taken Ryan and me with him in his suicidal attempt to elude the police.

"The Mullavey boy is dead?" Dad screamed, shocked. "Poor Pete and Bonnie; what'll they do! Oh, Jesus, I can't believe this!" Dad began furiously pacing, oblivious to the three of us and lost in his own disordered world. I had never seen him comport himself like this before, especially in front of strangers. "Bloody hell!" he screamed. "Why was he drinking? Why did he let that goddamn booze take his young life!" He looked at me, bewildered, as if he were wondering why I was not more shaken by Ryan's death, then continued his frenetic march around the room.

"Goodness, no!" Mom cried, putting her hand to her mouth in horror. "No, it can't be!"

"It isn't," I said, uttering my first words since coming home. "Ryan isn't dead."

Dad stopped moving. His chest was heaving and he stood there, gaping at me. I had always wanted to see real Ted McKendrick in action, but this was not who I had envisioned.

"The Mullavey boy is fine, Mr. and Mrs. McKendrick. He and your daughter were in the backseat. We have no reason to believe they were drinking. The driver, Gregory Francis Cheyney, was drinking heavily, as was his girlfriend, Cordelia Elizabeth Powell. The Mullavey boy had some cuts on his forehead and is being treated for a possible concussion, but he'll be fine, I'm sure."

"Oh, thank goodness Ryan is alive! Mom said, putting her right hand to her chest. "How is the girl?"

"She's in critical condition. Almost a goner too, ma'am," Officer Martinelli stated matter-of-factly, as if some time machine had placed him square in the middle of a "Dragnet" rerun.

Dad fell woozily into his recliner. "I don't believe what I'm hearing." He looked at me. "Darla, you could've been killed! Who the hell are these people, and why were you and Ryan with them?"

"How did this happen?" Mom asked the officer, not giving me a chance to respond to Dad's question.

"Well, ma'am, the Cheyney boy was speeding along Route 44 at about eighty-five miles an hour—"

"Jesus! Eighty five!" Dad said. Sweat was trickling down his face.

"—and when Officer Pankowsky put on his siren for the boy to pull over, he stepped on the gas and tried to disappear into the darkness. From what we know now, the young man had several previous DUIs and was driving on a suspended license. Next stop for him would've been imprisonment. We believe that he chose to risk his life, and the lives of his passengers, to avoid being arrested again. Unfortunately, that risk resulted in the loss of his life."

At that moment, the phone rang. Dad rose from his chair and continued talking to Officer Martinelli while Mom ran to answer it. "Hello, Melanie. Yes, Darla is home now. Well, dear, she and Ryan were involved in a car accident, but they're both okay. Yes—Okay, dear. Of course. I'll tell her. Good night now." She hung up the receiver.

"That was Melanie," Mom told me, stating the obvious. "She's been as frantic as we were. You can call her back in a bit, but just for a few minutes. She'll be waiting for your call."

"Did she say anything else?"

"No. Nothing but 'Oh my God.' "

"I'll be leaving now," Officer Martinelli said officiously, looking at my parents. "But a word of caution to you both. You may think your daughter is all grown up and doesn't need a lot of chaperoning, but as parents, it's your responsibility to make sure you know where she's going at all times, and with whom."

"Jesus!" Dad barked at him. "Do you think my wife and I just let her run wild? Hell, no!" I could see that my father's right leg was shaking violently." We never let Darla go anywhere without first knowing all the details, and then, and only then, do we grant her permission to do so. We're extremely careful when it comes to our daughter. We do always know where she's going, and we certainly do know with whom!" (I found this "we" talk interesting, since Dad was usually the sole granter of permission, but was now talking as if he and Mom made all their decisions jointly.)

"With all due respect, Mr. McKendrick," Officer Martinelli said, noticing that my father was on the verge of collapse, "on tonight of all nights, when parents should be especially careful about drinking and driving, your daughter got into the car of a drunk driver, one she had never even met before, right here in your own driveway. Quite frankly, you weren't nearly as careful as you should've been. I can see that you're both loving and responsible parents, but you need to be far more cognizant of what's going on in your daughter's life, and worry far less about your own New Year's Eve plans."

"My wife and I didn't have any damn New Year's Eve plans!" Dad snapped defensively, kicking the base of his recliner. "Do you think that we made our decision to let her go out tonight without carefully considering all the facts?"

"Again, sir, will all due respect, obviously you didn't consider them carefully enough. Well, good night now. We'll be in touch."

I hated this man. As if the accident itself weren't bad enough, he was going to undo all the progress I'd ever made with Dad. Most likely, when this ordeal was all over with, Dad would regress me back to the age of six, when I still needed his permission to cross the street. But that was not my prime concern at the moment. It was Dad. I watched him as he sank helplessly back into his chair, desperately trying to regain control of himself. In addition to his breakdown over the news, this man, who had prided himself on being the epitome of a responsible parent, had to endure a smug young police officer lecturing him on how he had failed as a parent. Dad, who often believed his parental skills to be beyond reproach, was now in the position of having to defend himself. It was all so ironic. My father was the last man on earth who needed to have the evils of alcohol explained to him. And for the officer to remark that he should worry more about me, and less about his own New Year's Eve plans, well, that was the icing on Dad's cake.

With all that had happened in the last three months, a part of me wanted Dad to know what it felt like to be blamed for something you really didn't do, and to understand the frustration involved in having your defense fall on deaf ears. But more than that, I just felt sorry for him, and above anything else, I was deathly afraid of what would happen once the officer left and Mom shut the front door behind him.

I had never seen him so upset, or quite so pensive. He sat there in silence for a long time, while Mom and I nervously waited for him to speak. Finally, convinced he could manage a conversation, he asked me to recount the evening's events, which I did for him in methodical, chronological order. Dad remained amazingly quiet while I spoke, not interrupting me once, as I had anticipated he would, though I could see he was still trembling. When I finished, he offered no comment or criticism. He merely instructed me to go upstairs to bed and get a good night's sleep.

I got up, walked over to my mother, and gave her a kiss. She reminded me that if I wanted to call Melanie back, I was only to talk for a few minutes. I agreed and looked over at my father. I didn't know if he wanted a good night kiss or not. Almost getting myself killed was probably the final straw for him and most likely he would not want any show of affection from me. I decided not to kiss him good night, and was absolutely amazed when I found myself doing so anyway.

Too exhausted to assume my regular eavesdropping post at the top of the stairs, I headed for my bedroom without a second thought. But when I heard my parents talking, I felt compelled to stop and listen to what they were saying.

"Ted, please say something. Your silence is unbearable."

There was a long pause before Dad began speaking.

"I've made a real damn mess of things, haven't I?"

"Goodness, no! This is not your fault."

"Oh, stop it, Maggie," Dad said, his voice worn. "Aren't you tired of trying to constantly shield me from my own failings? Doesn't it exhaust you? It does me."

"Ted—"

"All these years of my life, trying to be a model citizen and father. Just hoping that if I followed the rules, the past wouldn't come back and smack me over the head with a vengeance. Was I ever wrong…"

His voice trailed off. For a few moments, there was silence. I worried that they might be lowering their voices on purpose so I moved two steps down. Luckily, the action resumed at full volume.

"Oh, Ted," Mom said, "stop being a martyr; stop blaming yourself for everything that went wrong tonight. Aren't I a parent too? Aren't I allowed to share in the blame? Or are you selfishly going to hog all the guilt for yourself?"

"You didn't feel that way after Darla returned from the Halloween party, smelling like a distillery. You heaped plenty of guilt on me that night."

"That was entirely different," Mom said. "Please, Ted, let's talk rationally about this."

"Maggie, there are just some things a talk can't fix," Dad said angrily. "You're not my psychiatrist and you're not my mother, nor are you some fairy godmother with a magic wand. So give it up. Can't you even see who's standing in front of you? A damn coward, that's who. I've overcompensated to the point of insanity. I'm not the man you fell in love with; I'm some idiot who's been playing house with you all of these years. The man you fell in love with had character, gumption, a sense of adventure. No matter how flawed that son of a bitch was, he knew how to live. I don't even recognize the clown you're married to now, the guy who hides behind his red nose and floppy shoes because he's so goddamn afraid. Been afraid for years. Still afraid. And you know what? It's all been for naught, because no matter how good a father I have tried to be for Darla, I can't control the demons out there. Ultimately, life could still come crashing down around us at any time...thanks to me."

"Maybe it's time we faced those demons," Mom told him. "They might not be nearly as bad as we think. At least we'd know—"

"You know how I feel about that, Maggie," Dad cautioned her. "It's not worth the risk. Our lives don't need any more complications. Why invite trouble? It has a way of finding us all on its lonesome. Aren't things bad enough now? Jesus! Our little girl was almost killed tonight. With just a different twist of fate, it might've been Darla lying dead in that car tonight."

"Oh, honey, you're torturing yourself," Mom said, exasperated. "This is so unnecessary."

It sounded to me as if Dad wasn't even listening to her. He continued rambling on. "Am I too strict or not strict enough? I don't know anymore. Should I have stood in the doorway tonight and checked to make sure Darla and Ryan got into the right car? According to the young officer, who says I wasn't careful enough, perhaps I should've followed them in my own car to make sure they arrived at the party. Then maybe, I should I have waited outside and followed them home again. Anything short of that makes me a lousy parent, huh? I guess I don't have all the answers, but that rookie cop doesn't have them either. Who knows, Maggs—for someone who hasn't experienced much of life lately, I pretend to know quite a bit, don't I? Really, I'm just a suburban bore who comes home every night to his evening paper and a home-cooked meal."

"And just what does that make me?" Mom asked angrily. "Your boring suburban wife? Are you trying to tell me something? Am I not the woman you want to share your life with?"

"Damn it, Maggie, of course you are! It's me I'm talking about here. Maybe I'm not exactly what you had in mind! Maybe I've damn well failed you and Darla both! Maybe instead of coming home to your fancy meals, I should be taking you out to dinner more. Dancing the night away. Popping the cork on an occasional bottle of champagne. Living my damn life instead of being so afraid of it."

"I don't need to go dancing and—Where are you going, Ted?"

"I'm going out! It's New Year's Eve, isn't it? Isn't that what people do on New Year's Eve? Go out?"

"Ted—"

"That's my name, Maggie. Don't wear it out!"

"How childish...Ted, don't be absurd. Please come back!"

"Don't order me around!" Dad screamed. "I've had enough order to last me a lifetime!"

"Ted, please—"

To my shock, I heard the front door open and slam shut, and my mother crying hysterically, as she repeatedly called for my father to come back. I desperately wanted to comfort her but decided against it. I knew she would just clam up and go limp with fear at having to explain the meaning of their mysterious conversation. Besides, I was scared to death myself about what was happening to Dad. In the brief conversation I had just overheard, a side of him had emerged that I had never known before. I thought I had him all figured out— just a corny, self-controlled, kindhearted disciplinarian who used words like "shindig" and "whippersnapper." But now he was a sad, frightened, angry man who had run off into the night to do God-knows-what. I was exhausted from my own ordeal and sick with fear worrying about him. How quickly the tables had turned!

Between the lines of my parents' mysterious conversation were my own flashbacks of Greg and Corky, lying still in their seats, covered with blood while the glass fragments sparkled and danced in the glow of the officers' flashlights. I had never seen a dead person before. By now, maybe Corky was dead. I wondered what she was like when she was sober. Was she cheap and vulgar then too? I felt guilty for hating these people, yet I could not help despising them for what they had done and who they were.

I wondered if this ordeal would strengthen or end my relationship with Ryan. We had almost been killed together a couple of hours ago, and our mutual lack of poor judgment was having a devastating effect on my family and, most likely, on his. My life was falling apart and I didn't know who was to blame or how it had happened. I didn't care. I didn't even have the strength to call Melanie back. I just wanted to go to bed.

For someone with such an enormous propensity to dream of the grotesque, I should have realized that the evening's events were bound to bring on the most phenomenal of nightmares. To this day, I remain in awe of the brain's miraculous ability to extricate the most disturbing of thoughts, costume them properly in aberrant attire, and give them starring roles in dreams too deviant to comprehend. I have often wondered why an opposite phenomenon does not occur more often, one where the mind compensates for a person's daily woes and worries by offering up dreams filled with waterfalls and waterlilies, lush tropical gardens, sweet country roads, enchanted castles, and fragrant fields of flowers. For some people, this may be the case. I, unfortunately, have rarely been so lucky, a fact evidenced by the grisly dream that still haunts me from that terrible night.

The first thing I remember was Ryan, his head soaked in blood, lying along the side of a dark road in a heap of shattered glass. Sticking straight out of his forehead was a broken beer bottle, and an army of assorted, larger-than-life vermin was marching up his leg carrying picnic baskets, hurrying toward his head, where they planned to feast royally on his recently spilled blood. A female police officer was standing over him, holding Pierre and gleefully singing, "Today's the day the vermin have their pic-nic!"

"No!" I screamed. "He's alive! Leave him alone! And give me my bear, you dumb blue bitch, and take that beer bottle out of his forehead."

"Say please, Darla," the officer scolded me patronizingly, "or I'm not budging. And in case you don't know it, 'bitch' is a very bad word. I'm going to ask you to apologize for saying it."

"I don't want to apologize."

The officer now had Mom's face. "A simple painless little apology note will do. Is that too much to ask? Now, here's your bear, dear."

She handed Pierre to me and bent down to remove the bottle. The dead body was now Corky's. Just as the Mom officer touched the jagged edge of the bottle, Corky opened one eye, winked, and sang, "Whoa, feels good, baby, touch it in a special way."

"I think she's talkin' to me!" Greg laughed cavalierly, now standing beside the Mom officer. "Get lost, will ya? You don't own this freakin' road. I do. Heh! Heh!"

The Mom officer screamed and ran away, while Greg's face slowly began to disintegrate and a vile black substance began to bubble where there once was flesh.

"Gotta have a brewski!" he said, and reached down to Corky's forehead, where he grabbed a now full bottle of beer and began to drink it. Only the beer he drank was now thick, dark red blood, and Greg himself was now a faceless creature with oozing black slime pouring rapidly from every orifice of his body.

The next thing I knew, Greg, still wearing his leather jacket, had gotten his old face back, though it was now devoid of expression. He was sitting motionless in a wheelchair, holding an empty beer bottle in his hand, and staring blankly at the empty beer bottles on the floor that encircled the chair. He had only one leg—and had a beautiful afghan of many colors draped over his lap.

"He's brain dead," said an orderly from the nursing home. "I'll take him away."

"He was brain dead when I met him," I said sarcastically.

"That's nasty!" admonished Uncle Everett, who had appeared out of nowhere. "He was just trying to be a mentor to you. You're too young and stupid to know the ways of the world. Your father is a suburban bore who never took the time to provide you with real intellectual stimulation. You'll never be like my Nadine."

"I wouldn't want to be like her! I hate her."

"She's much more the lady than you'll ever be," Aunt Louisa said, also appearing out of nowhere. "Where are your manners, young lady? Aren't you going to plant one here?"

The scene instantly shifted to a beautiful park, which had been meticulously prepared for a wedding to take place. Unfortunately, when my brain shifted dream locales, it forgot to leave Aunt Louisa behind. She was still standing in front of me, tapping her cheek, and demanding her kiss.

"Plant one here, Darla! I'm waiting!"

"Well, you'd better find a magazine to read," I told her, "because it's going to be a really long wait."

"Really!" Aunt Louisa scowled in disgust. "It's no wonder that my lovely Nadine is going to be the June bride and not you!"

To my delight, my cousin June appeared in a gorgeous wedding gown and smiled at Aunt Louisa. "I'm going to be the June bride. Your daughter's a ditz!"

"Who in blazes are you?" Uncle Everett said, glowering at her with intense disdain.

"She's my cousin June. Isn't she beautiful? A June bride named June Montgomery. Won't that be lovely? What a lovely name too! Much lovelier than Nadine Montgomery. Yuk and double yuk to that one!"

Nadine, who had been vacuuming the finely manicured lawn with a giant Hoover, turned off the machine and came marching angrily toward June. "Give me my gown! I want my gown!"

"Give her the gown!" Uncle Everett chimed in. "Give it to her now!"

"Give me my gown, you little brats! I want my gown! Give me my gown! You're so handsome, Daddy. I love you so much. Daddy, make these brats give me my gown!"

"Give her the goddamn gown!" Everett shrieked at me. "Or I'll yank it off that cousin of yours! And when you've done doing that, I demand an apology!"

"But before you apologize to Everett, first, you'll have to write 'I'm sorry, Nadine' on the blackboard, one hundred times," Aunt Louisa said

153

authoritatively. "And legibly too. You won't leave my classroom unless it's legible."

"I hate you all!" I screamed. "I wish you were all dead!"

And with that, the locale shifted back to the dark and dreary roadside where Greg and Corky lay dead, holding hands. Next to them, covered in black slime and blood, were the Hoovers.

"It's all so sad," said Dad, who stood there next to me looking at the bodies. "I loved my sister very much. I wish you'd apologized to her, Darla. It's too late now. Now it's time for the funeral."

The next thing I knew, I was standing with my family in a very pristine funeral home. As I looked across the room, I saw a woman wearing sunglasses and a scarf over her head. She was waving at me as if she didn't want the others to see her.

Oh God, I thought. It's Aunt Rebecca! She's come back for the funeral.

I desperately wanted to tell my cousins, but they were way across the room with Aunt Didi and Uncle George.

My father turned to me. "It's time to say goodbye now, Darla. Don't dawdle."

Slowly, we walked toward the three open caskets. First, there was Everett's casket. Although his eyes were closed, he still wore his thick black frame glasses, and his pipe stuck prominently out of his tweed jacket pocket. I looked at him for a moment and moved to the next casket, where Nadine lay. She wore a beautiful white wedding gown, and a soft, delicate veil covered her face. A very handsome blond man, whom I presumed to be Ethan, stood weeping in the background. He looked up at me as I passed, with great anger in his eyes, as if I had personally caused her death.

Finally, I reached Aunt Louisa's casket. She looked very prim and proper in her flowered print dress with the lace collar. I looked at her for a very long time, wondering why Dad loved her so much, perhaps even more than he loved me. I felt happy that she was dead, but at the same time, I felt excruciatingly guilty for even entertaining such a thought. I knew it was wrong. I closed my eyes and prayed to God to forgive me.

When I opened my eyes, I took one long, final look at Aunt Louisa. Just as I was about to step away from the casket, she slowly opened her eyes, which were clouded by a muddy brown film, and in a hollow, barely audible voice, she whispered, "Plant one here, Darla," as a skeletal hand rose up from her side and tapped her ghostly white cheek.

It was in that harrowing moment that I woke up screaming. I looked at my digital clock radio and saw that it was 3:07 a.m. Within seconds, my father came racing into my bedroom. When he opened the door, I could tell from the light cast by the hallway lamp that he was still fully dressed.

He sat down on the bed and held me tightly in his arms. It had always been Mom who came running in the middle of the night. Having my father next to me felt strange, yet good.

"Are you all right, sweetie?" he asked gently.

"Uh, I think—" I said, still dazed.

"Did you have a bad dream?"

"No. I had a horrible one."

"Well, it's no wonder," he said, stroking my hair. "With the evening you've had, I would almost have expected it."

"How come you're still dressed?" I asked him softly, wondering if I might still be dreaming.

I could not see his face very well in the dark, especially since he was still holding me close, but I heard him sigh in frustration.

"I went out, Darla. I got home quite a while ago, but I was too upset to come upstairs to bed. So I stayed downstairs a bit and then I fell asleep on the couch."

"Oh," I said, trying to clear my brain and understand what he was saying.

"I haven't been able to get over almost losing you tonight. Just thinking about it has been unbearable."

"I'm sorry. It's all my fault."

"This isn't the time to talk about it. It's time for us both to get some sleep."

Something about him felt very different. I couldn't figure it out.

His Dadlike words were the same, and I wondered if it might be the tone of his voice, or perhaps the fact that he had gone out so very late at night and was still dressed in his day clothing.

"I'll see you in the morning," he whispered, getting up from the bed. "Nothing but sweet dreams from now on. And that's an order."

"Good night, Dad," I mumbled back to him.

As he shut the door and walked down the hall to his own room, I finally realized what was wrong. Dad, who had held me close for several minutes, had left the lingering scent of alcohol behind him on my nightshirt. It was a grotesque souvenir of a horrible night.

Although I could now clearly smell it, my brain could not fathom that my father, Ted McKendrick, had actually been drinking. Surely, I surmised, his visit must've been part of my nightmare. It seems that my brain was not happy simply torturing me with visual and auditory horrors; now it had decided to throw olfactory horrors into the mix as well.

I grabbed Pierre, who, thankfully, still smelled like a teddy bear, and instantly fell back to sleep.

CHAPTER 10

At eleven-thirty the next morning, I finally woke up from the all-night horror show that had been playing in my subconscious. I stared at the ceiling for several minutes, trying to remember, and to focus on all that had happened the night before. I sat up slowly in bed. My neck hurt badly and my entire body felt sore. I tried wiping the sleep from my eyes, but my eyelids felt as if they'd been glued shut with Krazy Glue.

Oh God, I thought, as I grabbed a fistful of nightshirt and introduced it to my nose. It's true. Dad was really drinking. But even with solid proof in the light of day, I still couldn't believe that my father had succumbed to the "evils of alcohol" he so despised.

About a half hour later, after a long hot bath to soothe my aching body, I made my way down the back stairs to the kitchen. I had four more steps to go, when I stopped short and sat down. I could hear my mother talking on the phone, and she sounded as if she were crying.

"I never wanted our life together to be based on fear. What's the point of that? Ted said it himself. He's overcompensated all these years, but it really hasn't changed anything. I mean, he's been trying to make up for something that really wasn't his fault, for almost seventeen years—and we've lost so much in the process. We've changed so much in the process. He said he doesn't even recognize himself anymore. And even though I hate the fact that he feels that way, I'm so afraid of what will happen if things were to change...if last night is any indication—oh Didi—I just don't understand how you and George have managed to deal with it so well...I know, but it seems like you do a better job of it than we do."

I was dying to run upstairs and pick up the extension, but I opted for waiting patiently on the stairs while my mother finished listening to whatever Aunt Didi was saying. Since I couldn't hear the other side of the conversation, the wait seemed eternal, but, finally, she began talking again.

"You're right, Didi. But when I look at Darla, and I see how young and inexperienced she is, it's hard to believe that Rebecca was just a year older when all of this happened. Even today, when I think about our sister, I still don't blame a lost teenager, I blame a vengeful adult because it's hard to imagine that a mere child could possibly have done so much damage. I know that's wrong, but Rebecca's actions bore a fear in our hearts that has never left; and for that, I feel such anger and...once, may God forgive me, I actually wished that she was still living in squalor, because she deserved it. Oh, Didi, I'm ashamed of myself for saying that, for even thinking it. I don't mean it. Not one bit. You know that. I'm just so angry. Where do you think she is now? What can her life be like? I wonder if she ever thinks about us."

I couldn't believe my ears. It made sense that my mother would be talking to Aunt Didi about my father, but at the very least, I expected her to be talking about me, and the fact that Ryan and I had almost been killed at the hands of a drunk driver. I expected her to be telling Aunt Didi how grateful she was that I had not expired in a pile of twisted wreckage, and maybe even ramble on about how frantic they both had been prior to my return, or perhaps relay how much the police officer had upset Dad. Something, anything, just to show she cared about me. But instead, she was talking about Rebecca.

I felt angry and jealous. If Rebecca were once again to be at the center of a family crisis, despite the fact that no one had seen her since before I was born (except for that time in the Alexanders' backyard), then I had a right to know what was going on. If I was old enough to almost get myself killed, I was old enough to know the truth. I didn't care how upset my mother was, or what repercussions she was suffering as a result of my catastrophic New Year's Eve date. This was the day I would finally confront her. It was the first day of a brand-new year and the perfect time, I decided, for the revelation of dirty family secrets.

I practically leaped down the four remaining steps and stumbled my way into the kitchen. Mom didn't see me at first, but when she finally turned around, she looked like a child who had been caught with her hand in the cookie jar.

"Darla, oh—"

She quickly ended her phone conversation, told Aunt Didi that she'd see her within the hour, and turned to face me. I vowed right at that moment that this was one conversation Mom wasn't going to tap dance around.

"How long have you been standing there?" she asked. Her usual welcoming smile was gone.

"You mean, 'How much did I hear?' " I challenged her.

She looked horrified. I had never spoken to her that way before.

"All right!" she said with a hint of anger in her voice. "Have it your way. How much did you hear?"

"I heard you talking about her again! Telling Aunt Didi how you blamed her for the past and how you wondered where she was now."

"Since when is it okay to eavesdrop?" she wanted to know. I wanted to respond with "whenever I can get away with it" but I gave her an angry stare instead. She looked exasperated. She wasn't nearly as adept at handling my insubordination as my father was. "Where in the world is this anger coming from?"

"I'll tell you where the anger is coming from!" I said, ignoring her first question. "I keep asking you about Aunt Rebecca and you keep telling me that it's all in the past, and that I shouldn't talk about her. Well, if that's the case, then how come you and Aunt Didi are always talking about her? Really, Mom, it's like you guys keep discussing the same old soap opera, except there hasn't been a new episode in, like, a billion years."

Mom, who was sitting at the kitchen table, started fidgeting with the pepper grinder. "Oh, Darla, don't be silly. Rebecca is our sister. Don't you think we wonder about what ever became of her, not having seen her in all of these years?"

I pulled out a chair and sat down at the table with her. "Well, how come if you're so worried about what happened to me last night, you're talking about her instead?"

Though she probably wasn't aware she was doing it, she took a napkin out of the holder and started nervously making a rose out of it as she spoke. "Darla, can't you understand that after what happened last night, after your father and I sat here for several desperate hours, wondering what in the world had happened to you, that we might've experienced some painful reminders about the past, about the many, many nights when my entire family sat up until the wee hours and worried about Rebecca?"

I didn't know how to answer her, though I was dying for further elaboration on a few things I'd overheard the night before. Mainly, I wanted to know what my father had meant when he said that life could still come crashing down around them, and what she had meant about facing demons. (The only demons I'd known any of us to have faced lately were the detestable Hoovers.) But I decided that I would really be pushing my luck if I made inquiries on not one, but two overheard conversations. I decided it would be prudent to choose only the most recent conversation as the object of my query, and also to answer my mother's question.

"Yeah, I can understand how everybody worried and stuff, but what did you mean about Rebecca doing so much damage, and how you still blame her for things and hope she's still living in—" (I still couldn't say "squalor" without choking on it) "—in poverty?"

Mom sighed and threw the napkin, which was not yet a rose, down on the table. It fell on the floor. She ignored it and snatched another potential rose out of the napkin holder. I could see that her composure was in jeopardy of near demise, but I was unsympathetic. I glared at her, waiting for an answer.

"Darla, you really have no business quizzing me on what you just overheard—accidentally on purpose. But I love you, and if answering your questions will finally put an end to all of this, well then, I suppose it's worth it. I must say, though, your overactive imagination is making a lot more out of this than really exists. No matter how I try, I cannot explain to you the horror of what Rebecca put us through. For years, all of us—Grandpa and Grandma, Aunt Didi and Uncle George, and your father and I—worried every single day of our lives that we'd get a call from God-knows-who saying that Rebecca was dead—from a drug overdose, a car accident, or God-knows-what. If you can even imagine the fear that your father and I felt last night, then think about having that same ordeal repeated over and over again for years. Goodness, it was a living hell!"

She did have a point. I'd never really thought about it that way before. I remembered the paralyzing fear that I had felt riding with Greg, and I couldn't imagine having to go through a similar torture on a regular basis, much less for years.

"Rebecca put such a fear into our hearts that we've never really been able to get rid of it. It was so hard to let go, Darla...you have no idea. But when she moved to New York, claimed to be pregnant, and then threw us all out of that horrendous place she was living in, well, there was little else we could do. We could've forced her to come back here, legally, but she was almost eighteen. Besides, she only would've run away again and that would have destroyed your grandparents. Really, all of this has taken such a tremendous toll on us over the years. Unfortunately, you've had to pay the price at times by having overprotective parents. Your father and I don't mean to compare you to Rebecca. Certainly it's not fair to you. But life isn't always fair. It's just that we can never seem to get her off our minds."

I needed to believe that she was finally talking to me like an adult. I decided to repay the favor.

"Maybe you should talk to a counselor or something," I suggested, wary of her response. "Do you think some sort of...therapy...would help?"

Mom, who had successfully finished her second attempt at flower making, laid the finished rose on the table. She picked up the pepper grinder and started caressing it with her right hand. I could tell she was trying her best to take control of the conversation, the way my father always did, but she was clearly struggling. I felt bad for her, but I felt even worse for myself and was bound and determined to finally get answers.

"I'm not against the idea," she said uncomfortably. "In fact, I've suggested it to your father from time to time. But he's not ready to face past demons, and going through therapy would mean bringing it all back again."

"But you just said it all comes back again anyway. So why would going through therapy be any worse?"

"It would be extremely painful, Darla. Can you trust me on that?"

"Yeah, I guess," I fumbled. My mother's tone made it clear that

161

no other answer was acceptable. But having now learned that Mom's references to "facing demons" meant going through therapy, I felt greedy for even more answers and wondered how I could find out what my father had meant about life crashing down on them. But luckily, I didn't have to ask.

"Darla, I'm sorry that old family history has hurt you so much, that we've allowed it to hurt you so much. I hope you'll understand that we're frightened. This car accident scared us to death. You simply have no idea."

I picked my mother's discarded rose off the table and began examining it. I liked having something else to focus on when I was about to approach a touchy subject. "Is that why Dad went out last night? Because he was scared?"

Mom dropped the pepper grinder on the table and almost jumped out of her skin at the noise it made. She stood it upright and grabbed yet another napkin.

"How did you know that?" she panicked.

"Dad told me! I had a really horrible dream about the accident and things. I woke up screaming and he came in my room. I asked him why he was still wearing his regular clothes, and he said it was because he was upset and had gone out for a while."

"Oh. I see," she said, playing with the pepper grinder again.

"So where did he go?" I asked, pushing Mom to the limit.

"I don't know," she said edgily. "I think to see a friend. Let's not concern ourselves with that right now, shall we? I think we have enough on our plate, don't you?"

"Always room for seconds," I joked. (I just couldn't help myself.)

Her eyes narrowed as if to silence me, then she continued. "Darla, you heard the way that Officer Martinelli spoke to your father. True, the young man was just doing his job, but what he said really upset your father. He made him feel as if he were responsible for what had happened to you. No matter how wonderful a father he has tried to be, the accident reminded him that life is short, and that in a matter of moments, it can all come crashing down on you. Being a good parent isn't always enough when it comes to protecting, or saving, your child. Rebecca taught us that. Some day, you'll be a parent, and then maybe you'll understand. Honey, I just don't know how else to explain it to you. I've tried so many times. You just won't believe me."

Mom seemed positively exhausted. She looked at me despairingly, as if she were pleading with me to end the inquisition, which I was more than ready to do. It was the first time in years I believed that she'd been really honest with me. True, she didn't admit that my father had been drinking, but I couldn't blame her for that. Besides, I didn't ask. It would be too devastating for all of us.

Somehow, the car accident had helped me to gain some insight into my parents and also to learn a little more about life in general. First, I learned that wrong decisions, even made for the right reasons, can have equally as severe consequences. With this in mind, it made sense that my father, who always made his decisions for "the right reasons," would be doubting and blaming himself when those decisions brought on unfavorable consequences, such as the near-death of his daughter. I also learned that intense fear can create powerful lifelong memories, and this knowledge helped me to better understand why the "Rebecca Years" had continued to affect all of our lives. The demons that I'd heard my mother speak of on more than one occasion were simply unhappy memories, which had manifested themselves into the habitual fear that Rebecca's life might repeat itself with me. This understanding didn't provide me with the deep, dark family secret I'd been digging for, but it did make a lot of sense.

My mother had seemed to understand all too well what counseling entailed, and I surmised that she had already been through it once in her life and was trying to get Dad to go through it now. My father, as was made clear by his exchange with Officer Martinelli, did not like anyone, especially strangers, making suggestions about how he should run his life. I understood why therapy was not an option for him.

A million thoughts ran through my mind. For one, I wondered why Rebeccaphobia only materialized in the McKendrick family, or at least to a much greater degree than it did in the Alexander family. Although my aunt and uncle had always been hush-hush about Rebecca, I'd seen very little evidence that they worried about April, May, and June in the same intense way that my parents worried about me. But maybe I was jumping to conclusions. Perhaps Rebeccaphobia explained why Uncle George had always sent the girls to private school. Maybe it also explained why Aunt Didi had filled my cousins' lives with a multitude of activities since the day they were born. What did I know? Maybe Aunt Didi and Uncle George did have the same fears. But they were completely different people than my parents, and, naturally, they would handle their fears in completely different ways.

I felt so grown-up and insightful, as though I'd really turned a corner. I decided to show my mother some mercy.

"Thanks for talking to me, Mom. You've really answered a lot of questions. I feel a lot better."

"Well, good!" Mom said, as a look of genuine relief washed over her face. "I'm so glad. Now, you get some food in your stomach. I'm going to see Aunt Didi." She pushed her chair back from the table and stood up.

"Yeah, okay. Mom?"

"Yes?" she said, warily.

"Where's Dad?"

"He had an errand to run. He'll be back later."

"Okay," I said, getting up from the table as well.

Mom smiled, and looking more like her old self, she kissed me on the forehead and walked as cheerfully as she could out of the room.

I felt as good as I could feel under the circumstances. Although I knew she had not told me everything about Rebecca, I had come to a place where I was finally beginning to understand why my aunt's past actions had such a strong influence on all of our lives. Surely the terrifying memory of the car accident would live forever in my mind, so how could I expect my parents to forget their own painful memories or—dare I use the same words—their demons? My mother was right. I did have an overactive imagination, but I concluded that it was a far better thing than not having one at all.

As my overactive imagination went back to work, thinking about

164

Ryan and worrying about what my father had in store for me, I poured myself a bowl of cereal and returned Melanie's call.

Melanie and I talked for over an hour. I gave her a detailed account of everything that had happened to me and apologized profusely for not returning her call the night before. Aside from being frantic with worry about me, it turned out that she had a disastrous evening of her own to contend with. Unbeknownst to Melanie, Jesse had chosen New Year's Eve as the perfect time to consummate their "deep love" for one another. For starters, he did not appreciate the fact that Melanie spent the entire evening worrying about the fate of her best friend, but he was even less delighted when Melanie explained that she had her own ideas about when and where she would lose her virginity—and to whom.

Many of my friends in school had faced similar dilemmas with their boyfriends, but what shocked me about Jesse was that he had planned for this romantic joining of two souls to take place in the large walk-in closet off his bedroom, and on top of his old sleeping bag from Boy Scout camp. A closed bedroom door, he had told Melanie, would arouse far too much suspicion. His way, they could "do it" in the closet with the door tightly shut, but leave the bedroom door slightly ajar, so no one would be any the wiser. At this point in their conversation, Melanie informed him that suspicion was the only thing he was likely to arouse that night, because it sure as hell wouldn't be her! That, unfortunately, escalated into a heated argument between the two of them, which ultimately led to a parting of the ways.

I felt absolutely terrible for her, although admittedly, a part of me couldn't help but be happy that we might have more time to spend together. And naturally, talking about boyfriends, love, and making love only made me think more about Ryan. I prayed that our relationship would blossom and grow into something really special. Although our New Year's Eve had been disastrous, I believed it had actually enhanced our relationship and brought us closer together. It was hard to let go of the feeling I'd had when Ryan held my hand tightly and reassured me that things would be okay. The warmth and comfort of his voice, of his body, were overpowering to me and, as I told Melanie, made me love him on a much deeper level than I ever had before.

Our conversation, which could've gone on for hours, ended because Melanie was exhausted, from crying and worrying all night and I needed to clear the line so that Ryan could get through.

My timing turned out to be perfect. Ryan called about ten minutes after I hung up with Melanie. He'd just gotten home a few hours earlier from the hospital, where he had to spend the night.

"I'm so sorry you had to stay overnight in the hospital," I said sympathetically.

"Well, better one night in the hospital than eternity in the cemetery, like Greg," Ryan pointed out. "I mean, I guess I'll get there eventually, but I'm sure not ready yet."

"Did you find out anything about Corky?"

"Yeah, she's doing better. She's still in critical condition and all, but this morning the doctors changed their minds and they expect her to live."

"That's good."

"Yeah," he said, sounding relieved. "At least I won't have to go to two funerals."

"You have to go to Greg's funeral?" I asked incredulously.

"Well, yeah, Darla. But worse than that, I have to go talk to his old man later about what happened. Man, I just spoke to him on the phone for a few minutes, and now I know why Greg was so messed up. His old man's a real trip. He's a drunk, I know that for sure, and I think he and Mrs. Cheyney have been divorced since Greg was a baby. Greg had been living with him in this beat-up yellow house on Brewer Street. You know, one of those places with spare tires and rusted lawn mower parts and shit all over the yard. What the hell am I supposed to say to this guy? I'm just really sorry that I got you into this mess, Darla. Will you ever forgive me? I swear, I never had any idea it would turn out like this. I'm so sorry!"

Although Ryan's deep remorse and pleas for forgiveness were music to my ears, I did not want him to grovel by any means, nor did I want him to think that his poor judgment had caused me to lose interest in him.

"Ryan, there's nothing to forgive. I can understand why you were sorta...I mean, why you didn't say no to him."

"Why I was sorta afraid of him? Is that what you were going to say?"

"Well, yeah," I admitted, relieved that he had a sense of humor about it. "You didn't force me into his car, you know. Of course, I wasn't very happy about the whole thing, but just like you, I went along for the ride. No pun intended."

Ryan laughed. "Gotta find some humor in all of this, I guess. But the bottom line is that you got into Greg's car for my sake. You didn't want to let me down. Damn, I feel really guilty."

"Well, don't. I wanted to be with you, so I went. It was my choice, Ryan."

There was a brief pause in our conversation, and I wondered if I'd gone too far by telling Ryan that I "wanted to be with him." To my absolute amazement, he responded in kind.

"I wanted to be with you too, Darla. I feel really good when I'm with you. You never talk about stuff like what kind of car I have, or how much money I can spend on you. And you don't nag me or bug me about when we're gonna get together. You're just really easy to talk to, and really nice. I don't know. You're just different from other girls. But good different... shit, you know what I mean."

I had never heard anything so romantic in my entire life, and as I reveled in my adolescent flights of fancy, I couldn't help but compare Ryan to Jesse. I could tell from Ryan's beautiful words that he would never want to "do it" in the closet on top of a musty old sleeping bag. He was far too romantic for something like that. When the time was right, a few years down the road, we'd probably get a room with a fireplace at a rustic, old country inn. There would be a chilled bottle of champagne awaiting our arrival and a patchwork quilt neatly folded at the end of a large canopy bed.

It was funny: here I had been so envious of Melanie's relationship

167

with Jesse, and as it turned out, Ryan and I would be the ones going on for the long haul. As Dad used to tell me, "Slow and steady wins the race." Maybe I hadn't given him enough credit for the wisdom behind his dumb clichés.

Ryan and I talked for another fifteen minutes, and I was so enthralled by his romantic declarations that I started taking notes so that I could repeat "the good parts" to Melanie, and to my cousins.

"We'll go out real soon, Darla. In my car. I promise. I really want to make this up to you, so start thinking about where you'd like to go."

"Great. I'm looking forward to it."

"No way! What the hell—" Ryan mumbled in a distracted tone.

"Ryan?"

"Yeah?"

"What are you talking about?"

"Shit, I can't believe it!"

"What?"

"Man, this is too much! Damn it!"

"What?"

"I'm lookin' out the window here—"

"Yeah?"

"And I just saw your dad drop off my old man. They must've been out together somewhere, talkin' about us. Damn."

"Are you serious?" I asked, feeling my aching body tense up.

"Do I sound like I'm kidding?"

"No, I guess not."

"Listen, Darla, I gotta run. I need to find out what's going on here. You take care, okay? I'll talk to you soon."

Not only was it a disappointing end to the most romantic conversation of my life, but I felt my anger toward Dad mounting again. I had no idea what he was up to, but I was certain it had something to do with ruining my life.

✳ ✳ ✳

My father arrived home about a half hour after I hung up the phone with Ryan, which enabled me to sustain a full thirty minutes of intense emotional upheaval, running the gamut from absolute rage to unbridled curiosity, in which I explored, analyzed, and criticized every possible reason he may have had for visiting with Mr. Mullavey. I decided that getting together for a serious talk was something that some fathers did naturally when their respective offspring were involved in the same troublesome situation, but if those two fathers happened to be ex-colleagues and old friends, well, then it was a given that such a meeting would take place. In fact, it was probably programmed in their dad genes.

I wondered if my father would even tell me that he'd been out with Ryan's dad, or if that fact, like so many other facts in my family, would be stamped confidential. But even if their meeting were to be kept secret, that certainly wouldn't be the worst-case scenario: far from it. There were far more dire possibilities, none of which I really wanted to explore at length. I decided to calm down, play dumb, and wait for my father to throw the first punch.

I walked into the living room just as he was coming through the front door. From the severe look on his face, I knew my luck was running against me, and I could barely contain my fear long enough to say hello.

Dad methodically hung up his coat in the foyer closet, rubbed his arms to get rid of the January chill, and walked into the living room to join me.

He sat down next to me on the couch. "Hello, Darla. How are you feeling?"

"Kind of achy. My neck hurts," I said, massaging the offending area.

"I left a message on Dr. Stanley's service last night that you need to see him as soon as possible. I want you to be fully checked out, X-rays and all."

"I hate doctors. I don't want to go."

"Darla, I'm not talking about dancing at some cotillion or gabfesting with your cousins. This appointment is not being arranged for your social pleasure. It's being arranged to ensure and promote your good health.

You will go."

I didn't have the foggiest idea what a cotillion was, but I figured it had to be something old-fashioned and corny that I would hate, and I did not consider getting together with my cousins to be "gabfesting," even though I wasn't one hundred percent sure what that meant, either.

"My neck doesn't feel as bad as I thought," I said, showing off my good posture as I sat straight up. "I'll be fine. I don't need a doctor."

"I'll determine what you need right now," Dad said in a fierce, no-nonsense tone. "Do you understand me?"

My father's entire manner was giving me the creeps. No matter what we had ever discussed or argued about in the past, there was always some sense of fair play about him. Even when he disagreed completely with my point of view, he always offered up some sort of plausible rationale to make me feel as if I had been given a fair shake. When I hurt his feelings that night at The Captain's Table, he had responded the next morning by calmly explaining his position and by listening carefully to my version of what had happened. Today would be different. There was an icy edge to his voice that clearly showed his refusal to take prisoners. He was a man with a mission, and there was nothing I could do or say to dissuade him.

"Yeah, I understand," I said, rising from the couch.

"We're not finished here, Darla. Sit down."

Reluctantly, I resumed my seat but turned my face so that he could not see the scowl on it, even though he was the designated beneficiary of it. Dad rose from the couch and took a seat in his recliner, where, like a true tyrannical monarch, he could impose harsher rule from the security of his throne.

"I've just come from a long visit with Peter Mullavey," he began.

"I know," I snapped, eager to let him realize that he hadn't pulled the wool over my eyes.

"I see," he replied, nodding his head as if that information explained my hostile attitude.

"Pete Mullavey is deeply disturbed about what happened last night. He'd met the Cheyney boy on several occasions and had warned Ryan not to get mixed up with him. Were you aware of that, Darla?"

"No," I spat contentiously. "So what?"

Dad bit his lip. He had that I'm-counting-to-ten-so-I-don't-lose-control look on his face.

"Well, that makes Ryan's decision to ride with him all the more alarming. Ryan knew exactly the kind of young man he was dealing with, and he deliberately put both of your lives at risk just for the possibility of banging his drums at some waterfront den of iniquity called Pier 23."

I knew I was in big trouble, having observed in the past that there was a direct correlation between my father's state of mind and his choice of words. When he was really angry, he would completely forget that my vocabulary was relatively limited compared to his, and he would use any word that popped into his head. In a reasonable state of mind, Dad was much more careful about choosing the proper words to get his point across, probably so that I could reap the highest reward from his incredible pearls of wisdom.

"Ryan didn't deliberately do anything!" I shot back defensively.

"Darla, he knew the young man was an alcoholic, and yet he still rode in the car with him and had you do the same. That constitutes a shameful lack of good judgment, wouldn't you say?"

He was acting so high and mighty he made me sick. And what a hypocrite he was, having spent the better portion of the early morning hours acting like an alcoholic himself.

"So Ryan made a mistake. Haven't you ever made one of those, or don't you even know what they are?"

I knew I was asking for trouble. He was already in a foul mood, and my sarcastic rebuttals weren't improving matters. Still, I couldn't seem to help myself. Not only was he violating my privacy, but I could sense that he was on the verge of destroying something very precious to me—my relationship with Ryan.

"Darla, you're treading on thin ice here. I'd advise you to stop. Right now." I said nothing, but challenged him with a fierce stare.

"You're obviously very angry at me for speaking to Peter Mullavey. I'm sorry you feel that way, but that's the way it is. For your information, Darla, it was he who suggested we get together. He's been terribly concerned about Ryan's association with this band for quite a while."

I shrugged my shoulders and grunted contemptuously. "Well, don't look at me. I'm not in the band."

"Darla—"

"Yeah, all right," I moaned, my left hand waving off another reproach.

Dad bit his lip again, then continued. "Pete Mullavey has long feared the possible use of drugs and alcohol by some of Ryan's fellow band members, but Ryan has vehemently denied it. Being a trusting father, and not having seen any evidence of alcohol or drug use with Ryan himself, Pete has reluctantly allowed Ryan to play with the band on weekends, providing that all of Ryan's school and work responsibilities were met first. Pete, however, had suspected alcohol abuse with the Cheyney boy, but Ryan had explained that the young man was not a member of the band and had convinced Pete that no one had very much to do with him. Well, Ryan did have 'something to do with him,' and that something almost got Ryan and my little girl killed."

I didn't know what he wanted me to say. Certainly, I wasn't going to agree with him, whether he was right or not.

"Last night was the straw that broke the camel's back," Dad continued. "Pete is extremely disappointed by Ryan's bad judgment, and he's very concerned about what might happen next, so much so, that he's decided to put a stop to Ryan's association with the band."

I felt terrible for Ryan, knowing how much his membership in the band had meant to him.

"In addition, Pete has made a decision to curb all of Ryan's extracurricular activities for the time being. Everything but his job at the supermarket. He wants Ryan to concentrate on nothing but his schoolwork. He feels that Ryan's priorities have been misplaced for too long lately. In just a year and a half, it'll be time for college, and Pete wants Ryan to concentrate on his grades so that he can be assured of making it to a good school."

From what Dad was saying, it was apparent that I was one of the "extracurricular activities" that Mr. Mullavey wanted Ryan to curb. I wondered how much Dad had had to do with this horrible decision. So far, I'd only heard what Mr. Mullavey wanted for Ryan, not what Dad wanted for me. I felt sick inside at the thought of not being allowed to see Ryan again. I couldn't believe that our fathers had conspired to break us up.

"So what are you saying?" I asked defensively. "That I'm not allowed to see Ryan anymore?"

Dad took a deep breath and looked down at the carpet. Even he knew this was unfair.

"I'm sorry, Darla. That's the way it has to be."

I sprung sky-high in my seat. "No way! You can't do this to me. And Ryan's dad can't do it to him, either."

"Darla, I agree with Pete. This is what's best. Personally, I find Ryan to be a fine young man, but he's been hanging out with an older crowd, one that hasn't been the best influence on him. He needs to settle down, reconsider his priorities, and crack the books."

It wasn't enough for Dad just being my father. He obviously wanted to "crack the whip" and be Ryan's father too.

"As for you, Darla, I just don't feel you're ready to handle a relationship."

"Why not?" I asked, crossing my arms.

"Well, for one, ever since you've been seeing Ryan, your mother and I have had to deal with one behavior problem after another with you. You've certainly never talked back to me like this before you met Ryan. I believe that being in a relationship is too stressful for you, and I just don't think that you have the ability to handle yourself maturely when things don't go your way."

It was so unfair, and my father was such a hypocrite.

"You were dating Mom when she was my age," I reminded him. "And you're five years older than she is! How do you explain that? Were you so mature? And please, don't tell me that times were different then. I hate when you say that."

He looked embarrassed, but he had no other answer for me. "You may hate it, but it's the truth."

173

"What do you know about being a teenager? Nothing!"

"Darla," he said, his voice rising, "I know it's hard for you to imagine, but I was a teenager once, spent seven years as one, whereas you've never spent one day as an adult. Now that gives me the better perspective on matters, wouldn't you say?"

I was seething; I hadn't seen that one coming and didn't have much of a response. But that didn't stop me from trying. "No, I wouldn't say! Besides, I doubt if you can remember all the way back to the prehistoric era!"

I know he wanted to laugh, but he held steady. "Darla, the die has been cast. The decision is made. Even if I were to reverse it, Pete Mullavey is sure to stick to his guns. I'm very sorry, honey. I know how much you care about Ryan, but the relationship is over."

"No. No, it's not! I love Ryan and we're going to be together! How dare you try to break us up! I hate you! And I hate Mr. Mullavey! I hate you both for treating us like children. If I don't do things perfectly, by your standards, then I'm not mature enough. That's not fair. That's stupid! You're not Mr. Perfection yourself. I love Ryan so much. You have no idea! You're so mean! I hate you! I hate Mr. Mullavey. You're both terrible fathers."

Dad sat there quietly while I carried on. I suppose he felt that I was entitled to rant and rave for a bit, and I could tell by the look in his eyes that he actually sympathized with me. But despite any sympathy he may have felt for my predicament, he, like Peter Mullavey, was also "sticking to his guns" and had no intention whatsoever of backing down.

"Darla, why don't you go visit your cousins? You need to do something to lift your spirits."

"Forget about my spirits!" I screamed. "Just make sure you don't lift any more of your own!"

Dad looked absolutely stunned. I was instantly sorry for what I had said and wished I could take it back. I wasn't even pleased with myself for retorting with such a clever witticism, as I normally would've been under similar circumstances. Despite the fact that my father had just conspired with Pete Mullavey to break up my relationship, I felt low and dirty for hurting him that way. Dad had been preaching the evils of alcohol to me all my life, and in one brief moment, I had exposed him as a hypocrite, and there was nothing he could do to deny it. He had tried so hard to teach me well and to set a good example, and I didn't have the maturity to allow him one indiscretion in almost sixteen years. Certainly, he had allowed me far more than that.

Dad didn't say a word. He looked ashamed and embarrassed, as if he were going to break down on the spot. The pain was unbearable, for both of us. I wanted to apologize but knew there would be no use in that—the damage was done. Finally, Dad rose from his chair.

"Be sure to let your mother or me know when Dr. Stanley's office calls. One of us will drive you to his office. I'll be back later."

Dad mournfully walked back to the coat closet, put on his coat, wrapped his camel-colored cashmere scarf around his neck, and slipped quietly out the front door.

CHAPTER 11

The snow fell hard that winter. It was a gloomy, cheerless time that debilitated us all, both in mind and in spirit. With one unplanned sucker punch, I had completely knocked the wind out of my father. More than anything, despite my anger, I wanted to stand him up, dust him off, and have him be my corny father all over again. But that was not to be. He moved through our home like a stranger passing through town, one who paid for room and board but who bothered no one as he padded softly about town: uncomplaining and mysterious, his family crumpled and forgotten in an old leather wallet.

This was the very first time I could remember that Dad had not come to me after one of our "incidents" (or arguments) to discuss the matter or to "clear the air." I prayed that he would. I wanted to tell him that he wasn't a horrible person for taking a few drinks, and that I still loved and respected him, even though he had hurt me deeply by joining forces with Peter Mullavey to destroy my relationship with Ryan. More than that, I wanted to understand why he was letting a few drinks destroy his entire life, his self-esteem, and his family.

Dad wasn't talking much and neither was Mom. The only conversation between them seemed to be about the stock market, which Dad had told Mom was "falling faster than the snow out there." I sensed that she was very angry with me for being the catalyst that had sent Dad plummeting, like the market, into the depths of depression. Twice, when she thought I didn't see her, I caught her looking at me, shaking her head in that "oh, Darla, look-what-you've-done" fashion. It was clear to me that she blamed me for humiliating my father and for all of the repercussions of that action that she was having to bear. But she was too cowardly to tell me that directly. And not once did she offer any truly sympathetic words about the forced breakup of my relationship with Ryan, except to mumble some hackneyed condolences about "how sad I must feel" and how I'll "be over it in no time." She must've forgotten that she was practically engaged to my father when she was my age. But I was just supposed to view the matter as one of the many pitfalls of being a teenager. She had disassociated herself from the whole mess, never once intervening on my behalf, or trying to find out, from my point of view, why the mess had taken place.

I often thought about Mom's phone conversation with Aunt Didi, in which she admitted blaming Rebecca "for everything." Now she was blaming me, whether she said it aloud or not. I wondered if Mom ever blamed herself for anything.

I didn't know how to sort out my feelings. Dad was the one who had "done me wrong," yet Mom was the one I felt angriest at, for her complete inability, or refusal, to walk a different path from that of my father. I recalled with anger the Hoover debacle, and Mom's constant prodding to write the "painless little apology note" so that everyone, especially her, would feel better. I inferred that it was probably my father who eventually determined that if an apology note was not sincerely written, then it need not be written at all, and that time alone would heal the Hoovers' wounds (as gaping as they were).

In addition to all this, I began to doubt the sincerity of my last conversation with Mom, the "honest" one that had left me feeling so good. My cousins approached me after school one day to let me know that out of the blue, Aunt Didi had made some casual revelations to them about Rebecca. April, in particular, was especially anxious to explore any leads that this new information might bring, but when we compared notes, we discovered that Aunt Didi's "revelations" were almost identical to Mom's.

It was positively eerie. We all agreed that our mothers were on to us and, unfortunately, one step ahead of us at all times. It was quite obvious that my mother, after talking with me on New Year's Day, had gone straight to my aunt and repeated the entire conversation. Together, the controlling Connor sisters had decided that Didi should reveal the same information to April, May, and June, thereby demystifying the whole matter and hopefully subduing our collective curious mind once and for all.

I didn't know what to make of my parents any longer. They both felt

177

like strangers to me, and as the days wore on, the situation got worse and worse. I was still having nightmares about the car accident, which were tangled up with recurring dreams about Ryan being lost and my trying to find him.

It took me weeks to realize that I wasn't only angry with my father and Peter Mullavey, I was angry with Ryan, too. What our fathers did was bad enough, but somehow I had expected Ryan to contact me, by letter, by phone, or perhaps even by sitting in his car and waiting for me to come home. My favorite scenario was one in which Ryan stood outside my bedroom window at night, knee-deep in snow, crying, "Wherefore art thou, Darla?"

I looked for Ryan around every corner, out of every window, up every tree, in every car, and in every mail delivery. He was nowhere to be seen.

January passed miserably into February. With Valentine's Day fast approaching, I prayed for a miracle.

The four of them descended on me at once, in my bedroom, on a Saturday morning, five days before Valentine's Day. They called themselves the "Cheer-Up Squad," and although they looked ridiculous in the assorted Army Surplus getup they wore, their comical invasion of my miserable life was just what I needed.

"At ease, soldiers!" April commanded. "Private Davenport! In the corner, on the chair! Be quick about it!"

"Geez, Darla!" Melanie playfully chastised me, as she followed April's orders and took a seat. "Don't you have any other clothes to wear besides these stupid gray sweats and this Mickey Mouse sweatshirt?"

"Gray is my color," I told her. "It reflects my mood. At least I'm not dressed like something that just dug itself out of the trenches."

"At least we got out!" Melanie retorted, making a face.

"Davenport! Shut up! No conversing with civilians! Privates May and June! Plant your military posteriors on the bed!"

June gave April a dirty look as she and May plopped strategically down on my bed, in exactly the place where April was pointing.

"What are you guys supposed to be, anyway?" I asked, enjoying the show. "GI Joe Monsters?"

"Just your average Army men, I guess," Melanie said, risking the wrath of her commanding officer. What do we look like?"

"I'm not quite sure, but you all look pretty funny," I said, sliding down the wall until I reached a comfortable position on the floor. "How come April's helmet has a light on it?"

"I told you she would notice," June said to April triumphantly.

"Oh, get a life!" April retorted, joining her sisters on the bed. "Move over," she said to June, pushing her toward the back wall with her left hand.

"April's wearing a miner's helmet," June teased. "She found it in our costume chest and thought it was our grandfather's old Army helmet. She thought the light was there so that the soldiers could signal each other when one of them had a good idea."

"I did not!" April giggled, swatting June on the arm. "But if that were true, and you were a soldier, you wouldn't have to wear one 'cause you've never had a good idea in your whole life."

"That's what you think!" June said knowingly, as if she had something up her khaki sleeve.

"What does it say on your helmet?" I asked April, while June, Melanie, and May quietly giggled to themselves.

"It doesn't say anything," April replied, confused by the giggles.

"Yes, it does," I said very sincerely. "It looks like it says 'Ze-tid' or something like that. Is that some kind of miner's code?"

"What?" April asked. "I have no idea what you're talking about."

The giggles from the peanut gallery grew louder.

"It says 'Ze-tid.' "

"Spell it," April demanded.

"All right," I said naively. "It looks like a backwards Z, T, I and a backwards 'D.' "

April jumped up and marched across my room to the mirror above

179

my dresser, then looked squarely at her own image, only to see the word "DITZ" emblazoned in big red letters over the light on her helmet.

June doubled over in laughter, followed by May and Melanie, who laughed almost as hard as the culprit herself. I took a good, hard look at April. There she was, standing defiantly before the mirror, wearing Army khakis and a miner's helmet with "DITZ" written on it. Her beautiful blond hair, which had been tucked up inside the helmet, had fallen to her shoulders, and her scowl had turned to a look of puzzlement as she tried to figure out how June had managed to pull this off. I hated to laugh at her, but I couldn't help myself because she looked so funny. April eventually thought so too, because she suddenly burst into gales of giggles as the ludicrousness of her own appearance finally dawned on her.

"Miner's code?" June repeated to me, when she was finally able to catch her breath. "Darla, did I hear you ask April if there was some sort of miner's code on her helmet? Would you like some help in deciphering it?"

"Oh, give her a break!" May said to June, as she grabbed a tissue from my nightstand and wiped the tears of laughter from her face.

"Maybe we should write 'Ditz' on that Mickey Mouse sweatshirt of yours, Darla," June suggested.

"Try 'Grunge,' " Melanie offered. "God only knows if Darla ever washes that thing!"

I quickly got up from the floor, grabbed my stuffed rabbit, Mr. Carrot Breath from the bed, and began hitting Melanie on the head with it. "I do too wash it!" I told her, as the rabbit's gray ears brushed across Melanie's freckled face.

"Prove it," Melanie said, holding her nose, and pushing Mr. Carrot Breath away with her right hand.

"Melanie has something that might cheer you up," May said brightly, interrupting our friendly fire. "But if it doesn't cheer you up, because we really can't be sure if it will or not, then we'll be here to cheer you up instead. We're the 'Cheer-Up Squad.' "

June looked oddly at May. "I told you not to sit so close to her at dinner. I think it's contagious."

I resumed my post on the floor, intrigued by what May had just said.

"Oh, leave me alone!" May told June, swatting her on the arm in the same manner April had.

"Yeah," April said giggling. "Worry about yourself. You're bustin' out all over, ya know!"

May and April, quite pleased with April's retort, took off their helmets and started imitating that horrible emcee from "Salute to Broadway" night, singing a mini-rendition of "June Is Bustin' Out All Over."

I was having the time of my life and by the song's end, I had all but forgotten what May had said, about having brought something that might cheer me up.

"So," Melanie asked, after the last note had been sung, "don't you want to know what I have hidden in my pocket?"

"Yes! What is it?" I asked, bouncing eagerly on the floor.

"Be patient," Melanie scolded me. "And sit still, woman! You act like you've got a wad of Silly Putty on your butt. And remember what your father told you: 'Good things come to those who wait.'"

May looked over at Melanie. "You're not going to torture her about this, are you?"

"C'mon, May," Melanie protested. "You don't think I'm just going to hand it over, do you?"

"Hand what over?" I asked anxiously.

"Melanie—" May reminded her, "we don't know what kind of news we're actually bringing Darla, remember? Maybe torturing her isn't the best idea."

Melanie looked almost disappointed. "Yeah, okay. I'll give it to her."

She reached in her pocket and pulled out a small white envelope that had my name written on it. Rising from the chair, she walked over and handed it to me.

"Here," Melanie said. "It's from Ryan. He gave it to Ben to give to me to give to you. Gee, Dar, I hope it's good news."

I held the envelope in my hands as if I were afraid it was going self-destruct. I honestly believed that the key to my entire future lay in Ryan's words, and I was deathly afraid to look, even though I had prayed for this moment for almost six long weeks.

"Are you okay?" May asked sweetly.

"I guess so. But I might not be after I read this."

"Open it already!" Melanie insisted. "This is torturous!"

"A taste of your own medicine is good for you," May told her, smiling.

Melanie looked embarrassed.

"All right. I'm gonna do it," I said bravely.

I opened the envelope and silently read the letter, which was written on a piece of white looseleaf paper:

Dear Darla,

You're probably pissed with me for taking so long to get in touch with you. I'm really sorry. My old man has really been on my case. New Year's Eve really freaked him out and he's been watching me like a hawk. He made me quit the band. I'm really bummed. Haven't done much but study and work at the supermarket. My mom's been real supportive, but what my dad says goes. You know how it is. I still feel really lousy about almost getting you killed. You were so nice about it, but I wouldn't blame you if you never wanted to see me again. My dad's told me a million times how I did you wrong. I'm really sorry.

By the way, I did go and see Greg's old man. The place was a trip. Looked like something out of a horror movie. More shit in the living room than in the yard. And the guy had gun magazines and porno movies up the wazoo. Man, it was unreal. I never liked Greg much, but I left there feeling really sorry for him. He never had a shot. Oh, by the way, I hear Corky's getting out of the hospital next week. Nice weather we're havin', huh? I don't mind the snow so much, but the ice is a bummer, especially for driving.

Well, I guess I better go. My dad's been sending away for every college catalog under the sun, and I'm supposed to look through them all and see where I want to apply. He's really on my case, but after meeting Greg's dad, I guess I'm kinda lucky. (But don't tell anyone I said that.) I really hope you're doing okay, Darla. I miss talking to you a lot. And seeing you, too. Take care. Love, Ryan.

When I finished reading the letter, I read it over a second time, much to the dismay of Melanie and my three cousins, who were dying to have its contents revealed.

"Well?" Melanie asked. "Was it a good letter?"

"I guess so," I said as I got up and handed her the letter. "I guess it's good, but I'm really not sure."

Melanie joined my cousins on the bed and eagerly read the letter while April peered over her shoulder. When they had finished, May and June read it together.

And then, for the next half hour, the five of us analyzed every word of poor Ryan's letter—over and over and over again. My cousins stood firmly behind Melanie, who did her utmost to convince me that it was a very positive letter. While she admitted that it wasn't the romantic missive I'd probably dreamed of, I needed to remember that most guys don't write letters at all, much less mushy, romantic ones.

May, who was always so sensitive to other people's pain, pointed out that Ryan seemed to be really down on himself for having involved me with Greg, and that as a teenage boy on the brink of manhood, he was embarrassed and possibly humiliated that his father had forced him to stop seeing me. She reminded me that girls aren't the only ones who can have low self-esteem, and that Ryan (no matter how cute he was) was obviously feeling really bad about himself.

But mostly, the five of us kept poring over all the "good parts" where Ryan had said that he missed talking to me, missed seeing me, and had even signed it "Love." I was thrilled to have some tangible proof in my hands that he cared, though I couldn't get over the nagging fact that he made no mention of us getting together again in the near future. But the girls all insisted that I take it one step at a time, and that it was better to have a guy like Ryan than one who promised the moon and delivered nothing. And when Melanie reminded me that Jesse already had a new girlfriend, "Dumb Debbie Dipshit," as Melanie called her, I felt very lucky to have what I did.

"So now what?" April said, as if she were gathering the troops for an undercover assignment. (All five of us were now crowded together on my bed.) "What's the game plan?"

"Game plan?" I asked.

"Yeah! Game plan. You're going to do something in response to Ryan's letter, aren't you? If you don't, Cuz, he'll think you hate him. Don't you remember what he said in his letter about not blaming you if you never wanted to see him again? You gotta do something!" April insisted.

"She's right," Melanie agreed, anxious to play Ethel Mertz to April's Lucy Ricardo. "We gotta do something!"

I found Melanie's use of the word "we" kind of touching.

"What do you guys think?" I asked, having no idea in which direction to turn.

"Well, I say we go back to the supermarket," April said with great assurance. "Except this time, we find a better costume!"

June picked up April's helmet, which had been lying on my pillow, and put it back on her head.

"Here, Sis, I think you need to wear your Ditz helmet. Gee, maybe you and Darla could go dressed in these costumes. You could keep your same costume and Darla could use mine. No one would suspect a thing!"

"I'm not kidding!" April said. "I'm serious—not about wearing these costumes, but I'm serious about going!"

"I don't think so," I told April. "That one experience was enough to last me forever."

April looked genuinely disappointed.

"C'mon, Darla. Please!"

"Why are you begging Darla to go?" June asked. "Sounds like you've got an agenda of your own."

"Omigod! I can't believe it! Omigod!"

"Shut up, Melanie," April scolded her, getting up from the bed.

"Omigod!"

"Shut up!" April said, pacing the room anxiously.

"What's going on?" May asked.

"I'll bet April's got a thing for my brother! Don't you, April? Omigod! How funny! Ben's got a crush on you, 'April in Paris,' and you've got a crush on him, 'Ben in Paris'! Omigod. How adorable!"

"I do not!" April said defensively, leaning against my dresser. "So shut up!"

Melanie, who had meant no harm, seemed a bit taken aback by April's condemnation.

"Sor-ree, April. Excuse me for living."

"It's all right," April said, picking up a bottle of my drugstore cologne and examining it curiously. "Just forget about it, will you?"

Melanie had discovered my cousin's secret, but April's embarrassment was obvious, and even June, April's number one tormentor, wasn't saying a word.

"Let's get back to our mission at hand," May suggested, eager to deflect the attention from April.

"That's a good idea," June agreed, proving that she could be kind to her older sister.

"Well, I think Darla should send him a nice Valentine," May said. "Just something sweet and simple with a note in it. Nothing too romantic that might scare him off."

"You could write a poem or something inside," Melanie suggested. "I mean, you're so good at writing."

"Yeah, but I'm not going to write Ryan a poem. What, are you nuts or something? How embarrassing!"

"I'm sending Jesse a Valentine with a little poem in it, and we broke up six weeks ago."

"Really? What kind of poem?" April asked Melanie, easing her way back into the conversation, as she resumed her seat on the bed. "What could you possibly say?"

"A lot!" Melanie assured her. "You guys want me to read it to you?"

"Sure," May told her. "And if you can recite it without torturing us

185

first, then we'd love to hear it."

"All right," Melanie conceded, reaching into her pocket for a piece of paper. "It's not as good as Darla's stuff, but I put my heart and soul into it. Remember that."

Melanie got up from the bed and stood before us. Then she read:

Dear Jesse:
Roses are red, violets are blue,
Why'd I go out, with a jerk like you.
Sex can be fine, when the time is right,
But not in your closet, on party night.
And not on that bag, all musty and gross,
I've seen scum before, but I don't get that close.
No way did you love me, tho' I was the best,
So enjoy Debbie Dipshit, I'm sure she'll say yes.
For me, I will wait till a time in my life,
When a decent guy wants to make me his wife.
So party on, dude, have your roll in the hay,
And forget about me on Valentine's Day!

"That's quite a poem!" May said. "Sounds like you really worked hard on it. In fact, it sounds like you spent weeks on it."

"Are you really going to send it?" I asked.

"Hell, yeah!" Melanie answered, sitting down again. "I want him to remember how clever and witty I am, not to mention beautiful, and I want him to think about what he gave up by being such a jerk."

"That oughta do the trick," June told her.

"Yeah," I said. "You're a one-in-a-million girl, Melody!"

We all laughed hysterically until Melanie reminded us of more pressing business.

"C'mon, guys, enough about me. We've gotta help Darla make a decision. That's what we're here for."

For the next couple of hours, the five of us discussed every possible response. After careful consideration, I decided to go with May's original suggestion about writing something nice and simple in a card, something that wouldn't scare Ryan off.

May, who was delighted that I'd agreed to take her advice, hugged me on her way out the door and said, "Don't worry, Scarlett, you'll think of some way to get him back. After all, tomorrow is another day."

As the troops departed into the snow, leaving me alone in the tormented silence that had become an integral part of my family life, I felt, for the first time in weeks, that perhaps a bright ray of sun would soon shine down and melt the ice away.

I didn't realize it at the time, but it seems that I wasn't the only one who had benefited from the Cheer-Up Squad's visit. That evening at dinner, Dad told me that the sight of his nieces and Melanie in "those ridiculous getups" was the funniest thing he'd witnessed in a long time.

"Your mother and I laughed ourselves silly," he told me. "I only wish I'd thought to take a picture."

I was delighted that my parents, especially Dad, had found something to laugh about, and I was grateful to the four of them for giving us some much-needed light conversation, even though the distance between us was still most definitely present.

With everything that had happened, I'd forgotten all about the pictures that Dad had taken on New Year's Eve. It wasn't until he mentioned taking pictures of the Cheer-Up Squad that I was reminded of the several undeveloped images of Ryan and me as a beautiful, loving couple that lay trapped inside Dad's camera. I considered asking him if I could develop the film, but I was afraid he'd think I was still obsessed with Ryan and tell me that it was better to let sleeping dogs lie. I decided it would be best to wait, because the last thing any of us needed was for my request to escalate into an argument. On the other hand, I couldn't wait too long to ask or the film would go bad.

That night after dinner, I read and reread Ryan's letter until I had every word memorized. When I had finished, I called Melanie to rehash everything we'd discussed earlier that day. Finally, I was as ready as I would ever be to compose the short note that would go in Ryan's yet-to-be-bought Valentine.

Dear Ryan:

I was really happy when Melanie delivered your letter. I've been wondering how you were, so it meant a lot to me that you wrote. Please stop feeling bad about what happened. We're both alive and well and that's what counts. I'm really sorry to hear about the band. I know how much it meant to you, and how much you miss playing with them, but I'm sure your dad will eventually change his mind. I'm keeping my fingers crossed for you!

Things have been pretty tough at my house. You know how stubborn fathers can be. I wish we could talk about it. I miss our conversations so much, and I especially miss seeing you. Anyway, I just want to let you know I'm thinking of you, on Valentine's Day, and always.
Love, Darla.

I hated every miserable word. I'd written ten-page book reports (and gotten an A on them) in less time than it had taken me to write and rewrite my letter to Ryan. One thing was for sure: unlike me, Ryan wouldn't be spending hours brooding over my letter, analyzing it, and choosing the "good parts." He'd probably skim over it briefly and then toss it into the garbage.

I had tried to cover every point the girls and I had discussed: letting him know I wasn't angry, being sympathetic to his band problem, telling him I'd missed our conversations (hint, hint), and being slightly romantic, but not too much so, right at the letter's end.

The next morning, April gave me a ride to the mall, where I picked out a Valentine for Ryan, a cutout of a big red heart that read simply "To My Friend on Valentine's Day." The inside was blank, leaving me lots of space to write my letter. It wasn't the most original card in the world, and it was hardly the most sensational, but it was sweet and simple and served my purposes well.

When I had finished selecting the card, I moved down the aisle to the birthday cards to see what I could find for my friend Rachel's sixteenth birthday. It was then that April stealthily snuck up on the "Someone Special" section, once I had moved away, chose a card, then rushed over to pay for it when she thought I wasn't looking.

Naturally, I was dying of curiosity, but I didn't dare ask her about it, knowing how easily she got embarrassed and remembering how angry she had been with Melanie for even bringing up Ben's name. Besides, the clandestine manner in which she bought the card clearly indicated that she didn't want anyone (except the recipient) to know about it. I wondered if she'd been having some sort of a relationship with Ben or if perhaps they were just starting one.

But all I really cared about was seeing Ryan again. Perhaps on Valentine's Day I would receive word that he wanted to see me, and together we would determine a place to meet. Even if that were not the case, and Ryan had no plans to ask for a secret meeting, receiving a Valentine from me would be more than enough incentive to prompt him into doing exactly that.

I left the mall with hope in my heart, as I counted the minutes until Valentine's Day.

CHAPTER 12

"To Our Daughter" and "To Our Niece" the cards read, but there was nothing "To the Girl I Love," or even "To My Friend." I tried telling myself that perhaps Ryan's Valentine would come late, maybe by way of Ben Davenport again, but my gut knew that it was not to be. I was terribly disappointed, but I simply couldn't bear the thought of going up to my room and crying my eyes out. That was practically all I'd done for the past six weeks, and I was bored to tears (no pun intended) with the red-eyed routine. Furthermore, I was feeling restless and agitated and knew that I needed a change of venue, one that would not induce claustrophobia and complicate my already fragile psyche.

As I wallowed in my own misery, I remembered what my father used to tell me as a child, whenever I had cried over not getting something I had wanted. In his cliché mastery, he had explained that it was a far better thing to give than to receive, and that whenever a person felt sad about what he or she didn't have, the best way to feel better was by giving to someone else who might have even less. Now, at the advanced age of fifteen, it finally sounded like a good idea, only I didn't know what I had to give that anyone could possibly want.

Then, miraculously, it dawned on me. I looked at the clock and rushed to the telephone. Luckily, I caught May just seconds before she was leaving her house. We arranged that April, who was in a hurry to get "somewhere mysterious," would drop May off at my house, and from there we would catch the bus to the nursing home, where April would pick us up later. May assured me that there was a card shop near the home where I could buy a Valentine for Victoria. I was really excited. I couldn't wait to see her again.

✳ ✳ ✳

Victoria's sweet face lit up like a Christmas tree when she saw me standing in front of her in the lounge with a single red rose and a

Valentine. It was amazing to me that someone who I barely knew could be so overjoyed by just seeing me, but I also was overjoyed by seeing her.

"Darla, my dear, you are a vision of loveliness. Please sit down." She motioned gracefully to an empty place beside her with her right hand. "I'm so delighted to see you again. You have no idea."

"Hello, Victoria," I said, settling in next to her on the sofa. "These are for you. Happy Valentine's Day."

She took the rose and the card into her frail hands as if they were an injured bird that she wanted to love and nurse back to health. Her eyes welled up with tears, and as the tears began to stream down her rosy cheeks, she slowly opened the Valentine. As she read the heartfelt sentiment inside, more tears began to fall, only this time, they fell from my eyes, too.

Dad had been right. It was far better to give than to receive. It occurred to me at that moment that even if I had received a hundred Valentines from Ryan, they could not have filled me with the same tremendous joy I was getting from just seeing Victoria's beautiful smile.

She thanked me profusely, telling me over and over again how I had given her such a beautiful memory to cherish forever. I almost felt guilty, as if I should've done more to be deserving of such great praise. I assured her that being there was my great pleasure as well, but she didn't quite seem to believe me.

"Now, my dear, I want to know all about what you've been up to since we last saw each other before Christmas. I'm very interested, you know."

Without realizing it, I winced at the thought of telling her all the not-so-nice events of my life since that time, then made a pathetic attempt to cover it up with a lazy smile. But Victoria wasn't buying any of it.

She looked resolutely into my eyes. "Darla, please listen to your aged friend, Victoria. True, my bones may be old and my back may hurt me most days, but I've lived for many years and know all too well that life is not always a bowl of cherries. Sometimes you just get the pits. Now, I'm not asking you to tell me anything you don't want me to know, but I do want you to know that it's not necessary to make 'Old Lady' talk with me for fear I'll fall apart. I'm a good listener and sometimes I can even give good advice. Even my son says so!" She laughed. "So I would be very happy if you let me help you with your troubles. Very happy, indeed."

She had me convinced, so, with some necessary omissions and slight equivocations, I told her all about Ryan and our New Year's date, including an abbreviated account of my subsequent despondency. She listened intently and never once interrupted me, not even when I faltered while recapping the catastrophic denouement of my voided romance. I had no doubt that everything I was saying really mattered to her, and that Victoria respected my problems as she would those of any adult. She was clearly disturbed when I told her about the evening's bloody end, but she did not seem any more confounded or disconcerted by my confessions than anyone else might be. That relieved me; at first I feared she might be too fragile to hear my news, but as it turned out, I'd made her feel wanted and needed by confiding so much to her.

After all had been revealed, we talked for a bit about the accident, and then about my strained relationship with Mom and Dad. Victoria, however, knew what was foremost on my mind. She gave me a delicate pat on the right knee and smiled. "I have a feeling that you're most concerned right now about the young man, Ryan. Am I correct?"

"Yeah. I would definitely say he's the main thing on my mind right now," I said, pleased by her acuity.

Victoria nodded, started to say something to me, then hesitated.

"What is it?" I asked, concerned.

"Oh nothing. I'm just wondering if you'll want to hear what's on my mind."

"Yes, I do," I said anxiously. "You don't have to make 'Young Lady' talk with me. I won't fall apart. I can take it."

We both laughed.

"I deserved that," Victoria said, smoothing a wrinkle on her violet-colored skirt. "Well now, if you're sure." She paused briefly, as if she wanted to choose the perfect words to begin. "Darla, have you ever heard anyone talk about 'being in love with love?' "

"I'm not sure," I said. I glanced briefly around the room and noticed that several of the residents were watching us. "What does that mean?"

"Well, dear, that's when a person, be they a man or a woman, falls in love with the idea of romance. Let's take a fictitious young lady, someone not unlike yourself, and let's see what she might be daydreaming about. To start with, maybe she's dreaming of an amorous first encounter, one where she's swept off her feet by a tall, dark stranger whom she meets on a gray and foggy day. Perhaps her fancy might extend to the courting stage, where she's wined and dined in the grandest of styles—complete with roses, love letters, and secret rendezvous—all the way up until that glorious moment when she and the very handsome stranger realize their deep love for one another, and vow to spend all of eternity together. Or at least the rest of their lives!"

Victoria chuckled to herself and continued. "Now, remember, daydreams can vary greatly from one person to another. For example, your daydreams might be very different from your lovely cousin May's. It all depends on whatever your particular idea of love and romance might be."

"Everything sounds pretty neat to me. I'll take all of it!"

Victoria laughed and I noticed how her eyes twinkled when she did so.

"Precisely my point! It all sounds 'pretty neat,' doesn't it? And this is where 'being in love with love' comes in."

"Yeah?" I said, hanging on her every word.

Victoria folded her hands and placed them emphatically on her lap. "Well, Darla, let's say our fictitious young lady dreams of these romantic scenarios day in and day out. In fact, it may be all she thinks about. Till finally, one day, she meets a handsome young man, a fine gentleman, whom she believes to be the very man of her dreams."

"Like me meeting Ryan?"

"Exactly!"

I noticed she suddenly looked a bit uneasy about continuing.

"Go on," I pressed. "I really want to hear what you're saying. I swear."

"Well, this young man may be very nice, and he may look like the man of her dreams, but more times than not, he's simply not 'the one.' But because this young lady wants so desperately to 'be in love,' she sees true love where it simply doesn't exist. Now mind you, she may like the young man a great deal, and he may like her, but there are many people who like each other who aren't destined to marry or to become soul mates. Oftentimes, the smart young lady may even realize all of this, but because she's fantasized about being in love for so long, she simply refuses to let go of her dream, thereby hanging on to the wrong man, and maybe even keeping the right man from finding her."

At that moment, I heard Melanie's voice in my head saying, "Duh, Darla, do you get it now?"

I did "get it," and I understood exactly what Victoria was so eloquently and kindly telling me. She was right. I was in love with love, and although I knew in my heart that Ryan wasn't "the one," I desperately wanted to hang on to him, and to my dream of him.

"How do you know when you've found 'the one,' Victoria?"

She smiled joyously. "Because it's so right that you don't even have to ask. The right man simply adores you and you adore him. And the right man will treat you like a queen—like his lover, and most importantly, like his best friend. He'll make you feel wonderful about just being yourself, and you won't have to work double duty to impress him. He won't try to change you or to mold you into someone else. And best of all, Darla, you won't have to look for hidden signs that he loves you. He'll make his feelings perfectly clear. In fact, they'll be written all over his face when he looks at you."

"Wow! That sounds pretty cool."

"Oh, it can be 'pretty cool,' " Victoria said and laughed.

"Did you find the 'right one'?" I asked eagerly.

"Certainly, and I married him, but I didn't find him on the very first try. Oh, far from it! I had to search for several years, and, naturally, I made a few mistakes along the way. But when I finally did find him, well, I knew instantly that he was a keeper."

Not since my grandmother had I heard anyone refer to another person as "a keeper." I hoped that Grandma Adelaide was watching, and that she liked Victoria as much as I did. Victoria had a special way of telling me the honest truth, a way that made me want to listen and to learn from her. Ironically, the same advice coming from either one of my parents would've been rejected immediately. But even armed with the knowledge that Victoria was right, that I was "in love with love," I wasn't ready to abandon my quest for Ryan, though I was ready to tuck her advice away in my brain for safekeeping. I knew that someday it would come in handy.

"I do hope I haven't overstepped my bounds," Victoria said with a hint of concern. "I would never want to do that."

"Oh no, you didn't overstep anything," I assured her. "I learned so much from you. I really appreciate it."

"Love is all around you, Darla. You don't have to look too hard to find it. And remember, love comes from many people—friends, family, and even old ladies like me. So when you find it, embrace it, and let it fill your heart. When you've got a heart filled with love, the right man is certain to find you."

I reached over and gave her a hug. I'd known her for such a short period of time, and yet I loved her already. From the corner of my eye, I saw that May was signaling me that it was time to leave soon. I took Victoria's hands in mine.

"We've gotta get going," I told her. "My cousin April will be here any minute to pick us up, and we've gotta be ready."

"I understand. Don't worry about me. I'll be fine. I just can't thank you enough for coming to see me today, and for bringing me these lovely remembrances of you. Now listen, Darla, I'm not going to pretend I wouldn't be very happy if you came back, but I would never want you to visit out of any sort of obligation. You're a beautiful young lady with a busy life to lead, and you can't be visiting old ladies all the time. Do you hear me?"

"Yeah, okay," I said, touched by her unselfishness. "I hear you. Bye, Victoria." As I walked away, I felt her smile follow me all the way out the door.

* * *

May was sitting on the bench in the vestibule of the nursing home, gazing reflectively through the large glass entrance doors, when I finally met up with her.

"April's not here yet. You might as well sit down. She shouldn't be too long."

"Okay," I said, taking a seat next to her. "How come you didn't come over and say hello to Victoria?"

She looked at me briefly, then turned away. "I don't know. She looked so happy just being with you. I didn't want to interrupt. I waved and blew her a kiss. Next time I'll say hello."

"Oh. Did you enjoy seeing the other residents?"

"Sure. I always do. They're wonderful."

"Yeah. They are," I agreed. "That's what makes it so sad to see them here. This is a real nice place and all, but I hope I never end up here. I don't think I could take it. I wonder how Victoria manages so well."

"She just does," May said, still gazing through the doors. "She has to. But having a friend like you really helps her."

May was definitely not her usual self. There was something distant in her voice, and it was very unlike her not to make eye contact when she spoke.

"May?" I said delicately.

"What is it?" she said tersely.

"Is there something wrong? You look really depressed. I'm used to seeing myself that way, but not you."

She turned and looked at me as if I'd just insulted her. "Why shouldn't I be allowed to get depressed once in a while too? You don't have exclusive rights on being depressed, you know."

I was totally taken aback by her response. "Well, yeah, May. I know, but—"

"But what, Darla?" she said, maintaining the edge to her voice.

"I dunno," I fumbled. "I've just never seen you like this."

"Like what?" she asked, as if purposely trying to alarm me.

"You know, sad and all."

"I can't be happy all the time. Do you know anyone who's happy all the time?"

"No, but—"

"But what? Really, Darla, just say whatever is on your mind. Everyone else does. Tell me how I'm supposed to be the 'mature one,' the Alexander sister who's 'wise beyond her years,' and that I should know better than to sit and sulk and be depressed. Even if I wanted to spend my life being cheery or cheering up other people, I'm not allowed to do so! No, I'm supposed to sing and dance forever, even if I don't want to—and it doesn't even matter if I don't always have a good time doing it, either. Maybe I just wanna go out and have some fun of my own. Maybe I wanna just be a teenager. Have you ever see a guy even look twice at me?"

"You're gorgeous, May. Everyone says so."

May turned away from me. "Guys don't think so," she said, looking mournfully out the doors again. "They look at April and June all the time but never once at me. I remind them of their mothers. What guy do you know who would want to date his mother? Huh? Tell me!"

I was dumbfounded by what she was saying. May was in deep pain, about so many things, and I felt guilty for having been so blind to it. She was always there for me when I needed a friend, and like a big baby, I was constantly running to her as if she were some kind of emotional buttress, someone who was older and wiser, and who did have all the answers. I couldn't tell her that she was ridiculous for thinking that guys might perceive her as their mother, when in a peculiar way, I did too. I reminded myself that May was actually younger than I was (though not by much), and I felt stupid for having been so stupid. And somewhere, in the middle of all her pain, having nothing whatsoever to do with me, I felt Aunt Didi's presence, ever so "gently" pressuring May to walk in the persona that she had created for her so many years ago.

"May, I'm so sorry," I said, clutching her left leg. "You've been the best friend in the world to me, and I really let you down. You always seemed so happy and so together and stuff. It just never occurred to me that you were so unhappy. I should've asked."

"It's not your fault, Darla. I've been trained to sleep with a smile on my face. You had no way of knowing I was so miserable."

197

"Yeah, May," I moaned, "but maybe I could've looked a little deeper where you're concerned, us being so close and all."

"It's all right, Darla. I'm sorry I let out my frustrations on you. It's not your fault. And besides, a lot of the time I am happy. It's just that lately, well, a lot of things are really bugging me. That's all."

"Do you wanna talk about them? Because I'd be glad to listen. I really would. I'm a good listener. But if you don't wanna talk, just tell me 'cause I can shut up too. I swear. I'm also a good shutter-upper!"

May smiled at me, looking a bit like her old self again. "You crack me up, Darla. I don't know what it is about you, but you crack me up. And thanks, I really would like to talk."

"Is it Aunt Didi?" I asked.

"April's applying to Juilliard, in New York City. Are you familiar with the school?"

"It's a famous music school or something, isn't it?"

"Yes. It's very famous. Our voice teacher, Miss Lund, taught there for many years. Anyway, April really wants to go there when she graduates, and that's great. I hope she gets accepted. She's got an incredible talent, not to mention ambition, and she should go there. If it's what she wants. June's hoping to go there one day too, and that just thrills Mom."

"But you don't want to go there, do you?"

"No," May said glumly. "No, I don't."

"I take it your mom has a problem with that?"

"Oh, Mom has a major problem with that! Are you kidding, Darla? She thinks she gave birth to a stage act, not to three daughters."

"What if April and June don't get accepted?"

May made a face and rolled her eyes. "Why do you think Mom does things like throw parties for Juilliard voice teachers and their prissy pupils? She's trying to buy their way in. But if her efforts don't pay off, I'm sure April and June can find another school. It might not be as prestigious for Mom, but there's still plenty of wonderful places they could go."

"Well, what about you? What does your mother say about you not wanting to go?"

"She says I'd be a fool to throw away a God-given talent like I have, and that I'd be an even bigger fool to throw away all these years of training that Daddy paid for! Can you believe it? Just because I'm not applying to Juilliard, she thinks I'm throwing my life away. God, Darla, she makes me so mad!" May balled her right fist and punched the arm of the bench we were sitting on. Her unexpected anger frightened me.

"What would you like to do with your life?" I asked, trying to calm her down.

"I'm not quite sure yet," she said wearily. "But I don't think I want to be a Broadway star. It sounds great and all, but I don't have the kind of drive and determination it takes to pursue that kind of life. It's just not me. I'm not a pavement pounder. That's what you have to do to succeed in show business, Darla. You have to pound pavements every day until you make it, and then you have to devote your entire life to it. I guess this is going to make me sound really boring and all, but I'd rather devote my life to raising a family. I do want a career, but I was thinking I might like to do some kind of social work, where I can help people—like the residents here who really need my help. Or maybe, I could pursue some kind of music education and teach kids how to sing and how to play instruments. I'm really not sure. I just want time to figure it all out. I am so sick of Mom trying to shove something down my throat that's not me. I didn't ask for all these stupid lessons. I know I'm lucky to have all this talent, but that doesn't mean I should have to pay such a high price for it and give up being me, does it, Darla?"

"No, May. It doesn't," I said sympathetically. "But that's not all that's bothering you, is it?"

"Not really," she moped.

"Is it what you said before? About guys not asking you out?"

"Well, they don't!" she said, looking as if she wanted to cry. "No one like Ben Davenport would ever write my name written a hundred times on a piece of paper. No way. Forget it. Maybe one of the residents here might write my name a hundred times, if he could, but not a guy my age. No way."

I was seeing a side of May that I'd barely known existed. I felt so angry with myself for not knowing how to help her. I wished it were possible to just run back inside and borrow some of Victoria's fine wisdom, as mine was sorely lacking.

"April's with Ben, you know. They've started seeing each other."

"I kinda thought so. That's really neat."

"Yeah," May said dejectedly. "Really neat."

I felt like an even bigger idiot. Obviously, April's newfound friendship with Ben was only making May feel worse about her lack of attention from the opposite sex.

"Don't get me wrong, Darla. I really am happy for April. It's just that—"

"I know, May. You don't have to explain. I understand."

I looked through the glass doors at the nursing home van, which had just pulled up to the side entrance. I watched as the attendants helped the residents out of the van and onto the sidewalk. The entire process of emptying the van seemed to take forever. Everyone moved in slow motion. I wondered what kind of outing the people had been on, if they'd had a good time, and how they could stand to come back to this place, where no one had any real privacy and where people were dying around them. One old woman in a black coat almost lost her balance on the sidewalk, but the attendants were quick to prevent her fall, as each one grabbed an elbow and held her steady. Even from a distance, I could see how much the near fall had frightened her.

The sky had grown a menacing gray since we'd arrived earlier. I looked at May, who was staring solemnly at the big evergreen trees that loomed in the distance. She didn't look as if she wanted to talk anymore. We sat there for several minutes, in silence, until I saw April pull up in Aunt Didi's car.

"She's here, May," I said, nudging her left arm.

"Okay," she said flatly. "I'm ready."

"May?"

"Yes?"

"I really love you a lot."

"Thanks, Darla," she said, attempting a smile. "I love you, too."

✳ ✳ ✳

"I'll walk you to the door," April told me when we pulled up to my house.

"You don't have to," I said, surprised.

"I really want to," April said, as she opened the driver's door and hopped out.

May, who had been sitting quietly in the front seat, turned around and smiled at me. "Thanks for everything, Darla. Happy Valentine's Day."

"Bye, May. Thanks for letting me come along. I'll see you real soon, okay? Call me if you need anything. I mean it."

I jumped out of the car, curious as to why April wanted to walk me to the door. I figured that she probably wanted to say something about May, or maybe confide in me about Ben. When we got to the front door, she pulled a big pink envelope out of her coat pocket and shoved it into my hands.

"Here, Darla. Happy Valentine's Day. I hope you didn't see me buy this for you on Sunday. I tried to do it real quick when you weren't looking. Well, take care. I'll see you later."

"Bye, April!" I called after her. "And thanks!"

I walked into the house, said a quick hello to Mom, and ran up to my room to read my cousin's card. I still couldn't believe that the Valentine she had purchased so surreptitiously was actually for me. The thought had never even crossed my mind.

Dear Darla,

You know how embarrassed I get saying things in person sometimes, so I just wanted to give you this card to let you know that you're the greatest cousin ever, and a wonderful person. I have the best time with you, and it's thanks to you for dragging me into that supermarket that Ben first noticed me, even if I did look like a wacko old woman at the time. He said it was my weird sense of humor that attracted him to me, and then he noticed my

great beauty and couldn't turn away such an unbeatable combination. Can you believe it? So I guess it's kind of obvious that we're seeing each other, and it's really thanks to you. Have a great Valentine's Day, Cuz. Here's the latest—you're the greatest.
Love, April.

I started to feel as corny and sentimental as my father, but I couldn't help but be touched as I read April's card. It had come as such a surprise, and I was starting to understand what Victoria had meant by love coming from many people, and how you should let it fill your heart. If anyone had told me the day before that I would not hear a word from Ryan, and yet in spite of that, it would be the best Valentine's Day ever, I never would've believed her in a million years. But it was.

CHAPTER 13

I began to wonder if there was a direct correlation between my family's frame of mind and the weather. Right after Valentine's Day, which turned out to be a good day for all of us, the sun started shining again, and that was followed by the melting of ice—both inside and outside our home.

My father had come home that Valentine's Day in an excellent mood, with a dozen red roses for my mother and a special Valentine's Day teddy bear for me. Actually, it was he who had given me my favorite bear, Pierre, many years ago. My father loved giving me "Teddy" bears because he'd been named after one. My paternal grandmother, Jacqueline Louisa Dale McKendrick, had named him Theodore just so she could call him Teddy Bear, as she knew from the moment he was born that he'd be just as cuddly as one.

His upbeat mood was so drastically different from that of the recent stranger who'd been lurking in our midst, that I wondered if it was actually authentic or was perhaps the result of some personality mutation that caused really depressed people to go on sudden, inexplicable "happy binges." But whatever the cause, my father was suddenly renewing his interest in photography and nature, listening to jazz recordings, reading novels, and taking Mom out to dinner on a semi-regular basis. He had somehow broken his old routine, and I wondered if it had anything to do with his recently revealed fear of having had become a "suburban bore." Jokes and silly anecdotes were now a side dish at every meal, topped with heaping spoonfuls of patriarchal mirth. Some days, I was left wishing for lighter fare—for the less frequent, smaller portions of intimacy that once defined my family life. But perhaps that was the point. Maybe, for the time being, Dad had intended for the laughter to mask our discomfort and disguise our pain. I tried not to let it bother me. After all, our house had become a home again, and that was all that really mattered.

Consequently, my father's new improved state of mind brought about similar changes in my mother. I was surprised when she met me at the back door late one February afternoon, bearing a very special gift of her own.

"Hello, Darla," she said, opening the screen door for me. "How was school?"

"It was pretty good," I said, walking in and dumping my books on the kitchen table. "I talked to my English teacher again about that internship at Merriman Papers next year. She said that as long as I keep my grades up, the job is mine. It sounds really cool. You get to work in all the different departments at the newspaper and stuff."

"And stuff what, Darla? Envelopes?"

"Get out of here, Mom," I said, opening the refrigerator door to grab a soda. "You know what I mean."

Mom laughed heartily as she took a seat at the kitchen table. She hadn't made jokes about my teenage speech habits in a long time, and only did so when she was in a very good mood. It was something my father enjoyed teasing me about as well.

"Sit down, Darla. I have a gift for you. I'm actually a little hesitant to give it to you, though."

I removed the flip-top from the top of the soda, dropped it inside the can, then took a seat. I pretended not to notice my mother cringing. (She was always so afraid I would swallow the little aluminum tab.) "Why would you be hesitant to give me a gift?" I asked curiously.

She faltered a bit. "Well, I'm not so sure it's really appropriate now, but I do think you might like to have them."

"Them?" She had my attention. "There's more than one gift?"

"Here, honey," Mom said, smiling, as she handed me an envelope. "I thought you might like to have these photographs of you and Ryan that your father took before that dreadful car accident. He finished the roll of film last week, when we were at the lake, and these pictures were on it."

"Wow! Thanks, Mom," I enthused. "I really wanted these."

I opened the envelope to look at the three photographs inside. In the first shot, Ryan's eyes were partially closed, and in the second, my smile was sort of crooked. But then I saw the third shot, an absolutely flawless snapshot of the two of us—together—as we were always meant to be. I

204

stared at the photograph for a very long time without saying anything.

"I knew you'd like that one," Mom said nostalgically. "I did too... Darla, I never really told you how sorry I am about what happened with you and Ryan. I know he meant a lot to you, honey."

"He still does," I reminded her.

"Of course," she said rather uncomfortably, straightening my school books. "At any rate, I knew you would want these."

"Well, thanks a million, Mom," I said, staring dreamily at the one photograph. "I was thinking of asking Dad about these pictures myself, but I didn't want to make things any worse than they already were. You know."

Mom paused for several seconds.

"Yes, I know...Darla, your father was very embarrassed and ashamed of himself for— "

"Drinking?" I asked, reluctantly putting the photos down.

"Yes, Darla. For drinking," Mom repeated, practically choking on the word. "It put him in a very bad frame of mind for several weeks. He wasn't aware that you had found him out, and the knowledge of that really set him back. He was ashamed and embarrassed that he hadn't practiced what he's always preached to you and feared that you had lost respect for him. Lately, he's resolved to look past that mistake, and as you can see, he's feeling much better. He should be telling you all of this, not me, but it's just too difficult for him. So I'm taking it upon myself, but I want you to know that he hasn't asked me to do so. He never would."

"I haven't lost respect for him. And I didn't mean to hurt him. It's just that he hurt me a whole lot and I wanted to hurt him back. But right after I said it, I wished I could have taken it back. I swear, Mom, I didn't plan it or anything."

"How did you find out?" she wondered aloud.

"I could smell it on him. When he came in my room after I woke up from that horrible dream."

"Oh. I was wondering...we were wondering."

I took a long, healthy swig of my soda. "So why does Dad think that he has to be so perfect all the time?"

"It's his way of staying in control, I suppose," she said.

"Well, it's stupid," I said in my wisdom. "Nobody can be perfect all the time."

"No, they can't. Nor can they always be in control."

I guzzled some more. "Mom?"

"Yes, Darla?"

"There's something I really need to know."

"And that something is—"

"How come Dad thinks drinking is the worst thing in the whole world? I mean, it was horrible what happened with Greg and all, but how come Dad hates it so much, and how come he got so depressed, just because he had a few drinks? And so angry at himself too?"

"Those are very good questions, Darla." She watched me nervously as I drank. I wish you wouldn't drink that soda so fast. It'll give you gas."

"Mom..." I moaned, taking another gulp.

I noticed she was eyeing the napkin holder and hoped she wasn't going to make those mindless paper roses again in order to avoid answering me. Thankfully, she refrained. "Good questions that deserve an answer," she said cheerfully, as if she were determined to maintain the high level of joviality that had settled so comfortably in our home.

"Yeah?" I said, hinting that she get on with it.

"Well, when your father and I were first married, he was under an awful lot of pressure for a young man in his twenties. For one, I was pregnant with you, and two, he had just started a new job that was very stressful and demanding. And then, of course, there was—"

"Rebecca," we said in unison.

"Well, yes," Mom said. She laughed awkwardly. "There was Rebecca. Anyway, back in those days, your father often had a few drinks after work to help him relax. One night, your dad and his friend Jim Penney were both drinking at the apartment we used to live in. I was working at the time, taking care of an elderly woman three nights a week, and Dad suggested to Jim that the two of them go out for a bite to eat. It was a very bad judgment call on both their parts. Jim, who was driving, had had even more to drink than your father, and on the way to the restaurant, he fell asleep at the wheel and struck another car."

"Oh my God!" I said, slamming my soda can on the table. "Was anyone hurt?"

Mom frowned as she grabbed a napkin and wiped a few drops of soda off that table that I'd spilled in the excitement. "Jim died two days later from internal injuries he had suffered, and the accident also caused a pregnant woman in the other car to lose her baby in the sixth month."

"Oh no! How awful!"

"It was more than awful," Mom lamented. "Your father blamed himself not only for having suggested the outing, but for the two deaths. He was so frightened by what had happened that he completely stopped drinking. For him, now, drinking is the worst thing in the world. Your father isn't against alcohol per se, for everyone, he's only against those who abuse it. The way he did."

"Is Dad an alcoholic?" I asked, wide-eyed.

"No, but he was a problem drinker back then who could've easily turned into one had he continued in that direction. That's what we were told by his doctor. It was your father's decision to simply never drink again, rather than to just drink responsibly. To this day, he still feels guilty about that accident. So you can imagine how he felt on New Year's Eve. Aside from everything else, it reminded him of his own terrible experience."

"Wow! That's incredible," I remarked, then took another large sip as my mother looked on disapprovingly.

Finally, everything was coming together, and for the first time I could really understand why my father had had such a fear of alcohol all these years. But there were still two nagging questions that puzzled me.

"So why didn't Dad tell me this before? It would've made everything so much clearer."

"Darla, it's not uncommon for people to avoid talking about things that they feel ashamed about. Your father is one of those people. I suppose he hoped he could get his message across without having to expose his past."

I took several more gulps of my soda, not stopping until I had polished off all twelve ounces. It was time for my second question, the one

I wanted to know most. Why, if my father was so against alcohol, which had been the driving force (no pun intended) behind both accidents, did he seek out the very evil that had brought him so much pain, as a source of comfort?

"Oh. Well, how come—" I began, crushing the empty can in my right hand.

"Why did your father go out drinking on New Year's Eve, when he despises it so?"

"Yeah, why?" I said, admiring my crushed aluminum sculpture.

"Because he was emotionally distraught, Darla, and although it sounds like alcohol would be the last thing he'd turn to, your father, out of sheer desperation, fell back on old habits. It's that simple. Luckily for us all, he came to his senses after the third drink and made it home safely. Thank God."

"Wow!" I said again, showing off my vocabulary. "Mom, are you going to tell Dad that you told me all this?"

"I'll tell him. But not tonight," she said, grabbing the can from me. "This is not a toy, Darla," she interjected. "Eventually I will tell your father everything we spoke about. Now, go upstairs, take these books with you, and finish your homework so that you can help me fix dinner later. Your father landed a big account today, and I want to cook a real fancy meal to help him celebrate. If I could just figure out what special treat to make him for dessert, I'd be set."

As Mom continued to speak, I wasn't sure if she was talking to me or to herself. "Ted really loves mocha chip fudge cake with all the trimmings...but maybe he'll be in more of an apple pie mood...à la mode, of course—but then again, he does adore a good chocolate soufflé. Of course, I could always make Mom's recipe for oven-baked rice pudding with raisins. Can't go wrong there. Decisions! Decisions! What shall I do! Yes, indeed, this will be a real fun evening!"

I gathered up my schoolbooks, and the photos of Ryan and me, and headed toward the back stairs. My mother stood there grinning at me at she put on her apron, looking nothing like the sensitive soul who had just divulged Dad's precious past to me. Within seconds, she had

208

changed from a nurturing mother deeply absorbed in the maintenance of her daughter's well-being to a vapid housewife preparing for battle in the local bake-off. Revealing my father's shame had frightened her, and she was responding to that fear by stepping back into her Betty Crocker persona. And once again, although she had dealt with my questions head-on, I still sensed that there was more to her revelation about Dad than met the eye, and that our discussion in itself was just another necessary task that she had now put to rest. I had no real reason to doubt her, but her explanations were just too pat and too perfect. But, naturally, they all made sense.

For the remainder of February, and throughout March, my life, which for quite some time had felt like a roller coaster ride through some familial house of horrors, had settled down and assumed the more mundane personality of a merry-go-round in the park. The carousel horses, analogous counterparts of my family and me, endured their daily ups and downs with ease, never once losing their pretty colors or their painted-on smiles. Round and round they went, always remaining a set distance from one another as they traveled for miles and miles without ever reaching any sort of destination.

Love, a marvel of the universe that sadly, I'd acquired a diminishing understanding of, took on vastly different meanings for those closest to my heart. For Mom and Dad, it meant the recapturing of something they hadn't felt for one another in years. It was heartwarming to watch as they tried to outdo one another with some sort of romantic gesture. How ironic that the agony and shame brought forth by the events of New Year's Eve had actually served as a catalyst in their renascent enthusiasm for a long-forgotten romance.

For Melanie, love was a game. The taunting sarcasm of her Valentine's Day poem to Jesse had brought on the much-desired results, though she would've denied to her death having done anything whatsoever to win him back. But once "won back," Melanie soon lost interest in him and his raging libido, and moved on to greener pastures, a studious, yet adorable, senior named Drew.

Even June had found a boyfriend, a tenth-grade track star named Tommy, who swore he would someday bring home the Olympic gold medal to her, if she'd only promise to wait that long.

But of all the relationships I'd been privy to know, the one I most envied was that of April and Ben's. They were two free spirits, who in their limited time together managed to forgo the usual high school dating routine for the more esoteric adventures that life had to offer. Whether they were exploring playgrounds, picnicking in rowboats, or looking under rocks for "new and unusual slimy creatures to gross each other out with," they enjoyed themselves, sharing an honesty rarely known to such young couples. While most of my girlfriends were plotting to "drive by his house and see if he's really there," or wasting valuable time calling (and hanging up on) the competition (as if that silly exercise in futility would actually eliminate their competitors' existence), April and Ben were busy deciding what mountains they would climb and what rivers they would ford.

Then there was May, who, like me, had no one in her life. I had hoped this fact would help May to see the two of us as kindred souls (thereby helping her through a difficult time), but that was not to be the case. According to May, I at least had wonderful memories, someone adorable had noticed me, and I was not some "dateless freak." May's pain and depression had come about so unexpectedly, and as the months wore on, I still had no better idea how to help her through it than I did that very first day she confided in me at the nursing home.

May was beautiful, as I had assured her countless times, but she wasn't the typical teenager. Only on very rare occasions did she come out with such phrases as "Oh my God (or Omigod)," "No way!," "Get out of here," "You know," "Gag me," "Skieve me out," or "Wow." And although it was June, the entertainer, who possessed the most obvious poise and charm during public appearances, it was May, the young lady, who truly had the greatest aplomb once the crowds had gone home and the sound of applause had faded into memory.

May spoke so eloquently, and with such maturity, that one easily forgot she was only a teenager. There was nothing matronly or boring about her, as she had once suggested in a self-deprecating moment; she was simply ahead of most teenagers (especially boys), and they knew it. Her maturity intimidated them (although she never meant it to), and I lacked the eloquence to tell her that (although I suspected she was well aware of it). I knew that someday men would fall at her feet, but at the time, it was clear that May wasn't interested in future predictions. She just wanted a date. She just wanted to "fit in," and like us all, she just wanted to be loved.

And then there was me. I thought about Ryan all the time, although the tears were fewer and farther between. Our New Year's Eve photograph, which I had since framed, sat prominently on my desk, a sad commemoration of what I had lost, or more accurately, of what I had never really had. Ryan's original letter had turned out to be his one and only attempt at communication with me, and I concluded that the harsh sentence that his father had imposed had not been nearly as painful for Ryan as I had initially thought. I also found it surprisingly easy to forgive my father for his role in the whole mess, as it became increasingly clearer to me that Dad's collusion with Peter Mullavey had little to do with the unfortunate outcome of my ill-fated romance.

I thought a lot about Victoria in those days, and about the hard lessons she had tried to teach me about true love. I wondered how she had known, in a matter of minutes, that I was "in love with love" and not with Ryan. What had I said that had given it away? How did she know when I didn't? Did everyone know? Were my cousins, and Melanie, just humoring me the entire time, laughing behind my back as they watched me struggle to revive a dying romance (if one could even call it that)? And why, if I were indeed convinced that Victoria was right and that I was not in love with Ryan, was I still mooning over a photograph of the two of us and hoping for an eventual reunion? It was an intense game of mental volleyball. One moment, I would find myself languishing in a state of mad, desperate desire, and in the next, I would be quietly suffering through the bittersweet remembrance of a once-sweet encounter, with the great hope of moving on. Surely, I thought, I must be crazy.

Eventually, I concluded that everyone needs some object of love to focus on, whether it be real or imaginary, and that loving Ryan was just my brain's way of functioning normally. But even after several hours of self-analysis and rationalization, which had brought me to such an insightful conclusion, I hated the idea of obsessing over him (which I knew was unhealthy) and vowed to stop doing so before it got out of hand. But in the end, no matter how sane or smart my logic, I simply could not forget the boy.

✳ ✳ ✳

To me, spring is the time when nature rejuvenates all of its beautiful colors. One by one the buds start blooming, and the animals prance and play as Old Man Winter hobbles away. In the air, a strange cacophony of sound floats past our ears. It is nature's band tuning up for spring—it is the blending of flora and fauna as they reacquaint themselves and say hello to old friends. And whether it really is or not, the world often feels like a happier place to those who have been saddened or discouraged by the gloom of winter.

That April, my father and I slowly began to trust each other again, and I had not only the benefit of his good humor, which had pervaded our home since late February, but the benefit of a more intimate father-daughter relationship as well. We had not yet discussed his brief re-acquaintance with alcohol, but I knew that such a discussion would come in time, and I felt no need to force the issue. As for Mom, her new romance with Dad had put joy back in her heart, and she once again felt like my mother, and not like the woman who had recited her carefully planned speeches to me, and who had moved so methodically in her efforts to protect my father, as well as herself. We were no longer carousel horses, bobbing up and down and going round, but real people, focused on each other's lives, who knew where we were going. So, aside from my lingering, nagging memories of Ryan, my home, once again, was a happy place.

The month of April was also a time for birthday celebrations. In early April, Aunt Didi, as per April's request, arranged an intimate "black tie" dinner party to celebrate April's seventeenth birthday. Ben and April, dressed in outrageous costumes and laughing themselves silly, role-played their way through the evening—pretending to be everything from duchesses and dukes to lonely old dowagers and their handsome gigolos.

In late April, the time of my sixteenth birthday, an elaborate surprise party was planned in my honor. On the day of the party, May was recruited to "keep me occupied," which she did by initiating a shopping trip and subsequent visit to the nursing home (much to Victoria's delight). It was April's job to drive us both back to my house when the time was right.

Unbeknownst to May, whose birthday wasn't for a couple of weeks, I was not the only one to be surprised. As the three of us entered my home late that Saturday afternoon, we were not only greeted by the sound of a crowd yelling "Surprise!" but by a banner proclaiming "Happy 16th Birthday, Darla and May!" Everyone I cared about (except Ryan) was there, and all of May's friends from her old private school, as well as from our mutual high school, were there as well. Naturally, I was thrilled to see all of my friends, but I was even happier to see the smile return to May's face when she saw how many loving friends, both old and new, had come to celebrate her life.

June, who had played a key role in planning the event, beamed as she saw our happy faces. On her arm was Tommy the track star, whose quirky smile and athletic build made June the envy of half the girls there. The other half envied April, as they coveted the charming and unconventional Ben Davenport, who with his pierced ear, ponytail, and patchwork jeans looked nothing like a supermarket clerk, and every bit like the lovable guy that he was.

Dad, not content to let Tommy and Ben have all the fun, charmed our friends by insisting that he'd never seen so many beautiful faces at one "shindig" before, and that surely they must be contestants for the Miss America Pageant whose bus had broken down in front of our house on the way to Atlantic City. He must have gone through four rolls of film that day, taking care to capture every face and every glorious moment.

Meanwhile, Uncle George, a shameless flirt, pretended to vie with Dad for his fair share of female attention. But he was a far more daring man than my father, and he always took matters a step further. What most of our friends didn't realize, is that Uncle George was notorious for teasing people, especially those whom he didn't know. On that particular day, I overheard him on three separate occasions ask one of our unsuspecting guests, "Who would you say is the better looking guy—me, or Mr. McKendrick here?" or very seriously he would ask, "Which one of us do you think earned his college tuition by working as a male model— me or Mr. McKendrick?" He was relentless, much to the embarrassment of April, May, and June, but nobody could argue the fact that Uncle George was the life of the party.

My mother and Aunt Didi, with help from Melanie, June, and April, had prepared a "scrump-dilly-icious" buffet dinner, but the mountain of gifts that lay waiting for May and me was almost more tempting than Mom's incredibly delectable, three-layer, thirty-two-candled birthday cake.

It was a wonderful day for me, not only because it was a gathering of the people I loved, but also because it was the proverbial cherry on a hot fudge sundae, topping off the past couple of months that had brought forth such a remarkable and welcome change in my home. And for May, whom I loved so much, it was a day that made her smile again.

Two weeks after the party, Aunt Didi dropped May off at our house for a visit, while she and Mom departed for their umpteenth shopping trip of the year. Aunt Didi, a thoroughbred clothes horse, was always trotting off to a mall for some particular outfit or accessory that she just "had to have." She was extremely discriminating about everything she wore, and even if the required item were something as commonplace as underwear, which nobody would even see, it was more usual than not for Aunt Didi to plan an all-day shopping expedition just to buy it.

Dad loved to joke and say that Mom and Didi were the victims of some Connor gene mutation that caused female siblings to shop excessively in pairs, and for no particular reason. But he understood full well that the shopping was just a way for my mother and Didi, who were without a doubt each other's best friend, to spend the day together. And it was also an excuse for Mom, who spent far too much time fussing at home, to get out into the world and enjoy a change of scenery.

I was delighted to have some time alone with May and couldn't wait to show her the photographs that Dad had taken at our birthday party. After having spent a good forty-five minutes going through them all, so that May could choose her favorite shots, we decided to walk down to the local Photorama and order reprints.

As we headed down the street, the warm sun hitting our faces, I looked over at May, hoping to see her beautiful smile that had resurfaced during the party. When she caught me looking at her, she smiled back at me, but her smile was fleeting as her eyes quickly turned toward the pavement.

I desperately wanted to talk to her, but I didn't want to burden her by asking a lot of questions or by forcing her to bare her soul to me. Remembering how Melanie and my cousins had cheered me up on several occasions by merely being light and funny, I decided that humor was the best way to drag May out of the doldrums.

"I've got the most incredible thing to show you," I bragged. "C'mon, you're gonna love this."

"What is it?" she asked curiously.

"Are you into lawn ornaments at all?"

May looked puzzled. "You mean like those lawn sheep and plastic animals and things that people stick in their front yards?"

"Exactly."

"Well," she said, as we continued walking, "I'm not personally 'into' them, but I do think they can be kind of fun to look at."

"Melanie and I love them!" I told her enthusiastically. "And every year around this time, we case the neighborhood looking for the tackiest, the most disgusting, and the most bizarre ones we can find. But actually, this is kinda early in the year. Some people wait until late May or early June to put their best stuff out. Like Mrs. Hathaway two blocks over. In about two weeks, she'll put out Snow White and the Seven Elves."

"You mean dwarfs, Darla," May corrected me.

"No, I mean elves," I said. "Remember that horrible storm we had three years ago? Well, it blew away her dwarfs, so now she uses some of her tacky Christmas decorations in their place. You should've seen what happened to Dopey!"

May burst out laughing and looked at me. "You crack me up, Darla. I don't know what it is about you, but you crack me up." She always said that to me, but I could never figure out why she found me so funny. "Listen," she said as we turned the corner, "I've got some news for you, though I feel a little funny about giving it to you. As Uncle Ted would say, 'I don't want to rub any salt into the wound.'"

"Is it about Ryan?" I asked, my love sensors already in the red zone.

"Well, yes," May said hesitantly. "April asked me to pass on some news."

"What news?" I asked excitedly, not having heard a peep from or about Ryan since his letter.

"April saw Ryan last night. When she went to pick Ben up from the supermarket. Ben and Ryan were standing outside talking when she pulled up to the front door."

I tried to be nonchalant but could not contain my excitement. "Oh my God!" I exclaimed, "as if May had revealed something vastly more interesting. "You're kidding! So what happened? Did April talk to him or what?"

"For a minute," May said.

"Did he ask for me?" I inquired, dancing ecstatically on the sidewalk.

May looked uneasy at the delirium she had unintentionally fomented. "He told April to say hello to you and asked if you were doing okay. He mentioned something about being really bummed over what happened, but he didn't go into it. But he did want you to know that he's playing with the band on the third Saturday of June, at Pier 23 at nine o'clock. But I think he's doing it behind his dad's back, so don't mention it to your parents, whatever you do."

"I won't!" I shrieked, grabbing her shoulders. "God, May, it sounds like he wants to see me again. Don't you think? I mean, why else would he tell April to tell me the exact time and date of the gig and all, if he didn't want me to come? I wish I could go, but there's just no way. Is there? Maybe I could sneak down there—nah—things are really going well with Mom and Dad and I don't want to break their trust and go through all that not-speaking-to-each-other junk all over again. No way. It was horrible. But damn, I really, really wish I could go."

"I wish you could too," May said sweetly. "I know how much it means to you."

"Yeah. It means a whole lot!" I said sulkily.

"How grotesque!" May shrieked.

I thought she was talking about my feelings for Ryan, until I realized that we had reached the house where several offending lawn ornaments lived.

"I'd love to know where to buy these things!" May said, laughing. Wouldn't it be a riot to plant a few of these in Mom's garden? She would totally freak. Like that day she saw Aunt Rebecca in the backyard. Too bad we don't really know what Rebecca looked like, or we could paint a lawn ornament to look just like her! It could be Mom's very own lawn sister!"

We both laughed hysterically at May's joke, and also at the thought of Aunt Didi finding such ornamental horrors in her beautifully manicured garden. In front of us, were eight lawn ornaments—poster children for the absurd and ridiculous. They looked a great deal like children's pinwheels, except each one had a plastic face in the center that resembled a Kewpie doll. As the breeze blew, the plastic vanes rotated gently around the faces in time with the wind.

"Aren't they creepy?" I asked.

"They sure are," May agreed, rather awestruck by the peculiar display. "Gives new meaning to the word 'kitsch.'"

"When we were here the other day, Melanie called them 'propeller heads.' That's what they look like, don't you think—just doll heads on sticks with those things rotating around them. Melanie said that the one on the end looked evil—like some spawn of the devil, and that on the next real windy day we have, it would go zooming around the neighborhood and spit in people's windows while they're sleeping. Imagine having that thing fly past your window at night! It's a bird! It's a plane! It's a doll head on a stick! It's a propeller head from the garden! I hate doll heads without bodies. They're so gross! Did you ever see that doll hospital on the corner of Clover Street? They've got porcelain doll heads in the window, all cracked and stuff, and there's like a million arms and legs strewn all over the place. Who would ever want to take their doll there to be repaired? It might come home with a different head or some other doll's legs or something. It gives me the jeebie-heebies."

"I think you mean 'heebie-jeebies,' " May said. "When I was younger, I used to think that the dolls came alive at night in those places."

"I'm still not so sure they don't! They probably grope around in the dark or something looking for their dismembered body parts. 'Hey, can anyone give me a hand? I've lost my head. I really need help. I don't have a leg to stand on.' How gross...oh, May, I wish I could go to Pier 23 and hear Ryan play. Wouldn't that be cool? I've never even heard him play before. I want to see him so much! It's not fair that I can't. I really want to see him. I really do! I wish there was some way I could."

"I understand," May said sympathetically. "If I'd had a guy like Ryan in my life, I'm sure I'd feel the exact same way."

Within seconds, the garish garden ornaments had lost their brazen appeal. And I, unfortunately, had all too quickly lost my ability to "crack May up" and to make her smile last longer than a moment. As the memories and desires for Ryan came flooding back to me, I noticed that May was already deep in her own private thoughts, and as the two of us maundered down the block, I vowed to help my cousin just as soon as I was able to help myself.

* * *

I could not get Ryan off my mind. He had come back into my heart with a vengeance. I did not want to consider the fact that he hadn't bothered to call me, nor the fact that he'd only sent word about the gig to me because he just happened to run into April. Instead, I was concentrating on the fact that Ryan had sent the message to me at all, and that in his brief conversation with April, he had made certain to give her the exact date and time of his gig. There was no way, I decided, he would ever have done that if he didn't want me to show up. And maybe, he had planned to call me himself but had run into April first. I even considered the fact that he didn't call me simply because he was embarrassed about what had happened and didn't feel he had the right to ask me for anything. But in all the months that had passed, I never considered the possibility that Ryan, in deference to his father, had agreed to steer clear of me. That was too unpleasant a possibility to even have considered.

Dad had always encouraged me to see the proverbial glass as half full, instead of half empty, and that's exactly what I was doing, although perhaps my twisted logic wasn't exactly what he'd had in mind.

I couldn't help but fantasize about sneaking down to the waterfront to Pier 23, and I imagined every glorious moment of a potential reunion with Ryan. But when I really thought about the possible consequences of such an action, and about how much it would hurt my parents, my fantasy remained just that—a fantasy. Besides, or so I thought, it would be impossible to get away with such a crime.

So when Dad broke the news to me at dinner, that he and Mom would be out of town the same weekend that Ryan would be playing at Pier 23, I thought it had to be fate—or at least fate with a very cruel sense of humor that liked to play tricks on lovesick teenagers.

"Your mother and I have decided to take a second honeymoon," Dad announced as he sliced the meatloaf. "Gosh, this looks good, Maggs."

"Well, actually, Ted, it'll be more like a first honeymoon. I certainly enjoyed our weekend in Atlantic City seventeen years ago, but it really wasn't much of a honeymoon."

"No. Especially when the water pipes burst and we had to evacuate the twenty-fifth floor."

"But thank goodness for the twenty-sixth floor," Mom said as she winked disgustingly at my father.

They both started laughing hysterically, so caught up in their private memory that they hardly noticed me.

"Your mother is right, Darla. About it not being much of a honeymoon way back when. But we're going to rectify that soon." Dad paused a bit uncomfortably and shuffled in his chair. He said something to Mom with his eyes and then looked at me.

"We'll be vacationing in New England for a week. We'll be going to Massachusetts and Vermont, and our final stop will be in Newport."

"Oh," I said, the light dawning. "You're going there."

Mom and Dad exchanged glances again. Determined not to break the good mood he'd been in for months, Dad smiled at me and continued to talk.

"Yes, Darla. We're going 'there,' to Newport, for your cousin Nadine's wedding."

I should've been grateful that my father's relationship with the Hoovers had resolved itself, despite the fact that I hated them so much, but a part of me felt angry and resentful that he'd allowed them to get away with being such despicable people and treating me like the dirt under their shoes. But at least I was not being blamed for any break in family ties, and for a brief moment, I considered the fact that my vacuous cousin had actually done me a favor by timing her precious June nuptials to coincide with Ryan's gig.

"I've arranged with Aunt Didi for you to stay at the Alexanders while we're gone," Mom said.

"I don't think that'll be a problem for Darla," Dad told Mom. He looked at me with a huge grin on his face. "I've never known you to turn down an opportunity to get together with your cousins."

"You can come here to pick up any clothing or other items you might need, but for the most part, your father and I would prefer that you spend your time there. School will be over by then, so there shouldn't be much need to come here, except maybe to water the plants. Is that understood?"

"Yeah. Okay...so I guess she couldn't stomach the thought of inviting me to her wedding too, huh?"

Mom and Dad exchanged looks again.

"Well, actually, Darla," Dad said, "it's quite the other way around.

220

You were invited to the wedding, but your mother and I knew that you wouldn't want to go, so we decided to use this time to take our second honeymoon. Were we wrong to make such an assumption? Perhaps you might like to attend the wedding."

"No way!" I retorted, appalled by the mere suggestion. "You were right. I wouldn't have wanted to go—no way, José!"

"Well, then, there's no problem. I will assume that your mother and I can trust you to take care of things while we're gone, and that you won't take advantage of our absence in any way."

I looked down at my meatloaf and noticed that Dad had given me a piece with part of the hard-boiled egg in it. I took my fork and poked at it, afraid to look directly at my father. He'd made that last comment in such a knowing, intuitive tone that I feared he was able to read my mind and knew precisely every tempting thought I'd had of going behind his back to see Ryan.

"I'm waiting for an answer, Darla. That piece of hamburger meat isn't going to answer for you, so I would prefer if you look at me and not at it."

"Yeah. Sure," I said, looking up at him.

"Yeah sure what?" Dad said, looking into my eyes.

"You can trust me."

He didn't seem convinced and continued to gaze suspiciously at me.

"I swear! You can trust me!"

"And there's to be no one in the house, except Melanie or your cousins, and even then for a short time. Agreed?"

"Yeah, fine."

"Excellent. More lima beans?"

"No, thanks. They're too chalky."

"Potatoes au gratin? They're awfully good."

"Yeah, okay. Just a few."

"And of course, Darla," Mom said, "I'll leave a complete itinerary of where we're going, and we'll call if there are any changes. But we're not leaving for several weeks, so there's no need to fuss over that now."

221

"I'm really happy to know we'll be able to trust you, Darla," Dad said, gently poking at my conscience. "This family has come a long way together lately, and trust is the glue that will keep us together."

In an odd way, I was actually happy about Dad's corny, not-so-subtle reminder for me to behave. Sneaking off to see Ryan was a real temptation, and I needed a something solid, like my father's faith in me, to keep in line. I needed something to focus on, something that was much bigger than Ryan and his band, something to help me remember why I shouldn't go and something to remind me of what I had to lose.

He was right. Trust was everything.

CHAPTER 14

In the weeks that followed, I finished the tenth grade with an impressive GPA and received the good news from my English teacher, Connie Barnes, that an after-school internship at Merriman Papers would be mine in the fall. I was proud of my achievements, but most especially of the fact that I'd gotten the prestigious internship on my own merit, and not by the likes of some pompous, patronizing pig like my Uncle Everett.

I had tried in earnest to wipe the Hoovers from my mind, but I was reminded of my intense loathing for them when my parents announced that they would be attending Nadine's long-awaited dream wedding. Secretly, however, I hoped that when they saw Everett at the wedding, one of them would tell him about my internship, proving to him once and for all that I hadn't needed his contacts in the "dog-eat-dog" world of journalism. How ironic that he had indeed treated me like a dog, one whom he expected to grovel and beg for the useless bone he had dangled before me.

But my rage was short-lived, as I had far better things to concern myself with that summer than repugnant relatives. For one, early that June, my friend Rachel's mother, Sarah Levinson, had offered me a part-time job at her family's bakery, which was only seven blocks away from my home. That, in addition to my semi-regular babysitting jobs, offered me enough money to get through the summer, with a little left over for a rainy day.

I continued to ruminate about Ryan, in the days leading up to my parents' vacation and to his gig, but I'd long given up any serious thought of sneaking off to see him. My parents were beaming with pride at my recent accomplishments, and I was enjoying the positive attention from them. I had even begun to think realistically about college and life after high school, whereas six months earlier, I had been anxious to delay my inevitable segue into adulthood. My life was falling nicely into place, and while I happily anticipated my junior year, I couldn't help but take a hiatus from such a mature way of thinking and simply look forward to the lazy pleasures of summer.

Mom and Dad left for Martha's Vineyard on a Friday night, with plans to return home a week from that Sunday. I couldn't wait to spend nine days with my cousins. We always had such a wonderful time together, and their love and friendship helped to soothe my only-child aches and pains. To me, April, May, and June were my sisters—they just lived in another house and had different parents.

In just a few short days, my extended guest status enabled me to understand even more than I already had just how different our parents really were. My parents, who were quite serious about guiding me in a positive direction, never tried to push me toward career choices that deviated from my own desires. But things were a bit different at the Alexander home. I began to see exactly what May had been talking about that day at the nursing home, when she so diligently explained to me what was involved in a show business career, and how she was not prepared, nor had any intention of preparing herself, to go that route.

But despite May's feelings, Aunt Didi had worked long and hard that winter to book the girls into a summer stock production at a theater just outside town, one known to be visited on occasion by New York producers and talent scouts. Rehearsals were to begin the last few days of June, with performances running the last week in August.

One night at dinner, while April and June were expressing their enthusiasm for the production, May respectfully pleaded with Aunt Didi to let her do "something else for a change," explaining how her absence from the production would not hurt April's or June's chances of being discovered in any way. But my aunt wouldn't hear a word May was saying. Instead, she insisted that May would have "plenty of time" to do other things and that this production might be one of the last chances the Alexander girls would ever have of performing together at such a prestigious place, since April would be leaving for school in a year.

Two days later, when it was apparent that Aunt Didi's final edict on the matter was having a devastating effect on May, I overheard April tell her mother that she also didn't see any reason why May had to be in the production if she didn't want to be. While it was obvious from the conversation that April preferred May's participation, it was also clear that April, unlike her mother, had the good sense to see how forcing the issue was hurting May. But Aunt Didi, unwilling to budge, insisted that May would be "just fine" once rehearsals started, and that April shouldn't encourage her sister to "foolishly drop out of the show."

Apparently, June agreed with her mother, because later that day, I was present when she chastised April for speaking to Aunt Didi on May's behalf. June believed that May just needed "cheering up," and she told April that she believed May might become even more depressed if left alone all summer to "sulk." But in reality, it was June's fear of losing her older sisters, and of breaking up the "act," that prompted such devout allegiance to her mother's way of thinking.

I, of course, though bursting at the seams with my own opinion, kept my mouth shut for fear of having the Alexander welcome mat pulled out from under my feet—at least by Aunt Didi and June.

And then there was Uncle George, who figured the least prominently into the girls' affairs. He often worked late at the office and so wasn't privy to the heated discussions that took place at the dinner table. When he was home, heated discussions were usually avoided.

Uncle George was fiercely devoted to his daughters' well-being, and to their bright futures, but unless something required his personal attention, he seemed content to step aside and let Aunt Didi take charge of the girls' lives. Unlike his wife, he had no burning desire to see his daughters' names emblazoned on Broadway marquees, unless, of course, it was what they really wanted. He was just concerned that they had good educations and good morals and that they never used foul language like he did.

* * *

225

Although the Levinsons' bakery was within walking distance of my house, it was not within walking distance of the Alexanders', so that Thursday, May, who now had her driver's license, picked me up from work at three o'clock.

She was unusually quiet that afternoon and barely said hello to me as I got into the car. My attempts at making conversation seemed futile, and I had an uneasy feeling in the pit of my stomach. Not knowing what to do, I asked her if she'd mind coming back to my house with me, because I wanted to talk to her about something in complete privacy. I didn't give any further explanation, and she never bothered to ask.

"Can I get you a soda?" I offered as May sat down on the couch.

"No, thanks," she said glumly.

"May?"

"Yes?" she said flatly.

"Please talk to me. I'm so worried about you. Please let me try and help."

"I don't know what you can do, Darla. My life is a mess. You can't fix it."

"Is it that summer stock production that your mother's forcing you to be in?"

"That's just part of it," she said, as if she had no desire to talk, then picked up one of Mom's needlepoint throw pillows and started hugging it for comfort. I felt completely helpless but remained determined to reach her.

"Will you tell me what else is bothering you?"

She didn't even seem to hear me.

"Please, May," I said, gently touching her right forearm, "tell me what you're thinking."

May looked straight into my eyes. "If you felt sad and lonely, Darla, would you want to get up on a stage, in front of five hundred people, and sing your heart out?"

"Well, if I got up on a stage and started singing in front of five hundred people, pretty soon I would be lonely, 'cause they'd all get up and leave."

226

May smiled weakly, but she was too depressed to laugh.

"But seriously," I continued, "the answer is no. I would hate it. I don't even like saying hello to people when I'm in a bad mood, so I sure couldn't imagine singing for them. Maybe you could talk to your mom again and get her to change her mind."

"Mom's more interested in changing her clothes," May said resentfully. "You have no idea how many times I've tried talking to her. I just don't know how to get through to her. It's like talking to a stone wall. You'd think she'd be happy that April and June want to be performers. You'd think that two out of three daughters in the business would be enough for her. But no, Mom's not happy unless everything goes exactly as she planned it. Do you remember that day in your bedroom, when April got really angry and defensive after Melanie figured out that she and Ben had a thing for one another?"

"Sure! How could I forget?"

"Well, it wasn't because April's shy, like you might think, Darla; it's because she was afraid to let anyone know about her relationship with Ben—until he insisted she bring it out in the open."

This was really getting interesting. "Why would April be afraid of anyone knowing about her and Ben? He's such a great guy!"

"Because Mom hates for us to have boyfriends. They threaten her. They threaten the act. They threaten the perfect little world she thinks she's created for us. But, of course, Mom would never admit that if you asked her." She looked ponderously toward the mantle, then at me. "You know something? I think Dad teases Ben and Tommy so much because it's his way of making the guys feel welcome. Mom only tolerates them, but you can tell she wants them to go away."

"She can't want you guys to be spinsters all your life!" I said, surprised.

"No, but if it were up to Mom, she'd want to pick the men we marry. And if it were up to Mom, none of us would have a boyfriend until we'd finished college. That's for sure."

"Maybe you could talk to your dad about this."

May looked despairingly at me. "Mom would make me feel like

227

I'd committed a mortal sin if I did that. One time June went to Daddy for permission to go somewhere, because she thought Mom would say no, and boy, was that a mess. Daddy actually gave June permission to go wherever it was, and Mom accused June of stabbing her in the back and then had a big fight with Daddy about it."

"But what about what you, April, and June want? Maybe it's time to just tell your mother that you're taking control over your own lives."

"That's easy for you to say, Darla," May corrected me. "She's only your aunt!"

"But, May," I persisted, "it's one thing if you perform in this stupid summer stock production against your will, but what about choosing a college—and a career? Are you going to go to some performing arts school just to please your mother? You'd hate that!"

May burst out crying. "No, I'm not. But I don't know what to do! I just wish I could talk to Daddy about it."

"Then do it!" I encouraged her. "Talk to him!"

"Mom'll kill me," she wept. "She doesn't want him to be a real father to us. She feels personally offended if we don't go to her for everything. Well, I'm sick of going to her. I want my father now!"

"How come he lets her do that?" I asked suspiciously.

"I don't know," May said wearily, her tears subsiding. "It's like she's blackmailing him or something. Every time he intervenes she gives him the evil eye, and then he skulks off into a corner somewhere and starts mumbling curse words."

"Wow!" I said, lost for a more appropriate response. "That's weird."

May clutched the pillow to her stomach as she began rocking back and forth. She was in extreme agony, and once again, I hated myself for not knowing how to help her.

"May, I hate to see you so unhappy. I want you to have a good time again, like you did at our birthday party a few weeks ago."

"I didn't have a good time at that party!" she blurted out. "I just pretended I did! I'm a professional actress, remember?"

I was stunned, not to mention a bit hurt. I looked at her in sheer bewilderment. She stared back at me defiantly, and then, as if she'd had a change of heart, lowered her head in shame.

"I'm sorry, Darla. I didn't mean to hurt your feelings." She paused and grabbed a tissue from the coffee table to wipe her eyes. "But I still didn't have a good time."

"But all your friends were there!" I protested. "All seven million of them. You were laughing and smiling the whole time. I don't understand how you couldn't have had a good time. I mean, it's impossible!"

May smiled sweetly at my naiveté. "But I didn't, Darla. I faked it so I wouldn't hurt everyone's feelings. I've been taught to fake smiling since I was a little girl, back when Mom used to enter us in those dreadful beauty pageants and talent shows. We've all been taught to smile on cue. It's our legacy from our mother."

"How come you had such a terrible time at the party?" I asked, still reeling from her revelation.

"Because Darla, the whole evening was humiliating from beginning to end."

"It was?" I said, baffled. "How come? I wasn't humiliated. Should I have been? Oh God, May, I hope I didn't make a fool of myself by having a good time."

"Darla," May said, shaking her head lovingly at me, as if I were too dumb to get it. "There was nothing for you to be humiliated about."

"So what was so humiliating for you, then?"

May started crying again. "Think about it, Darla. Think about April and Ben, and then about June and Tommy."

"Yeah? I'm thinking about them. So?"

"Now think about me, May, the Alexander sister that guys never look at 'cause I remind them of their mothers—maybe even their grandmothers!"

"That's ridiculous, May."

"There I am, at my sixteenth birthday party, and both of my sisters have boyfriends by their sides, but meanwhile, it's my party and I've barely been asked out on a date in my entire life! Don't you find that humiliating? How do you think that made me feel in front of my friends from the academy, my old school? Like a complete failure! Like an idiot! Like the ugliest girl in the world! I felt stupid enough being at April's dinner party without a date, but at least that was her party and the whole world wasn't there. But at my own party? I wish it hadn't been a surprise party. Then maybe I could've paid some guy to be with me, and to pretend that he found me halfway attractive!"

By this time, May was absolutely hysterical and out of control. I sat down next to her on the couch and held her for a very long time, while she sobbed and sobbed and sobbed. Finally, after about ten minutes, she stopped crying and looked at me apologetically. Even in her misery, she was worried about my feelings.

"I'm sorry, Darla. You didn't ask me to come over to your house just to watch my imitation of Niagara Falls. I didn't mean to burden you."

"You didn't burden me! And I asked you to come here so we could talk about what was bothering you. I'm just glad you felt you could be open with me."

"Yeah. I know. But I still feel bad dragging you down with me."

"You're not dragging me down. How many times have I cried on your shoulder? A million probably. You're so beautiful, May. I know you don't believe me, but you would never have to pay any guy to be with you. Don't even think that! In fact, I think you're even prettier than April or June."

"No, you don't. You just said that because you pity me."

"Pity you? Are you kidding? I've admired you my whole life, May. I've always wanted to be like you."

"No way, Darla."

"I mean it. I swear! You're gorgeous, and you have so much class. You always know how to talk to people, and you don't say stupid things the way I do."

"Well, I'm sure you'll change your mind about that after today."

"No, I won't. I admire you even more, seeing what you've had to go through and stuff. I used to think I was the one with all the parent problems, and that you guys just sat around and had fun all day."

"The grass is always greener, Darla. Believe me."

"God, May," I said and laughed, trying to cheer her up. "You sound like my father! But really, I do admire you—so much!"

"Thank you for the compliment," she said, drying her eyes. "I admire you too, and I think you handle yourself just fine."

"Like on Thanksgiving? When I screamed at those stupid Hoovers? You wouldn't have done that!"

"No," May replied. "I would've sat there like a lump and let them insult me. I wish I had your guts, Darla. You're honest, and you're not afraid to speak your mind. That's what I admire most about you."

I was stunned. My honesty had gotten me into trouble so many times during the past year, that it was the last thing I expected someone to admire about me.

"I don't think my parents would agree with you on that one."

"You never know." May smiled. "They're both so proud of you. I know it."

"May...I hate to bring up our party again, but you gotta remember, I didn't have a date either, and even though I really missed Ryan, I didn't feel humiliated or anything, just because April and June had dates."

"I know, Darla. But people don't compare you to your cousins, the way they compare me to my sisters. I stuck out like a sore thumb. And besides, everyone knows you had a boyfriend. That makes all the difference in the world."

I was immediately sorry I'd brought up the subject again.

"Speaking of my 'ex-boyfriend,' " I told her, choking on the word "ex," "Ryan's gig is on Saturday. Just a little more than forty-eight hours away!"

"I know," May said sympathetically. "I was thinking about it this morning. It's so weird that Nadine's wedding is on the same day, isn't it? Gee, I don't think I've seen Nadine since I was eight years old."

"Well, don't complain about it," I teased her. "Just be thankful you're not related to her. Now, she's one cousin I don't admire! I hope she has a horrible hair day on Saturday. I hope her overpermed hair splits into a thousand different directions and she looks like a tumbleweed head, and I hope it rains all over Rhode Island. I hope she flushes her engagement ring down the toilet by mistake. I hope the fingernail on her ring finger breaks right before the ceremony, and that all her other nails break at the reception and fall into the wedding cake. I hope she falls into the wedding cake! I hope all the Hoovers fall into the wedding cake! I hope that Nadine finds out that Ethan's been lying about his last name and that it's really 'Doofball.' Don't you think that's a nice name, Nadine Doofball? A June bride named Nadine Doofball. How lovely!"

The color started returning to May's cheeks, and I knew she was not faking the smile that began to form on her lips.

"You crack me up, Darla."

"And I hope Uncle Everett bores everyone at the reception, all three hundred of them, and that they all go home early just to get away from him. I hope his rented tuxedo pants split in the back while he's dancing. I hope Aunt Louisa's cheek caves in from tapping it so much, and I hope Nadine gets her period right in the middle of taking her vows!"

"Darla, you're terrible!" May laughed.

"I can't help myself! I just hate her so much. She thinks she's better than me. She always has. I wish you could've heard the way she spoke to me—the way they all spoke to me."

"They sound awful," May said. "I'm surprised you managed to stay calm for as long as you did. I've never liked people like that, who think they're so superior to everyone else. And believe me, being in show business, I've met a lot of them."

"Nadine's always had to have the best of everything," I snickered, "probably since the day she was born."

"Was she born with a silver spoon in her mouth?"

"I don't know about any spoon in her mouth. But she sure speaks with a forked tongue!"

May laughed.

"Honestly, I don't know what kind of spoon she was born sucking. I mean, the Hoovers aren't millionaires, but I guess they've saved every last cent for their precious Nadine. She's been spoiled rotten her entire life. Whatever Nadine's ever wanted, she's gotten. Mom told me that she's worn designer clothes since she was three, and that Aunt Louisa used to hire an interior decorator to redo Nadine's bedroom every couple of years—whenever she got sick of her wallpaper, I guess. Can you believe it? 'Oh Mumsie, dear, I say, that floral pattern is beginning to grate on my nerves. How about you and Dadsie popping for some stripes? Get the decorator in here, will you? Be quick about it, Mumsie, or I might have a palpitation or two!' Sheesh, what a priss!"

"You're crazy, Darla!"

"And get this," I told her, "for her sixteenth birthday party, Uncle Everett bought her a brand-new car, and then threw her this incredible party. The invitation was printed on parchment paper, you know, the stuff that looks real old but isn't, and her parents rented out some historic castle for the afternoon. If you ask me, they should've found the dungeon and left Miss Priss there to rot. Anyway, Dad said that 'the whole shindig must've set Everett back a pretty penny.' I can't even imagine what they're spending on her wedding, especially since she's marrying some rich guy whose mother has fine lines or something. Mom didn't show me Nadine's wedding invitation, because she knows how much I hate that vacuum head, but it's probably dripping in eighteen-carat gold or something equally as disgusting. You wanna bet?"

"Do you know where it is?" May asked. "I'd love to see it!"

"Me too," I said mischievously. "I guess it's gotta be in the second drawer of Mom's desk. That's where she keeps all her invitations and important papers and stuff."

"Go get it," May encouraged me. "Let's take a look."

I ran over to Mom's mahogany writing desk, which was in the far corner of the living room, and began carefully sifting through her papers so as to not leave any evidence behind that I'd been snooping. It was only a matter of seconds before I found the invitation, and I rushed back to May's side so that we could examine the contents of the pale pink envelope together.

May looked intently at the calligraphy on the envelope. "What do you think it cost to have someone address all these invitations?"

"Big bucks, I'm sure. Let's look at the invitation and see if it's printed in gold."

"Hurry up, Darla. I'm dying of curiosity."

I reached into the envelope, but there was no matching invitation to be found.

"Damn. It's not here," I grumbled.

"Darn!" said May, disappointed. "You know, they probably took it with them because it had all the pertinent information on it, like the time and place of the wedding. We should've thought of that."

"Yeah, you're right. Wait! What's this?"

Inside the large pink envelope was a much smaller white envelope. Curiously, I pulled it out and turned it over and saw that my name was written on the front of it.

"What the hell is this?" I said, reeling back in horror at the sight of "Darla" written in Nadine's perfect handwriting.

May and I looked at each other in shock, as if we'd just come across buried treasure and didn't have a clue as to what to do with it. A note from Nadine was the dead last thing I expected to find, and I couldn't begin to imagine what it might say.

"I guess you should open it," May said skeptically.

"Yeah, I guess you're right," I told her. "Besides, if I hold it any longer I'll have Nadine's cooties all over my hands."

May burst out laughing and watched me with fascination as I opened, and then read, the note.

"Well?" she said eagerly, after I'd had ample time to read and reread it. "What does it say?"

I was too shocked and upset to answer her. My entire body began to tense up with rage, and it wasn't long before tears of anger began rolling down my cheeks.

"May I see the letter, Darla?"

I didn't answer her.

"Darla! Are you all right?"

"She betrayed me, May! I just can't believe she would do this! I trusted her! This is unbelievable! God, I hate her!"

"Who?" May asked anxiously. "Nadine?"

"No! My mother! I hate her and Nadine!"

May couldn't believe her ears and took the note to see for herself. It read:

Dearest Darla,

After such a disastrous Thanksgiving at your house, I never imagined that I would be writing this note to you and personally requesting that you attend my wedding. But life is filled with surprises, my dear cousin, just like the surprise attack that you launched on my parents and myself this past November when we were guests in your home.

So I'm sure you can understand why, after such a distasteful incident, I could not have imagined you to have the intestinal fortitude it takes to apologize for such a childish wrong. Therefore, I was truly touched and truly surprised when my family received your sincere letter of apology last December. Although you didn't come out and say it, my parents and I are well aware of the green-eyed monster in you, and it's never been a secret to any of us that you've always been a bit jealous of the luxuries life has bestowed on me, and most of all, of the gifts that God has given me. Having this knowledge, and being a mature, educated woman of the world, how could I not allow you a foible or two as you travel down the rocky road of life? And so, I come full circle to what my sweet mother has always taught me, "To err is human, but to forgive is divine." I forgive you, Darla, we forgive you, and we all hope that you will come to Newport in June and share in my happiness.

With love, your cousin Nadine.

May looked at me in horror. "Darla, tell me this letter doesn't mean what I think it means!"

"It means my mother betrayed me!" I said furiously, grabbing the letter back from her and looking at it again.

"I thought you told me at Christmas that your parents had decided against forcing you to write an apology. I thought they told you it 'wasn't necessary' or something like that."

"Well, they didn't force me to write it, did they?" I told her, boiling with rage. "Mom just wrote it for me! Wasn't that kind of her?"

235

"Wow!" May said, consoling me. "This is such a terrible betrayal! I can't believe that Aunt Maggie would write an apology letter and sign your name! What in the world would possess her to do that?"

"Her obsession with pleasing Dad, I guess. Remember I told you how upset he was about what happened at Thanksgiving, and how he was so afraid that he'd never see that prissy cheek-tapping sister of his again?"

"I remember."

"So I assume that Mom, who's never happy unless Dad's happy, decided to forge my name to some phony apology letter and make everything 'hunky-dory' again. At my expense, obviously."

"How completely manipulative!" May said vehemently. "I never thought Aunt Maggie did things like that. This sounds more like something my mother would do!"

"Mom and Aunt Didi aren't as different as you think they are. They just do their controlling in different ways. Your mother has a big mouth and bosses people around to their face, and my mother acts real helpless and weak and tricks you into thinking she's giving in. Then, when you're not paying attention, she stabs you—wham—right in the back. And then, while the blood is gushing out of your body, she twists the knife, just for good luck!"

"Really?" May gasped.

"Doesn't this prove it?" I asked, waving Nadine's note in the air.

"It sure does," she agreed.

"God!" I screamed. "What the hell do you think my mother said to her? Can you believe that all this time, those slimy Hoovers thought I had apologized to them? Well, not for long they won't be thinking it. I'll see to that! And how can Mom and Dad have the nerve to make such a big deal out of being able to trust me, when I can't trust them? Dad must've been in on this too, you know. They've both deceived me! And here I am, trying to be Little Miss Perfect to please them! And for what? God knows how many other times they've done something horrible like this!"

"Well," May concluded, "when you think about it, I suppose it does make sense that your mother would do something like this. After all, she spends enough time with my mother to have learned her manipulating from the best. They both make me so angry I could scream!"

"Me too!" I said, as the tears continued to roll down my cheeks.

"Darla?"

"Yeah?"

"Let's stop letting our mothers manipulate us. And let's do what we want for a change!"

"Like what?" I asked, intrigued by yet another side of May I'd never known.

"Let's go to Pier 23 on Saturday night and see Ryan."

"Oh my God, May! Are you kidding?"

"Do I look like I'm kidding?"

"You've got to be kidding!"

"I'm serious, Darla. Let's go to the waterfront and have some fun!"

"We'll never get away with it."

"Why not? I'm sure we can come up with a good cover. Come on! You want to see Ryan, don't you?"

"May, I want to see him more than anything! You know that."

"Then what's stopping you?"

"I don't know. I guess the promise I made to Dad before they left. When I swore he could trust me and stuff."

"Like you could trust them?" May baited me.

"Yeah, right! Why should I stick to my word when they don't stick to theirs? When they betray me and lie to my face!"

"No reason I can think of," May said passionately. "None at all."

It was hard to believe that I was talking to May. She had always been so mature and so well behaved, that I had mistakenly perceived her as someone who would pass right through adolescence without so much as a scraped knee or a rebellious moment. She was the very last person in the entire world that I ever would've expected to coax me into disobeying my parents—much less by going to a place as wild as a waterfront club.

"How come you want to go so bad?" I asked curiously.

"Because I just do!" she said defiantly. "I want to go somewhere without April and June. I want to be someone different than boring May Lynne Alexander, dateless freak. I want to do something, just for once in my life, that my mother didn't arrange and knows nothing about. And I want to help my cousin do something that's really important to her. Aren't those good enough reasons for you, Darla?"

"Yeah, May, sure. It's just that—"

"It's just that you've never seen me like this and you think I've completely lost it, right?"

"No..."

"I'm fine, Darla. I really am. I just want to start being me. Okay?"

"Okay, May."

"Then we're on for Saturday night, right?"

"Sure! God, May, what'll I wear?"

CHAPTER 15

It didn't take us long to set the wheels in motion for our outing to Pier 23. The following day, Melanie, who sympathized with our respective humiliations at the hands of our mothers, readily agreed to serve as our alibi for Saturday night. It was simple: May and I would tell Aunt Didi that we'd been invited out for pizza and a movie with Melanie and her boyfriend, Drew. It was perfect timing, Melanie said, because she and Drew really would be out for the evening, and there was no place for Aunt Didi to call and check on us, even if she wanted to.

Melanie did warn us, however, that even if our cover fooled Aunt Didi and Uncle George, there was still the problem of our getting into Pier 23, being only sixteen years old and way below the legal drinking age. There was bound to be some "hulking ape" at the door who checked ID, and when he "grunted his request," we had better be prepared "to show him our stuff" or to "flirt our way" inside.

May couldn't help but point out the irony in Melanie's warning, since she believed that looking and acting older than her years is what had caused a good deal of her problems in the first place. But all we needed, according to Melanie, was "a lot of makeup and a little attitude," and we could slip unnoticed into any place we wanted.

Everything I had learned from Victoria about love and infatuation went right out the window. I could barely contain my enthusiasm for seeing Ryan again and fantasized about every possible reunion scenario imaginable. My favorite, however, was one in which Ryan, from behind his set of drums on the stage, noticed my face in the crowd. For a moment, he would blink, wondering if it could possibly be me, seeing that I looked so much older—and so incredibly alluring. His eyes would remain fixated on me, and mine on him. Finally, after what seemed an eternity, the band would take a break and we would run, mad with anticipation, into each other's waiting arms. In fact, we would be just like the slow-motion lovers in my favorite television commercial, except we'd have to make due with a rock club instead of a lonely beach as the site for our fantastic reunion.

But as much as that implausible scenario delighted me, I started feeling extremely anxious about the whole plan of action. Still troubled by the events of New Year's Eve, I reminded myself that Pier 23 had been one of Greg Cheyney's favorite haunts (and maybe still was!) and that my father's descriptions of the waterfront element might be a lot more accurate than I had wanted to believe. I considered backing out at the last moment, but since the outing was being planned for my benefit, I didn't dare tell May or Melanie that I had reservations about going, and about defying my parents. It would be far too embarrassing, especially when they'd both gone so out of their way to help me.

To intensify my confusion, one of Dad's many worn clichés, "Two wrongs don't make a right," kept echoing in my mind, reminding me that I had no good reason to do what I planned to do. But armed with some tired clichés of my own, such as "One good turn deserves another," I ordered my brain to cease and desist any further thought of obeying my duplicitous parents.

So it was arranged. May and I would leave the Alexander home around five o'clock on Saturday, go to my house to get dressed, have a little dinner, and then head down to the waterfront around nine-thirty that evening—in Aunt Didi's car.

I had a miserable night's sleep that Friday, and my nervousness and agitation were clearly reflected in the series of dreams that I had, all of which were about Ryan, May, and my parents. The dreams were far more realistic than the usual nighttime apparitions that often visited me, and each one depicted a different version of my anticipated reunion with Ryan, and of my subsequent "murder" at the hands of my father.

By the time I woke up the next morning, I was completely exhausted and felt a strong sense of foreboding that warned me to change my mind before it was too late. But the warning to stay away was incongruous with my heart, which wanted to go. With minimal effort, I convinced myself that it was not uncommon to be influenced by one's dreams, and that any evil portent tugging at my sleeve was surely just a result of that.

After a shower and long walk in the bright June sunshine, I felt much better, and by the time May and I got to my house at five thirty, armed with beauty aids to enhance (and age) our "natural beauty," I felt nothing but excitement as I looked ahead to the evening.

By nine o'clock, our makeovers were completed. May, whose shoulder-length blond hair was normally pulled back in an ordinary ponytail, suddenly looked nothing like the conservative teenager that she was, and everything like some superstar model who'd just flown in from Milan or Paris for the weekend. I was amazed at the dexterity and speed with which she set her hair with electric curlers, and blown away when she teased her hair to look just like the model's style on the cover of Cosmopolitan. By the time she had finished applying her makeup, even May, in her slinky black dress and wild hair, had to admit that she truly was gorgeous, and there was absolutely no question in either of our minds that she could easily pass for an adult.

I, on the other hand, had been quite worried that I wouldn't be able to duplicate the feat, but by the time May had finished with my makeover, we both agreed that I also looked older than sixteen. My chestnut brown hair, which I always wore down, was slicked back in some "high-fashion ponytail" that May had seen in Vogue, and my makeup was severe enough, without being "too much," that I was easily able to defy my card-carrying membership in the teenage kingdom.

Getting into Pier 23 was a breeze. The bouncer, whom Melanie had so eloquently predicted to be a "hulking ape," seemed more interested in showing off his biceps than in checking identification at the door. While he flexed and flaunted his muscles to a small audience of appreciative young women, May and I confidently walked through the front door as if we'd done so a thousand times before.

Once inside, however, our confidence began to wane as we looked around the enormous room and wondered where to go next. Ahead of us to the left was a giant horseshoe-shaped bar that extended almost the entire length of the room. To the right of the bar, at the very front of the room, was the stage. Even from a distance, I could see the pilings and the heavy rope that had been used to transform the stage into a "pier." In front of the stage was a dance floor, and behind the dance floor, closer to where we were standing, was a cluster of tables, where food and drink were being served.

"What do we do now?" I said to May.

"I don't know. Do you want to get a table?"

"I don't think so," I told her, raising my voice so that she could hear me over the loud music. "The tables are all a million miles from Ryan, and besides, the people on the dance floor are blocking the view of the band."

"You're right," May said loudly, directly into my ear. "You can't really see the band at all from these tables. But geez, you sure can hear them! Well, I suppose we should just walk up to the front of the bar and stand around, since I doubt we'll be able to get a seat. That's about as close as we're going to get to Ryan. Unless, of course, you want to sit on the stage with him. Maybe you could dangle your feet off the pier."

"Very funny," I shouted.

"All right then," May said, trying to conceal her nervousness. "Let's go."

As we walked along the right side of the bar, toward the front of the room, I began to feel more and more sick to my stomach with each passing step. Pier 23, a rowdy, raucous rock club for the twenty-something set, was a long way from the elegance and sophistication of The Captain's Table, which was just a few doors down.

As we walked the length of the bar, I could sense that people were staring curiously at us. As "gorgeous" as we looked, we were inappropriately dressed among the T-shirts and torn jeans, and I couldn't help but notice that many of the club patrons had tattoos, pierced noses, or hair color that had obviously not come from Mother Nature's palette. How ironic that May and I had worked so hard to fit in, only to be more out of place than we'd ever been. When we reached the front of the bar, there was no

242

place else to go, so we stood there anxiously, trying to pretend that we felt at home in the smoky surroundings.

Neither May nor I had any inclination to drink alcohol, but I desperately wanted a soda to hold, just to give me something to do. I hadn't yet mustered up the courage to look at the band, but even a peripheral glance in their direction told me that my fantasy, the one involving fixated eyes and passionate glances, was not only ludicrous, but physically impossible. Ryan was much farther away than I'd imagined, and from where he sat behind the drums, there was little chance of him locking eyes with anyone, except a scraggly-haired keyboard player wearing a spiked dog collar, and I doubted he was very interested in doing that.

Just as I was about to scream over the escalating decibel level to ask May how we should go about putting in an order, a good-looking guy in his late twenties appeared out of nowhere and offered to buy us drinks. He was impeccably dressed, and although he reeked of expensive cologne, I sensed that he was very much at home with the regulars who frequented Pier 23. There was a dangerous twinkle in his eyes when he smiled, one that warned those paying attention to run, not walk, in the opposite direction. But it was that same smile that made it hard not to feel an attraction for him or, as Melanie would've put it, "wild animal magnetism." In spite of his penetrating eyes and streetwise stance, he seemed genuinely kind, especially after he booted two of his buddies off their bar stools so that May and I could sit down. I'd felt uncomfortable standing in the boisterous crowd, dressed in my suburban finery, so I was very grateful that he'd come along and given us a place to hide. With three-quarters of myself now covered by the bar, I was able to breathe a sigh of relief as the churning in my stomach subsided.

Soon after we'd taken our seats, side by side at the bar, our newfound host stood next to May and introduced himself to us as Hatch. It was definitely an unusual name, and although under normal circumstances I would've asked about its origin, I wasn't about to scream over May just to make small talk. Besides, from the way he was staring at her, it was quite evident that I wasn't the one he wanted to talk to. That was fine with me.

243

I had a safe place to wait for Ryan, and from the look on May's face, she seemed positively enthralled that such a handsome guy was practically falling all over her.

Hatch never said another word to me after introducing himself, nor did he acknowledge my presence again. Instead, he stood on the opposite side of May in such a way that she was forced to turn her back on me in order to speak to him. I didn't mind being left out of their conversation, but as time wore on I began to feel rather uncomfortable about Hatch himself. There was something disturbing to me about the way he looked at May, and eventually I realized that his cocky grimace bore an uncanny resemblance to the leer that Uncle Martin had given Melanie when he first feasted his ogling eyes on her in our dining room. But Hatch was so good looking that it had taken a while longer to notice the seamier side of his smile.

The more I watched him, the more uncomfortable I became, especially since I could not see May's face or gauge her reaction to him. While I was staring off into space, wondering what, if anything, I could do, I noticed a very sweet-looking guy on the opposite side of the bar, who was looking very intently at me. The curious part of it all was that he looked at me as if he knew me. That was impossible, I determined, since he didn't look remotely familiar, and I was sure I would've remembered meeting such a cute guy—especially one with dark curly hair and such kind eyes. It was amazing, but I really could see the goodness in his eyes, even from several feet away and even through his round gold-rimmed glasses. I guessed him to be about twenty-one or twenty-two. Oddly, he looked to be more a fish out of water than I did, and I could tell from his facial expressions that the loud music was hurting his ears. Naturally, I wondered why he continued to sit there and torture himself with sounds so obviously unpleasant to him. The popcorn he was munching on couldn't be that tasty. Actually, I wasn't enjoying the loud music either, but at least I had a very good reason for listening to it.

Then, from the corner of my eye, I noticed someone else staring at me, a young woman, who was sitting about two feet away from him, also on the opposite side of the bar. At this point, I began to question my sanity, wondering why I had suddenly acquired this bizarre sense of déjà vu, or more accurately, a case of paranoia in which I thought total strangers knew me. Perhaps, I consoled myself, it was a temporary case of nerves.

Whatever the reason, I was quite sure that I didn't know this woman either, only there was something oddly familiar about her that I couldn't quite put my finger on. She also appeared to be in her early twenties, and unlike the cute guy, she seemed very much at home in her raucous surroundings. She kept lighting one cigarette after another and had the oddest habit of continually touching her head, as if she were self-conscious of her very short hairstyle. It was clear from the way she swayed her body to and fro, as she sung along with the lead guitarist, that she was wild about the band.

For several minutes, my gaze went back and forth between these two people, until a third person caught my eye. I guessed her to be about eighteen or nineteen. She had wavy blond hair and seemed to know everyone in the place. Unlike the other two, however, she didn't even glance in my direction. I was sure I had seen her before, but once again, I had no idea where.

I followed her with my eyes as she walked around the end of the bar and over to the dance floor, which was closer to where I was sitting. As I swung around on the bar stool to look at her, I noticed her very shapely legs and short skirt. This was a first for me, as I'd never recognized anyone by the shape of their legs before, but I instantly flashed back to the Halloween party, when I first saw a "bag of groceries" with very shapely legs talking to Ryan. It was her. Lisa. Ryan's ex-girlfriend. He had mentioned then that she had connections at Pier 23, so naturally, she'd be here at his premier engagement. Boy, was I stupid! They were back together again. No wonder I hadn't heard from him. What a moron I was!

I desperately wanted to discuss this revelation with May, and suggest that we leave before I made a total fool of myself, but Hatch had monopolized her so completely, that I was literally afraid of what he might do if I tried to speak to my own cousin. And, of course, there was a part of me that wanted to stay, no matter what, and take my chances at reuniting with Ryan. So I said nothing to May and continued to watch Lisa prance around the dance floor until everyone had noticed her cute little outfit and her oh-so-petite body. I hated her.

After dancing two long numbers, Lisa walked across the dance floor toward the band and continued on until she arrived at the left side of the stage, where she could see Ryan and blow him a kiss. I felt my blood boil as I seethed with rage over this girl who was going to single-handedly destroy everything I'd dreamed of for so many months.

I looked at May again, hoping she'd be momentarily distracted and I could get a chance to talk to her, but no such luck. Hatch had engaged her in intense conversation, and although I couldn't hear a word of what he was saying, I knew from the look in his eyes that he was putting on an act, and that his intentions toward her were anything but honorable. Being able to see nothing but the back of May's head, I wondered if she was as worried about that as I was. I simply had no idea.

An hour had passed since we'd arrived, and although I wasn't counting, I couldn't help but notice that Hatch was a very heavy drinker. I wondered again about his name, and whether it had evolved from such activity, as in "down the hatch," but I was so concerned about May, and so anxious about Ryan, that I quickly forgot about it. Moments later, the lead guitarist announced that the band was going on break, and for the first time since we had sat down, May turned around and smiled at me.

"I guess this is the moment you've been waiting for!" she said, squeezing my right hand for good luck.

I looked briefly at Hatch, and I could see he was annoyed that May had taken even a momentary hiatus from their conversation.

"Yeah," I whispered to her. "But his ex-girlfriend is here, Lisa, and I have a sickening suspicion that we've changed places and she's not so 'ex' anymore—and that I am!"

"Oh no! Gee, Darla, I hope that's not the case. But maybe you're just jumping to conclusions. They could just be friends, you know."

"Yeah, right," I said bitterly. "That's why she blew him a kiss while he was playing. 'Cause they're good buddies."

May frowned sympathetically. "Well, just wait and see. Okay?"

"May," I said, hoping to detain her a moment or two longer before she turned around again, "are you feeling okay about this guy?"

Hatch must've sensed that I was talking about him, because he gave me a piercing look, one that warned me to keep my mouth shut.

"Sure," she said unconvincingly. "He's okay."

"What do you mean by 'okay'?" I asked, taking pains not to look in his direction again.

"Well, I'm not interested in him that way, Darla, if that's what you're thinking. He's too slick for me, and he brags a lot. But he's kind of interesting. He runs his own business. He's sort of like an agent, and he books bands and different acts into clubs. He said he might be able to help April and June get some bookings. Me too, if I want them."

"I don't know, May," I said uneasily. "Something's not right about him."

She smiled as if to reassure me. "Don't worry, Darla. I'm not planning on taking him up on any offers. If anyone knows how I feel about performing right now, it's you. It's just kind of interesting to hear what he's saying. And he does think I'm beautiful, unlike the guys at school, so that's got to count for something, doesn't it?"

"Trust me, May, if the guys at school saw you looking like this, they'd be all over you too. I swear. Just be careful."

"I'm fine," she said confidently. "You worry too much."

I noticed out of the corner of my eye that Hatch was no longer standing behind May, but I didn't bother to point it out to her.

"May, listen," I said imploringly. " I can't get rid of this bad feeling. I mean, I thought he was real cute and stuff at first, when he got us these seats and all, but now he kinda gives me the creeps. And don't you think he drinks too much?"

"Geez, Darla, May said, her eyes widening. "You sound just like your dad."

"I know I do. But still...just be careful, okay?"

She was right. I did sound like my father, and I wasn't quite sure how I'd gotten to that point, but suddenly, the things he had warned me about were making a lot of sense. And as Victoria had explained to me during our last visit, it was much easier to have good instincts and clear vision when you were on the outside looking in. My "good instincts" may have been sorely lacking where Ryan was concerned, but I had no problem whatsoever in seeing that Hatch was bad news.

Just as I was about to plead with her one more time to be careful, I saw Hatch approaching us with a bewildered Ryan at his side.

"Oh, God!" I choked. "He's got Ryan with him."

Hatch walked right over to me and sharply said, "Isn't this who you came here to see?"

Ryan's bewildered look turned to shock as he finally recognized my face under all the makeup, and Hatch instantly seized the opportunity to divert May's attention back to him. I was learning fast, and there was no doubt in my mind that Hatch had located Ryan not for my pleasure, but solely for his own devious purposes.

"Darla!" Ryan said, as if I were the last person he ever expected to see. "What in the world are you doing here?"

Before I could answer, he reached over and gave me a perfunctory kiss on the cheek, which, sadly, I was grateful for.

"You look great, Darla. It's just that...well, I'm just really surprised to see you. How did you know I was here?"

I felt very hurt that he'd even asked the question. Obviously, he hadn't been crossing his fingers and praying that I would show up, as I had hoped would be the case, but at the very least, I would've expected him to remember talking to April.

"April gave me your message," I reluctantly explained.

"What message?" he asked, looking completely bewildered.

I was humiliated. "The message that you were playing here tonight. Remember? You told April to tell me about your gig here—the night you ran into her at the supermarket, when she was picking Ben up from work?" I was desperate for any glimmer of recognition he might give me.

"Oh, right," he said, remembering. "That was a hundred years ago. Gee, I was just making conversation. I never really thought you'd show up here!"

I was at a loss for words. I was sure I was going to start crying and make a complete fool of myself. But Ryan, proving he had a modicum of sensitivity after all, noticed the hurt look on my face and made a somewhat gallant attempt to soothe my ruffled feathers.

"But I'm really glad you did come," he said in the nick of time. "I hope you didn't take what I just said the wrong way. It's just that I never imagined you'd be able to sneak past your parents and get down here. You know what I mean. How did you guys get in, anyway?"

"It was easy," I told him. "The guy at the door was too busy flirting to even notice us."

"Didn't the bartender double-check your ID?"

"No," I said naively. "But I'm only drinking soda."

"Yeah, Darla, but they usually do anyway. You're supposed to be twenty-one to even sit at the bar."

I shrugged my shoulders. "I dunno. That Hatch guy ordered our drinks, and the bartender just gave them to us."

Ryan looked nervously at Hatch, then back at me.

"Oh...Darla, tell your friend to be careful of that guy."

"She's not just my friend, Ryan. She's my cousin. That's May."

"No way!" Ryan said, twisting his neck around to take a second look. "That's May Alexander? She looks so different! Wow! She's hot! Well, anyway, Darla, if you think Greg was bad, this guy's a lot worse. Greg was just screwed up and shit, but he never deliberately set out to hurt anyone. He just didn't care who got caught in the crossfire—like on New Year's Eve. But this guy, shit, he'll do anything and everything to get what he wants."

Ryan was really beginning to frighten me. Although he was only confirming what I'd already feared, to hear him tell it, Hatch was a lot worse than even I had suspected.

"What does he want?" I asked nervously.

"Right now, I'd say he wants your cousin. Girls are like property to him. He thinks he owns any girl who gives him the time of day. And even those who don't. And he deals, too."

"You mean drugs?"

"You don't see a deck of cards in his hands, do you? Yeah, drugs."

I felt like a complete idiot for asking such an obvious question.

"Listen, Darla, I hope you won't take this the wrong way, but I really think that you and May should go home. This really isn't a good place for you. I feel kind of guilty about you being here, and I'd feel a lot better if you guys were safe at home. I really gotta run now, but see that guy over there, in the Hawaiian shirt? That's Jack. He's the manager here. When you're ready to leave, he'll get someone to walk you to your car. Okay? Just get your cousin away from that guy. I'm dead serious."

"Sure, Ryan," I said, disappointed that our conversation was coming to an abrupt end.

"I'm really sorry, Darla. I just didn't know you were coming and I've got shit to take care of and people I gotta talk to."

"I understand," I said mournfully.

"I'll call you sometime, though, and we can catch up on things. Oh...and by the way, you're not gonna mention to your dad that you saw me here, are you?"

"Of course not, Ryan. Do you think I would actually tell my father that I was here?"

"Yeah, right," he said, probably feeling as stupid as I had just moments ago. "That was a pretty dumb question." He heaved a sigh of relief and smiled awkwardly at me.

I could see Lisa at a distance, scanning the crowd for Ryan. I really didn't want her to find him with me. It would've been far too humiliating to watch her paw at him, then drag him off somewhere for a moment of passion that should've been mine. I just wanted to leave and for the whole disastrous evening to come to an end. I was deeply disappointed by the outcome of all my careful planning—and in my fantasies remaining just that—but I felt a curious wave of relief come over me as I finally realized, without a shadow of a doubt, that Ryan and I were never to be. It was the closure that I needed to move on with my life, although I was too young, and too hurt at the time to recognize it as such.

"It was great seeing you again," I managed to say. "The band sounds great."

"You take care, Darla," he said. He smiled and kissed me on the cheek. "And get home safe. Please!"

"Bye, Ryan," I said despondently. "See ya."

At that moment, I understood why wounded animals often seek out a quiet place to die when they are sick or injured, and I wondered if I could find such a refuge at Pier 23. Although the ladies' room seemed like my best bet, I neither wanted to separate from May nor walk alone through the crowd. Not knowing what to do, I sat at the bar and sipped sorrowfully on my soda as I glanced around the room.

By this time, Ryan had made his way to the opposite side of the bar, and I spotted Lisa, just as she breathlessly managed to catch up with him. He spoke a few words to her, kissed her on the lips, and then pointed to someone in the crowd. Lisa took off in the opposite direction, and I was more surprised than ever when I saw Ryan approach the cute guy across the bar from me—the one who so obviously hated the music. I figured they had to be friends or co-workers, but I didn't much care anymore. I just felt sick and I wanted to leave.

Eventually, the band started playing again. Growing more frustrated by the moment, and feeling alone and frightened, I decided to risk angering Hatch by telling May that I wanted to leave. But before I could do so, I was jolted back into cowardice as I saw Hatch trying to coax May into having a drink. Although I couldn't see her face, it was very clear from her hand gestures that she wasn't interested, but it was also clear that Hatch was very determined to change her mind. I didn't know what to do, only that I didn't dare let May out of my sight.

"Carla? Is that you?"

I turned to my left, my back now to May and Hatch, to see who was speaking to me.

"Carla?"

"It's Darla," I said, looking curiously at the woman with the very short hair whom I'd noticed earlier. She stood in front of me, smiling like an old friend, and I noticed that her leg was bandaged in some sort of orthopedic contraption, and that she was getting around with the aid of a crutch.

"Oh, right. Darla. I remember now. Well, how have you been? Doin' okay?"

"I'm sorry. Do I know you?"

"I'm Corky. Corky Powell. Don't you remember me?"

"Oh God! Corky! You look so different."

"Yeah. I know. I had a head injury and they had to shave me. My hair is just starting to grow back. Man, I hate it, but at least I'm alive. Look, they cut off all my nails, too... I almost bit the dust, you know. I almost croaked right there on the side of the road."

"Yes," I said uncomfortably. "I heard. I'm so glad you're okay."

"I fractured my leg in a zillion places, and I'm pretty fucked up inside too, but the doctors all say I'll be okay."

"I'm glad to hear you're going to be all right. You're really lucky, though. It could've been much worse."

"Yeah, you're right, it could've. But that don't bring my old man back, though. He's dead, and I'm bald and crippled. Life's a bitch."

"I'm just so sorry, Corky. I really am."

"Well, I'll tell you...Darla, right?"

"Yes," I said, wondering what was on her mind.

"I know you and me don't have much in common, and it's not like we're best buddies or nothin', but I feel real crappy about you and Ryan almost bitin' the dust. I really do. See, ya gotta understand—Greg's old man beat him and all, since he was a little kid—so that's why he drank so much, and, well, I'm sure you probably thought he was the scum of the earth, but he really was a good guy, when he wasn't drinking, and he took real good care of me. I really miss him, Darla. I miss him so much. I was gonna have his baby, ya know. But I never even got the chance to tell him. Now I've lost them both."

At that moment, Corky's tough exterior vanished completely. She looked as if she were going to cry, although I knew she had an image to protect and would never do so in public. But I did sense an urgent need for comfort—a cry for friendship — even if it was as transitory as the moment that took Greg's life and changed hers forever. It was a scene I never thought I'd play, but I hopped off the bar stool and gave her a hug. Hungry for affection, she hugged me back as if I were her best friend.

"Thank you," she said, displaying a softness I'd been certain didn't exist. "You're a real sweetheart. I don't have any family, not really, and there's nobody I can talk to. Nobody wants to hear that you're lonely and your old man's dead. Believe me, Darla, they don't."

"Gee, Corky, I wish I could say something to cheer you up. Ryan told me that Greg had a really tough life, and we both felt really bad for him. I swear. I'm sorry you're hurting so much. I really hope you'll find someone to love you again. You know, when you're ready and stuff. And, really...I'm so sorry to hear about your baby."

"Thanks. That's really nice of you to say."

"And by the way, for what it's worth, I think your hair looks really cute this short. It shows off your face. You're very pretty."

"Really? You think so? I don't feel very pretty."

"I can understand that," I sympathized. "When I'm upset, I don't feel very pretty, either."

"You're upset now, aren't you?"

"Is it that obvious?" I asked plaintively.

"I watched you from across the bar when you were talking to Ryan. You looked pretty bummed when he walked away—and I guess it can't help none that she's here."

"No," I admitted. "It doesn't."

"So I thought I'd come over and say hi. I was gonna come over earlier, but I wasn't real sure if I should. Under the circumstances, I wasn't sure if you'd wanna see me."

"I'm glad you came over to say hello. I'm glad we got a chance to talk, and I'm really happy to see that you're recovering and stuff."

"I think someone wants to talk to you, Darla," Corky said, looking over my shoulder. "So I'm gonna split and let you do your thing. Take care, and watch your back here. This ain't no prom dance."

"Bye, Corky," I said, turning around to see who wanted to speak to me, praying that it would be Ryan or May. To my surprise, it was the adorable guy from across the bar, only he was looking far more agitated than adorable.

"Hi, Darla. You probably don't remember me, but we did meet before. I'm Sam Darcy, Ryan's cousin."

"I'm sorry," I said, as though it were getting to be a habit. "I really don't recognize you at all."

"I don't think you ever saw me with my head off. I mean, I was the gorilla—at my brother Keith's Halloween party."

"Oh sure! I remember talking to you. Gee, I'm just surprised you recognized me. I looked pretty unusual that night, and I sorta have a lot of makeup on tonight. Even Ryan didn't recognize me at first!"

"Actually, I really didn't know who you were. I just knew that you looked familiar; Ryan clued me in. Listen, Darla, you can tell me to mind my own business, but Ryan also gave me the lowdown on Hatch, you know, that guy your cousin was talking to earlier. So naturally, I was worried when—"

Panic-stricken by Sam's clear use of the past tense, I turned to check on May, realizing in horror that my back had been turned to her for ten minutes. Not only were she and Hatch gone, but someone else had already taken May's seat. In that split second, I felt the most horrific sense of foreboding and fear that I'd ever felt in my life. A dread came over me that seemed even worse than the final moments before Greg had crashed the car on New Year's Eve.

"Oh God!" I screamed, not caring who heard me. "Where's my cousin? Where's May?"

"I was watching them," Sam told me, "and the minute that girl with the short hair came over to talk to you, and you turned your back, that Hatch guy grabbed his drink and led your cousin off by the arm. She seemed confused, like she really didn't want to go with him."

"No!" I cried hysterically. "That bastard! Where did he take my cousin? Please help me, Sam! Please!"

"Try to calm down, Darla. I'll do anything I can to help. First of all, I don't think they left this place, because I saw them walk alongside the stage, toward the back. Maybe there's a room back there. I just couldn't see any more than that from where I was sitting. Anyway, I thought I'd better come over and let you know what was happening."

"He's going to hurt her! Please!" I beseeched him. "Help me; I don't know what to do!"

"Is everything all right here?" the man in the Hawaiian shirt asked as he rushed toward us. "I'm Jack Stelford. I'm the manager here."

I wasted no time answering him. "Hatch took my cousin May somewhere! And she's only sixteen!"

I saw a look of unadulterated panic sweep Jack's face. "Do you have any idea where they went?" he asked, pounding impatiently on the bar.

"I saw them walk behind the stage," Sam told him. "That's all I know,"

"Just wait here," Jack said to me emphatically. "I'll be back."

"I'm going with him," Sam told me. "Do what he says, Darla. Wait here."

And with that, he took off to follow Jack. I stood there, sobbing, as I watched both men run up along the side of the stage and disappear into the blackness behind it. Within moments, Corky came limping back over to me, with a deep look of concern on her face.

"What's wrong, Darla? You look horrible! What were you talking to Jack and that other guy about? Why are you crying?"

I was sobbing so heavily that I could barely answer her. Leaning on my empty bar stool with her left arm for support, she did her best to hold me steady with her right arm.

"Calm down, honey. Talk to me."

"Do you know Hatch?" I asked tearfully.

"Sure I know him. Most people that hang here do—whether they want to or not. He was just here a few minutes ago, talkin' to some blonde. I saw them split while we were talking. Why d'you care?"

"She's not 'some blonde,' Corky. She's my cousin May. And she's my age. I'm afraid he's going to hurt her."

"Holy crap, Darla! I don't know if the SOB'd actually hurt her, but let's put it this way, Hatch ain't a happy camper when he don't get what he wants. I learned that the hard way."

"He hurt you?" I asked weakly, petrified of her answer.

255

"Let's just say that I went along with his game plan," she said diplomatically. "He's a mean drunk and I didn't wanna try his patience."

"You mean you—"

"Yeah Darla," she said. "I gave it up. Let him do his thing with me. That was three years ago. Before I met Greg. Hell, Hatch don't even remember bein' with me, and if he does, you'd never know it. Bastard never even says hi. Just as well. He just used me. He's a pig. Don't look like one when ya first meet him, but he's a pig all the same. The biggest oinker in this place. Turns kids on to drugs by tellin' them he's some big-time agent or something. Whatever garbage pops into his head at the time."

Despite the fact that Corky was scaring me to death, I was glad she'd come back over to be with me.

"Please," I moaned despairingly as reality inched closer. "They've gotta find May. They've just gotta!"

Corky reached over to the bar and grabbed a handful of cocktail napkins. "Here, Darla, wipe your face, hon. You've got mascara all down your chin and all. Hey, I'm sure Jack and that other guy will find her. Don't worry. She'll be okay."

"It's all my fault! If anything happens to May, I'll never forgive myself. She's just the sweetest person in the whole world. I swear she is!"

"I'm sure she is. C'mon, hon. Wipe your face."

I took the napkins and tried to clear off the streaking mascara, but it was impossible to concentrate on what I was doing. Corky smiled sweetly as she wiped my face for me. I could feel a million eyes watching me, but May's life was at stake, and I couldn't have cared less if I was making a spectacle of myself.

When Corky had finished cleaning my face, with all the gentleness of a loving mother, I felt terribly guilty for once having hated her so much. With all her rough edges, I could see that she was actually a very nice person. But my thoughts of Corky's good nature were fleeting as I grew sicker with worry over the fate of my cousin.

"Hey, here comes that other guy!" Corky alerted me. "Maybe he's got some news."

I looked up to see Sam hurriedly making his way through the crowd toward us.

"Did you find May?" I asked him, before he could say a word.

"We found her, Darla. She's in Jack's office now. She's very shaken, but I'm sure she'll come through this in one piece."

"What happened?" I asked, looking into his eyes.

"Just come with me, okay? I'll take you to her."

I looked at Corky. "Please come with us."

"Are you sure?"

"Positive," I told her.

I barely remember walking through the crowd to get to the manager's office, but I will never forget the moment when I first saw May again. In a split second, I knew exactly how my parents must've felt on New Year's Eve when the officer had escorted me home, so frightened and disheveled, and I understood instantly how a person could feel so relieved and so horrified all in the same moment.

May sat on the couch with her eyes looking downward in shame. A stranger's sweater was draped over her shoulders, and a woman I'd never seen before was caressing May's arms and speaking softly to her. May looked far worse than I had expected, and although I was relieved not to find her completely hysterical, I became doubly concerned when she looked up at me—stunned, fearful, confused, and lost. Her face was streaked with mascara and tears, just as mine was, her gorgeous blond hair was twisted halfway around her neck, and her black evening dress was savagely torn.

When she saw me, she looked up and extended her arms without saying a word, as her eyes begged me to come to her. As I rushed over to her, the woman at her side quickly got up and made room for me to sit down.

I threw my arms around May and held her as tightly as I could. We sat there for the longest time, weeping and holding each other for dear life.

"What the hell did he do to her?" I heard Corky ask Jack. "Where'd ya find the son of a bitch?"

"He had taken her to the storage area—behind the stage," Jack said

257

reluctantly. "Sam and I got there just in time."

"What did he do?" Corky asked furiously.

"I'd rather not go into it now, Corky," Jack told her. "I'll explain it all to her parents when they get here."

I don't know why it came as such a shock to me, but in all that had happened, I'd never once thought about Aunt Didi and Uncle George, nor did I want to think about what would happen once they arrived. I tried repeatedly to talk to May, but she would only respond with her eyes, and as the minutes ticked by, she began to slip deeper into herself. Corky hobbled over to the couch and with great difficulty took a seat on the other side of May.

"This is my friend Corky," I told May. "She knows Hatch and she understands what a bad person he is."

Corky looked at me and smiled, as a few bittersweet tears fell from her eyes. I knew she was touched that I had called her my friend.

"I'm really sorry, May," Corky told her. "Would you let me talk to you for a moment?"

May, with a blank look in her eyes, slowly turned to look at Corky.

"Hatch is a real...well, he's a horrible person," Corky explained, making an obvious and unnatural effort to use respectable language for May's sake. "He's hurt a lot of people. He's a liar and a user— and believe me, to know him is to hate his guts. Problem is, he ain't a bad-looking dude, and he uses that to get people to trust him and to like him at first. But that never lasts very long. People see right through the son of a—I mean, people see right through the guy. He hurt me once too, you know. Years ago. Don't even remember doin' it, either. Hurts so many people he loses count."

May continued looking at Corky, although the expression on her face was unreadable and I couldn't tell if she understood what Corky was saying or not.

"Listen, hon, you don't need me to tell you that he's a bad guy. You found that out for yourself. But I want you to know that none of this shit—I mean, nothin' that happened here tonight is your fault. So promise me now, ya ain't gonna take this out on yourself. You're a really sweet girl—just like your cousin Darla. I can tell that just from lookin' at you. And sweet girls usually blame themselves for what bastards like Hatch do. I used to be a sweet girl once. I'm not anymore, though."

Corky reached over, as best she could, and gave May, who was unresponsive, a hug. As she got up from the couch, with the help of her crutch, she turned to me.

"You take care, Darla," Corky said, trying to camouflage her pain. "I gotta go. I'm dyin' for a smoke."

"Take care, Corky," I said, genuinely sorry to see that she was leaving. "Thanks for everything you've done for me tonight."

"No, thank you, Darla. Thanks for not hatin' my guts. And just remember, nothin' that happened to your cousin is her fault. You just keep remindin' her of that, okay? More than likely, she's gonna forget it."

Corky walked out of the office, nodding at Sam, Jack, and the woman whom I assumed to be Jack's girlfriend.

"Where the hell is our daughter?" I heard Uncle George scream, just outside the door.

Frightened, I jumped up from my seat and hurried to the corner of Jack's office, where I stood cowering. I don't know why, but I thought that if I removed myself from May's side, it would lessen Aunt Didi's rage toward me. Jack poked his head out in the hallway and beckoned Aunt Didi and Uncle George inside. Aunt Didi practically knocked Jack down as she barreled into the office and made a beeline for May.

"My baby!" Aunt Didi cried as she ran over to May and hugged her. "What happened to you? My poor baby!"

I thought for sure that May would want her mother more than anyone at this moment, but she didn't. She sat there rigidly, while Aunt Didi fawned all over her and wiped the smeared makeup from her face.

"What the hell happened to my daughter?" Uncle George screamed at Jack. "Do you know that she's only just sixteen, and so is my niece? What the hell kind of a place are you running here, letting teenagers come in and sit at the bar? Have they been drinking?"

"No, sir. I don't believe that they—"

"Didn't someone check their goddamn identification at the door? I could have this place closed down, you know!"

As Uncle George barraged Jack with a fusillade of questions, not giving him a chance to answer any of them, Aunt Didi sat and rocked May in her arms, getting visibly more agitated when she saw that May was neither speaking nor responding to her.

"What happened to my baby?" Aunt Didi screamed at Jack.

"She was attacked in our storage area," Jack said, hating every word he spoke. "A man named Paul Hatchford, whom your daughter had been speaking with at the bar, brought her back there on false pretenses and attempted to rape her. Sam Darcy here and I—well, we managed to find them before any more damage could be done."

"Where's the goddamn son of a bitch now?" Uncle George roared.

"Long gone, sir. I tried to run after him, but I was more concerned with—"

Uncle George pounded the wall with his left fist. "Have you called the police? How many goddamn rapists frequent this filthy joint? Just give me an average. Five, ten? Come on. Spit it out!"

Jack stood there uncomfortably and let Uncle George continue to berate him.

"Enough to start a goddamn softball team, or what?"

"Mr. Alexander, please," Jack said, standing his ground. "This isn't helping your daughter. And yes, I've called the police. They're on their way."

"Talk to me, baby," Aunt Didi kept repeating to May. "Why are you dressed like this? Why did you come down to this awful place? Oh, look at your beautiful hair! What did that animal do to you?"

May didn't answer, much less make eye contact with her mother, and I began to wonder what was upsetting Aunt Didi more—the fact that a man had tried to rape her daughter, or that May wasn't answering her questions.

As Uncle George continued to shout at Jack, Aunt Didi fumbled through her pocketbook for a hairbrush, which she then used to undo May's tangled locks. For several minutes, she continued to groom May, treating her like a prized cat who was being primped for the judges. May, who had been unresponsive up until that point, suddenly knocked the brush violently out of her mother's hands and went running across the room to her father, throwing her arms around him and hiding her face on his chest.

Aunt Didi looked horrified and hurt, and as Uncle George changed from a screaming maniac into a loving father, Aunt Didi turned and acknowledged me for the very first time.

"Sit down!" she screamed. "Now, where are Melanie and her boyfriend?"

"What?" I said, unclear about what she was asking me, as I took a seat on the couch again.

"I said, where are Melanie and her boyfriend? Isn't that who you were supposed to be with tonight?"

I looked at the floor.

"I see. So I take it you were lying to us. Is that how I'm to take it?"

"I guess so," I mumbled.

"You guess so? What the hell did you bring my daughter down here for anyway?"

"Well—"

"Well, what?"

"Ryan was playing in the band," I told her, still looking at the floor.

"Ryan was playing in the band?" Aunt Didi repeated incredulously, her voice steeped in anger. "Let me make sure I've got this: my daughter dressed up like a sex kitten and was attacked in this filthy place by some depraved psychopath, just so that you could hear that boy, the same one who almost got you killed, play in a goddamn, stinking rock band? Is that the way it is?"

She reached over and forcefully grabbed me by my shoulders and began shaking me. "Did you enjoy the music, Darla? Was it fun seeing Ryan again? Was it worth it? Was it worth my baby almost getting raped, maybe even killed? The way I heard it, you promised your parents you would start behaving. You told them they could trust you. Obviously, that was a complete lie. It's just been one thing after another with you. You're fast on your way to becoming as worthless as your aunt Rebecca!"

261

And with that, she let go of me as if I were a rotten piece of garbage that she couldn't bear to touch anymore. I fell backwards and hit my head against the wall, but Aunt Didi didn't even seem to care.

"Get up!" she shouted. "I promised my sister I'd look after you, and I can't break my word."

I sat there on the couch, crying hysterically as I rubbed the sore spot on my head, but feeling even more pain at the horrible things she was saying to me. She didn't seem anything like an aunt, or anything like a person who had ever loved me at all.

"Get up, Darla! Now!"

"I don't want to go with you!" I said, sniveling.

Aunt Didi grabbed my right arm and yanked me up from the couch. I could tell by the sympathetic look on Sam's face that he wanted to save me from her, but he was certainly not about to take on Aunt Didi.

"You'll be hearing from me!" Uncle George thundered at Jack one final time as the four of us walked out of the room. "You can count on that!"

CHAPTER 16

We'd only gotten a few paces out of the door when two policemen, who asked us to return to Jack's office for an interview, greeted us. May was still not able to speak, though surprisingly, she did respond to most of the officers questions by nodding her head yes or no. As for me, I could do nothing more than relate everything May had told me about Hatch, and to give the officers the chronology of events as I remembered them.

No one said a word to me on the ride home from Pier 23. And although I was sitting right next to Uncle George in the front seat of his car, I might as well have been invisible, for all the attention that he was paying to me. Hatch, on the other hand, who really wasn't there, was clearly there in spirit, or at least in Uncle George's mind. All the way home, I watched as my uncle mouthed obscenities, banged his fist repeatedly on the steering wheel, and turned his head in an animated fashion, as if he were having a real conversation with a person he wanted to murder. Thankfully, he had the good sense not to speak above his agitated whisper, thus taking care not to traumatize May any further.

In the backseat, Aunt Didi was busy pleading with May: "Tell Mama what happened," and "Tell Mama how you're feeling." My cousin was not able to do so, but I was, and I desperately wanted to "tell Mama what happened." I wanted my aunt to understand just how her controlling personality had driven May to initiate our outing to Pier 23 in the first place (and all just for the sole pleasure of defying her and her unscrupulous sister Maggie). But I'd suffered enough abuse from Aunt Didi for one evening, and besides, it was May's privilege to tell her all of that, not mine. Still, I couldn't help but feel a growing resentment toward my aunt, especially after the way she had treated me in Jack's office. Her words "You're fast on your way to becoming as worthless as your aunt Rebecca" played over and over in my head. I could not understand why she would say something so ugly to me, and although it was not foremost on my mind at the moment, I could not comprehend why she hated Rebecca so much—just for being a wild teenager—so many years ago.

263

But my mind drifted back to May, whose troubles were far greater at the moment than mine. I wished that I could be the one comforting her, and that Aunt Didi had heeded Uncle George's advice and driven her own car home (the one May and I had driven down in). My aunt, however, wasn't about "to leave her baby's side," not even for a split second; she had made that quite clear.

As we pulled up to the Alexander home, I could see April's and June's grim faces at the bay window. Before Uncle George could even get the key out of the ignition, April and June, clad in their nightshirts, came tearing out of the house.

May, by this point, was near catatonia as Aunt Didi helped her out of the car. Her sisters, obviously horrified by her empty stare, gasped, as I had, upon seeing her for the first time. Shaken, they led May into the house, inundating her with questions for which she had no answers. I trailed meekly behind, feeling somewhat like a stray dog who hated the shelter she was living in but who had nowhere else to sleep.

Once inside, Uncle George raced off to his study to make some phone calls while April and June helped May onto the couch, taking a seat on either side of her. Aunt Didi, still obsessed with May's appearance, tore off to the bathroom to get a washcloth, intent on washing any visible signs of tragedy from May's tormented face.

"Let me sit next to May," Aunt Didi demanded of April as she returned to the living room with a wet washcloth and towel.

"I can do that, Mom," April protested, reaching for the washcloth.

"I'll take care of my daughter," my aunt said huffily. "Would you get up, please?"

As April reluctantly rose from the couch, May, still looking vacant and lifeless, grabbed April's wrist with her right hand—a clear indication that she preferred April's help to that of her mother's.

"All right then, you do it," Aunt Didi angrily consented, practically throwing the washcloth and towel at April.

"How did this happen?" June asked her mother, ignoring me completely.

"I'll tell you how it happened!" Aunt Didi shouted, looking over at me as I cowered in the corner. "Your cousin Darla was so desperate to see her old heartthrob, Ryan, play music in that godforsaken hole, that she dragged your sweet sister down there with her. Then, she was so damn busy making goo-goo eyes at him that she failed to notice when some drug-dealing weasel hauled your sister off into a back room with every intent to rape and do God-knows-what-else to her!"

"Oh May! You poor baby!" April moaned as she washed May's face clean.

"How could you take her there, Darla?" June cried, looking at me for the first time. "How could you put May in so much danger?"

"It wasn't like that. I didn't know what was going to happen! Don't you think I feel horrible about everything? I love May so much!"

"Well, I hope you don't love me too!" June snapped. "I don't want to end up dead or raped!"

"That's not fair, June," April said softly in my defense, as she continued to tend to May.

"It's the truth!" June told her, as she turned her gaze back in my direction to give me the dirtiest look she could manage. "If Darla cared one bit about May, she never would've used her like that—just to get a ride to see Lover Boy play in a band!"

"June—" April insisted. "Stop it!"

I couldn't help but notice that Aunt Didi seemed proud of June for what she was saying to me—and happy that June was so ably continuing what she had so inappropriately started. Just as Aunt Didi had done all the girls' lives, she was living vicariously through her daughters. She knew there was a limit to how much she could berate me, being my aunt and my mother's dear sister, but June, who was merely a teenager, could say any horrible thing she wanted and no one would blame Aunt Didi for it.

"Don't tell me to stop it!" June snarled at April. "If the shoe fits, Darla needs to wear it."

April was furious. "Listen, June, forget about the shoe or put a sock in it. Right now, May needs our help. She doesn't want to hear you and Mom saying nasty things to Darla. There's nothing to be gained from that. I'm not happy about what happened either, but your behavior is

265

disgusting. So cut it out!"

April turned to May, who had begun rocking back and forth again, and lovingly stroked her hair, ignoring June and her mother completely. Aunt Didi fidgeted nervously, and I sensed that she was annoyed that April had not only refused to relinquish her seat on the couch, but that in her wisdom, she had put a halt to the verbal bullets June had been firing at me. I was at a complete loss for words. I desperately wanted to defend myself, but I couldn't think of any way to do so without having it sound like I was blaming May. Going to Pier 23 had been a bad decision on both of our parts, and as I'd learned from past experience, it didn't matter which one of us had initiated the idea, we both were responsible for going along with it. I was furious at Aunt Didi for making up her own warped version of the facts for June's benefit. Also, I knew of no way to tell them that May had actually enjoyed Hatch's attention at first, and that I had tried to warn her about him and that she had refused to listen. No matter how I phrased it, it would come out wrong. And as much as I despised the bum rap I was getting, it was far preferable to doing anything that might incriminate May.

"Get up, June," Aunt Didi demanded, realizing that there was another seating option she hadn't thought of before. "Let me sit next to May."

June obligingly jumped up from her seat, but May cringed and huddled closer to April as Aunt Didi went to sit down on the other side of her. Realizing that her attempts to coddle May were futile, Aunt Didi stood back up again, looking frustrated and embarrassed.

"I'm going to talk to your father," she told April and June. "Watch your sister."

Feeling like a roach at an exterminator's conference, I decided I would resort to a death-defying stunt in hopes of crawling out alive.

"Aunt Didi?"

She turned and glared at me, as if I had no right to even speak her name.

"Can I call Melanie or a taxi and get a ride back to my house? I think it would be better if I didn't stay here."

266

Her eyes narrowed viciously. "My daughter has been attacked and she needs immediate medical attention. Do you think I'm going to concern myself with where Darla McKendrick prefers to spend the night? I promised your mother you would stay here with us, so don't you dare bother me again with another ludicrous request for a change in venue. Besides, God only knows the trouble you'd get into if I let you go home alone. Forget it!"

And with that, she marched off toward Uncle George's study. April, though she had defended me earlier, refused to even glance in my direction, and June, who was more than happy to look my way, gave me nothing but evil glares when she did. I was more concerned with what May was going through, however, and disheartened by the realization that neither April nor June would allow me to help in any way. Understanding that my presence was completely useless, and feeling defeated and unloved, I slunk upstairs to the guest room.

I had been lying in bed for about ten minutes when I heard the front door shut, followed by the sound of Uncle George's car pulling out of the driveway. Moments later, I heard June scream "Where are they taking her? Why can't she stay here?" and although I could not make out what she was saying, I could hear April frantically trying to calm her down.

From what Aunt Didi had said earlier about May's requiring medical attention, I assumed that they were taking her to the hospital, possibly to find out why she wasn't talking and to make sure that Hatch had not harmed her physically. My instincts, naturally, were to fly down the stairs and join April and June, but I could not bear any more rejection and misery, especially from my cousins.

So I stayed in bed, alone and frightened. Frightened for myself, and frightened for May. The guest room was hot and muggy, and my body was covered in a sweat that only intensified my anguish. But I didn't dare use the extra bed in April's air-conditioned room, as I had done all week. Instead, I just lay there in the oppressive summer heat, replaying every horrible moment of the evening, and recalling how in just a matter of days, my life had crumbled to pieces like a stale donut. Almost everyone whom I loved and counted on had betrayed me. It began with my mother, who had lied to my face and stabbed me in the back, then with my father, who had happily consented to her machinations, just to get back in the good graces of his wretched sister and her family. My parents' collusion in writing the phony apology letter defied every value they had ever instilled in me. Who and what could I believe in anymore?

Then there was Aunt Didi. I had been used to her hot temper, and to her unorthodox methods, ever since I was a child. But while I could forgive her for telling me that Squalor was a town in New Mexico, I could not forgive her for practically throwing me against the wall, calling me "worthless," and making up lies about me.

But that was not the worst of it. The one constant in my entire life, the one thing I could always count on to cheer me up, was the love and support of my three cousins. To them, I was now the scourge of the earth, at least where June and April were concerned, and May, whom I'd come to love the most, was probably locked up in a psychiatric ward screaming silently for someone to facilitate her escape.

My thoughts then moved to Ryan, as I belittled myself for having chased after him, and for being too naive to realize that he'd reconciled with Lisa. I recalled my very first conversation with Sam, at the Halloween party, when he had confided to me that Ryan had originally left Lisa because of her possessive and flirtatious nature, then "guaranteed" me that Ryan would never go back to her. Obviously, Sam was as wrong about Ryan as I had been. I didn't really care anymore. Besides, that party was a lifetime ago. Ryan was a lifetime ago. I was sick of thinking about him.

My thoughts drifted back to my parents, as I tried to anticipate their reaction upon arriving home the next day, but my brain was on overload and could not handle any more—at least in my conscious mind. It was some time around then that I fell asleep and that my unconscious mind took over, taking on the grim task of sorting out everything that had happened and everything that I was feeling, then meshing it all together in yet another debilitating nightmare.

As nightmares often do, this one started out harmlessly enough, carefully imitating real life so expertly that I didn't realize I was dreaming. Instead, I found myself lying on Aunt Didi's rose-pattern percale sheets (the ones with the high-thread count), thinking about everything that had transpired on that miserable June night. Suddenly, I heard a tap at the window, then another one. It didn't sound like the kind of tap a person makes when he wants to get someone's attention, but like the kind of tap you hear when something is hitting the window—like a branch or a pebble that's been thrown.

I was too tired to open my eyes and look, but I knew I should find out where the noise was coming from. It took my eyes a moment to adjust to the darkness, and at first I didn't recognize the object at the window. But the tapping sound came again, and this time my eyes popped wide open, as to my horror, I saw a doll's head on a stick, with Nadine's face and the devil's horns, spitting tiny black crystals at the window.

"Omigod," Melanie screamed, appearing out of the blackness. "I told you those things were evil. Run for cover, or cover your eyes. But please, Darla! Do something before that she-devil eats you alive!"

Before I could react, I saw the windowpane transform into Aunt Louisa's face, and as she uttered the dreaded words "Plant one here, dear," Nadine's devil head quickly turned into an angel's face, halo and all, as it lovingly spit little red heart sponges at Aunt Louisa's cheek.

"Now, that's what I like to see! That's what a good girl does," Aunt Louisa said as she turned toward me to show off her cheek. To my utter repugnance, I saw a large black hole on the side of her face, with a tiny human hand coming out of it.

"Help me, Darla!" I heard May's voice cry. "I'm trapped in here. Where's the escape hatch? I'm scared! I need to escape Hatch! Help! He's going to rape me!"

Just as I was trying to figure out where May's voice was coming from, I saw a miniature version of May frantically climbing out of the black hole in Aunt Louisa's cheek. To my dismay, a miniature Hatch was not far behind her. But once May extricated herself from the black hole, she resumed her normal height, while Hatch, appropriately, remained small.

"Both of you are going to be sorry you ever messed with me! And you," Hatch screamed at May, "you led me on, you slut!"

Having nowhere to run but the closet, which was already filled with boxes of Uncle George's legal briefs, May and I opted to hide under the sheets. I don't know how many minutes had elapsed in dream time, but when I finally had the courage to come out from under the sheets, everything was quiet. Everyone was gone but me. I looked around the room, just to make sure it was as I'd remembered it, when suddenly, the most horrifying squeal imaginable came from under the bed. There was nothing left to do but clutch the pillow and pray.

Then, with a quick warning thud, a large round object came rolling out from beneath the bed, which I soon recognized as Sam's gorilla head. For a few seconds, it rolled around on the floor, seemingly jockeying for the most desirable position in which to stop and get a good look at me.

"Hi, Darla! You probably don't recognize me without my body, but I'm Sam Darcy, Ryan's cousin."

"What happened to your body?" I choked.

"That awful flirt Lisa took it. She just walked right up to me and said, 'I want your body, Sam!' I tried to protest, but she just took it. You know, I was really attached to my body and I fear I'm going to be rather useless without it. I think you'd better warn Ryan. She wants his body too!"

"Well, she can have it! I'm through with Ryan forever. He's a jerk and a waste of my time!"

"Omigod, Darla!" Melanie said, reappearing by my side. "What are you going to do with this gorilla head? Play soccer or what? Maybe you should just put it on a stick and plant it in that lady's garden with all the other propeller heads. If it were closer to Halloween time, I'd say carve out the inside and make a pumpkin out of it. Just make sure those little brats on your street don't squash it to death and leave pumpkin cooties all over the lawn!"

As I turned to look at Sam's head, and to gauge his reaction to Melanie's ghastly suggestions, I noticed that it had died. Within seconds, another head, one that was completely bald, came rolling out from under the bed. It had three holes in it and looked just like a bowling ball. A quick glance told me that it was Corky.

"Greg's dead, and I'm bald and crippled. Life's a bitch. Ain't it, Darla?"

"Eeewwww gross!" Melanie screamed. "Skieve me out! What happened to her body?"

"Hatch took it. And he's gonna take that blond chick's body if you don't protect her," Corky warned. "Roll me back under the bed. I'm dyin' for a smoke."

"No one's smoking cigarettes in my house!" Aunt Didi screamed, as she burst into the room with June and April behind her. April, all snugly in Grandma Adelaide's old brown coat and wearing the "Ditz helmet" June had made for her, glared at me in disgust. "You're not the greatest anymore. You're awful!"

"I told you!" June snickered at April. "But you wouldn't believe me. Darla put May in danger because Darla doesn't care about anyone but herself."

"That's not true! May just wanted to be noticed," I explained in earnest. "That's why she talked to Hatch. She thought he was a nice guy at first."

Miraculously, Sam's dead head came back to life. "Your cousin is beautiful, Darla. She could go out with me any time. And I'm rather unattached at the moment, as you can see."

"You hairy hunk of worthless junk!" Aunt Didi shouted, kicking Sam with her expensive Italian shoes. "Get out of my house, and take my worthless niece with you. Go to Squalor, New Mexico, and live happily ever after in the filth you've created. That's where you both belong!"

Sam looked at me with tears in his gorilla eyes. "Darla—I have a headache 'this big,' " he wailed. Then he rolled back under the bed, along with Corky, and disappeared.

"Everything that happened to May is your fault!" June cried. "And that's why we all hate you! And we'll hate you forever!"

"Don't talk that way to Darla!" admonished a pint-sized Uncle Martin, who was standing on the bed holding hands with Hatch. "She's a one-in-a-million girl. Even my son Hatch thinks so!"

"That rapist is your son?" Aunt Didi cried in disbelief. "Well, if he is, he's illegitimate, I'm sure."

"I smell alcohol," June said. "Is someone here drinking?"

"Not me," lied Hatch. "Never touch the stuff!"

"Me either!" said a very intoxicated voice. "Spirits are evil and they make people do bad things."

"Ted McKendrick!" Aunt Didi snarled in disgust. "You old drunk, you! No wonder your daughter is so worthless. She takes after you and your worthless sister-in-law."

"How could you do it, Daddy?" I cried. "How could you tell me not to drink and then do it yourself? How could you let Mom forge that apology letter? How could you lie to me! Nothing you've ever told me matters anymore. You don't matter, Mom doesn't matter, and I don't matter."

As my father bent his head in shame, I looked in Grandma Adelaide's old mirror on the dresser, hoping to see my own image, and in doing so, to determine my value. But all I saw in the mirror was a blank face, devoid of features, devoid of a soul. Quickly, I touched my face to see whether my eyes, nose, and mouth were still there. Luckily, everything seemed to be intact, but oddly, the image in the mirror did not reflect this.

I turned to "face" the assorted characters around me. "Can't anyone see who I am? Can't anyone see me at all?"

No one answered me, and in a moment, they were all gone. I looked in the mirror again. I was still faceless. I couldn't figure out whether I was invisible to them, or whether they were invisible to me. I just knew that I had no face and that no one loved me. And as I touched my face again, desperate to feel alive, I could feel the tears pouring down my cheek. I simply had to be real. I was crying.

It was then that I woke up, covered with sweat and drowning in tears, as I lay lonely and frightened in Aunt Didi's rose percale sheets.

CHAPTER 17

By nine o'clock the next morning, despite a disastrous night's sleep, I was fully dressed and ready to go home. The only problem was that I had no way to get there, and under the circumstances, I didn't dare ask any of the Alexanders for a ride. I was perfectly willing to walk the four-mile distance to my house, but I knew it would be tough sneaking out unnoticed, and with my luck, I was bound to get into even more trouble for doing so.

It felt so odd to be avoiding the family that I loved so much, but I could not bear the thought of incurring Aunt Didi's wrath again, nor did I want to think about June saying unkind words to me or April refusing to look in my direction. I had no idea what I might expect from Uncle George, but I wasn't prepared to find out.

Luckily for me, I wasn't forced to debate the issue for too long. At nine fifteen, as I sat on the bed contemplating my fate, there was a knock on the guest room door.

"Come in," I said cautiously.

"Hi, Darla," April said, standing in the doorway.

"Hi, April," I said, happy to see her despite the circumstances.

"I heard you moving around in here, so I figured it would be okay to knock. You could've slept in my room last night, you know. I'm surprised you didn't melt away in this heat."

"Well," I began, not knowing what to say, "I felt kinda—"

"Yeah, I know," April said, saving me from the awkward task of having to finish my sentence.

"How's May? Is she okay?"

April frowned and looked as if she were going to burst into tears. "Not really. I don't think she's okay at all."

"Oh, God!" I said, feeling guilty for having even been born.

"Mom and Dad took her to the hospital last night. The doctor said that she's suffering from something called posttraumatic stress syndrome and that's why she's not talking. She's got to stay there for a while. Probably till she starts talking again."

"Can I go see her?"

"I don't think it would be a good idea," April said firmly.

"I really think I could help her. I mean, I was there and—"

"Darla, I don't think it would be a good idea. Just trust me on this. Okay?"

I wasn't about to argue with her, but I felt hurt and frustrated that she wouldn't listen to me.

"I feel so rotten about what happened to May. I swear, I never would've gone to Pier 23 if I had any idea this would happen. I mean, I know my father told me it was a bad place, but you know my dad, he thinks half the places on this planet should be off limits to me. I just figured that if Ryan was playing there, it had to be okay."

"I know," April said, leaning against the door jamb. "After all, I'm the one who originally passed on Ryan's message to you. I just wish I'd never run into him that night, and that you and May had never gone to that awful place. But I don't agree with Mom and June, Darla. I don't think that you should take all the blame for what that maggot-sucking creep did to my sister. But I'll tell you one thing, you should thank your lucky stars that nobody tried to hurt you too."

"I wish I had been hurt! I wish May and I could switch places. I wish it were me in that hospital bed instead of May. I swear, April. That's the God's honest truth."

"I believe you, Darla. But what would be the point of that? That wouldn't solve anything. The whole horrible evening just shouldn't have happened—to either of you, okay? I just can't figure out why you guys went to that dive in the first place."

It occurred to me that perhaps I should tell April everything that happened and explain to her in detail how the whole mess had come about. But no matter how I looked at it, doing so still felt like a betrayal of the worst kind to May. She deserved to tell the story in her own words, not in mine, and although I was dying to get everything off my chest, I knew I had no business exposing what May had told me in confidence just to save my own hide with the Alexanders.

"I'm sure May will be okay soon. She's a strong person."

"She's not as strong as she pretends to be," April said softly.

"I know," I said, trying to convince myself. "But I still think she'll be okay."

April and I looked at each other in awkward silence, having no more to say.

"Would you mind giving me a ride home?" I finally mustered up the courage to ask. "My parents will be back early this evening."

"Yeah, sure. Are you ready to go now?"

"I just have to get the rest of my stuff out of your room," I told her, feeling as if we were parting company forever. "Then I'll be ready."

"Okay," April said dully. "I'll meet you downstairs."

By the time April dropped me off at home, I was emotionally spent. Except for her commenting to me about the futility of yet another pizza parlor opening in her neighborhood (as we passed by the offending establishment), there was no conversation between us. It was all I could do to thank her for the ride and get my suitcase quickly out of the car. Naturally, I wanted to ask that she send my love to May, but I feared she would refuse my request, or nod insincerely, and I was not up for any more rejection. I just wanted to get away from her and go inside my own house, where I could feel some semblance of belonging—as short-lived as it might be until my parents found out what had happened.

The house felt oddly quiet, as if no one had lived in it for years. It was hard to believe that my parents had been gone only a little more than a week; it felt like forever. I couldn't quite admit it to myself, but I missed them terribly. As angry as I was at what they had done, I needed to reassure myself that unlike the Alexanders, my parents loved me unconditionally, and just maybe, they would understand that I was hurting too.

I took my things upstairs and went into my bedroom to call Melanie. But as I began to dial her number, an overwhelming fatigue came over me and I knew I wouldn't have the strength to talk to anyone without first taking a nap.

I slept soundly for almost five hours, in a sleep devoid of nightmares, and it was some time around three o'clock when I woke up, completely disoriented and very hungry. After floundering listlessly around my room for a good fifteen minutes, I made my way downstairs and fixed a ham and cheese sandwich. As I went to take the first bite, it dawned on me that the cold cuts had been in the refrigerator for at least ten days. Food poisoning seemed like the last thing I needed at that juncture, so I threw the sandwich into the trash can and decided to forget the whole idea of eating. It was far too much trouble. Even the milk was sour.

There was only one problem: I was still starving. So, for another twenty minutes, I agonized over my predicament, checking and rechecking the pantry for some tasty item that I hoped might magically manifest itself. Deciding finally on the nourishing choice of sour dough pretzels and diet soda, I sat down at the kitchen table, dialed Melanie's number, and prepared for a marathon phone conversation in which I would emerge feeling worlds better.

To say I was devastated when Mrs. Davenport told me that Melanie had just left with Drew would be an understatement. I didn't know what to do with myself. I was restless, bored, irritated, unhappy, and lonely.

I took the pretzels and soda up to my room. After polishing off most of the pretzels and gulping down my soda, I decided to play a few games of solitaire on my bed. Finding little solace in a lone deck of cards, I got up and took a walk around the neighborhood. That entertained me for about twenty minutes, until the heat (and thinking about my problems) got the better of me, so I decided to come back inside, take a shower, and watch some TV. Naturally, there was nothing on that interested me in the least: boxing, an old war movie, golf, a political debate, and a documentary on American farmers.

Finally, after several more hours of mindless activity, monumental boredom, and incessant worry, I heard the front door open, followed immediately by the sound of my father's voice calling upstairs to me.

✳ ✳ ✳

276

"Darla!" he called a second time. "Are you up there?"

"I'm here, Dad," I answered as I came down the stairs to greet him.

Dad smiled broadly at me, threw his arms around me, and gave me a great big hug the moment I reached the landing. I was surprised by the ferocity with which I hugged him back, but I wanted to memorize every loving moment of our exchange. I knew that once I told him what had happened, I would never know my father's love again.

Seconds later, Mom came bursting through the front door weighed down by assorted shopping bags.

Oh, Darla!" she exclaimed, dropping her packages and extending her arms. "I'm so happy to see you!"

Dad released his grip on me and smiled. "I guess it's only fair to give your mother a turn."

I was happy to see her as well but found it difficult to offer the same fond embrace that I'd used to greet Dad. The loathsome and condescending courtesies that Nadine had expressed to me in her letter danced tauntingly in my memory, and Mom was clearly to blame for allowing Nadine the pleasure of expressing them.

"How are you, Darla? Is everything all right here in the house?"

"The cold cuts are bad and the milk is sour."

Mom laughed. "I think that can be remedied, honey. Why don't we all go into the living room?"

"That sounds like a good idea," Dad agreed. "I'll get the rest of the luggage later."

Both of my parents were still smiling at me after we took our usual places in the living room. Dad, all snug in his easy chair, rubbed the upholstery as if he were saying hello to an old friend.

"It's good to be home," Mom said, looking around the living room as if twenty years had passed since she'd been there. "Everything looks just as I remember it."

Her words of nostalgia, after a mere ten-day absence from home, seemed rather ludicrous to me, but I quickly remembered that I'd felt almost the same way when I'd come home just a few hours earlier.

"How was your trip?" I asked, purposely avoiding any direct

mention of the wedding, but hoping they'd tell me anyway.

"New England is a beautiful place," Dad said. "Picturesque, full of charm, and as American as your mother's apple pie. I hope we can go back there someday soon, only the next time, I'd like you to go with us."

"What's Newport like?" I asked, subtly encouraging them to mention the wedding, hoping against hope that they'd have something disastrous to report.

"Newport is lovely," Mom said. "Lots of boats, lots of shops, lots of beautiful mansions, and—"

"Lots of money!" Dad laughed, finishing her sentence. "You'd better believe it!"

"Were the people nice?"

"Didn't meet all that many native Newporters," Dad explained. "Most of the people your mother and I met there were guests at Nadine's wedding, and I'd say the majority of them came from elsewhere."

"So were they nice?" I asked, determined to hear Dad tell me that Nadine's entire guest list was comprised of little more than a bunch of snotty social-climbing sociopaths banded together to watch one of their own as she edged up the gilded ladder of greed.

"Nobody challenged me to a duel or threw their lobster tail at me," Dad teased. "Of course, there was that woman who tripped your mother because she didn't like her shoes."

"Really? What happened?"

"Your father's just having some fun," Mom said. "Don't pay any attention to him."

"Oh," I said, embarrassed by my gullibility.

"I'll tell you all about the wedding and the trip another time, Darla," Mom offered. "Right now, I want to hear how you're doing."

The moment of truth had arrived and the fun was over. I looked at my parents' adoring faces for the last time. I would never again see the proud gleam in Dad's eyes, nor the nurturing smile on my mother's face.

"Something really bad happened while you were gone," I told them, looking down at the floor.

"Would you like to tell us about it?" Dad asked.

"You'll hate me forever once you find out," I warned him.

"I don't think that's possible, Darla. Now, why don't you tell me what happened."

"You'll hate me!" I insisted.

"All right, Darla," Dad said slowly. "I'm going to be very up front about this. Your mother and I have just come from George and Didi's house. We'd gone there first thinking that's where we'd find you. Your aunt told us everything that happened. We know that May was attacked by someone named Hatch and that she's in the hospital, and that the purpose of the trip was for you to see the Mullavey boy play in a band."

I needed a moment to process what he'd just said. "Aunt Didi told you all that and you were still glad to see me?"

"Of course we were glad to see you. You're our daughter and we love you very much."

"Really?" I asked incredulously.

"Darla," Dad elucidated. "We've all been through quite a lot this year. We've had our good times and more than our share of the bad. While we were away, your mother and I did a lot of soul searching, and we asked ourselves what we could do to keep the lines of communication open in this family. What we realized is that we couldn't expect you to listen to us if we didn't listen to you. So I'm going to put aside my anger and my fatherly impulse to rant and rave, which is quite strong at the moment, and ask you what you have to say about all of this. Now, how's that for your new and improved dad?"

It was hard to believe that my parents knew everything that had happened, and yet they were still calm, rational, and loving, especially my father.

"Go on, Darla. Tell us what happened," Mom said gently.

"Well—" I stammered. "Things sorta started a couple of weeks ago when April ran into Ryan at the supermarket. He asked her to tell me that he was going to be playing with this band at Pier 23, and—"

"And it just happened to be the weekend that your mother and I were going to be away?" Dad asked, stiffening.

"Well, yeah, but I had no intention of going. I swear!"

279

"Something must've happened to change your mind," Mom interjected.

"I guess it did," I said, looking directly her. "A lot of stuff happened."

"I see. Anything in particular?"

I had been dying to confront Mom with what she had done to me, but suddenly, I was losing my nerve.

"We're waiting, Darla," Dad said, drumming his fingers on the armrest.

"I know," I replied nervously. "I just don't know where to start."

"The beginning is usually a pretty good place. Why don't you try that?"

I took a deep breath and continued. "Well, the first thing that happened was with May. I shouldn't be telling you all this, but she's been really depressed lately and angry with her mother. For one, May doesn't want to be in that summer stock production, and she doesn't want a career in show business either. But Aunt Didi doesn't care what May wants."

"Go on," Mom said, as if she weren't the least bit surprised by my revelation.

"So one day, when May was really depressed, I asked her to come here so we could talk in private. I wanted to cheer her up and thought she might want to talk without having to worry about Aunt Didi listening in."

I looked up briefly to see my parents' reaction. They were hanging on my every word.

"Anyway," I went on, hoping someone would interrupt me, "I started talking to May about Nadine, and we got on the subject of the wedding. May wanted to see Nadine's wedding invitation, so I looked for it in Mom's desk drawer."

It took my mother only a few seconds to realize where I was heading. Instantly, her pleasant expression disappeared and was replaced with a bizarre look of terror, appropriately accented by one of her famous throat-clutching gestures. Dad, who appeared to be totally bewildered, looked at Mom and then back at me.

I wasn't sure what to say next. I had rehearsed my showdown with Mom numerous times, but in light of what Hatch had done to May, and of the ensuing repercussions, Mom's crime, though still reprehensible, no longer inspired me to employ draconian measures in order to seek my revenge. Besides, one look at her face told me that she was already suffering and I hadn't even gotten to the "good part" yet. But that by no means excused her wicked behavior, not as far as I was concerned.

"Oh Darla. Goodness gracious," she said, as her hands fluttered nervously in the air.

Dad looked baffled as he watched Mom's quirky parade of gestures. It felt good to reign superior over my parents, although I knew it was only temporary.

"Does someone want to tell me what's going on here?" Dad asked impatiently.

Mom sighed again and put her open palm to the side of her face. She reminded me of Jack Benny, the old comedian whom Dad enjoyed watching in reruns. I wanted to remark aloud on the resemblance but I didn't think Mom would appreciate it.

"What the hell's going on here, Maggs?" Dad asked her, obviously recognizing her odd movements as a sign of distress and showing signs of the old Ted McKendrick again. "Darla, would you like to tell me?"

"I'll show you!" I said, suddenly feeling very courageous.

Mom sighed despairingly, watching in angst as I got up and marched over to her desk. It took me no time at all to retrieve Nadine's letter, which I promptly presented to my father. I still had no idea of what role, if any, he had played in all of this, but it was clear from his bewildered expression that he knew nothing of Nadine's letter to me.

"Oh, Jesus!" Dad exclaimed when he'd finished the letter. "What in the world is going on here? Maggs, tell me you didn't do what this letter suggests you did."

"That's exactly what she did!" I said victoriously. "Mom forged an apology note to Nadine and made a complete fool out of me in front of all the Hoovers!"

"Calm down, Darla," Dad scolded me.

Mom started wringing her hands and sniffling. As I predicted, it was only a matter of seconds before the tears came.

"I'm sorry, Darla. I'm sorry, Ted. It was such a stupid thing to do. I knew it was wrong, but I was desperate to bring peace back into our family. Honestly, I don't know what possessed me to do such a dreadful thing."

My mother started crying like a baby. To me, her tears seemed like a mere ruse to deny me of any feelings of victory that I was entitled to have, and I felt my anger begin to grow again. I was the one who deserved Dad's sympathy, not Mom, and I wasn't about to let her steal my thunder. I had to do something to get his attention. I decided to try on several new words that I'd learned in my tenth-grade English class, to see if they fit. It was my hope that the use of more sophisticated vocabulary would enable my father to see me in a more adult light.

"I don't even want to imagine the falsehoods that Mom attributed me to in her phony missive!" I said with great emotion. "Certainly not!"

Mom and Dad shared a surprised look. Within seconds, I saw the corners of my Dad's mouth curl up, as they often did before he broke into hearty laughter. Mom stopped crying, and the terror in her eyes quickly changed to what Dad always called "that delightful little twinkle that I first fell in love with."

I was devastated. Not only did my attempt to use my new vocabulary words fail to impress my parents, but it had backfired on me as well. Mom was going to try to use this charming little scenario to deflect the attention from her and thereby weasel her way out of the most despicable act she'd ever committed. I was determined not to let her get away with it.

"Go ahead and laugh if you want!" I challenged her. "Laugh your head off! I'm sure that's exactly what the Hoovers did when they got your letter."

My parents knew I was on to them, and their faces quickly resumed their previous expressions. I was gaining ground.

"Darla," Mom said. "I'd like to explain."

"First tell me what you wrote to them. I want to know every word that I said!"

"Darla—" Dad warned.

"Don't I have a right to know what I said to the Hoovers?"

"I don't think that's really the issue right now."

"Oh really, Dad? Well, I beg to differ with you!" I said, surprising myself by using a corny adult phrase that had never come out of my mouth before. "I think I have a right to know what I supposedly said. I mean, did I lay it on thick, did I tell Nadine how wonderful she is and what a stupid child I had been, or did I just grovel at the Hoovers' smelly feet?"

"Darla! This is not the time for this! Your cousin May, in case you have forgotten, is lying in a hospital bed, mute and emotionally distraught after being violated and almost raped. The contents of your mother's letter hardly seem to be our priority right now. Now, I've offered you a chance to tell your side of the story, but if you insist on going off on this silly tangent, then we might as well cease all communication efforts and go to bed. I've been driving for God-knows-how-many hours and I'm tired as hell. Do you read me?"

"Yeah. I read you," I repeated, fighting the urge to mock him.

"Anything you'd like me to repeat?"

"No. I got it."

"Fine. Then why don't you continue with your story so that your mother and I can understand just what happened."

"Yeah. Okay," I conceded, taking a couple of extra seconds to brood over Dad's admonishment. "After I read Nadine's letter, I got really upset and started crying and screaming because Mom had betrayed me. May felt really bad for me, and that's when she suggested that we go to Pier 23, you know, because I was so mad at Mom and she was so mad at Aunt Didi. May thought that it was our turn to do something we wanted for a change."

"Going to Pier 23 doesn't seem like the kind of activity that May would opt for, given her druthers."

I had no idea what "druthers" meant, but I hoped that someday it wouldn't creep into my vocabulary by mistake. It was embarrassing enough to have said "I beg to differ" at the ripe old age of sixteen, and though I was all for improving my vocabulary, I didn't need any more corny words or phrases thrown into the mix.

"May didn't want to be May anymore. At least she didn't want to be the same old May boys never looked at. She wanted to be glamorous and sexy."

"Oh goodness."

"You don't seem very surprised by all of this, Maggs," Dad said to Mom.

"I'm not surprised, Ted. Not really. I warned Didi about this many times, but she didn't want to listen."

I was dying to ask Mom to elaborate on what she was saying, but I knew I would be instantly chastised for doing so.

"Go on, Darla," Dad implored me.

"I know you're not going to believe this," I said, looking at both of them, "but I really didn't want to go. I mean, I wanted to go, but I knew it wasn't a good idea and I was kind of afraid. But then we got Melanie to help us, and we made plans and stuff, and I was too embarrassed to back out. I mean, they were both trying so hard to help me see Ryan. I would've looked like the biggest dweeb in the world if I'd said no."

It was apparent by my father's expression that he had the same confusion about "dweeb" as I'd had about "druthers," but he didn't bother to ask for a definition either.

"So anyway, we got all dressed up and May drove us to the waterfront. The bouncer at the door was flirting with these girls, and I guess because we looked so old, he didn't even bother to check our ID."

"That's great!" Dad shouted angrily. "Can you believe that, Maggs?"

Mom shook her head in despair.

"What happened next?" Dad wanted to know.

"Well, May and I didn't know what to do when we got inside. It was really noisy and crowded and everyone was staring at us because we were so dressed up. Most of the people there just wore jeans and had tattoos and stuff, so I guess we kinda looked out of place."

Dad rolled his eyes in disgust.

"Anyway, we decided to stand around the front of the bar because it was the best place to see the band. That's when we met Hatch and he offered us two seats at the bar. He looked okay at first because he was so clean-cut and didn't have ripped clothes and weird hair like most of the people in there."

I could tell that Dad was fighting to stay in control. With each word I spoke, he looked angrier and angrier, but he was obviously determined to let me finish. For the next fifteen minutes, I explained in detail how I had come to distrust Hatch as the evening wore on, how I had pleaded unsuccessfully with May to be careful, and how Hatch had taken May away as soon as I had turned my head to speak with Corky. Both of my parents were visibly shaken when I described how May had looked in the aftermath of her attack, but neither of them interrupted my story until I got to the part about Aunt Didi throwing me against the wall and telling me that I was fast on my way to becoming as worthless as Rebecca.

My mother was aghast. "Darla, are you absolutely sure that's what your aunt said to you? Is there any way in all the confusion that you might've misheard her?"

"That's exactly what she said, Mom. I swear. I'll never forget."

She was stunned. I had a captive audience and I knew it. With my parents paying rapt attention to what I was saying, I went on to finish my story, taking care to include every horrible thing that was said to me at the Alexander home and how I was virtually told by April to stay away from May.

"Darla," Mom said, "if indeed that's what happened, it's simply not acceptable. No, not at all."

She paused and squirmed anxiously in her chair. "Neither is what I did by writing that letter to the Hoovers. But I'm exhausted, Darla, and as your father told you, we've been driving for hours and hours today. There just isn't the time tonight to give any of these matters the attention they deserve. Why don't you and I continue this conversation in the morning?"

"Really?" I said, doubting her sincerity. "We'll talk about the letter?"

"Really. I promise."

285

I didn't quite believe her, based on past experience, but I knew that if she didn't stay true to her word, I could always quote her and shame her into talking to me. Naturally, I wasn't especially gung-ho to talk about what I had done wrong, but I also knew that I wasn't going to get off scot-free just because my parents were tired.

"Well, I'm going get the rest of our luggage and call it a night," Dad announced, rising from his chair. "Maggs, don't we have a gift for Darla?"

"We certainly do!" Mom said, jumping up from her chair and running over to the hordes of shopping bags she had brought inside. She rummaged anxiously through her store-bought treasures, beaming with pleasure when she found my gift.

"It's a stuffed sailboat!" Dad grinned.

"Oh, Ted! It's a throw pillow, in the shape of a sailboat. It's not a stuffed sailboat."

My parents giggled as Mom handed me the pillow.

"This is really cool. Thanks. I like it a lot."

"I'm glad. I have some more gifts for you, but I'll look for them in the morning—when we have our talk."

Maybe Mom really was sincere. I would soon find out. Stuffed sailboat in hand, I kissed them good night, and went upstairs to sleep in my own bed, in my own house, where I would be safe and sound, knowing how much I was loved.

CHAPTER 18

Dad left for work bright and early the next morning, and by nine fifteen, I was downstairs at the kitchen table with Mom, anxious to have the talk that we'd scheduled the night before.

"Well, I feel one hundred percent better after a good night's sleep," Mom told me as she sipped her coffee. "I don't know why I was so exhausted—after all, it was your father who did all the driving—but I guess it has something to do with crossing state lines and getting up so early in the morning."

"Yeah, I guess," I said, hoping that her inane chatter wasn't going to replace the significant conversation that I'd been promised.

"But I suppose you'd rather talk about the awful thing that your mother did," she said, looking pleasantly at me.

I couldn't read her. I didn't know if she was trying to make me feel guilty for wanting to resolve the matter, or if she was simply admitting to her mistake. But for once in my life, I wasn't going to dive head first into the water without checking to see how deep it was. I looked at my mother blankly and waited for her to give me some indication of where she was coming from.

"Goodness, Darla, you're looking at me as if I've grown a second head overnight. Are you so surprised that your mother can admit to making a mistake?"

"Do you really mean what you said last night? That you were wrong to write that letter? Or did you just say that 'cause Dad was listening?"

My mother's pleasant expression immediately disappeared from her face. I instantly regretted my question, realizing that I'd insulted her good intention to come clean and had hurt her feelings in the process.

"I'm sorry, Mom," I said sincerely. I wasn't trying to be mean. I swear."

"I know that," Mom said, putting her coffee cup down, then looking at me with sadness in her eyes. "Under the circumstances, I don't blame you for doubting me. And I'm not trying to avoid discussing this with you either. I just don't know how best to explain it."

That said, Mom appeared to sink momentarily into some sort of meditative trance. "Well, let me ask you this, Darla," she said after deep contemplation. "Since you met Ryan last September, have you done anything that you've regretted—to get his attention, or to get him to like you?"

"Well, sure!" I said, as if she'd asked me the world's stupidest question. "I went to Pier 23 to see him! He's back with his old girlfriend, Lisa the slut, and he barely even remembers telling April to say hello to me. Talk about the most humiliating moment of my life, made only a billion times worse by what happened to May afterwards, and then by what Aunt Didi did, and June, and April. Of course I regret it!"

"I'm sorry, Darla," Mom said sweetly. "I know what a terrible evening it was for you, and even more so for dear, sweet May. But we'll get back to that subject in just a bit. Right now, I'm curious to know if there was anything you've done to gain Ryan's affections that you now regret."

I didn't quite grasp her point, but the supermarket incident came quickly to mind.

"Well, I guess dressing up like an old lady and going to the supermarket was pretty stupid."

"Anything else?" she inquired delicately.

"What do you mean?" I asked. I was not enjoying her line of questioning at all.

"How about New Year's Eve? Didn't you tell me that you got into that Cheyney boy's car because you were afraid that Ryan would leave you in the driveway if you told him how frightened you were? That he would think you were just a 'little kid' if you protested?"

"Yeah. I remember," I said, a bit resentfully.

"Well, that decision almost got you killed, didn't it?"

I couldn't quite figure out how Mom's frank and open discussion about the Hoover letter had turned into a retelling of all the idiotic things that I'd done to win Ryan's affection.

"How come we're talking about me now? What do my feelings for Ryan have to do with writing a letter to the Hoovers?"

Mom took the coffeepot off the hot pad and poured herself a second cup. "Well, honey, I'm trying to show you that people often do very stupid things to be with someone they love, or to make someone that they love happy. You've made many mistakes with Ryan in the name of love, and I made a stupid mistake by writing that letter to the Hoovers, in the name of love for you and your father. I know it's no excuse, but I was desperate to put this family back together, especially when Christmas was so near, so I wrote a short note to the Hoovers and then convinced your father to let you handle the matter in your own sweet time. He was pretty tired of the bad feelings too, so it didn't take much to convince him. And by the way, I promise you, I didn't do any 'groveling.' Now, what would you think if I called Louisa and explained to her that you didn't write the letter—and that I did? Would that, and a really big apology, be enough?"

"Yeah. Sure, Mom."

"Then give me a great big hug and I'll call Louisa later in the day."

"She might hate you!" I warned.

"I don't think so," Mom said and laughed. "But I'm willing to take my chances."

As I leaned over in my chair to hug my mother, grateful for a fairly painless resolution of the matter, I started thinking about May and about how a painless resolution of her problems would be next to impossible. I tried to imagine how frightened she must be, lying silent in a hospital bed while all sorts of distorted images and voices battled for center ring in her head. I surmised that she must be feeling a terror not unlike my nightmares—only that her pain was real and wouldn't go away when she opened her eyes. Hatch was not a monster whom her brain had conjured up to deal with subconscious demons; he was a real person, an unlikely symbol whom May had chosen to prove to herself that she could be as beautiful and as independent as she'd always dreamed of being. Had May not been desperate to prove something to herself and to her mother, she never would've allowed someone like Hatch to lure her into his evil trap, and then to violate her soul with one brutal tear of a party dress—and God only knows what else.

"Mom, I'm so worried about May. I don't know what to do."

289

"I don't know what to do either," she said nervously, trying to steady her right hand that was holding her coffee cup. "I haven't been able to take my mind off that poor child. I was thinking of going to see her later on in the day, if it's allowed."

"The Alexanders don't want me anywhere near her," I said bitterly.

"I'm sure that nobody blames you for what that awful man did, sweetie," Mom said, unaware that she was spilling her coffee onto the table. "You were probably just an unfortunate scapegoat in this ugly mess. Oh, goodness. Look what I've done." Mom sighed, put down the cup, and jumped up to fetch some paper towels.

As I watched Mom grab a handful of towels, then frantically wipe up the spillage, I wondered why she was comparing me to an escaped goat. I figured it had something to do with being perceived as a naughty animal that destroyed things and then ran away, therefore deserving little more in life than proverbial tin cans to munch on.

"I'm sure it would be fine if you went to see May in the hospital," Mom said, throwing the coffee-soaked towels in the trash, then resuming her seat." We just have to check first and make sure that the doctors say it's okay. If you'd like, we can go shopping later and choose a gift for May. How does that sound, honey?"

"But, Mom, the Alexanders don't want me to visit May, no matter what the doctors say!"

"I'm sure that Didi and George would be delighted if you paid May a visit," Mom said, daring to drink the coffee left in her cup.

"Think again, Maggie." Aunt Didi's voice resonated from the patio, as she looked at Mom and me through the screen of the kitchen door. "I'll thank you not to decide what will or will not delight me and my husband."

Mom, startled, looked at me, almost spilling her coffee for the second time as she put the cup down on the table. Then, Aunt Didi opened the door and came charging into the kitchen, destroying the long overdue conversation that I was having with my mother, as she once again injected her verbal poison into my veins and made me shiver with fear. Only this time, I had my mother to protect me.

290

"Oh Didi, really!"

"Maggie, don't you dare give me that 'Oh, Didi' routine. A week ago, I had three beautiful, happy, healthy daughters, eagerly preparing to participate in the theatrical opportunity of their lifetime. What do I have today? Well, I'll tell you. I've got one daughter lying in the psychiatric ward of the hospital, suffering from unspeakable trauma, and I've got two others at home crying their eyes out and refusing to participate in anything until their sister has fully recovered from her brutal attack. And to make matters worse, that animal who ravaged my daughter is nowhere to be found, while the inept morons who call themselves police officers can barely track down a jaywalker—much less this rabid creature who no doubt is hiding in a sewer somewhere, polishing his genitals and getting ready to pounce on his next victim. I've got a husband who is going stark, raving mad, fancying himself to be a sheriff's posse of one, and who's determined to find that spineless son of a bitch and hang him up by his cowardly balls in front of City Hall. So don't 'Oh, Didi' me if you want to live!"

Mom and I just looked at each other. Aunt Didi was a tough act to follow.

"And would you like to know how this all started? It started with your daughter, Maggie, your daughter who somehow convinced my daughter to toss all caution to the wind and drive her down to that waterfront dive."

Mom took a moment to collect her thoughts and looked at Aunt Didi. "Darla did not convince May to drive her to Pier 23. If you must know, it was May who convinced Darla to go. The truth is that both of our girls should have known better, but to everyone's great misfortune, especially May's, they did not. However, as ill advised as their mutual decision was, it is not Darla's fault that her cousin was attacked. Clearly, the blame for that lies squarely on the shoulders of that detestable man."

Aunt Didi looked as if she were going to spit nails. She picked up a wooden spoon from the ceramic utensil holder on the counter, pounded it three times into the palm of her hand, and threw it into the sink, breaking my juice glass that sat waiting to be washed. Then she began furiously pacing the kitchen, while Mom and I sat at the table, observing her madness. Finally, she stopped moving and looked dangerously at Mom.

"You will never convince me Maggie, ever, that my daughter May initiated that outing to hell! Never!"

"It's the truth, Didi."

"My daughter would never do something like that! Your daughter, on the other hand, has committed a multitude of sins this past year, far too numerous for me to recount at this moment."

"Which brings me to ask you a question," Mom said, impressing me with her gumption. "Did you tell my daughter that she was 'fast on her way to becoming as worthless as her Aunt Rebecca?'"

Aunt Didi looked at Mom and then at me. "Haven't you stirred up enough trouble for one week?"

"I'll take that as a yes," Mom said furiously. "And I'll thank you never to speak that way to my daughter again."

The two sisters just stared at each other, as if they were waiting for the bell to sound before they began fighting again. Finally, Mom took a deep breath, as she tried to do her best to calm things down.

"Didi, May is a very sweet girl whom we all love very much. I can understand that it's difficult for you to picture her actually wanting to go to that wretched place. But neither May nor Darla had been there before, and neither one of them knew what to expect. Goodness, let's not forget that they're inexperienced sixteen-year-old girls. But think about what you're saying—even if Darla had convinced May to blindly follow her lead, do you think May would've dolled herself up like that, and spent so much time talking to that awful man Hatch, if it wasn't what May felt comfortable doing? Surely your girls have minds of their own! Or don't they?"

I could tell from the look on Aunt Didi's face that she did not want to hear what Mom was saying, or even to contemplate the possibility that Mom might be telling the truth.

"You can rationalize and twist this sordid mess any way you want to, dear sister, but I will never believe that my daughter was there by her own choice. What possible reason could she have had, except to please Darla?"

"I warned you about this, Didi! I've warned you so many times that it's not funny. But you never wanted to listen to me."

"What the hell are you talking about, Maggie?"

"I told you to let those girls find their own way, and to let them dance to the beat of their own drummers—not yours. May was very upset at being forced into this summer stock production, and even more upset because of your constant insistence that she pursue a performing career. She initiated this outing to Pier 23 because for the first time she wanted to be in charge of her own life. Now, surely you can understand that."

"Darla!" Aunt Didi barked at me, ignoring Mom completely. "We invited you with open arms to stay in our home, and that made you privy to some very personal family conversations. I'm very disappointed that you would take a conversation that you heard at our dinner table and turn it into something ugly, just to slither your way out of accepting responsibility for what you've done."

"This doesn't have anything to do with what I heard at dinner," I said, eager to defend myself. "And I'm not slithering! May told me many times that she didn't want to do the show. She was really depressed about it too."

I felt guilty divulging any of what May had told me in confidence, but I thought it was necessary, and I believed that May would approve, knowing the bind I was in.

"Darla, I think I know my daughter better than you know your cousin. May is a temperamental performer. It's not unusual for her to make noises now and then about wanting to do something else, but when she's on stage and the curtain goes up, she's in seventh heaven. There's no place she'd rather be. And don't you believe any differently. Performing is in her blood."

"Well, maybe she had a transfusion when you weren't looking," I said fearlessly.

I saw Mom quietly put her hand to her mouth to suppress a giggle. Aunt Didi was not amused. She leaned against the sink and glared at me as she calculated her next move.

"Didi," Mom said diplomatically, "why don't you sit down at the table and join us? It would be a lot nicer than just standing there, giving us the evil eye."

Aunt Didi did not like it when anyone tried to downplay her anger. "I don't want to sit...Margaret!"

"Well, then, have it your way...Deirdre!"

At that precise moment, it occurred to me that although the average person did garner her fair share of wisdom as the years pressed on, even the most mature of individuals was likely to revert back to childish means of retaliation when the going got rough. For the first time, I could picture Mom and Aunt Didi as children, squabbling over some trivial matter while Grandma Adelaide unsuccessfully tried to placate them. I decided that without a doubt it must've been my aunt who did all the instigating. My mother was noticeably the mature one.

"Maggie! I cannot believe that you condone what Darla has done to my daughter! Why isn't she being punished? Just what in the hell are you and Ted planning to do about this?"

I could see Mom's hackles go up. "Darla has done nothing to May! How dare you even intimate that she has! I'll say it once again. The girls made a mutually bad decision, and May was hurt. But it's not Darla's fault! Now, I know you're angry, and that's certainly understandable, but as for what Ted and I are going to do about this...well, that's McKendrick family business. I know you need to blame someone, but making my daughter culpable isn't going to help May get well any faster. Now, I've—"

"You're damn right I need someone to blame! And if it hadn't been for your daughter's obsession with Ryan Mullavey, all three of my girls would be happily preparing for summer stock right now."

I wanted to ask Aunt Didi if May's attack was really what was bothering her, or if perhaps it just might be that all three of her daughters had to bow out of the production. But I knew it was a cruel question, and probably not true, so I wisely kept it to myself.

Apparently, Mom was having the same thought, but she managed to phrase it a bit more delicately than I would've been able to.

"Didi, will you forget about that darn show! This is the second time you've mentioned it. The show is what you wanted. Maybe it's not what all of your girls wanted! Why don't you ever let them decide how they want to spend their summer?"

"And that is Alexander family business!"

"Didi," Mom said, lowering her voice authoritatively, "you can't go on running the girls' lives forever. If you don't learn that now, it's going to be disastrous later on. Look what happened with Rebecca!"

I couldn't believe my ears, although by this point, I should've been used to it. There she was again, Rebecca, right smack-dab in the middle of another problem, one that had absolutely nothing to do with her. I prayed that in their anger, one of the Connor sisters would reveal the real truth, which, I knew instinctively, was still buried deep.

"Okay then!" Aunt Didi fumed, picking up the wooden spoon again as if she were going to hit Mom with it. "You want to talk about what happened to Rebecca? Let's talk about how you convinced Mom to take away the one thing that Rebecca loved, because you had something better in mind for her...and, well, we both know what happened after that, don't we? We both know what destroying someone's dreams can do to them!"

"To this day, Deirdre, I still don't know where Rebecca's dream ended and yours began. It's certainly not my fault that Rebecca grew up too fast. If she'd been allowed to play with children her own age, instead of being dragged around to talent shows by her sister, or made to practice silly song-and-dance routines in the basement, maybe she would've developed normally and not turned into a...well, maybe things would've been different!"

"It's not what I gave her that destroyed her, Maggie: it's what you took away!"

"You taught her how to flaunt her body when she was five years old! What in God's name did you expect would happen?"

"I was only ten years old myself!" Aunt Didi screamed. "What the hell did I know about flaunting bodies! What do you think I was, some adolescent tart? Get real, Maggie!"

As I listened to my mother and Aunt Didi argue, with the same back-and-forth intensity that one might watch at a final Wimbledon match, I frantically tried to piece together the clues. All I could really figure out was that Aunt Didi was a stage sister long before she was a stage mother, and that as a child, she had tried to push her youngest sister toward the bright lights of fame, just as she'd done in recent years with April, May, and June. Only I'd never heard so much as a whisper about Rebecca's having any talent, much less any show business aspirations, so it seemed odd that this information could be so relevant and yet had never surfaced before in any of Mom's so-called confessions.

"Rebecca deserved to grow up like a normal child!" Mom said loudly, uncharacteristically pounding her fist on the table. "Not a doll for you to play with, or for you to design and manipulate, but a child, who finds her own way by exploring her own curiosities, not those of her older sister."

"I did not treat Rebecca like a doll!"

"Oh yes, you did!" Mom said seething with anger. 'Dance, Rebecca! Sing, Rebecca' Goodness, you were just like that Gypsy Rose Lee person's mother. You even named one of your daughters June!"

"Well," Aunt Didi bellowed, "now you're just being silly, Maggie. You're not making any sense at all. And I certainly didn't name June after some stripper's sister, and you know that."

"Oh, pardon me for forgetting!" Mom said childishly. "April, May, and June were your little calendar girls. Too bad you didn't have July, August, and September to push around too!"

In my opinion, Mom was inching closer to being as mean as Aunt Didi and I didn't like seeing that side of her. To my dismay, I feared I would have to rethink my theory about Mom being the more mature sister, if her infantile prattle continued.

"Well, at least I didn't punish my husband by refusing to get pregnant again!" Aunt Didi shouted.

I couldn't believe what I was hearing. Suddenly, Mom and Aunt Didi grew very quiet, as if they'd just noticed me for the first time. Obviously, in the heated moments that had preceded Aunt Didi's unusual and shocking statement, they had completely forgotten that I was in the room.

"Oh, goodness!" Mom said, turning white as a sheet as she clutched her throat. "Darla!"

"Why don't you go upstairs or something?" Aunt Didi said, glaring at me. "Let your mother and I have this out! Now, go!"

"Don't you dare order my daughter around in her own home!" Mom retorted, releasing the choke hold she had on her own neck. "I won't have it!"

"Fine!" Aunt Didi growled. "Then I'll go! And I don't want anyone in the McKendrick family to come within a mile of my child's hospital room. Is that understood?"

"Oh, Didi," Mom pleaded, rising from the table. "This has gotten way out of control. Why don't we resolve this before we both say more ugly things that we're sorry for?"

"You're right, Margaret! This is out of control! I'm out of control! And you know what? I like it!" Aunt Didi started waving around the wooden mixing spoon like a lunatic on the fringe.

"Stop that, for goodness sakes," Mom screamed. "Before you break something else!"

Aunt Didi marched over to the wall where Mom's decorator kitchen clock hung. "You mean like this ugly clock?"

"Didi—please!"

"Please my ass! Here's what I think of you, and here's what I think of this repulsive timepiece...this dime store exclusive you're so fond of."

Before Mom could clutch her throat or make one final plea, Aunt Didi whacked the face of the clock with the base of the spoon, shattering the crystal into a million pieces.

"My clock! My beautiful clock!"

"Get out of here, Aunt Didi!" I screamed, surprising myself more than anyone. "Leave my mother alone!"

"I'm going!" she snarled at me. "And you just make sure you stay away from my daughter ...from all of them. We've had enough of the McKendrick family to last us a lifetime!"

297

As my mother stood there crying, surveying the shattered mess, I watched as Aunt Didi went flying out the back door, like a wicked witch making a race against time to get to her broomstick before the meter maid could ticket her for double parking. It was unfathomable to think that she was now our enemy, and that my mother's best friend and confidante had wreaked such devastation on our family.

For a moment, I started to wonder if perhaps Aunt Didi wasn't right after all. Maybe it was my fault. Maybe my feelings for Ryan and my poor judgment were to blame. I didn't know anymore. I walked over to my mother and threw my arms around her, trying desperately to comfort her as she cried.

"I love you, Mom. I swear I do."

She smiled briefly through her tears and looked lovingly at me. "I love you too, honey. Now, go on about your business. I'll clean this up."

"No, Mom. I really want to do it."

"I need to be alone right now. Didn't you want to pay a visit to Melanie today?"

"Yeah, Mom, but—"

"Go then, honey. I'll see you later."

I kissed Mom good-bye and walked out the back door. As I rounded the rear of the house, toward the side yard, to my surprise, I could see my aunt's car still parked on the street. Even from where I stood in the distance, I could see her sitting in the driver's seat, sobbing, and banging her head on the steering wheel.

Despite my anger, I wanted to spare her the embarrassment of being seen, so I cut through our neighbor's backyard to the next block, thereby allowing Aunt Didi the courtesy of not having to pass her wayward niece on the way home.

When I reached Melanie's house, I found a landscaping crew hard at work in the Davenport front yard. Being quite shy in such situations, and not wanting to walk past a bunch of shirtless, sweaty men, who I feared might make intimidating remarks or attempt to engage me in embarrassing conversation, I decided to walk up the driveway and enter through the rear of the house.

I had the oddest sense of déjà vu when I looked through the door off the kitchen and saw Grace Davenport, Melanie's mom, sitting at the kitchen table with her head bent in sorrow. Although I couldn't be sure, it appeared that she was crying. For a moment, she reminded me so much of my own mother as I'd just left her. I wondered if perhaps Aunt Didi hadn't recently paid Mrs. Davenport a visit as well, possibly to chastise her for Melanie's small, albeit vital, role as cover in our infamous visit to Pier 23.

But that was too ludicrous a notion to take seriously. Besides, Aunt Didi was probably still parked back on my street, banging her head against the steering wheel, or playing bumper car with other drivers as she drove home.

I didn't know what to do. I hated the idea of knocking on the door and forcing Mrs. Davenport to face me in her tearful state, but I also couldn't bear the thought of having to infiltrate the band of bare-chested wonders on the front lawn just to get to the front door. As I stood there deciding my course of action, I heard Melanie's voice call to me from the second-floor bathroom window, which was right over my head.

"It's a door, Darla. The idea is to open it and come inside."

"Very funny!" I said, squinting at the sun, as I looked up to see her.

"What are you waiting for? You want one of those hunks out front to escort you inside or what? Did you see the butt on the blond guy, the one in the green shorts? Omigod, is that a butt to die for or what?"

"God, Melanie. Shut up!" I scolded her. "Do you want him to hear you?"

"I don't care. Don't be such a prude. Who cares if he hears me or not? He knows he's got a nice butt. And I'll bet he does a hundred squats a day just to keep it firm like that."

"Melanie!"

By this time, Mrs. Davenport, hearing our voices, had noticed me at the door and walked over to let me in. She was a gorgeous woman, tall, with short dark red hair, and was one of the most charming and vivacious people I'd ever met.

"Darla! Come in, honey. How long have you been waiting out here?"

"Oh, not long, Mrs. Davenport."

"Oh, gracious," she said and smiled. "I hope you didn't see me sitting at the table in my weepy-eyed condition."

"Well, sort of," I replied, not knowing whether to give her a definitive no or yes answer. "I didn't want to knock and disturb you. Is everything all right?"

"Everything is fine!" she said with great conviction. "Just fine. I'm feeling a bit sentimental today, that's all. Now, go on upstairs and see Melly. She's been waiting for you."

Melanie was still in the bathroom when I got upstairs, standing in front of the mirror, plucking her eyebrows, and wincing as she extricated each tiny hair from her forehead.

"Having fun?" I teased, as I stepped into the bathroom to greet her.

"You know what, Dar? You should go pluck yourself! Then you'll see how much fun it is!"

"I hardly ever pluck my eyebrows. I really don't need to."

"Well, you're lucky you don't have a Neanderthal for a grandfather. Have you ever seen my dad's father? He is so hairy. I have his genes to thank for this grueling ritual. Of course, my mom's side of the family is responsible for saddling me with these gazillion freckles."

"I think they're cute."

"You would, Darla, until you had to go through life with a connect-the-dots game permanently etched on your face. Then we'd see how cute you think they are! Well, I'm all plucked out. Let's go in my room and talk."

"Is everything all right with your mom?" I asked Melanie as we entered her bedroom and plopped down. "She was sorta crying when I got here."

"Omigod, Dar: I completely forgot to tell you about my sister. Do you remember how Brenda was going to work for my mother's interior decorator friend, Simone La Française or something, after she graduated from college?"

"Sure."

"Well, Brenda's boyfriend, Dave, just got a job on Wall Street and guess who's going to New York with him, and guess who got herself a job as an apprentice for this really fancy decorator on Madison Avenue?"

"Wow, you're kidding! Brenda's moving to New York?"

"Yeah, and my mom's kinda...well, she's really bummed out about it. She thought Bren was gonna stay here forever. I mean, she's happy for her and all, but it was just all so sudden and she really hasn't had time to adjust to her firstborn flying the coop."

"You mean leaving the nest?"

"Duh! Does it matter?"

"I guess you'll miss Brenda a lot too."

"Of course I will. But Bren promised I could visit whenever I want. So it'll be fine. I won't miss her that much," Melanie said unconvincingly. "I'm more bummed about Drew going to college in Boston. I don't know what's going to happen to our relationship once he's gone. Anyway, I hope he doesn't come back saying 'pock the caaah' the way they say it up there. Wouldn't that be a trip!"

"You worry about the strangest things," I said, resting my back against the wall in an attempt to get comfortable.

"Speaking of worrying," Melanie said, taking the spotlight off herself, "I know how freaked you've been about May. Have you heard any more about her condition? Do you think your aunt will let you see her?"

"Oh God, Melanie. No way! And you wouldn't believe what just happened this morning!"

"What? Tell me!"

Melanie listened attentively, dotting the verbal landscape with an occasional "Omigod" as I recalled the morning's events to her, finishing my tale with a colorful description of Aunt Didi's grand finale, the smashing of the kitchen clock.

"Your mom must be devastated! Geez, I can't believe your aunt got violent with a clock. Why would she do something like that?"

"I don't know. Maybe she was just killing time."

"Fun-nee," Melanie said, as we shared a quick laugh. "You oughta be on the stage! There's one leaving in an hour!"

"That's original! My father used to tell that stupid joke all the time!"

"I know. Who do you think I learned it from?"

We both laughed.

"But seriously, tell me about May. Is she any better at all?"

Suddenly, I hated myself for having taken even a moment to laugh. I had no business making jokes, not for any reason at all. I twisted my face and looked at Melanie. "No, she's no better. Not from the little my aunt told us. It doesn't sound like she's any better at all. And I'm sure that Aunt Didi's just making it worse. I'll bet you she's fawning all over May with this 'Talk to me, baby' stuff, like she did the night that it happened. I'll bet you anything that it's just making May go deeper into herself, so she doesn't have to deal with her mother. She's the one who should be kept out of May's room, not me!"

"She banned you from seeing May?" Melanie asked, as if she hadn't heard correctly.

"Aunt Didi told Mom that she didn't want any McKendricks going within a mile of May's hospital room."

"Omigod, Dar! She's gone bonkers! What a bitch on wheels!"

"You can say that again," I moaned.

"I wouldn't let her keep you from seeing May."

"What do you think I'm going to do, Melanie? Sneak into May's room when she's not looking?"

Melanie smiled dangerously at me. "Why not? I'll help you."

"I don't think so, Mel. I'm in enough trouble already, wouldn't you say? I don't think it's probably such a hot idea...but, of course, I really do think I can help May...nah, with my luck, I'd get caught and then burned at the stake."

"What's your aunt going to do? Curse you out in front of May or beat your face with a wooden spoon? Your aunt may be a bitch, but she's not stupid. She knows May would never forgive her for that."

"I don't know. I've done some pretty stupid things lately. Maybe I better cool it, you know?"

"Well, I'm not gonna push you, Darla, at least not today. But if May's not better in a few days, I'd seriously think about doing what you can to help her. I'll even drive you to the hospital, whenever you want. Promise."

"Thanks, but I'm just gonna wait and see. Maybe Mom and Aunt Didi will make up and then I won't have to sneak around."

"And maybe Drew will grow a butt like that guy in the green shorts has! But I wouldn't hold my breath. Not after what you told me!"

I stayed at Melanie's house for another couple of hours, discussing every topic du jour at least three times, and taking special care to fill her in on the latest clues surrounding Rebecca and her mysterious past. I could've easily stayed all day, but I became consumed with worry about my mother's state of mind and felt a strong pull toward home. True, I had left at Mom's insistence, but I figured that she'd had enough time alone to cry and might be needing someone to talk to in her state of anguish. Ironically, the person Mom always went to for support in such times was Aunt Didi, and though I perceived myself as little more than a consolation prize, I hoped that my love alone would be enough to cheer up my mother.

✳ ✳ ✳

For four days after Aunt Didi's visit, Mom barely said a word to anyone, tending to her household chores in a robotlike fashion. She didn't speak unless she was spoken to, and even then, would reply in a barely audible whisper using only the minimal words necessary to offer a response. It was devastating to see her so unhappy, but I soon realized that only Aunt Didi could fix what was broken.

Initially, I had tried to coax Mom into talking things out, but when I found my words to be reminiscent of Aunt Didi's "talk-to-me-baby" babble, I resolved to let Mom come around in her own time. Dad, who was very sweet and loving, instinctively gave Mom the space that she needed, but I suspected that he felt shut out, and I knew that he had to be hurting too.

I continued to work part time at Levinson's bakery. I had hoped that my job would take me away from my troubles, but business was slow most afternoons, so I was left alone at the counter with the bagels, challahs, and assorted rye breads, while Mrs. Levinson worked in the back with her husband. Rachel, who was originally slated to work alongside me, had happily gotten a last-minute opportunity to teach athletics at a local day camp during the week.

I had nothing but time on my hands. Time to contemplate every miserable moment of days past. Time to play an unending game of "what if" with myself, and time to re-create every waking horror I'd experienced. Over and over again, I wondered how things might have been different had I not fallen prey to Ryan's charms or run off to Pier 23 with May. No matter how I looked at the situation, I was to blame. If I hadn't screamed at Nadine and Everett on Thanksgiving, Mom would never have forged the apology letter, and there would have been no condescending letter from Nadine to use as an excuse for disobeying my father's strict orders. May would not have been viciously attacked, and Mom and Aunt Didi would still be the best of friends. In my defense, I had never been to Pier 23 before that night and certainly didn't know what to expect. But to my discredit, I had known that the club once served as a second home to Greg Cheyney, so it stood to reason that Pier 23, even dressed in its Sunday clothes, was likely to be a far cry from the palatial ambience and grace of The Captain's Table.

My mind was a cornucopia of clutter, a veritable junk drawer stuck in the open position, forcing me to confront every pitiable piece of paper, every rubber band, every paper clip, and every dismembered piece of hardware taking up space. The more I tried to clean it out, the more junk I found—baubles, buttons, and baby pictures, old junk mail, keys, and earrings without mates. I desperately wanted to close the drawer, if only for a brief respite, just so I wouldn't have to look at the mess, but nothing worked. I was doomed to face my problems, if not in the form of waking thoughts, then surely in the form of another monstrous nightmare.

As if I didn't have enough on my mind, worrying about May and Mom, thoughts of Victoria began to fill my head. I hadn't seen her since the day of my surprise birthday party, and although it wasn't much more than a month ago, I was sure she felt abandoned and unloved. Besides that, I missed her. I had grown to love her, and in a way I needed her more than she needed me. She accepted the tales of my teenage blunders without criticism, she understood what I was too embarrassed to say aloud, and she helped to fill the empty space that Grandma Adelaide's passing had left in my heart so many years ago.

I was sure that Victoria would know how to heal my family's broken heart—or at least know how to make it start ticking again. She would know how to make May better, and she would know just what to say to Mom, even to Aunt Didi. I just had to see her. Besides, I couldn't wait to tell her that I'd finally gotten Ryan out of my mind, though, unfortunately, I paid too high a price in doing so.

I decided that I would take the bus to the nursing home just as soon as possible. Naturally, the notion of riding buses led me to think about getting my driver's license, which my father had promised we'd talk about when he returned from vacation. But things being as they were, I didn't have the nerve to bring up the subject. I was lucky enough to have escaped punishment, but surely he was not about to authorize a learner's permit as a reward for my disobedience.

On the fifth day after my aunt's impromptu visit, on a Saturday, my mother's quasi week-long silence ended with a bang. Rachel had just driven me home from the bakery, and as we sat in the car laughing about her hilarious adventures as a day camp counselor, I suddenly saw my mother emerge from the back of the house and walk frantically to her car, which was parked in the driveway. Practically ripping open the car door, she began furiously looking for something in the backseat, her keen eyes failing to notice that Rachel and I were parked in the street. After several moments of what appeared to be a frenzied and unproductive search, Mom slammed the car door shut and stormed off toward the back of the house, colliding head-on, seconds later, with the cluster of trash cans on the side of our house.

"Damn it!" Mom screamed as she picked up two fallen trash can lids and banged them together. "Damn it to hell!"

Rachel and I looked at each other.

"I thought your mom and my aunt Rose were the only two people in the world who didn't curse," Rachel said, "Guess not, huh?"

"Guess not," I repeated, dumbfounded.

"I think my Mandy Hirschfeld-crotch-full-o-poison-ivy story can wait. Maybe you'd better see what's eating your mom. She looks kind of wired, Darla, if you know what I mean. Hope your dad doesn't stay at the golf course too long. Your mom might need him."

"You're not kidding," I said, slightly embarrassed by my mother's public impersonation of the Energizer Bunny on drugs. "Thanks for the ride, Rach. Maybe I'll catch you on Tuesday."

As Rachel pulled away, I raced up to the house, tracing my mother's steps to the back door and into the kitchen. By the time I got there, Mom had already made an atypical mess of the pantry, furiously opening drawers and cabinets and throwing aside anything that got in her way.

"Mom! What's wrong?"

"It was here yesterday, Darla. That's all I know. It was here yesterday. I'm sure I brought it in from the car and put it in the pantry. But it's not here today, and I just can't imagine where it went."

"Mom, please. Calm down," I said, leading her by the elbow to the kitchen table. "Why don't you sit down?"

"I don't want to sit, Darla! I want to find it! I want to find it now. Okay?"

"Find what, Mom? Maybe I can help you."

"My clock! My new clock. I bought it yesterday to replace the one that Didi—"

Mom started crying hysterically, giving in to the comfort of the kitchen chair as she fell into it, sobbing.

"Oh Mom. I'm so sorry," I said, at a loss for more reassuring words. "It'll be all right." I pulled up a chair and sat next to her.

"I'm afraid not," she said, her head bowed sadly. "I don't think the

McKendricks and the Alexanders will ever be family again."

"Don't say that, Mom!" I begged, shaken by her dismal prediction. "Things will get better. Aunt Didi will get over it. She always does."

"Don't you remember how she acted on Monday?"

"How could I forget?"

"Well, she was ten times worse today!"

"You're kidding!" I shrieked. "You saw Aunt Didi today?"

She looked up at me. "Oh, Darla. I made such a big mistake going over there. But knowing how muleheaded Didi can be, I thought I'd never hear from her again if I didn't do my best to rectify this terrible situation at once. And so I swallowed my pride and took it upon myself to make the first move toward reconciliation. I thought I was doing the right thing. I really did."

"Was Aunt Didi still 'muleheaded'?" I asked, repeating the rather odd word I'd just heard.

"Worse!" Mom said vehemently. "She was a complete jackass!"

I looked strangely at my mother. In a way, it felt good to hear her release all the anger she had pent up, but I wasn't quite used to her new vocabulary.

"Darla, don't look at me like that. I only said 'jackass.' And that's exactly what Didi is acting like. A total jackass! As your father would say, 'If the shoe fits!'"

"What did she do?" I was eager to know.

"The same thing she did on Monday. Only more of it. She called me names and insulted me. Only this time, she threatened to take out a restraining order against our entire family—including your father—if we didn't keep our distance. Oh, Darla, it was simply dreadful! And if that wasn't bad enough, April and June were at home and heard everything. They even saw their mother chase me out of the house with that old broomstick she keeps in the closet to remove cobwebs from the ceiling."

"Probably the same one she had double-parked the other day," I mumbled.

"What did you say?" Mom asked curiously.

"Oh nothing," I said, then blurted out, "Mom, why do you think

Aunt Didi's acting like this?"

"Who really knows, honey. I suppose she's frightened to death about May and she needs someone to blame. When I arrived there this morning, April, June, and Didi had just returned from the hospital. Apparently, May isn't showing any signs of improvement. Goodness, that poor child. It's all so terrible. I so wish I could see her."

The wheels in my head started turning at warp speed. Instinctively, I looked up at the wall to see what time it was, completely forgetting that the clock was missing. Glancing casually at Mom's wristwatch, I saw that it was four o'clock, and I figured that Melanie should be home from her lifeguard job at the country club and would be more than willing to drive me to the hospital.

I had nothing to lose. Mom's relationship with Aunt Didi was in cinders, and I could no longer justify staying away from May. After all, my own parents had not forbidden me from seeing her, so who would I be defying but Aunt Didi, who at the present time deserved no respect at all for the way she was treating us. And since the Alexanders had been to the hospital earlier, it was unlikely that they'd be there now. The coast was clear and I was ready—I could not let May rot in the hospital one minute longer without trying to help her. I loved her, and I owed her.

At four thirty-five that afternoon, as Melanie and I walked from the visitors' parking lot toward the main entrance to Pennwater Memorial Hospital, I suddenly felt my great courage and determination shrivel into pathetic cowardice. Now I could barely put one foot in front of the other as I dreaded what I had come here to do.

"Wait," I said to Melanie, who was several steps ahead of me. "Just wait a minute, okay?"

Melanie turned around and looked at me. "I know, Dar. Hospitals give me the creeps too."

I was grateful that she hadn't chosen that moment to tease me.

"I feel so guilty saying this," I choked out, "but the thought of going inside makes me sick."

Melanie walked back toward me and looked at me sympathetically. "I know, Dar, but May's inside, and she needs you. Wouldn't the thought of leaving her make you even sicker?"

She was absolutely right. I quickly remembered the first day that I'd gone to the nursing home, and how May had cheerfully coaxed me inside by threatening to sic the tickle monster on me. Had it not been for her extraordinary sense of compassion and charity, which brought me to the nursing home in the first place, I never would've met my great friend Victoria, nor would I have learned so many valuable lessons. What could I be thinking? I looked at Melanie, took a deep breath, straightened my shoulders—and led the way inside to the hospital lobby.

Melanie had called the hospital in advance to get May's room number, determining that the fewer questions we asked once inside the hospital, the fewer eyebrows our presence was likely to raise. We boarded the elevator unnoticed, and when we got off at the fifth floor, Melanie quietly took a seat in the lounge while I nervously made my way down the corridor toward Room 556.

At any moment, I half-expected the penetrating screams of deranged patients to echo through the hallways while perhaps an orderly or two chased an escaped patient down the stairwell. But everything was quiet and serene—vastly different from the chilling vision of the fifth floor that I envisioned prior to arrival—and I prayed that I could make it to May's room without being seen.

Just at the precise moment I was approaching my destination, I heard a woman's voice behind me yelling, "Young lady! Excuse me. Young lady!" I was doomed for sure. I turned around to see a nurse walking briskly in my direction and pointing her left index finger at me as if that gesture alone would detain me. Annoyed, I stood there and waited for her.

"Your name wouldn't be McKendrick, would it?" she said severely.

"Uh—" I said, groping for words.

"Because Mrs. Alexander left strict instructions that nobody from the McKendrick family was to visit Miss Alexander. And she specifically

309

mentioned a young woman named Darla who fits your description."

I had a split-second decision to make. There was no time to contemplate my options.

"I know Darla," I said confidently. "She's my best friend."

"Oh," she said suspiciously. "Then who might you be?"

"Melanie Davenport," I said without missing a beat.

"Well, I'm sorry, Miss Davenport," the nurse said with a mean smile, as if she were enjoying her authority, "but you can't visit Miss Alexander either."

"Why not?"

"Family only!" she bellowed.

"Well, I'm almost family!"

"You're either family or you're not!"

"But—"

"I've got no time to debate this with you, young lady."

"My brother Ben is engaged to May's sister April. They're getting married next summer. So that makes May and me practically sisters-in-law or something!"

" 'Practically' being the operative word," the nurse said and snickered. "You still can't go in there."

"Oh, come on! What if Ben and April elope tonight? Does that mean I can visit May tomorrow? Come on. That's ridiculous!"

"Well—" the nurse stammered, at a loss for unpleasant words.

"I just spoke to Mr. Alexander an hour ago," I lied, taking advantage of her temporary speechlessness. "He told me that Mrs. Alexander and her two daughters had been here this morning, and that this afternoon would be a perfect time for me to visit. Should I call him back and tell him you won't let me in? What's your name?"

Just as she was about to reply, a doctor rushed down the hall yelling, "Ethel! 503. Stat!" and with a quick snarl, she huffed and puffed down the corridor after him.

The moment of truth had arrived. I was inches away from seeing May and there was nobody to stop me. Feeling almost courageous, I put my smile on and walked into her room.

I don't know what I expected, but I was not ready for the lifeless form with the long blond hair that lay on the bed, staring straight ahead into nothingness. If anything, I had thought that May's face might reflect the agony that she had to be feeling, as it did that awful night, but never did I imagine her entire being to be so silent. It was eerie. A chill raced down my spine.

I didn't want to just stand there, staring invasively at May as if she were a zoo animal, so I quietly walked over to the corner of the room and pulled a chair next to her bedside. She had no reaction whatsoever to my presence. I immediately understood why Aunt Didi was so frightened and angry, although I still did not condone her behavior.

"Hi, May," I said softly. "How are you? It's Darla."

There was not even a glimmer of recognition in her eyes. She was still staring straight ahead at the empty wall. To my surprise, my thoughts moved to a different time and place, and I found myself standing on Grandpa Henry and Grandma Adelaide's street, next to the old abandoned house on the corner. As a child of six, I remember asking my father why the grass was so long and why nobody lived there. He had tried to explain the fundamentals of unsold real estate to me, but I could not grasp the concept that every home did not have a family living in it. It made no sense. I remembered pleading with Dad to let me look in the windows, and I remembered how horrified I was to see the empty rooms and to feel the abundance of nothingness that surrounded me. Each time we visited my grandparents thereafter I would relive the same feelings of sadness as I saw the house on the corner, empty and deteriorating—from lack of love and lack of life.

"I've missed you so much, May," I said, gently touching her left hand. "And I've been so worried. So are my parents. We're all worried about you and we all love you."

There was no response.

"I've got so much to tell you. And I've got some new clues about Aunt Rebecca. I'm dying to hear what you think! It's really incredible. And guess what? Mom apologized for forging the note and Melanie's sister is moving to New York. Melanie's okay with it and all, but she's more bummed about Drew going to college in Boston. I guess she must really love him and stuff, but for the last couple of days she's been talking nonstop about this guy with the great butt who mows her lawn. But get this, she found out that his name is Irv. That totally freaked her out. I mean, would you expect a guy named Irv to have a great butt? I sure wouldn't."

May slowly turned her head toward me. She looked directly at me, though still without emotion.

"May?"

A lone tear fell from her right eye.

"Oh God, May! What is it?"

"I waited for you, Darla. You never came."

A rush of tears came pouring down my face. I grabbed her hand and started sobbing. "I'm so sorry, May. I really am."

She just looked at me, as if she were waiting for something in particular, but I didn't quite know what it was.

"Why didn't you come, Darla? Why didn't you come before now?"

"Your mother wouldn't let me. She doesn't even want my parents to visit you."

May looked oddly at me, as she continued to lie still on the bed.

"I swear, May. That's the truth. Aunt Didi blames me for what happened to you. She and my mom had a huge fight—two of them, in fact—and now Mom thinks we'll never be family again."

May looked confused and disoriented, as if she were having a hard time following the conversation.

"Are you okay, May?"

"Mom wouldn't let you come here?" she repeated hazily.

"Yes! She hates me, May. She told me I'm becoming as worthless as Aunt Rebecca, and today she told Mom she's getting a restraining order out against our entire family if we go anywhere near you."

May looked as if she were desperately trying to process what I was saying. After several minutes of this apparent confusion, I saw the old familiar look of anger return to her eyes—the same look that I'd seen the last time we'd discussed her mother. I instantly felt guilty for having said so much against Aunt Didi, but I also felt that I had a right to defend myself, to tell the truth, and to let May know that my absence had not been of my own choice.

"How come you're here now?" she asked.

"Because I couldn't stand to be away from you anymore! And I almost didn't even get to see you today. Some ugly old nurse named Ethel with clodhopper shoes and a hair net tried to stop me. She asked me if I was Darla McKendrick and told me that Mrs. Alexander didn't want me to visit her daughter. So I told her my name was Melanie Davenport, and she goes, 'Family only. You still can't visit her,' like a real bitch. So I told her that my brother Ben was engaged to your sister April, and that made us practically family."

"Ben and April got engaged?" she asked, wide-eyed.

"No. Of course not. I just made it up. To get in here."

May averted her glance and began staring at the blank wall again. I knew I was losing her and didn't know what to do.

"Please, May! Don't just lie there like a zombie! They'll keep you here forever! Don't you want to go home? Don't you want to sleep in your own bed? Do you like having Nurse Ethel stick needles in your arm and treat you like you're crazy or something? Stop acting like this!"

"I just wanted to be pretty," May said softly. "I just wanted to be liked! What did I do wrong?"

"You didn't do anything wrong!" I said helplessly.

She turned and looked at me. "Yes, I did. You even tried to warn me. Don't you remember, Darla?"

"It's not like that, May. I mean, a lot of people tried to warn me about falling for Ryan. Did that make me wrong for loving him? You were just being nice to Hatch. It's not like you were even interested in him that way. It's not your fault that he was such a pig. I thought he was real cute at first too."

"So why were you able to see through him when I couldn't?"

"Because he wasn't saying a bunch of nice stuff to me and complimenting me every two seconds. You know what that's like, May.

I mean, it's a lot harder to see what a creep a guy is if he's telling you how beautiful you are. You know that."

"No, I don't," she moaned. "I'm stupid!"

Corky's last words to me came racing through my head: "Nothin' that happened to your cousin is her fault. You just keep remindin' her of that. More than likely, she's gonna forget it."

"May, you've gotta remember that it's not your fault. That guy Hatch has hurt a lot of people—and kids too. He's a drug dealer. He's a loser. You can't blame yourself for that! What if that had happened to me? Would you think I was stupid?"

May slowly sat up in bed. I could see her entire body coming to life again, as if she had just risen from a long sleep. She began rocking back and forth, the intensity of her movements becoming more severe by the second.

"I've never thought you were stupid," she said, as the tears began to roll.

"Well, you aren't either, May! You're one of the smartest, most wonderful people in the whole world."

May's chest started heaving. She looked at me in desperation, and as she began to unlock the pain she had hidden inside, her eyes became electric with rage. She continued to rock, nearing a ferocious crescendo, while her fingers, twitching in a madbrained dance, began ravaging her golden blond hair until it became as tangled and tortured as the memories that haunted her.

I had dreamed of being the one to bring May out of her silence, but I was not prepared for the aftermath of such a feat and had no idea how to handle my poor cousin who was consumed by her own hysteria.

"May, please calm down," I implored her. "Please!"

She momentarily took her hands out of her hair and looked at me, breathing heavily as she prepared to speak. "He made me touch him, Darla. He grabbed me by the wrist and forced me to touch him. I tried so hard not to. But he was so strong. I swear to God I tried. You believe me, don't you?"

"Of course I do!"

"I want to wash my hands!" she cried, looking at her hands as if they were crawling with vermin. "I can't stand looking at them knowing they touched him. It makes me sick!" She shook her hands wildly. "He told me I led him on, and that I was only getting what I asked for. He called me disgusting names and pushed me down on this dirty table. He ripped my dress and told me that if he had to, he was going to rip all of my clothes off me to get what I owed him. Then he kept saying, 'Don't fight me, sugar, tomorrow night you'll be begging me to do it all over again!' I felt like I'd crawled out from a sewer. He made me feel so low!"

"He's the one who crawled out from a sewer, May. Not you, May, not you!"

"Then he put his hand up my dress and said, 'You're gonna love this, baby. Get ready to feel the love.'"

"No, May—"

"Then he started to climb on top of me, while his hand was still touching me, and then—"

May slid her hands up to her temples, and she began squeezing her head, in what appeared to be a desperate desire to stay in control.

"I never thought this would happen to me, Darla. I only thought these kinds of things happened to bad girls. I must be a bad girl, too. I can still feel his hand touching me...I can still hear the things he said to me... they were so awful. He used such awful words. I'll never say them aloud. Never, never!"

"You don't have to, May. You never have to."

"Even when those men came in to save me, he kept touching me, and touching me and—"

By this point, May had wound herself up to a state of full-blown hysteria. She took her hands from her head and grabbed a pillow, clutching it desperately as she began rocking back and forth more wildly than she had before. "Do you know what he said to those men when they came in?" she cried through her tears.

"What?"

"He told them that they could have a turn, too, but that he was going first. He said he liked virgins, especially since they were so hard

315

to find anymore, and that they were more satisfying than a cold beer on a hot day. And then he laughed like he'd said the funniest thing in the world and told the men they could watch if they wanted."

"Oh no, he didn't!" I cried.

"I'll never be clean again, Darla. Never ever."

"What happened then?" I asked.

"The man in the Hawaiian shirt called him a filthy child molester and a son of a bitch, and then he punched him, while the younger guy pulled me away. That's when Hatch ran off with his nose all bloody, and they took me to the office. I think the man in the Hawaiian shirt wanted to go after him, but he was more worried about helping me. I couldn't even stand up. I was so scared and so humiliated."

"I'm so sorry, May."

"Can you believe it, Darla? He told them they could have a turn, too! Please help me! I wish I could stop thinking about it!"

"Thank God that Jack and Sam came in when they did. And that they're such nice guys."

"I know. But I'm still dirtied for life. He touched me and he made me touch him. I want to wash my hands. I want to wash my whole body. Over and over again. I'll never be clean enough. Never, never! Help me, Darla! Help me!"

As I reached over to embrace May, I felt a hand grab the back of my shirt and jerk me away from her.

"Get away from her!" Aunt Didi screamed, as she pushed me out of the way. "Oh, May, my poor baby."

I was sickened that Aunt Didi had chosen that moment to burst upon the scene. And just as I expected May to push her mother away and to reach for me, she threw her arms around Aunt Didi, buried her head on her mother's chest, and began crying, "Help me, Mommy! Help me, Mommy!"

I was heartbroken. Perhaps it was totally irrational of me, but I resented May for clinging to her mother. I hated the fact that Aunt Didi was finally getting what she wanted. She didn't deserve May's love. She didn't deserve to be needed. After all, I was the one who understood

May, and I was the one who had been there with her. Had it not been for Aunt Didi's machinations and manipulations, none of this would've happened.

My aunt had betrayed everyone in the family, and now May was falling helplessly into her motherly trap. It wasn't fair. On some level, I understood the power of the mother-and-daughter bond, and how it could defy all logic at times, but I couldn't help resenting the fact that May had succumbed to its power and that wicked Aunt Didi was emerging the victor.

It was selfish and wrong of me. I knew that. This wasn't a game and there were no victors. I should've been happy just to know that May was on the road to recovery. I had prayed for this moment, and now I was bemoaning the fact that it had not turned out exactly as I had imagined. May needed her mother's love to heal. She could not recuperate without it. Why, then, was I wishing that she would reject her mother and come running into my inexperienced and feeble arms? How ironic that I understood my mother's longing for Aunt Didi and yet I could not accept May's.

I watched the two of them as they clung to each other. It occurred to me that while some people drown in their tears, Aunt Didi and May were creating a river, in which they would row themselves safely to shore. Their tears were long overdue, and I was sure they were crying for hurts both old and new, and for pain both real and imagined. But whatever they were thinking, and whatever they were feeling, one thing I knew for certain was that they did not want me around, and I did not want to stay. I felt invisible and unwanted, just like I had that last night at the Alexanders' house. I couldn't stand the thought of Aunt Didi throwing me out, or Nurse Ethel coming in to "take a bow" for having called Aunt Didi to alert her of my presence.

I took one last look at May. I loved her so. I loved Aunt Didi too, although at that moment, I was loath to admit it. And as I stood there watching them, wondering if we'd ever be "family" again, I said a silent goodbye and quietly left the room.

CHAPTER 19

In the days that followed, Melanie became our pipeline to the Alexanders. Through Ben, she found out everything that was going on and relayed it to me, and I, in turn, relayed the information to my parents. My mother was especially appreciative of Melanie's efforts but confided to me that it was humiliating having to rely on her daughter's best friend for word about her own family. She was right. I would never have admitted this to Melanie, but a part of me resented her being privy to Alexander family news when my family wasn't. It was my place to impart such news to her, not the other way around. But the situation was hardly Melanie's fault, and things being as they were, I was very grateful for her help and had no intention of biting the hand that fed me.

Three days after my visit to May, we heard that she was sent home from the hospital and would be receiving regular therapy on an outpatient basis. Dad said that the Alexanders had me to thank for bringing May around, and that sooner or later one of them would realize that, and maybe then this silly cold war would come to an end. I was completely miserable about the whole situation, but I managed to find some solace in the fact that my father was finally proud of me for having taken a risk, rather than punishing me for it.

The prognosis for a reconciliation, however, was looking bleaker by the moment. With each passing day that May didn't call, I became more and more convinced that her family had successfully turned her against me. As for Mom, she would've been happy to break the ice and pay the Alexanders a visit, but she had been twice burned by Aunt Didi and told me that she had no intention of subjecting herself to that kind of abuse and degradation again. There was nothing to do but wait.

It was a terrible time for all of us. When I wasn't blaming Aunt Didi for the misery she had caused, I was blaming myself, heaping guilt on top of anger and anger on top of guilt. I was a mess. Dad tried everything in his power to cheer Mom and me up, reminding us every day that hope springs eternal and that we should all hold on to positive thoughts. But even Dad lost hope when Melanie reluctantly gave us the news that June's July birthday bash had come and gone without us. It had always been a tradition in our family to celebrate June's birthday on the Fourth of July. Naturally, this year, the party had been postponed because of May's hospitalization, but all of us had secretly hoped that the occasion, when it was celebrated, would be the catalyst that brought the family back together again.

✳ ✳ ✳

It was the longest July of my life. Never in my wildest dreams had I imagined that the summer sun could burn so interminably long and that I would be counting the days until school started again. Melanie told me that I should have my head examined for wanting to enter the "hallowed halls of yearning" any sooner than the law demanded, and then she suggested that I call my family doctor to make sure that whatever I had wasn't contagious.

But Melanie understood exactly why I wanted to go back to school. School was the only place that I'd be able to see my cousins again, unless, of course, Uncle George and Aunt Didi decided to send them back to private school. That seemed an unlikely prospect, though, even under present circumstances, as all three of the girls were happily settled in their new academic surroundings and would be less than eager to dust off their old uniforms and conform once again to the strict regimen they'd left behind.

There was little to do but wait. I tried hard not to burden Mom and Dad with my unhappiness, since they were also suffering, but it was hard to keep my pangs of depression and boredom to myself. It was especially difficult when Dad kept asking me such leading questions as "How was your day, honey?" and "Tell your old man what's on your mind." I would usually answer him with such bon mots as "Lousy" and "What else?" until finally, he gave up asking and just smiled at me instead.

I was on a fast track to nowhere, selling bakery goods by day and moping around by night. Each day seemed a bit worse than the day before it, and by the end of July, I found myself as obsessed with the Alexanders as I had been with Ryan.

Almost daily, I would think of visiting Victoria and perhaps benefiting from her wise perspective on life's enigmas. But somehow, telling her about May's attack and the ensuing family decline just didn't seem right. I resolved to simply call her from time to time.

Dad had pretty much stepped away from it all, rarely mentioning the situation and going on about his business. Generally, he did not like to deal with problems that he could not find immediate solutions for, because doing so made him feel inadequate. Rather, he liked playing the charging white knight, running to rescue the damsel in distress in her hour of need. For my father, understanding the villain made it easy to apprehend him and to bring him to justice. Only in this case, there was no villain. Just a family in tatters. A family that needed help.

Needless to say, I was very surprised when he approached me in early August and suggested that we go out for a father/daughter lunch to discuss "the state of family affairs." I was thrilled, not because I thought he could solve matters, but because he cared enough to try and showed it by planning something special with me.

Dad seemed a bit nervous as we took our seats in the corner booth.

"Well, this is nice, isn't it?" he said, as he opened the menu. "Hope they've got a nice club sandwich here. That's just what I'm in the mood for. A club sandwich and chips. How about you?"

"I dunno," came the scintillating response.

"Well, have whatever you like, Darla," he said, burying his head in the menu.

It felt so odd being with my father, but I couldn't quite figure out why. Maybe it was the fact that we'd never been alone in a restaurant without my mother before, and now, here we were, about to embark on a new journey and work together to deal with a family crisis.

"I think I'll have the Caesar salad with the grilled chicken," I said.

"Sounds like a good choice for a summer day," he said cheerfully.

"Yeah. I guess." I was at a loss for words. I didn't know how to get our very important conversation started, but I hoped we'd talk about more than appropriate menu selections.

Dad smiled at me. "Darla, I have a surprise for you that I think you're going to like."

I quickly scanned the room. "Are we meeting May here?" I asked excitedly.

"No, honey. It's nothing like that, unfortunately. It's about your learner's permit. Your mother and I have talked, and you have our permission to apply for it anytime you'd like."

"Really? That's great," I said, disappointed that May wasn't my surprise but delighted all the same by my father's news. "Thanks a lot, Dad. I really appreciate it. It's just that—"

"Seeing May—seeing all of your cousins—is what really would've made you happy today."

"Yeah," I said mournfully.

"I understand." He smiled knowingly. "You know, Darla, it's times like these that really—"

"Can I take your order, hon?" the waitress with the huge hairdo asked as she chomped on a piece of gum and looked into my father's stunned eyes. "Did you see the specials on the board outside, or do you need me to tell them to you?"

"We're ready now," Dad told her, as he quickly gave her our order. "And I'd appreciate it if you'd bring the drinks along as soon as possible."

"Oh sure, hon. No problemo," she said, then cracked her gum.

"Problemo?" Dad and I repeated in unison as she walked away.

"You know, Darla," he said curiously. "She reminds me of someone."

"Maudie!" I gasped. "She's so much like Maudie! Look at her, Dad!"

"She's a one-in-a-million waitress!" Dad laughed. "You're absolutely right. She does remind me of Maudie. It's no wonder I couldn't recall her name. Martin and Maudie. Now, there are two people I'd just as soon forget!"

I was feeling worlds better. The waitress, whoever she was, had taken the edge off our mutual nervousness, and for me, being with Dad was beginning to feel more natural.

"It sure feels good to have something to laugh about. Doesn't it, honey? Can't say there's much to laugh about lately. At least not in our house. Or in Didi and George's house, for that matter."

"I feel like things are never going to work out. Aunt Didi's going to hate us forever, and she's going to make sure that April, May, and June hate us too."

He reached across the table and squeezed my left hand, smiling. "I don't think so, Darla. Didi is a lot more hotheaded than your mother, but I'll guarantee you that she's feeling the pain of this separation every bit as much. You've just got to be patient, though I know that's easier said than done."

"I'm sick of being patient," I told him.

I was hoping that Dad wasn't going to tell me once again that "patience is a virtue." It was a cliché he often used, and it always made me think of the Lughead's sister, Patience Ludwig, who was three years our senior and who was anything but virtuous.

"You know what they say," Dad said right on cue. " 'Patience is a virtue.' "

Well, I thought, as my mind wandered off, there was nothing virtuous about climbing into the back of a Ford pickup truck with half the members of the football team. Nor, I remembered, about loosening one's bikini top so that it would fall off "accidentally" after diving into the country club pool, just to get the attention of a hunky lifeguard. And certainly, there was nothing virtuous about trying to seduce your calculus teacher whose class you were failing, by offering to make him "feel good" after a long, hard day.

"Patience is a slut," I said out loud, literally speaking my mind.

"What?" said Dad, his eyes popping out of his head.

I gasped. "Sorry, Dad. I was just thinking about the Lughead's sister, Patience. She was the school slut. Until she graduated. I mean, she's probably still a slut, just not the school slut anymore."

322

Dad tried to hide his amusement. "I see. And I thought we were only talking about family problems."

"Well, yeah. We were," I said, embarrassed by my unintentional outburst.

"You know, Darla, I've always told you that 'time heals all wounds.' And I really believe that in most cases that's true. Problem is, sometimes we don't always feel like waiting for time to do its job. I have no doubt that eventually, your mother and your aunt will find their way back to one another, as will you and your cousins, but unfortunately, the only advice I have to help you in the meantime, is to get on with your own life. Which is precisely why I want you to learn to drive and to go on with all the plans you've made for yourself. You've got an exciting year ahead of you at school and an internship at Merriman Papers to look forward to. Please, don't let this summer's events take over your life."

"Do you think I'm being controlled by what happened?" I asked him.

"You're certainly being weighed down by it, honey. That's for sure. And that's understandable and natural. I just don't want you to stop living your life, or to let your depression over family matters manifest itself in more serious ways."

I wasn't exactly sure where Dad was headed.

"Peer pressure can be hell," Dad continued. "I may seem like an old man to you, but it wasn't that long ago that I was your age."

"What do you think I might be pressured into doing?" I asked defensively.

"Well—" Dad fumbled. "Look at Patience Ludwig. She was obviously a victim of peer pressure."

"Uh-uh. Dad! She wasn't the pressuree—she was the pressurer. Nobody pressured her into inviting half the football team into the back of a pickup truck for some post-game touch-up-and-downs. No way."

"Darla—I doubt that."

"It's the truth, Dad. She initiated everything. Then she tried to get her girlfriends to do it with the other half of the team, her rejects, but only one of them went along with her, Rhonda Dashern, also a slut. The other two dumped her 'cause they didn't want to get bad reps and have their names smeared all over the walls of the boys' bathroom like hers was."

My father looked positively baffled. Without meaning to, I had thrown him completely off track. "How would you know what's smeared on the walls of the boys' bathroom, Darla?"

"Turkey club!" the waitress announced, putting the plate down in front of Dad. "Hope you don't mind white toast instead of rye. We just said goodbye to rye, at least for today. See that man over there, the one with the red shirt? He got the last two pieces of rye. Now, technically, your order went in first, but the kitchen processed his first because he ordered a ham and cheese, which didn't require frying bacon or making toast."

Dad looked at the waitress as if she were speaking a foreign tongue. He was already processing more information than he had bargained for, thanks to me, and hadn't a clue how to respond to her useless twaddle.

"Do you want me to repeat that, sir?" she asked, chewing vociferously.

"No. Don't repeat it. Just give my daughter her salad and we'll be fine."

"Yeah, okay," she said, putting my plate down. "Enjoy your meal."

"What were we talking about, Darla?"

"Peer pressure," I reminded him. "And Patience Ludwig."

Dad took a big breath and a sip of iced tea. "Right. Well, Darla, I believe I was going to say something to the effect that there are many things that young people can be pressured into. Like drinking and taking drugs."

Dad and I hadn't discussed the evils of alcohol in a long time, and I wondered if he was finally going to mention his most recent experience with alcohol on New Year's Eve.

"You've told me about this so many times!" I groaned. "Not again!"

"It's time that I clear the air about something." He paused, then started in. "You must've found your old man to be quite a hypocrite,

324

lecturing you about drinking and then having a few drinks himself after your experience on New Year's Eve. While it's true that under the right circumstances, there's nothing wrong with a responsible adult having a few drinks, I haven't always been a responsible adult. Your mother told you about my friend Jim Penney and how he died. It's a shame I'll live with forever. I just want you to understand, Darla, that if I could so easily fall back into that trap, you can fall even easier—because you have no shameful memories to stop you."

I looked at him sympathetically. I had no words.

"I'm sorry, Darla. I didn't bring you here to lecture you. I brought you here because I love you, and I wanted to ask you to give yourself permission to live your life and be happy. That's all."

"Thanks, Dad," I said, wondering if he'd done the same for himself.

"Our family's relationship with the Alexanders will heal. Just give it time."

"Yeah. Okay, Dad."

The conversation significantly lightened after that point, and we ended up really enjoying each other's company. After leaving the restaurant, my father decided that it was such a beautiful day that the two of us should go for a ride in the country and take full advantage of the blue skies and warm sunshine. Our first stop was the lake, where we fed the resident ducks and walked the circumference, followed by a visit to a nearby farmhouse, where we bought corn and tomatoes and were treated to a tour of the barn by the farmer himself. Afterwards Dad drove to the day camp he had attended as a child and was absolutely delighted to find that the camp was still operational, even thriving. The camp director gave us permission to walk around, and Dad insisted on showing me the spot where he had fallen and broken his right arm as an eight-year-old.

It was a glorious day. Looking back on it, I don't know why we never found the time to repeat such an outing, or why we had never had one previous to that day. When I thought about it, none of my girlfriends or my cousins ever spent the day alone with their fathers, except for my friend Juliana Marsini, and that was only because her parents had recently divorced.

325

Although my afternoon adventure with my father did not erase my pain, it filled me with love and reminded me that I indeed belonged to a family who wanted me. And for a brief moment, that was enough to put a halt to my obsessive compulsion to dwell in the house of Alexander.

The very next day, I started to enjoy what was left of the summer. For starters, I called Melanie and accepted her family's invitation to join them at the house they were renting at the Jersey shore. Since May's attack, I had been reticent to go anywhere, laboring under the fear that she might phone while I was gone and that if I wasn't home to take the call, I would miss out on my last chance to ever see her again. Melanie, who claimed that my sanity had been kidnapped by aliens from the planet Guiltoid, finally helped me to realize the ludicrousness of that notion, as did Dad, who continually reminded me that "watched pots never boil," and that "life is for living."

After arranging time off from work with the Levinsons and listening to the sage advice from those who loved me, I packed my bags and headed for the roar of the ocean.

The next two weeks were idyllic. Life seemed wonderful again, and I felt as if my troubles had been swallowed up by the pounding waves and washed out to sea. Melanie, who had just made an agreement with Drew to "see other people" while he was away, happily upheld her end of the bargain (before he had even left!) by scanning the beach for guys with great butts. One guy in particular caught her fancy, a lifeguard named Tim, but unfortunately for Melanie, she couldn't "check him out" because he was "sitting on the merchandise" all day long. One day she got the brilliant idea that I should pretend to be drowning, just to get him down from his lifeguard post, but I refused to do so, wondering what aliens had kidnapped her sanity.

On the fifth day of our vacation, we met a set of identical twins from Texas, Cody and Casey, who fell "madly in love" with Melanie and me, respectively, and we with them, for all of four days. On the ninth day of our vacation, it was Melanie who decided that having a cowboy boyfriend identical to mine was just "too weird for words," and that the remaining five days of our vacation were better spent cruising rather than schmoozing with two guys from San Antonio whom we'd never see again "in life." I agreed with her wholeheartedly, and together we decided to go visit the guys and "let them down gently."

When we got to their beachfront home, we were surprised to find that the front door was wide open, yet there was no sign of Cody and Casey. We continued to knock for several minutes, but there was still no answer. Then, hoping for a clue of some sort, we peered through the screen door into the living room but saw nothing unusual besides a trail of clothing on the floor. I surmised that they were probably downstairs doing laundry, but Melanie was not convinced and suggested that we take a walk around back to see if they were on the beach.

They were on the beach, all right. Naked behind the fence that separated their picnic area from the public area and engaged in serious foreplay with two buxom blondes, who for some reason, were each wearing one half of the same bikini.

We quickly ducked back around the corner, out of sight, and several "Omigods" and "Oh my Gods" later, after catching our collective breath, we discussed the idea of breaking up the action by pretending to be insanely jealous and creating a tempestuous scene worthy of an Academy Award. At first, the idea really intrigued us. We were both curious to find out what four naked people would do in a panic, but Melanie quickly decided (and I agreed) that the whole situation was just "too skievy to even deal with."

On the way out, however, now knowing that the pile of clothing on the living room floor had been shed en route to conjugal paradise, and not on the way to the washing machine, we quickly snuck in the front door, grabbed every garment in sight, then promptly discarded all of it in the first trash can we could find along the beach. We weren't exactly sure why doing so gave us such great pleasure; we only knew that it did, and that we would remember it forever.

I suppose it was seeing Cody, naked and face down on the

"bottomless blonde," that temporarily cured Melanie of her obsession with butts, because for the rest of the time, she never mentioned any guy but Drew. As for me and my eternal quest for true love, seeing both Cody and Casey just minutes before sexual intercourse not only frightened me, but reminded me of just how easy it was to get into trouble when you think you're having a good time. On the other hand, I wasn't blind or dead, and there was something terribly exciting about it all, but it just didn't seem right for me yet, especially in light of what had happened to May. Much to my delight, our beach cruising came to an end, and the last days of vacation were spent basking quietly in the August sun.

CHAPTER 20

The moment I got home I could feel all the pain again. Mom, who had been ecstatic about my "getting a chance to go away," was even more ecstatic about my return. Without Aunt Didi in her life, her days were long and lonely, and although she tried, it was awkward and embarrassing for her to explain to people just how terrible things really were. For the most part, she avoided her friends altogether, pushing away any and all comfort they might've brought to her.

I was home less than fifteen minutes when she asked me if I'd seen April at the shore. She said she'd been praying that April had come down to the Davenports' vacation home with Ben and that we'd had an opportunity to at least begin talking things out. To her great disappointment, I explained that Ben had stayed behind to work, and that although he had made two weekend visits to the shore, he did not bring April with him. I'm sure she was wondering, as was I, if April's absence had anything to do with my being there, but it was an unpleasant thought that was better off not being borne into a discussion.

There was not much to say that hadn't been said before. For the first time, I began to feel more sorry for my mother's despair over the situation than for my own. In just two weeks, I would be returning to school and my days would be filled with activity again. For Mom, there was little else to do but think about Aunt Didi and to dust furniture that was already sparkling clean. While my mother had a multitude of activities that she enjoyed, such as sewing, reading, and restoring antique furniture, she lost interest in everything the moment she got depressed.

I didn't like it, but I began to realize that my mother's moods often served as a barometer by which I decided what mine should be, and that if I didn't do something fast, I was likely to end up down in the dumps with her. Hard as I tried, I was completely unsuccessful in my attempts to escalate her mood, so, determined to keep my own spirits from falling again, I paid a long overdue visit to Victoria.

As much as I loved being with Victoria, I could never get over the uneasiness that I felt each time I entered the nursing home. Although it was clean and bright with cheer, there was always that all-pervasive, always-present smell of disinfectant that seemed to be a staple of every hospital and nursing home I'd ever been in. Victoria had once referred to it as "hospital perfume," and out of politeness, I pretended that I hadn't noticed the unsettling aroma. But Victoria was keenly aware of my discomfort and could often sense my dread at being surrounded by the old and frail bodies preparing to die.

On my first visit, that same day I had met Victoria, I had actually drawn a Charles Addams-like cartoon in my head, just moments after the old woman had died and her daughter's screams had filled the hallway. The Grim Reaper, a dark and mysterious character swathed in nurse's white, stood in the lounge and pointed to an old man, shouting "Next!" as two orderlies opened a casket behind him. At the time, I had been rather aghast to realize that my conscious mind was becoming as adept as my unconscious in dreaming up such ghastly scenarios and horrified upon subsequent visits to realize that I could not shake the harrowing image I had created.

Luckily, going inside did become a bit easier. I soon came to realize that many of the residents were very much "alive" and were still vibrant, exciting people like Victoria, whose bodies simply wouldn't allow them to live on their own anymore. Even so, I was never really at ease with the place, and that made me feel extraordinarily guilty. How could I resent going inside for a brief visit, when these poor people were doomed to live out their lives inside? What kind of wretched person was I?

Victoria was gifted at understanding my fears even though I had never expressed them. On this particular day, she had asked me to come to her room. She said that it would be more private than visiting in the lounge. I knew, however, that she was trying to protect me from the other residents who often looked longingly at me and begged me with their eyes to make them a special part of my life too. In fact, the last time I had seen Victoria, on the day of May's and my sixteenth birthday party, she had told me to always do my best and to stay true to my values, stressing that I should never feel guilty for not being able to do more. I distinctly remember her telling me that I was better off taking care of my small corner of the world, and doing it well, than trying to save the planet. Keeping those words of wisdom in mind, and forgiving myself for any feelings of trepidation, I entered her room with a smile and a bouquet of flowers.

She was sitting in one of two mauve-colored cloth chairs when I arrived. Noticing the flowers in my hands, her eyes sparkled and she smiled. "Those can't be for me! Not again."

"They certainly are," I said, as I handed her the bouquet and gave her a hug.

"They're very beautiful, Darla, and it means so much to me that you always bring me flowers. But honestly, child, don't spend your hard-earned money on me."

"Oh, don't worry, Victoria," I said. "I didn't spend any money on the flowers. I stole them from the front desk on my way inside."

Victoria looked momentarily alarmed, then grinned as she realized I was teasing her.

"Gotcha!" I said.

"You certainly did." She laughed heartily. "Would you put these flowers in that blue vase for me?"

Victoria's eyes followed me around the small room as I filled the vase with water and placed it on the small table between the two chairs. "Thank you, Darla. They're just beautiful. Now, tell me, who is your lovely cousin visiting today? Mrs. Cornwell? Mr. Selak?"

My face dropped to the floor. Before I had time to pick it up, Victoria noticed.

"Darla," she said, knitting her brow sympathetically. "Is something wrong?"

"May's not here today," I said slowly, taking a seat in the empty chair. "In fact, I haven't seen her for a really long time."

Victoria looked exceptionally concerned. "Something is very wrong, isn't it?"

"Yeah. I guess it is," I said hesitantly.

"Do you want to talk about it?" she asked gently. "I'd be glad to listen."

"Yeah, but I just got here!" I protested, trying to tell her in my clumsy way that I wasn't about to dump my problems on her, a mere two seconds into our visit.

"I see," she said, shaking her head wisely. "You'd rather we exchange pleasant chitchat for a half hour and talk about things that don't really affect either one of our lives. I have those conversations every day. There's one nurse in particular who always tells me what the weather's like outside. I suppose she feels I'm incapable of looking out the window to see for myself. I don't know; I so rarely get outdoors that it hardly matters what the weather's doing these days. Anyway, do you understand what I'm getting at, Darla?"

"I think so. But it seems like every time I come here, I'm telling you my problems. Don't you get bored listening to me?"

She laughed again and shook her head. "What bores me, is when I have nobody in my life who regards me as a thinking, functioning human being. What bores me is having people talk to me as if I were a two-year-old child. Just the other day, a young doctor came in here to see me. He gave me a thorough examination, yet he never spoke one word directly to me. Instead, he told the nurse all about what ails me, and purposely did so in medical jargon, just so that I couldn't properly understand the state of my own condition. Isn't that something else?"

"That's terrible! Can't you get another doctor?"

Victoria shook her head negatively. "The young man is on staff here. Unless I want to pay extra for someone to come from the outside—"

"Isn't there another doctor on staff?"

"They're not much better. And I suppose I could scream and yell about it, but that would only elevate my blood pressure and make me sick, and that action would probably result in that same doctor coming back here to check on me."

"But can't you say something, without yelling?" I pressed.

"Oh, I said something, all right. I complained to the director. We'll see. Maybe she'll do something about it. Time will tell. Anyway, now I've told you my troubles. I've 'laid it all on you,' as they say. So please, but only if you feel like it, dear, tell me what's hurting you so."

It was odd. I had thought about this moment for so long. I knew I'd eventually be confronted with an opportunity to tell Victoria what had happened to divide my family, yet each and every time I pondered doing so, I had expressly decided against it. But now that I was face to face with her, telling her felt right. I desperately needed an adult perspective, and my parents, being directly involved in the situation, were certainly not able to see matters objectively, or to offer any new insights.

There was one thing that still bothered me, though, and that was divulging the details of May's attack. But with a little ingenuity, I was able to tell Victoria an abbreviated story that minimized May's role and focused more on my mother and Aunt Didi. I also explained to Victoria how my aunt Rebecca had survived a dreadful adolescence that somehow had left an indelible mark of shame on the family honor, created an air of mystery with my generation, and served as a bone of contention among the adults in my family. And without airing all of our family laundry, I managed to elucidate on Mom's inventive way of answering my questions so that absolutely nothing new whatsoever would be revealed to me.

"You certainly have some colorful characters in your family," Victoria told me, trying to lighten the load I was carrying. "Perhaps your aunt Didi would be able to make some headway with my young doctor friend."

"You're not kidding! She'd probably beat his bag in with Mom's wooden spoon. And that's only if he was lucky!"

Victoria and I shared a brief laugh.

"Oh, Darla, how I wish I had an easy answer for you. It has always pained me so greatly when I hear about families in turmoil. Life is so short, yet people who love one another will spend years not speaking. They have no idea how precious time really is until there's no more of it left."

"Dad always says that time heals all wounds, but it sounds like you've got to waste a lot of it before you get healed."

"You have no idea how right you are." Victoria smiled. "And from everything you've told me, it seems as if far too much time has gone by already. Not so much between your mother and her sister, but between Rebecca and the entire family. I'm certain that what you say is true. There must be much more to this story than your mother has told you."

"Then why doesn't she just tell me everything and get it over with? What's the big deal? Wouldn't that be easier than having me bug her all the time?"

"That I can't tell you, but I'm sure she's not hiding anything intentionally. It sounds as if the past is simply too disturbing to talk about."

"Dad must be completely wrong about time healing all wounds because nobody's seen Aunt Rebecca since before I was born, and there hasn't been any healing going on that I can see."

"It's very difficult to heal in absentia, Darla. And I think that's the key."

"What do you mean?" I asked curiously.

"I would imagine that Rebecca, wherever she might be, is living with a very different reality of what happened way back when."

I was intrigued. "How do you know that?"

"I can't say for sure, but that's usually the case. Time can heal wounds, all right, but it's a lot more difficult if the parties involved haven't spoken. I believe the only way for any of this mess to get solved is for everyone to come together and talk. I mean really talk! That means your mother and Didi first, then your aunt Rebecca and both of her sisters."

I felt both hopeful and hopeless in the same instant. "But nobody knows where Aunt Rebecca is! They haven't even looked for her! It's been so long; I mean, they'd never find her now. And I'm not so sure they'd want to."

"Maybe some day you'll find her then." She smiled warmly at me, as if she was certain of every word she'd spoken.

"Gee, Victoria," I said glumly. "I don't think so."

"You never know, Darla. But in the meantime, live your life to the fullest. Make every day an adventure and enjoy the challenges that life brings you—and never run from them."

"Dinner is being served now, Mrs. Ashbury," the nurse said as she poked her head in the door. "I'm here to take you to the dining room. Better say good-bye to your granddaughter before your food gets cold."

Victoria smiled, but her eyes frowned. "I suppose I'd better listen to her. And I wish you were my granddaughter."

"How come you have to eat dinner now? It's only five o'clock."

"This is when they serve it, so it's now or never. Now, you go along and remember what I said. And don't worry about rushing back to see me, but do give me a call and let me know how you're doing. Enjoy your new year at school and enjoy your life. And please, dear, try not to worry too much."

I gave Victoria a kiss goodbye and watched as the nurse smiled mechanically, helped her into a wheelchair, then took her out of the room. I wondered how Victoria could so generously encourage me to view life as an adventure, when her own life was little more than a sad routine. But I didn't think about it for too long, because I knew Victoria would be angry with me for letting her hardships bring me down. The best thing I could do for her was to take her advice and to grab life by the proverbial brass ring.

I looked quickly around Victoria's room and felt strangely uplifted by all the family photographs that sat on her dresser. Perhaps she wasn't so alone after all.

As I walked out of her room, I saw Victoria at the end of the hallway, just outside the dining room. The nurse had stopped to talk to someone and had not taken Victoria inside yet. Her face lit up once again, as it always did when she saw me, and as she blew me a kiss and waved cheerfully at me, I felt that life truly was worth living and that anything was possible. All I had to do was try.

CHAPTER 21

The rest of the summer passed without incident. Mom slowly came out of her depression, and I worked overtime at the bakery to earn some extra money before school started. I no longer minded the long hours, since Rachel had finished her camp counseling duties and was now working alongside me.

Melanie continued to fill us in on Alexander family news, and we were all delighted when she told us that May was getting stronger every day and would be returning to school. Hatch, as word had it, who we now knew had quite a police record, had fled the state and was nowhere to be found. Uncle George, however, still relentless in his pursuit of him, was constantly in touch with law enforcement officials from all over the country in an effort to "bring the bastard to justice."

Despite her numerous efforts, though, Melanie could still not find out how the Alexanders were feeling toward us. Ben was extremely tight-lipped in revealing more than necessary, and although he was sympathetic to our troubles, his loyalty was to April and her family.

Naturally, we didn't need Ben Davenport to tell us that the outlook for reconciliation still looked bleak. But we were hoping that Aunt Didi had laid down her sword, and that April, May, and June were missing me at least half as much as I was missing them. What haunted me, though, was why May hadn't telephoned me, not even once, just to say hello. She didn't seem to hold any grudges toward me when I had visited her in the hospital, so I had only to conclude that she had somehow been turned against me, or even worse, had changed her mind about me on her own.

There was nothing I could do but wait until school started. Dad, with an uncharacteristic dearth of clichés to offer, had little left to say on the matter, and Mom, whom I sensed had pinned all her hopes on the younger generation, was also impatient for school to begin.

Talking to my cousins again seemed indeed to be my family's only hope, and I began to more fully understand what Victoria had meant by it being difficult to heal in absentia. She was absolutely right. When I really thought about it, it seemed impossible that our family could ever regroup under present circumstances, not if they continued to stand obstinately in different rooms, to live separate lives, and to isolate themselves by foolish pride. With that kind of attitude, the current standoff could easily last into the next century. Truly, it would take a miracle to get everyone together again. And as for finding Rebecca and bringing her home to heal, well, that was simply too much to hope for.

Labor Day had both its good and its bad points. What I didn't like about it was that we had to "celebrate" yet one more holiday without the Alexanders, and what I did like about it, was that it meant school was less than twenty-four hours away and that a new chapter of my life would finally be starting.

It had always been a tradition with my brain to handle my preschool jitters by writing a series of one-act dreams for my subconscious to play out while I was sleeping. Although I was usually prone to nightmares, these dreams, for the most part, were fairly tame. Often I would dream that I'd arrived late to school and that nobody was there, or even worse, that the Lughead was in all of my classes—and that she'd been assigned the seat right next to mine.

But this year, there was a lot more on my mind than the first day of class. My family's future hung in the balance, and because I had indirectly caused the familial walls to crack, it was my responsibility to repair the damage. I knew that I had to make peace with my cousins before Aunt Didi would ever consider talking to Mom again, but I began to wonder if my mother would be so quick to forgive her. With all the time that had passed, and after two unsuccessful attempts to make peace, I'd seen my Mom's hurt feelings turn to anger, and just recently, she had finally gotten closer to her friends, pretending sometimes that she no longer needed Aunt Didi at all. Of course, while a part of me was thrilled to see her open up to other people, another part of me was frightened. I couldn't help but think that if too much time passed, my mother's friends might fill the void too adeptly. Perhaps then she would forget all about the Alexanders and then everyone, especially "muleheaded" Aunt Didi, would simply move on with their lives, severing any and all ties forever.

With the weight of the world on my shoulders, I feel asleep and my brain went to work.

✳ ✳ ✳

I was standing in a field of buttercups when I noticed the tremendous stone wall that loomed in front of me. I couldn't quite make out who they were, but I could see that four people were sitting on the right side of the wall and that one person was sitting on the left. As I inched closer, I recognized the lone person as Mom, and on the left, I saw my three cousins clinging to some creature with a mule's head and a woman's body.

Mom, who was gaily swinging her feet against the wall, looked at the creature and started to sing: "Didi Alexander went to town, a head just like a pony, put her foot right in her mouth and gobbled macaroni. Macaroni, eat it up, macaroni mule head—"

"Mom, stop!" I screamed, as she stubbornly repeated the verse. "You're just going to make her even angrier."

I turned to look at the muleheaded creature and wondered if this genetic anomaly was going to kill my mother on the spot or simply continue to glare menacingly at her. As for Mom, her face now looked like her old kitchen clock, and her real face lay deathlike on the grass, like a Halloween mask that had been deliberately discarded.

"What time is it, Mom?" June asked the creature.

"It's wooden spoon time! Tick tock. Let's smash a clock!"

"Don't hurt me Deirdre, please!" Mom screamed, putting her big hand on her head, as her little hand clutched her throat. "What have I ever done to you?"

"Hickory dickory dock. The maggot ran up the clock. The clock struck one, and Maggie was done. Hickory dickory dock."

"No! Please, Aunt Didi!" I screamed. "Please don't hurt her! Leave my mother alone!"

But just as I was pleading for mercy, the wall beneath my cousins began to slowly crumble, and I feared that everyone might be killed if someone didn't do something. Then, out of nowhere, Victoria walked blithely onto the grass, assessed the situation, looked at me, and said, "It's very clear what's happening here. There's too much weight on the right side of the wall. Perhaps two of your cousins should sit on the left and even things out. If not, I'm afraid this whole family might die."

"Oh, God, Victoria. No!"

"I'm afraid so, dear. Especially if that creature persists in swinging that spoon. Someone might just get hurt, including the creature herself."

I looked up at the creature. Her mule head was gone and now she was just Aunt Didi—and she was scowling at me. The giant wooden spoon she'd been swinging had turned into an old broomstick, and I prayed that she'd fly away on it, and leave us all in peace. But she didn't. She just sat there and stared at me. Then the wall began to collapse even more—and May started rocking back and forth—and April and June started screaming—and the sounds of the falling rock grew louder, muffling their cries—and Aunt Didi's scowl turned to tears—and Mom's clock face had smashed all by itself—and the pieces were crumbling—and Victoria, who had all the answers—had disappeared into a thick yellow fog that had obliterated my view of the wall completely. I was alone and there was nothing or no one left.

"Mom! Are you all right?" I yelled, flailing my arms wildly. "I can't see you!"

"You're going to be late for your first day of school if you don't get up now."

"I don't care about school. I have to make sure you're okay."

"Darla!" Mom said shaking me. "Wake up, honey. Summer's over."

I opened my eyes and looked up at my mother, who was smiling at me.

"Mom. I'm so scared."

"I know, honey. Go hop in the shower and wake yourself up. I'll see you downstairs. We'll talk for a moment before you leave. All right?"

She walked out of my room. I drew a calming breath, then looked toward the open window. Summer was over and so was my nightmare.

339

School would begin in a little more than an hour, and ready or not, my life was waiting.

✳ ✳ ✳

It was no surprise that the Lughead, for the fifth year in a row, was in my homeroom class. Alphabetically speaking, Ludwig and McKendrick were too close not to be thrown together, and I had often wished for an invasion of transfer students with names like Lukas, Lyle, Mahoney, Mason, Mayfield, and McDaniel who could put more alphabetical distance between us, and thus bump me up to another homeroom. But that was just a fantasy.

So once again I was stuck looking at her face, bemoaning yet another school year that I would have to endure her vaunted claims and childish taunts.

"Hello, Darla," she said, knowing damn well that I hated talking to her. "And how was your summer? Did you work at all? I did administrative work for Congressman Schuyler. How about you? Where did you work?"

I looked at the odious braggart before me, debating whether or not to answer.

"Wait don't tell me!" she said, holding her palms up in a halting position. "You babysat! Gosh golly, gee whiz, and all that, I hope they were good little boys and girls."

I desperately wanted to correct her but knew she'd have even more fun criticizing the Levinsons' bakery, and I didn't want to hurt Rachel, who was also in our homeroom and possibly within earshot.

The Lughead chuckled to herself and shook her head. "Can't put babysitting on your college apps, you know. Not exactly what they're looking for! Ha ha!"

"And what makes you so sure they're looking for you, Amy? What did you do for the congressman that was so great? Open his mail? Order his lunch?"

The Lughead momentarily retreated, and I knew I'd called it correctly. Unfortunately, she quickly regrouped. "I dabbled in legislative

340

affairs, made crucial appointments, and most importantly, had the learning experience of a lifetime. What did you do, Darla? Change diapers and sing lullabies to some suckling infant? Or did you play hopscotch and make peanut butter and jelly sandwiches for some spoiled brat?

"The only brat I've spoken to in months is you, Amy. And I didn't babysit, if you must know. I was put in charge of a retail operation, in which I gained a great deal of business knowledge and was given substantial responsibility. What were you put in charge of? Shredding evil files?"

"Oh, grow up!" the Lughead said, knowing that she'd been defeated and being too slow to think of a comeback. "Some people never change!"

And as the pot who'd just called the kettle black sat down, the teacher called the class to order and began her standard first-day speech. Under normal circumstances, I would've stewed over my encounter with the Lughead, or perhaps gloated over my perceived victory, but I was consumed with thoughts of seeing my cousins again, especially since I knew that such an encounter might be no more than moments away.

If June had not dropped her books on the way to third-period algebra, she would've been gone by the time I rounded the corner. Rather than simply stand watch while she collected them, I knelt down and began to help.

"Darla," she gulped, as she took the copy of Pride and Prejudice out of my hands.

"Yeah, it's me," I said, lost for words.

We both stood up and looked at each other. I thought about how June had treated me after May's attack and wondered if and how she'd changed over the summer.

"Thanks for helping me," she said, as she turned to walk away.

"God, June! Is that all you're going to say to me?"

She looked fearlessly at me. "What do you want me to say?"

It took every ounce of willpower not to burst into tears. "Do you still hate me?" I asked, as students rushed by us in both directions.

"I don't hate you, Darla," she said, looking angry as her arch enemy, Sheila Shillingsworth, "accidentally" bumped into her as she passed.

"Then why won't you talk to me?" I asked, annoyed by the distraction.

"What do you want me to say?" she said, looking seethingly down the hall after Sheila.

"I don't know. Maybe 'Hello. How are you? How was your summer'?"

Sheila out of sight, June turned her focus back to me. "You ruined my summer. Why should I care how your summer was?"

"June, please!" I said, leaning back against a locker and unintentionally banging my head. "Can't we talk about this?"

"The bell's ringing, Darla. Can't you hear it? Do you want us both to be late for class on the first day of school? I'll see you later."

And in one angry flash she was gone. I started to cry but quickly wiped the tears from my eyes, taking care not to smear my makeup, and rushed down the hall to Mr. Willow's English class, arriving just seconds before he called it to order. To my utter surprise, there was one seat left in the back of the room, and it was right next to May.

She smiled warmly at me, and as I took my seat, she touched me gently on the arm, instantly taking away some of the pain that I was feeling at the hands of her younger sister. More than anything I just wanted to hug her and tell her how much I'd missed her, but class was in session and that was not possible. I just smiled back at her and waited impatiently for forty-five minutes until we were free to talk.

Luckily, it was lunchtime when class ended, which meant that neither May nor I had to rush off to another class.

"It's good to see you, Darla," May said, as a flurry of students exited around us. "I never really got a chance to thank you for coming to the hospital. I don't know if you realize it or not, but your visit really helped me."

"I heard that you'd gone home a couple of days later, so I was hoping that I had. But I wasn't really sure, not having talked to you at all."

"You're probably wondering why I didn't call you, aren't you?"

"Well, yeah, May," I said, fidgeting with my pencils. "I'd be lying if I said I wasn't. I mean, you know why I didn't call you."

"I know," she said, lowering her gaze shamefully. "Because of my mother. And because of what happened between my mom and your mom. It's so awful, Darla. And it's really all my fault. If I hadn't been so stupid—"

"Stop it, May! I told you, it's all Hatch's fault, not yours. And if you don't want to blame him, then blame me for wanting to see Ryan so bad. Just don't blame yourself."

"I'll try not to," May said quietly, as she gathered her books and papers. "Anyway, I really am sorry that I didn't call. I haven't had one moment of privacy since I got home. They all hover over me like mother hens. I guess I'm lucky that I'm loved so much, but sometimes a person just needs to be left alone. Anyway, I just thought it was better to wait until I could see you in person, but I should've realized how the silence might upset you. I'm really sorry. I haven't exactly been myself, and you just can't imagine what it's been like in my home. For one, Mom is absolutely miserable without your mother, but she won't admit to it at all. Instead, she just goes around screaming at people—especially my father. They fight every time Dad comes home—which isn't often these days. And he's a lunatic about what happened to me. It's horrible. You should hear him. It really scares me. And then there's June. She's been really depressed."

"I just saw her in the hall. She hates my guts."

May smiled ever so slightly. "No, she doesn't, Darla. She's just having a bad time right now. For one, she and Tommy broke up at the end of school last year, and that hurt her terribly. It was so unexpected. She didn't even tell us right away. She said that she was embarrassed to tell anyone that she'd been rejected — especially since he left her for Sheila Shillingsworth. We weren't programmed for rejection, you know. And if that wasn't enough to handle, June was really counting on the three of us appearing in that summer stock production. When I decided not to do it, she got really angry with me. She felt like it was the last chance the three of us had to perform together and that I had destroyed our swan song...I think that's how she put it. Anyway, after that horrible night at Pier 23 when I was attacked, June developed a terrible case of the guilts for all the mean things that she'd said to me earlier. Since that time, she just hasn't dealt with anything very well. And if that weren't enough, she's been totally freaked out about April going to Juilliard next year and leaving her behind. I think she's kind of scared that life will never be the same again. Up until now, we've always been the Alexander Three. Now, we're all kind of headed in different places. As far as you're concerned, I guess June just needed someone to blame, and you were an easy target."

"Great," I said, scribbling mindlessly on the inside cover of my English notebook.

"Oh, she'll come around, Darla. I told you, she's just scared. You know how it is: Mom's always taken care of everything for June, her 'baby,' and now that the real world is saying 'Hey, look at me,' well, June's having a hard time accepting that."

May was amazing, and despite the way June had just hurt me, I couldn't help but be touched by May's compassionate defense of her actions. She was so intuitive and bright beyond her years.

"How are you doing?" I asked. "I've been so worried about you."

"I'm getting better. At least I can sleep through the night. At first, I was having horrible nightmares. Have you ever had a really awful nightmare?"

"Uh, yeah, you might say that," I said, not having the strength to commiserate at full power. "You could say that!"

"Then you know how frightening they can be. I've been going to see this lady, Maria. She's a therapist, and she's helped me get through a lot of this."

"I'm really glad," I told her. "How's April?"

"April's fine," May said proudly. "She's grown up so much. I think it's because of Ben; they're just so great for one another. Don't get me wrong; April's still April, but Ben's sort of unditzed her, if you know what I mean. I wouldn't be surprised if they got married someday. You know, maybe five or six years down the road or something."

"That's really nice." I paused and scribbled some more. "How about your mom? Do you think she'll ever want to talk to me or my mom again?"

"Oh, Darla, she loves you both so much; I know she does. But my mother is such a control freak, and she just can't stand the fact that all her stage mothering backfired. I've told her a million times that it was my idea to go to Pier 23, but she'd rather blame you for being obsessed with Ryan than blame herself for being obsessed with controlling our lives. I'll tell you, your mom must've really struck some kind of nerve, because April and June told me that she chased her out of the house with a broomstick."

"Yeah, she did," I said, pleased that May had gotten wind of her mother's rotten behavior. "The old broom with cobwebs all over it."

May looked mortified. "Yes, I know."

"Well, it's pretty silly to sit here in this empty classroom," I said, having finished my artistic endeavor. I closed my notebook and smiled at her. "You wanna have lunch together?"

"I'd really love to, Darla, but I told June I'd have lunch with her."

"Oh," I said, feeling like raw sewage.

"Listen, we can have lunch tomorrow. How's that? And even the day after if you'd like. Come on. Cheer up."

"I'm sorry, May. I don't mean to put you in the middle. Not after what you've been through. It's just that, I dunno, it feels so ugly, June not wanting to talk to me and all. It just feels really ugly."

"I know, and I'm really sorry. I'll keep talking to her. That's all I can do."

May was still her sweet self—that much hadn't changed—but with Aunt Didi and June still out for blood, I held out little hope for reconciliation. And, of course, I'd yet to know where I stood with April, but I wasn't about to press May for any more information. As for Uncle George's feelings, it was clear he wasn't thinking about anyone but Hatch, and wouldn't be, until "the bastard" was behind bars. For everyone's sake, I hoped that Hatch would be caught soon; then maybe Uncle George would stand still long enough to see the madness in his family and maybe be the one to put a stop to it all. But that was just another of my many fantasies. I knew that.

I hugged May good-bye, and told her that I'd look forward to lunch the next day. Then I thought about Dad and his lectures on seeing the glass as half full, instead of half empty, and as I walked toward the cafeteria to look for Melanie, I felt very blessed and very lucky to have May back in my life.

✳ ✳ ✳

Very little changed in the days that followed. May and I continued to be close, and while outwardly she appeared to have recovered fully, I could clearly see how the attack had changed her. She no longer talked about wanting to have a boyfriend or someone to care about her. Her one valiant attempt at being a woman had ended in such tragedy that she had no idea where or how to start again. Ironically, the boys at school had finally started to notice her, which sadly, made May turn inward even more.

May also developed a new closeness with my parents and often came over to see them, despite the obvious objections Aunt Didi may have made had she known. With her unwavering faith in family, May maintained her belief that someday soon we'd all be together again, which was music to our doubting ears. But while she opened up to us, she no longer went to the nursing home to visit the residents. Her "joie de vivre" had been trampled on, she explained, and there was simply not enough joy in her heart to share with others.

June continued to have little more to say to me than she did the first day of school, although on a good day, she struggled to be civil and even once told me she "loved my outfit." I was angry at June for being so angry with me, but ever since May had explained her sister's emotional conflicts, I had resigned myself to wait until she was able to come around.

Up until that point, I had always seen June as "older" than April. But now, with the flip of a page, everything had changed. April, who once relied on giggles to get her through a difficult situation, had blossomed into a self-confident young woman, while June, with so much public poise and grace, had little idea how to handle an audience of one.

Although April was far friendlier to me than she had been that past summer, she seemed preoccupied with other things and was painfully aloof without really trying to be. I had hoped that we could speak about May's attack and get it over with once and for all, but April never mentioned the subject, thus limiting our talks to very pleasant, yet insignificant, matters.

More than anything, though, I just wanted May to be okay again and for everything in our family to be the way it used to be. But the only things around me that seemed willing to change at all were the autumn leaves, and as Melanie had so bluntly stated, it seemed like there was a greater chance of her being the first woman on the moon than of my family reconciling our differences. I had to admit, she was probably right.

CHAPTER 22

In early October I got my driver's license, fell madly in love with a boy named Michael (who moved to Vermont in early November), and finally began my internship at Merriman Papers.

As Connie Barnes, my tenth-grade English teacher had explained to me, I would be working two or three days after school, with perhaps an occasional evening by special request. My duties would include researching facts, proofreading, filing, answering phones, and maybe even writing obituaries. I would be under the direct supervision of the Pennwater Post's assistant managing editor, Amelia Johnson, and more than likely would be working with a fellow intern or two on selected projects.

Miss Barnes' description of the internship, as it turns out, had more than adequately prepared me for my role at the paper, but she had failed to mention one small fact to me, which consequently, resulted in a horrifying revelation on my very first day of work.

As Mrs. Johnson was giving me a tour of the office and simultaneously explaining my duties, her assistant came rushing in to tell her that she was wanted immediately in the managing editor's office. She quickly apologized for the interruption and, before taking flight down the hall, told me to have a seat and wait for the Post's other high school intern to come in and "show me the ropes" while she was gone. I naturally complied, and as I sat waiting at the desk, reading the editorial page of that day's edition, a horrible sound filled my ears, one that, unfortunately, I was all too familiar with.

"Hello, Darla. How are you? Amelia told me you'd be working here. Quite frankly, I was surprised. I thought you'd be back at Levinson's Bakery—uh, I mean 'retail establishment'—getting more of that 'great responsibility' and 'business knowledge' you so proudly spoke about. Business knowledge, my prune Danish! Big whoop! Geez, Darla, did you think I wouldn't find out that you worked at a …bakery!"

"And what's wrong with working at a bakery, Amy?" I said, closing my newspaper. (I really wanted to roll it up and hit her with it.) "It is how the Levinsons earn a living, and they're not exactly in the poorhouse. I would think you of all people, having dough for brains, would understand that."

The Lughead looked defiantly at me, as if I had a lot of nerve swinging back.

"Well, if I were you, Darla," she said, sitting casually on top of the desk next to me, "I wouldn't be so quick to insult the one person you're going to need to show you around this place. This is my second year here, you know. Ms. Barnes accelerated my admission into the program last year due to my excellent class record and my 4.0 GPA. One can't do much better than straight As, can one? How in the world did you get in? Wait, don't tell me. You went for the big B. You begged! 'Oh please, Miss Barnes, pick me! Pick me! Pretty please with sugar on top! Please let me go to the newspaper and play ace reporter!' "

The Lughead burst out laughing, and I contemplated, but quickly rejected, the idea of quitting the internship on the spot. I certainly wasn't about to let her emerge victorious and ruin the "humble beginnings" of my great career. Whatever it took, I would tolerate this mutation of human decency that dallied menacingly before me.

"I'm sure that Mrs. Johnson will show me what I need to know," I said confidently.

"But she asked me to do that, Darla," she said with a supercilious grin on her face. "Don't you remember?"

"Well, I guess I'll just have to tell her that you wouldn't cooperate. After all, you don't even know that you're supposed to sit at a desk, not on it!"

The Lughead didn't quite know how to walk that rope, so she went in another direction. "I call her Amelia, by the way," she said, swinging her feet cavalierly against the side of the desk, oblivious to the thumping sound they made. "We're on a first-name basis. We have been since the day I started working here."

"Congratulations. What do you want me to do? Strike up the school band? So what, Amy? I mean, who the hell cares, the man in the

349

moon?"

"Oh, grow up!" the Lughead growled, a clear but unintentional sign that she was conceding the round. "Try and be professional, Darla. This isn't an after-school play group, you know."

I looked at her, sitting on top of the desk, and wondered if she even knew what the word professional meant. But not wanting to sink further to her level, I decided it was best to redirect my brain back to its initial focus: the newspaper business.

"Is this the desk I'll be sitting at all the time?" I asked, trying to make intelligent conversation.

"It all depends on what reporter you're working with. If you stay in Editorial for a while, you'll sit here. I happen to be working for the entertainment editor now, Jessie Angelino, so I'm in her office down the hall."

Thank God, I thought.

"Do you know what the morgue is, Darla? And no, I don't mean the one with the dead bodies and the creepy coroners lurking around."

"I know exactly what it is. That's where they keep all the old newspapers and photo files, stuff like that."

"Yeah, right. So you better learn how to use it. And when you take phone messages for the reporters, don't screw up or you'll be outta here like yesterday's donuts."

"Thanks for telling me," I said, wondering when Mrs. Johnson would return.

"Darla," the Lughead said with devilish delight, "tell me something. I've just been dying to know—"

"What is it now, Amy?"

"Is your aunt Rebecca still living in squalor?"

"Amy!" Mrs. Johnson said, reentering the room. "What kind of question is that? If by some unfortunate chance, Darla does have an indigent relative, it's certainly not your business to talk about it, especially not for the purpose of entertaining yourself and humiliating Darla. I'm surprised at you. This seems very out of character for you."

I was devastated that the Lughead still remembered my horrible faux pas in Miss Todd's history class, but I was delighted that Mrs. Johnson had gotten a kaleidoscopic view of the Lughead's true colors—a rainbow of which she fiercely hid from adults in authority.

"I know how that must have sounded, Amelia. I'm very sorry. Darla and I go way back, you see, and I was simply referring to something—"

"I'm hardly interested. And you've got work to do. Jessie needs you to go downstairs and find some photos of the celebrity marathon last fall. Pronto. I'll take over here. Oh, and Amy, next time you need to sit down: use a chair!"

I wanted to explode with laughter but didn't dare. The Lughead had dug her own grave, jumped in, and she deserved all the dirt that Ms. Johnson had heaped on top of her. As she left for the morgue, I smiled with delight at Mrs. Johnson, who, by the way, asked me to call her Amelia.

As it turned out, I didn't see too much of the Lughead after that day, and when our paths did cross, she pretty much steered clear of me. I imagined that she was still licking her wounds from the accidental TKO, but I kept my guard up anyway, knowing that she might come out of her corner swinging at any moment.

I began to enjoy the internship more and more as my confidence grew, and I was thrilled when Amelia asked me to write obituaries. Even though it was one of the least glamorous jobs a "reporter" could do, I was still happy to see my words in print.

"People are dying to have Darla write about them!" Dad had joked at the dinner table, and when Mom and I laughed hysterically, Dad, pleased with our enthusiastic response, repeated his clever turn of phrase for weeks—to everyone and anyone who would listen. Later, Amelia told me that every obituary writer had probably heard the same "clever" line in one form or another. I didn't have the heart to tell Dad, though, who had since relegated his bon mot to the McKendrick Hall of Fame, whereupon it would lie in wait for unsuspecting dinner guests in the many years to come.

✳ ✳ ✳

Despite my hectic schedule during those days, I still found the time to visit Victoria and to learn from her what no schoolbook or internship could ever teach me. She'd lived an amazing life, as had her six older siblings, now deceased, and each and every one of their stories seemed a novel in itself. As it turned out, Victoria's oldest brother, Edward, had been a writer for the New York Times. When she told me about his life and work, explaining how he had struggled against a multitude of odds to become successful, I was inspired to new heights and determined to make even more out of my internship and subsequent career.

But for me, the best part of talking about Victoria's brother was that she was sharing her family history with me, and in turn, I began to feel more and more like her friend and confidante, and less and less like the little girl who lived down the lane. Victoria, always true to form, continued to maintain a keen interest in the well-being of my family, never prying or pressing and always managing to offer me a little piece of hope to take home with me as a souvenir of our visit. Every time I visited her, without fail, she expressed her belief that someday we would all get together to heal and that Rebecca would come home to reunite with the family to whom she belonged.

I didn't have the nerve to share with Mom what Victoria had said about Rebecca. Doing so would have been a form of self-incrimination, an admission that I'd broached the taboo subject with someone beside herself. But one day after school, as my mother was folding laundry in her bedroom, I stopped in for a chat and ended up telling her about Victoria's wish for the McKendricks and the Alexanders to get together again.

"From Victoria's lips to God's ears," Mom said, folding one of the pink candy stripe towels that matched her bathroom. "You know, Darla, I've been thinking. I know I've said a hundred times that it's Didi's place to call me, but Thanksgiving will be here in a few weeks, and if she's feeling half as bad as I am, maybe she'll want us all to have dinner together. So just maybe I should call her. What do you think?"

"Gee, Mom, I don't know," I said, as I rummaged through the laundry basket for my favorite jeans. "I mean, I know Aunt Didi wants exactly the same things that you do, that we all do, but she's so stubborn.

352

But who knows if she'll ever give in. You know how she is."

"Muleheaded! And you're very perceptive, Darla." She looked at the jeans I had just recovered. "Oh, don't take them now, honey. I want to patch the knee for you."

"Mom..." I groaned. "No way. I like them like this."

She shook her head resignedly. "Right. I'd forgotten. I suppose I'm just trying to take my mind off that muleheaded sister of mine. Oh, honey, I wish I knew what to do."

"You know what, Mom?" I offered. "I think you should just think it over for a few days. And then, if you still feel like calling, just go for it. You know what I mean?"

"I'm very proud of you," she said, grabbing another towel. "You're turning into quite a remarkable young woman. You know the one good thing that's come out of this separation?"

"No. What?" I said, folding my jeans.

"I've learned even more just what a terrific friend I've got in my own daughter and that I can rely on her for good advice in times of need."

I was really touched by Mom's sentiment, but she had a penchant for getting really mushy at times, and I could feel a hug coming on the size of Texas.

"Thanks, Mom. That's really nice. Listen, I've got a ton of homework to do, and I have to read the last three chapters of Catcher in the Rye and then write this report on Salinger. So I'll talk to you later, okay?"

Mom knew a fast getaway when she saw one and smiled knowingly at me as I grabbed my jeans and headed for the door.

"I'll let you know what I decide to do, Darla," she called after me. "And thanks again for the sound advice. You're—"

"Yeah, I know, Mom," I said, as thoughts of nefarious Uncle Martin played in my head. "I'm a one-in-a-million girl."

"Something like that," she said as her eyes sparkled. "Go on, now. You wouldn't want to keep J.D. Salinger waiting, and I've got some serious thinking to do."

✳ ✳ ✳

353

Five days later, on a Saturday, as I sat on my bed reading Wuthering Heights, I could hear my mother wailing in the hallway, her voice getting louder as she neared my door.

"Mom?" I called out. "Are you okay?"

Redfaced and agitated, she entered my room.

"Three strikes and you're out!" Mom said. "Isn't that what they say?"

I closed the book and laid it on the bed. "Heathcliff can brood without me. What's wrong, Mom? You look like you've just been hit by a runaway train."

"No," she said ferociously. "Just by a runaway sister leading a mule train."

Mom paused and began trembling. "Darla, I want you to make me a promise. The next time I even consider approaching Didi again, I want you to stop me. Chain me to the bedpost if you have to! Lock me in the cellar! I don't care. Whatever it takes. Just don't ever let me near that woman again." She walked over to my bed and plopped down next to me, exasperated.

My heart sank. I had been hoping against hope that Mom had made some headway with Aunt Didi and that we'd all be together by Thanksgiving.

"What happened?"

"I don't know," she said helplessly. "Things started out all right. When Didi opened the door and saw me standing there, for a moment, I thought she was actually glad to see me. She even looked like she might hug me, but obviously she thought better of that." I could hear the disappointment in her voice.

"Yeah. Go on," I said, edging closer to her.

She smiled at the gesture. "So, I asked her if we could talk. She said okay, and we went into the family room and closed the door. Before I could even get word one out of my mouth, Didi says, 'Well, Margaret, I hope you're here to apologize.' I told her, Darla, quite frankly, that I had nothing to apologize for. 'Oh, yes you do!' she expounded, as if I were a naughty child. Then she started berating me for having insisted that it was May's idea to go to Pier 23. I told her that I was sure May must've confirmed that notion, but Didi, in blind denial, insisted right back that the only reason

May would've suggested anything is because she thought it was what you wanted her to do."

"That's not true, Mom. It's what May wanted to do. For her own reasons."

"I told her that. Which, of course, led right back into the whole mess about me wrongly accusing Didi of pushing the girls too hard. Then we got into the whole thing about Rebecca and her theatrical aspirations turned rotten. We moved from there right to that awful night Pier 23, and the horrible way she spoke to you in the manager's office—and before you know it, the accusations were flying and I was being verbally tossed out of the house."

"Well, at least she didn't chase you out with that broom again," I said emphatically.

"Now, there's something to be thankful for!" she said, not knowing whether to laugh or cry.

"Were the girls home?" I asked.

"I don't think April and May were home, but June was. She had come downstairs looking for her mother and probably heard us screaming at each other. I felt so sorry for the poor child. She was standing in the living room crying as I left. Looked just like she wanted to reach out to me, but naturally, that was impossible."

Mom and I talked for a long time that day. Like a one-woman tennis match, she went back and forth, first blaming herself for being stupid enough to attempt reconciliation with Aunt Didi, then blaming Aunt Didi for being so obstinate and blind. When she was finally through telling me the story, in every conceivable form, she took my hands firmly in her own and looked at me with great purpose.

"I'm not going to let this destroy us, Darla. It may weigh us down at times, but it will not destroy us. Do you hear me?"

"I hear you, Mom," I said, then smiled.

As the tears trickled down her face, I reached over and put my arms around her, giving her back the Texas-size hug that I had cheated her out of, just a mere five days before.

CHAPTER 23

Mom's latest go-round with Aunt Didi may have done little for their relationship, but the following week, things started improving ever so slightly between June and me. I began to notice that her eyes were no longer angry, but instead, seemed filled with a longing to be friends again. One day, she even surprised me with a warm introduction to a friend of hers, but I sensed a reluctance to go further and a fear that she had gone too far.

April, however, had begun calling me "Cuz" again and appeared practically her old self once more as she occasionally joined me for lunch or stopped to chat in the hallway.

As for May, our relationship continued to blossom. She was worn down, though, from all that had happened, so we both decided to leave the subject of Hatch alone for a while and to talk about more pleasant things. As for the sad state of affairs between our respective mothers, there was little to say except to lament the fact that once again we would be spending Thanksgiving apart. If anything seemed to weigh heavily on May's mind at that time, it was the ongoing tension between her parents at home, which, according to May, was ripping apart what little sense of family they had left.

As for me, things at my home were never better. Two weeks before Thanksgiving, Mom asked me if I'd like to invite Victoria to join us for dinner. I had often thought of inviting her to my house, as neither of my parents had ever met her and both were quite anxious to make her acquaintance. But I couldn't shake the nagging fear that once the three adults had met, I would become an outcast, a lone child, superfluous in the company of adults, where suddenly Victoria would seem more like their friend than mine. I set my fears aside, however, as there was no getting around it: asking Victoria to Thanksgiving was really a marvelous idea.

When I called to extend the invitation to her, she wept with joy, and when my father and I went to pick her up at the home, she literally glowed with elegance. Her silver hair was swept up beautifully, accented by a delicate pearl hair comb, and in her dark blue dress trimmed in antique lace, she was the epitome of beauty and refinement. Dad told me later that he "fell in love with her" on the spot and kindly requested, with a twinkle in his eye, that I didn't mention that small fact to my mother.

The evening turned out to be everything that the previous Thanksgiving was not, and our home was filled with love and joy. I had never seen Victoria move in the real world before, and the grace and dignity with which she embraced my parents and our home was something I'll never forget. Not only did she have impeccable manners and irresistible charm, but she never once forgot that she was my friend, and she took advantage of every possible opportunity to tell my parents what a "treasure" I was and to extol my "many virtues." Normally, such a display of affection would have embarrassed me to no end, but it gave Victoria so much pleasure to tell my parents (and they to hear it), that I decided I would simply have to bear the burden of hearing myself described with a plethora of praise.

In early December, Amelia Johnson pulled me aside one afternoon to compliment me on the "spectacular job" I was doing at the Post, and to let me know that by early spring, I might be ready to cover a school board meeting or two. I was delighted by her encouraging words and looked forward to the challenge of moving past obituaries.

Around that same time, I also began lusting madly for a twenty-three-year-old copywriter in the advertising department named Jared Thompson. He seemed to enjoy my company in the fleeting moments that we were together, but he was busy sowing his youthful oats and had not a moment to waste with a sixteen-and-a-half-year-old high school intern. Even I, in my romantic naiveté, was able to see this, thus enabling me to recover fairly quickly from that particular crush before it reached Ryan-esque proportions.

And then there was Billy Bradshaw, a classmate of mine, who

somewhere between chemistry lab experiments fell hopelessly in love with me and felt the need to express himself by leaving occasional love notes in my locker. Unfortunately for me, the only chemistry between us gurgled in a test tube. That left me with the unpleasant task of telling Billy the words no romantic suitor ever wants to hear: "I like you as a friend, but—" He took it well eventually and after a suitable period of grief moved on to a more fulfilling relationship with Carly Myers. Although I had yet to find true love, especially in time to get a date for New Year's Eve, having won Billy's affections made me feel better about my appeal as a woman and boosted my self-confidence, which, needless to say was shaky at times.

All things considered, excluding the small matter of my family being in tatters, life seemed downright livable.

Dad was delighted to hear that Victoria's son would be flying in from Oregon over Christmas, but he was personally disappointed that she would not be spending the day with us. He had liked her "more than words can say" and told me that he'd selfishly been hoping that she would light up our Christmas just as she had brightened our Thanksgiving. But that was not to be, and so we planned for a quiet celebration, in which the three of us would enjoy a quiet Christmas dinner.

May had told me that she wanted to bring her gifts over after dinner, but under the circumstances it was doubtful she'd get a chance and our gift exchange would probably have to wait until the next day. So when the doorbell rang during dessert, we were thrilled that May had made it over after all.

When I opened the door and found all three of my cousins standing there, my first reaction was to jump for joy, but when I saw the look of mutual devastation on their faces, I knew something dreadful had happened. My parents, by this point, had come into the living room to greet them and were equally struck by the sight of their tear-stained faces.

"Aunt Maggie!" June shrieked, as she rushed into my mother's arms.

"June, honey," Mom said, wrapping her arms around her, "what's wrong?"

"Oh, Uncle Ted, it's just so awful," April cried as she ran over to Dad and embraced him. "You won't believe it."

"God, May, what happened?" I asked, wondering if I really wanted to know.

May burst into tears and threw her arms around me. Everyone was hugging everyone else and the tears were flowing like celebratory champagne, but my parents and I still had no idea what was going on. All that I could come up with was that maybe the girls had told their mother that they wanted to pay us a Christmas visit and that a major battle had raged in response.

"Come on, sweetie," Dad said to April as he gently led her to the couch. "Please sit down and tell us what happened."

Everyone eventually took a seat, but my cousins were all sobbing profusely, taking intermittent breaks to glance at each other as if to say, "You tell them."

Finally, June looked right at my mother and choked out the words, "Dad told Mom he wants a divorce for Christmas."

"Oh, gracious, no!" Mom screamed and clutched her throat.

Dad looked too nonplussed to speak, and I couldn't do much more than mumble "Oh—my—God."

"And we think he's got a girlfriend too," April exclaimed, taking over for June, who was too distraught to continue. "Dad didn't show up for Christmas dinner until it was almost over, and as soon as he walked in the door, Mom accused him of being with her. Then she said, 'I'll bet you didn't even bother getting me a gift,' and Dad said, 'Didi, if you give me a divorce for Christmas, you can have anything you want!' Then he looked at us and said, 'I'm sorry, girls. I'm so very sorry. You'll never know how sorry I really am. I love you all so much.'"

Mom's hand had crept up her neck and was now covering her mouth.

"I don't know what to say," Dad muttered, shaking his head in disbelief. "I just don't know what to say."

I didn't know what to say either, but all I could think about was how glad I was that Victoria had had other plans for Christmas. Hearing about my family's problems was one thing; being at the center of them was quite another.

"It's my fault," May blurted out. "Things were bad before, but they got a lot worse after I was stupid enough to get myself almost raped!"

"May!" Dad said adamantly. "That is absolutely, positively not true! The crime committed against you has nothing to do with the problems in your parents' relationship, nothing whatsoever. And I'm sure I speak for both George and Didi when I say that. Now, we've got enough heartache going on in this family without you shouldering the burden or taking blame." He softened. "Do you hear me, sweetie?"

May shook her head affirmatively, but I doubted that she believed him.

"Everything's falling apart," June sobbed. "I'm not going to have any family left at all." She paused and looked at me. "I'm sorry I was so mean to you, Darla. You know how much I love you."

I ran to the loveseat where June was sitting and gave her a hug.

"I knew things were bad," April told us as I comforted June. "But I never thought they'd get a divorce."

"Why does your dad want a divorce?" I asked. "I mean, doesn't he love your mom anymore, or is he just mad at her for something?"

"I don't know. At first I thought it all started when Dad got real obsessive about finding Hatch and stayed away so many nights. But now I don't think that's the case at all. I mean, they were fighting way before that. Anyway, tonight, after Dad told Mom he wanted a divorce, he turned and went into the living room and Mom got up and followed him. You should have heard the way she was screaming at him. Then she asked him how he could destroy our family like this, and he said that he was sick and tired of being her punching bag, and even more tired of soaking in her family dysfunction like a wet sponge. Then he said that he'd had it up to here with being blamed in perpetuity for one lousy mistake."

360

"What mistake was that?" I asked confusedly.

"I don't know, Darla. All I know is that they were screaming at each other, and the last thing Dad said when he stormed out was, 'Why don't you go find Rebecca and have it out with her for a change!' "

My parents looked at each other so quickly that I feared they'd get whiplash. I looked at my cousins. I couldn't believe what I'd just heard. I had almost gotten used to finding Aunt Rebecca at the center of McKendrick family problems, but now she was invading the Alexanders' home with equal intensity. I was sure that my mother and father understood Uncle George's comments a lot better than we did, but things were bad enough without my unintentionally making them worse by asking my parents to reveal something that might hurt my cousins even more.

April, May, and June stayed with us for several hours, and we consoled them as best we could. A couple of times I heard my mother mumble "Poor Didi," and I knew how desperately she wanted to call her sister. I thought about Mom's request, to chain her to bedpost or lock her in the cellar if she ever thought of calling Aunt Didi again, and hoped I wouldn't be presented with the dilemma of having to chain my mother to anything. Besides, in light of what had happened, maybe all bets were off and she would no longer want me to stop her from making that call.

However, all speculation ended when Aunt Didi called around eleven o'clock. When Mom answered the phone, Aunt Didi started off by saying, "Margaret, I'd appreciate it if you'd send my children home." Before Mom could offer her condolences, Aunt Didi finished by saying, "And if you blab one word of my personal problems to anyone, I'll kill you. Merry Christmas!" Then she slammed down the phone.

Uncle George moved out of the house in early January, and Aunt Didi slid into a deep depression. Things being the way they were, I figured Aunt Didi would cling to the girls like never before. Instead, she did just the opposite, retreating into her own little corner of the world, quietly putting up her "Do Not Disturb" sign, and ushering out all the insanity no longer within her control.

More and more, the girls came to rely on Mom for their motherly needs. Aunt Didi never so much as whispered in protest. In fact, I believe that she really appreciated what Mom was doing and counted on her to be there for the girls when she couldn't.

"Didi is very, very tired," my mother had explained. "She needs to be alone, and she needs a good, long rest so that she can see things clearly again. And when that day comes, maybe she can start to put all the pieces of her life back together."

My mother truly believed in her heart that Uncle George still loved her sister and that he would come home again. But when April confirmed the fact that he was indeed seeing someone else, another attorney in his firm, I was not able to share Mom's optimism. Still, I hoped for the best.

My cousins were pretty amazing through all the upheaval. Ironically, even though her parents had split up, June actually seemed happier than she'd been in a long while and even began calling April "Ditz" again, the pet name she hadn't used in ages. Once, I asked my mother to interpret June's improved state of mind. She explained to me that what June had probably missed the most was the closeness of her two sisters and her one cousin, and now that she had that closeness back, she felt secure that at least one aspect of her life was still the same. And perhaps, Mom had added as an afterthought, June was just a bit happier since all the fighting had stopped.

I didn't quite understand all of what my mother was saying, because I couldn't imagine feeling anything less than devastated if she and my father had split up. What she said made a lot of sense, though, and it did support one of Dad's favorite sayings—something about not understanding what other people are feeling until you've walked several miles in their shoes.

CHAPTER 24

In late March, true to her word, Amelia Johnson asked me if I'd like to cover my first school board meeting on a Thursday night. She explained that the meetings usually ran between eight and ten o'clock, and that I would have approximately one hour and forty-five minutes to get back to the paper and finish my story by deadline. She said that she was sufficiently impressed by my writing skills, which were "getting better every day," and that the opportunity to cover a meeting was well deserved.

I was ecstatic. The next day after school, when I reported my good news to Connie Barnes, who was still supervising my internship, she gave me a big hug, congratulated me on getting such a great head start in the business, and said that she had every faith in my ability to excel.

Unbenownst to either one of us, the head of a Lug had been lurking in the doorway during our conversation. Lying in wait for an opportunity to pounce, she waited until Miss Barnes had left the classroom, then descended on me.

"Hello, Darla," came the familiar sickening sound of her voice. "Sounds like you're pretty up on yourself these days. Ridin' high, as they say. Giddyap, horsey!"

The girl had a real talent for making my stomach turn sour. "What should I be doing instead, Amy? Banging my head on the blackboard and wishing I were you? God! Give it up, will you?"

She looked at me with a delicious smile on her face. "So, you're going to be covering a school board meeting. Wow! Whoopee and all that! Pretty exciting stuff. Let's see. First they might talk about the new curriculum—that's always a shocker—and if you're really lucky, they might begin nominating people for the school board committee. They'll say all kinds of fascinating things you can quote, such as, 'I second that' and 'I nominate Bill Smith for treasurer!' Be sure to get it all down correctly, Darla. You wouldn't want to misquote anyone."

"I think maybe you're jealous, Amy," I said matter-of-factly.

The Lughead flung her head back and laughed hysterically. "Darla, Darla, Darla. When will you ever learn? Me, jealous of you? Honestly, get real. Is a Cadillac jealous of an Edsel? I think not. And apparently, as usual, you're totally ignorant about what's really going on."

"And what might that be?" I asked, inadvertently egging her on.

"Well, you've heard of the rock group Bad Hair Day, haven't you?" the Lughead asked, shifting her weight from the right to the left, as if having to explain taxed her. "And their lead guitarist, Rick Anson Hispants? The guy that smashes guitars during every performance? He's so cool."

"Of course I've heard of him," I said apathetically. "Who the hell hasn't?"

"Well, then," she said, putting her hands on her hips, "you probably know that they're coming to town next Thursday—the same night as your little board meeting, I believe. But what you obviously don't know, Miss Ignoramus, is that Jessie Angelino has asked moi to go with her when she covers the concert. Do the words 'backstage pass' mean anything to you? How about 'post-concert party'? Man, I am so psyched. Jessie even said I could bring my sister."

"Oh, really?" I said devilishly. "Well, I'm sure Patience will look forward to meeting each and every member of the band."

The Lughead looked mortified. There was more truth to that comment than she cared to admit. But she pressed on, pretending not to have heard me." Anyway, Darla, it's going to be the opportunity of a lifetime."

"How so?" I asked quizzically. "I thought you wanted to be a political correspondent. How will this help?"

"Because, you myopic lag-behind, Mr. Leon Withers, from Merriman's New York Mirror, will be at the party, and he's known for inviting la crème de la crème of the interns to visit the New York operation each summer. Don't you get it? I cozy up to him, get myself invited to New York, which will be trés facile being a two-year veteran, make some contacts, and voilà, je suis on my way to becoming a political correspondent. Case closed, Einstein!"

364

"That sounds like a lot of fun, Amy, but it's not like you're going to get any writing samples for your portfolio. After all, it'll be Jessie covering the concert, not you. You'll just be tagging along."

"Oh, grow up!" she fumed. "Haven't you heard a word I've said?" She turned on her heels and walked out of the classroom. "New York, New York, a wonderful town...The Amy is up, and the Darla is down."

I scooped up my books, chuckled to myself, and rushed off to find Melanie, who was always in the mood for a good Lughead story.

The school board meeting began routinely enough, and although I was far from stimulated by the talk of budget proposals and new reference books for the middle school library, I was determined to do the best job that I could. After all, this would be my very first byline, and as Dad had warned me, I would never get a second chance to make a first impression. I never imagined, however, that one school board meeting would have such a drastic impact on me and on the future of my family.

It all started when Frank Huckings, who chaired the meeting, opened the floor for discussion on the school district's new antidrug campaign, right after introducing Clyde W. Rooney, who, he announced would be "guiding our children into a safe and drug-free future."

"You've got to be kidding!" wailed a lone voice from the back of the room. "Clyde W. Rooney, my ass!"

Everyone turned around to see who the eloquent dissenter was, and a large, strapping man in a denim shirt, Bob Lilley, stood up and started flailing his arms wildly. "You're not leading my kids to the bathroom, you two-bit hypocrite! Not over my dead body!"

"Sit down!" a woman ordered angrily (who turned out to be Mrs. Rooney). "Or drop dead then. One or the other. Just shut up!"

On the dais, Clyde W. Rooney looked very nervous.

"I'll sit down when I damn well decide to sit down. Right now, I'm going to tell everyone just what kind of slime this committee has elected to teach our children the evils of drugs. Clyde W. Rooney, recreational

365

drug user of many years, that's what kind of slime! Marijuana, barbiturates, you name it. This son of a bitch uses them all."

"That's a lie!" screamed Mrs. Rooney, rising from her chair.

Clyde Rooney started to say something, but instead his mouth snapped shut, like a dummy whose ventriloquist had quickly let go of the string too quickly. Meanwhile, everyone in the room began talking, and it became increasingly difficult to hear what was being said.

"Now, hold on, Bob," Frank Huckings yelled over the crowd. "Just where do you get your information?"

Bob Lilley, looking as if he were going to explode, said, "My nephew Jason is in jail. On a drug charge. Wanna know where he bought the stuff? From Clyde W. Rooney, local drug dealer. Sells mostly out of Conrad's Tavern on Waverly. Everyone seems to know that, except you, Frank. He puts up this concerned citizen front to throw us off track and to keep the cops off his dealer ass!"

"That's a lie!" Mrs. Rooney yelled, waving her right forefinger spitefully at Bob Lilley. "A bold-faced lie!"

"Listen, lady, either you don't know a druggie when you're married to one, or you're using that poison yourself!"

Clyde Rooney stood up formally from the dais. "You want to keep talking, Bob? Then why don't you tell everyone how you screwed Matt Hansen's wife two years ago, when he was laid up with pneumonia and your own wife was mixing it up with her friends in the Cayman Islands. I think we'd all prefer fact to fiction tonight!" His eyes swept the crowd with authority. "How about it everyone?"

With that, Bob Lilley practically leaped over the people sitting next to him and flew to the front of the room, where with one mighty punch, he flattened Clyde W. Rooney and knocked him out cold. Mrs. Rooney began screaming bloody murder, Frank Huckings took a swing at Bob Lilley in defense of Clyde Rooney, and chairs and dirty names began flying like Frisbees on a beach. Within ten minutes the ambulance arrived (not to mention the police) and Clyde Rooney was taken to the hospital, where he was later operated on for a brain hemorrhage. Luckily for everyone, he survived.

Meanwhile, in another hospital in Miami, Florida, Rick Anson Hispants, lead guitarist for Bad Hair Day, was lying in a hospital bed, also recovering from brain surgery the day before. Hispants, it seems, in a drug-induced euphoria, had gotten too carried away with his guitar smashing at the end of the concert. In a blaze of fuchsia light and purple smoke, he had inadvertently smashed his guitar over his own head rather than slamming it onto the floor, thereby knocking himself out cold. He was then rushed to the nearest hospital, where he almost died during surgery, as a mob scene of sobbing fans kept vigil outside. Needless to say, Bad Hair Day canceled the final leg of their concert, and it stands to reason that certain people who had looked forward to using a backstage pass were sorely disappointed.

Things only got better after that. In what Amelia Johnson called a "first for the paper," a story written by an intern would appear on the front page. That intern, of course, was me. For weeks, I was congratulated by schoolmates, teachers, and coworkers, and even treated like a celebrity by my own parents. And although my intern status did not allow me to write any of the follow-up stories, I was assigned to work with the investigative reporters who did write them, tirelessly uncovering more scintillating details about the town's shocking school board scandal.

But the best part of all, was that Leon Withers, before he returned to the home office in New York City, had invited me to visit Merriman Papers that summer, and to be his special guest for lunch at the Russian Tea Room, the famous restaurant on West Fifty-seventh Street.

The Lughead could barely look in my direction. Without even trying, I had flattened her, the way Bob Lilley had flattened Clyde W. Rooney, and she had no taunting retort or pathetic comeback. A couple of times, when I passed her in the hallway at school, I heard her mumble things like "scuttlebutt monger" and "pain in the scuttlebutt" under her breath, but that was the extent of our communication on the subject.

✳ ✳ ✳

Right after April's eighteenth birthday, Uncle George and Aunt Didi agreed to go for counseling in the hopes of saving their marriage. Uncle George's office liaison had gone back to her estranged husband, and although Uncle George refused to move back home with Aunt Didi, he said he was willing to give the marriage "one more shot."

According to the girls, my aunt began to slowly ease out of her long winter depression, and although she still had not reconciled with my mother, we all hoped that such a day might not be long in coming, especially if all went well with Uncle George.

Meantime, life went on. May and I both turned seventeen, April graduated with honors, and shortly after school ended, much to the delight of everyone, May resumed her visits to the nursing home.

For me, eleventh grade had zoomed right along, and with one year of high school left to go, I was busy contemplating my future. My parents and I had talked a lot about Mr. Withers's invitation to visit the New York office, and although my father said that I could go, we really hadn't worked out the logistics of how and when that would happen.

As it turns out, Brenda Davenport, who lived in New York, had invited Melanie to visit her for two weeks in August. When Brenda got wind of my newspaper story and subsequent invitation to visit Merriman Papers, she insisted that I join Melanie and take full advantage of the opportunity. As thrilled as I was, I felt a bit reluctant to impose on their time together, but Brenda explained that she would be working much of the time and that she would feel "worlds better" if Melanie were not left alone all day long.

Dad, being Dad, thought long and hard about the idea of my going to New York for two weeks, which, he said, "can be as scary as it is exciting." He also wasn't keen on the idea of my "wandering around aimlessly" with Melanie. So Melanie, quick thinker that she was, arranged for him to speak with Brenda on the phone. Brenda explained to Dad that she lived in a pretty safe neighborhood, one that was crowded with people both

368

day and night, and that she would make sure that neither Melanie nor I ventured out alone once the sun went down. She also assured Dad that Melanie had visited New York several times before, was well aware of the "lay of the land," and knew how to get around.

He took several days to mull it over and to discuss the situation thoroughly with my mother. Finally, at the end of June, he told me that an "exemplary year of school deserved an extra-special reward," and since April would be living in New York come September and we would surely be going up there to see her, I might as well get that first visit under my belt.

I was so excited that I could barely sleep nights. During most of July, I worked at Levinson's Bakery to earn money for the trip, and on August 4, with a pocketful of money and a heart filled with hope, Melanie and I boarded the train for New York.

CHAPTER 25

The train pulled into Penn Station at eleven thirty-five, and within ten minutes, Melanie and I had lugged our bags upstairs and hailed a cab to Brenda's apartment on East Sixty-second Street. From the moment I saw Madison Square Garden, Penn Station's next-door neighbor, I fell madly in love with New York, and as our cab jostled its way uptown through the crowded, colorful streets, I was so tense with excitement that I barely knew where to look first. When I told Melanie that I felt as if I were on a safari and that I was looking at all the wildlife through a car window, the cab driver yelled back, "You ain't kiddin', babe." Then, he proceeded to tell us just how wild life in New York could really be. Later, when he dropped us off at Brenda's and noticed how young we were, he apologized for any inappropriate remarks he may have made, warned us to be careful, then sped off with his new fare, a painted "lady" in leopard hot pants who quite nicely proved the cabbie's point.

Brenda lived on the third floor of a small apartment building right off Second Avenue. Because we arrived during the workday, she had instructed Melanie to use her own set of keys to get in. It took Melanie about ten minutes to get both the top and bottom locks open at the same time (a task more daunting than it appeared). This wouldn't have been so terrible, had we both not been stricken with an urgent need to use the facilities.

Once settled inside, it took Melanie all of a minute to show me around the one-bedroom apartment that Brenda shared with her boyfriend, Dave. Never having been to New York before, much less inside a typical New York apartment, I was absolutely dumbstruck by the tininess of the kitchen, a mere indentation in the wall that housed a small refrigerator and a stove and that had barely enough counter space to core an apple.

"This is the kitchen?" I asked Melanie, and although I could tell she was tempted to give me a sarcastic answer, she admitted that she'd had the very same reaction on her first visit. The "guest room," as Melanie had explained, was the convertible sofa we were sitting on, and she warned me that the honking of horns outside was likely to continue throughout the night, and that I might have some trouble sleeping.

Sleep, however, was the last thing on my mind. All I wanted was to soak in the energy and electricity of New York. Brenda wasn't due home for six hours so Melanie suggested that we go somewhere in the neighborhood for lunch and spend the day shopping. As it was planned, the following two days were to be spent at Merriman Papers, and after that, we had ten days to explore New York to our heart's content.

When I called Leon Withers' office the next morning to confirm my arrival, his secretary, upon learning that I had come to New York with a friend, invited Melanie to join me for my two-day tour of the New York Mirror. I was absolutely delighted, as was Melanie, who admitted to me that she hadn't been looking forward to spending the two days by herself.

On the first day at the paper, Mr. Withers had a small emergency at the printing plant in New Jersey. Not wanting to disappoint me, he took us with him by limousine. While he tended to business, we were given an executive tour of the operation, and later, upon returning to Manhattan, he treated us to a wonderful late lunch at the Russian Tea Room.

The next morning, the moment we arrived at the paper's headquarters on West Fifty-seventh Street, we were introduced to a reporter, Mark Brazelton, who was to be our host for the day. He let us sit in on a morning story meeting with him and later arranged for us to be given a tour of the morgue and the newsroom. After lunch, he brought us back to his office, told us to make ourselves comfortable until he came back, then gave us several copies of the Mirror to peruse.

About one-thirty, Mark came rushing back into the office, looking rather frantic, and yelled over to me, "Darla, please, do me a favor and look in the Manhattan phone book for the number of a Lawrence B. Connolly on Houston Street." I did so and wrote the number down for him. Snatching the slip of paper from me, like a relay runner grabbing a baton, he mumbled apologies for having to abandon us, then raced through the busy office in heated pursuit of his story. To this day, I have no idea why he had to leave, as I was far more intrigued by the Manhattan directory than I was by Mark's sudden exit.

"Darla, you can close the phone book now," Melanie chided me as I my eyes moved up and down the page.

I ignored her and kept on reading.

"Darla!" she groaned. "What in the world are you doing?"

"Shhh! I'm looking for something," I said urgently, as my eyes scanned the page.

"I hope it's not a good story," Melanie joked. "Because you won't find it in there. Phone books have great characters but lousy plots. Really, Dar, if you're that hard up, I can lend you a novel."

"God, Melanie! It must be fate. Look at this!" I shrieked, ignoring her attempt at humor as I tapped my right index finger excitedly on the page. "Just around the corner from Connolly. Can you believe it? It must be a sign. You know, Mark asking me to look up a guy named Connolly, a name that just happens to be right—"

"What in the world are you talking about?" she asked, looking over my right shoulder to see what the excitement was all about. "Omigod! Connor! Listings for Connor! Omigod, Darla. Tell me you're not thinking what I think you're thinking! You're not looking for her, are you? Rebecca?"

"Why not?" I said, as the adrenaline rushed through my veins. "You don't think she could still live in New York, do you?"

"Sure, why not?" Melanie said. "If I lived here, I might never leave."

"Yeah," I reasoned, "but you wouldn't be living in squalor. Maybe Rebecca moved out of New York to get her life together."

"I don't know, Darla. Maybe she stayed and got it together, too."

Melanie and I read through every listing for Connor in the Manhattan phone book. Unfortunately, there wasn't one listing for Rebecca Connor or even for an R. Connor.

"Well, easy come, easy go," Melanie said, trying to console me.

"No. No way, Mel," I said willfully. "I'll admit, I never thought of looking for her before, but now that I'm here, why not give it my best shot? C'mon. Are you with me on this?"

"Are you serious?" Melanie asked in wide-eyed wonder. I could tell by her quirky facial expressions that her brain had gone into overload trying to process my plan, and I wondered if I shouldn't heed her stunned reaction as a warning to stop right there. But then I thought about Victoria. I recalled what she had said about not being able to heal in absentia, and about Rebecca coming home again some day. I suddenly realized that Victoria's words, like Bob Lilley's fist in Clyde Rooney's face, were all part of the master plan to bring me to New York to find my long-lost aunt.

"I'm dead serious, Mel," I said, clutching her right arm. "Will you help me?"

I could almost see the wheels in her head still turning at warp speed. "Of course I will!" she finally answered, as the mechanisms finally ground down to a functional velocity. "This is too cool for words. But where do we go from here?"

"I dunno," I said, as reality knocked me conscious. "Good question."

"You know, Dar, maybe your family doesn't want her found."

"Well, I can't worry about that now," I maintained doggedly. "And I'm certainly not going to call home and tell my parents what I'm planning. My father would yank me home by the scruff of my neck if he knew what we were up to. And Mom would probably lose it completely!"

A few minutes later, a young reporter named Sandra, whom we'd met earlier, noticed that we had our heads together about something and stopped to ask if she could be of any help. I explained that I was looking for a relative who had lived in New York seventeen years ago, and that even though it was a long shot, I wondered how I might go about looking for her.

"Whew! That's a tough one," Sandra said. "If you can find your aunt after all this time, I think Leon might be inclined to give you a job on the spot as an investigative reporter."

"Seriously, Sandra," I said. "How would I start looking?"

"Seriously? Well, first I'd look in all the New York phone books."

"What do you mean, all the New York phone books?" Melanie asked. "How many are there?"

"There's one for each borough," Sandra explained. "One for Queens, one for the Bronx, Brooklyn, Staten Island; you know. Mark's got them all in his office. I'd start there. And you might even check some of the North Jersey books. But honestly, girls, even if she is listed, there's a good chance that she got married and is listed under her new name."

"Yeah, you're probably right. Wow, I'm such an idiot!" I said dejectedly.

"If you don't find her in any of the borough phone books, you might check in the morgue," Sandra suggested. "We've got phone books there going back years. At least you can find out if she was ever listed at all, and then you'll have an address to go on. I know it's not much, but it's a start. Oh, and one more thing: you might call information and ask for a listing. If she's here but unpublished, at least you'll know that too."

"Thanks a lot, Sandra. That really helps."

It took Melanie and me about a half hour to eliminate all the current listings. In the Brooklyn book, we thought we'd hit pay dirt when we found our first listing for R. Connor. But when Melanie called and asked for Rebecca, the woman on the other end of the phone screamed at her, accused her of having an affair with her husband, then threatened to burn down Melanie's house. I, however, had the good fortune to call R. Connor in the Bronx, who told me, "If there is a damn Rebecca in my house, tell me where she is, because, honey, I ain't had a woman in years!"

After we had exhausted almost every possibility and gotten a few more wrong numbers, we headed to the morgue, where luckily, we were able to locate a fifteen-year-old Manhattan directory.

"What's Rebecca's middle name?" Melanie asked as she read through the listings.

"I dunno. Uh...wait, I think it's Carolyn, after my grandma's sister."

"This could be her," Melanie said with cautious excitement, her eyes focused on the book. "R.C. Connor on Amsterdam Avenue."

"Is Amsterdam Avenue in lower Manhattan?" I asked. "I remember Mom saying she lived in lower Manhattan."

"Well, actually, Dar, it's not. Amsterdam Avenue is on the Upper West Side. But this phone book is only fifteen years old. Wasn't it almost eighteen years ago that your mom and aunt came here to see her? She could've easily moved uptown in those three years."

I felt defeated. "R.C. Connor isn't a very unusual name, is it? I mean, there could be hundreds of people named R.C. Connor."

"Yeah, there could. But there's not. There's only one. I'm game if you are, Dar. It's your call. We can hop a cab right now and go over there."

"Beats sitting around here reading Mark's old newspapers. Let's leave him a note, thank Mr. Withers, and make tracks outta here."

When the cab let us off in front of the massive apartment building on Amsterdam Avenue, the improbability of finding Rebecca hit me even harder. I couldn't figure out how standing in front of a building where she might've lived some fifteen years ago could possibly help us in locating her. It seemed completely futile to even try, but Melanie suggested that we walk through the courtyard to the outer lobby and read the names on the buzzer panel in the hopes of finding a clue. I couldn't imagine what kind of information we could possibly find, short of big red letters proclaiming "Rebecca Connor Lived Here," but I decided there was nothing to lose.

There must've been a hundred names inside, making our search all the more impossible, but Melanie suggested that we read every one of them, just in case Rebecca still lived there, or maybe, in case she had moved but her name had never been taken off.

After several minutes, an elderly woman pushing a small hand cart with groceries entered the lobby and eyed us suspiciously.

"I've never seen you girls around here before. Who ya lookin' for?"

"Uh, my aunt, Rebecca Connor," I stammered.

"Never heard of her," she said crossly.

"Do you know everyone in this whole big building?"

"Of course not," she snapped. "But I still never heard of her."

"Well, we don't think she lives here anymore."

"Then why don't you look for her somewhere else?" she said, glaring at me.

Melanie and I looked at each other.

"We don't know where else to look," Melanie said. We were hoping that somebody here might know where she lives now."

The woman's face tensed. "What the heck are you girls planning to do? Knock on every door in the place? I'm in 9B. Don't knock on mine. I told ya, I ain't never heard of her. And don't be tryin' to follow me inside. You want in, you get buzzed in. But don't spend all day here. You make people nervous doing that. Wanna find someone who remembers her? Go ask the super. That ol' bag and her worthless kid been here forever. She got a mind like a steel trap, though. Knows everybody's damn business. 'Cept mine, thank the good Lord."

And with that, she turned her key in the lock of the glass door that separated the inner lobby from the outer lobby, carefully pushed her cart inside, and quickly shut the door so that we couldn't follow behind her.

"Sheesh, Mel. What do we look like? Ax murderers?"

"She's just old and paranoid, Dar. You probably can't blame her, living in New York so many years. So listen, what do you think about buzzing the super?"

"I think it's a great idea. Especially since it's the only one we've got."

It took us another ten minutes to locate the right buzzer, but luckily, we got an immediate response over the intercom.

"Yeah, who is it?"

"My name is Darla McKendrick. I'm wondering if I could talk to you. I'm looking for a relative of mine and I think she used to live here."

"You're not selling anything, are you?"

"No, I swear I'm not."

"Somebody's always trying to sell me something. And we don't

376

want no menus, either."

"Really, I'm looking for my aunt."

"Who's your aunt?"

"Rebecca Connor."

"Rebecca, huh? You better not be lying."

"I'm not. I promise! Please, I need your help!"

"All right. I'll buzz you in. Make a right when you get inside and go all the way down to the end of the hall. I'm 1G, on the right. And you better not be selling anything."

"Are these people really paranoid or what?"

"Forget about that, Darla," Melanie said, punching me in the arm. "Geez, it sounds like she knows Rebecca!"

The door buzzed open, and we walked cautiously down the long hallway. As we approached 1G, the door opened slightly, and we saw a gray-haired woman peering over the chain to take a look at us.

"Hi there," I said.

The woman looked us up and down.

"Didn't know there was two of yous coming in. Well, I suppose you look harmless enough. All right. I'll let you in. After all, I got Baby Boy to protect me."

Melanie and I shared a look as the woman opened the door and ushered us inside.

The room was considerably larger than Brenda's small apartment but in a sad state of disrepair. The brown wall-to-wall carpet was paper thin in places, covered in others by cheap nonmatching throw rugs, and the couch and love seat appeared to have been mauled by a band of renegade cats. Newspapers were strewn all over the couch, and I counted at least five ashtrays that hadn't been emptied and nine squashed cans of Coors beer throughout the room. The noxious smell of cat urine filled the large room, although I noticed only one cat, a large black-and-white tom, sleeping in the open window. On one wall, painted on black velvet, was a picture of five bulldogs shooting pool, and on another wall, above a small desk, was a faded photograph of John F. Kennedy in a black frame and a garish watercolor of Elvis in a red one.

The woman coughed up a phlegmlike substance in the palm of her hand, then tried to wipe it inconspicuously on her flowered muumuu before motioning toward the couch. "Take a seat, girls. Don't mind the papers."

Melanie looked squeamishly at the couch and then at me as we reluctantly sat down.

"I'm Libby Ainsworth," the woman said as she settled into a ragged old recliner with a broken footrest. "And you girls?"

"I'm Darla McKendrick," I said nervously, "and this is my friend Melanie."

"And you're looking for Rebecca Connor," she asked again, as if she expected me to change my story now that I was inside her apartment.

"That's right," I said, resisting the temptation to take a second look around the room. "Do you know her?"

"Does she owe you money?" Libby asked, looking down at the skirt of her dress and noticing the gelatinous throat matter was still there.

"No. I told you," I said, my stomach churning. "She's my aunt."

"I see," she replied, apparently satisfied that I was telling the truth. "Well, I don't know how I can help you, Darla. She moved outta here some six or seven years ago. Can't say as we've kept in touch."

"What can you tell me about her?" I asked anxiously.

"She's your aunt, isn't she?" Libby said, her right hand attempting to rub the offending phlegm into the material. Why you asking me?"

"I've never met her, " I explained, flashing a quick look of horror Melanie's way. "She moved to New York years ago, and now my family's trying to find her."

"Yeah? How come?" Libby asked suspiciously. "She owe *them* money?"

"Oh no!" Melanie burst in excitedly, much to my relief. "You see, Darla's mom is putting together this really big family reunion. Her dream is to have Rebecca come home again, has been for years, poor woman, so we're looking for Rebecca in hopes that we can make Darla's mom's dream come true. We want it to be the best surprise she's ever had."

"I see," Libby said, clearly moved by Melanie's story. "Wish Baby

378

Boy cared that much about his mother. You're good kids."

Melanie looked at me and rolled her eyes.

"Still, though," she said, rubbing her hands together as if she'd just squeezed some lotion into her palm, "don't know what I can tell you. I do know she was going to school for somethin' er other, but I got no idea where. And she worked in this boutique over on Broadway. I think it was on Seventy-second Street, no, maybe Eighty-seventh Street. I'm not sure."

"Do you know the name of it?" I asked, lurching forward.

"Heck no," Libby said, now vigorously scratching an itch on her inner right thigh. But maybe Baby Boy would know. He had kind of a crush on her, and I know he went over there a few times, just to say hello and all that. Rebecca, though, she didn't have much time for him. Can't say as I blame her. He's my son and all, but he can't seem to get off his fat ass and do much work. Stevie 'Ain't Worth Shit,' that's what people call him. Hell, half of them don't even bother calling us for repairs no more. Don't wanna let Baby Boy in their apartment. Can't say that I blame them neither."

Melanie and I, had we looked at each other, would've howled with laughter, but this was serious business, so we avoided making eye contact.

"Let me see if he remembers that boutique. BABY BOY!!! Can you come out here?"

"Whattya want, Ma?" a male voice boomed from the other room. "I'm watchin' 'Car 54.' Muldoon just—"

"Get your fat ass out here, Stevie. Now! We've got company. Two pretty girls have come to call."

I saw peripherally that Melanie had covered her mouth so as not to laugh, and I casually did the same. We glanced toward the hallway where we'd heard the male voice, but nobody appeared.

"Baby Boy! If you don't get your rump out here, I'm comin' in after you."

"Yeah, aw right, Ma!" came the annoyed response.

Within a minute, "Baby Boy," a three-hundred-pound, unshaven, unkempt thirty-something-year-old in a moth-eaten white T-shirt and baggy jeans, appeared in the living room.

"Stevie, say hello to Darla and Melanie."

Stevie looked us up and down. "Hello, girls," he said, as he wiped his runny nose with his right forearm.

"Hello," we said as quietly as possible.

"Stevie Skievey," Melanie muttered under her breath.

"Stevie, these girls are looking for Rebecca Connor. Do you remember where that boutique was that she worked?"

"Yeah, I remember," he blubbered. "Seventy-seventh and Broadway. Right next to the deli. They got great subs there. Don't skimp on da meat like old man Mueller on Eighty-first Street."

"Gag me!" Melanie mumbled.

"Don't it have a name?" Libby asked him.

"I don't know, Ma," he whined. "C'mon. Dis is one of my favorite episodes. It's the one where Toody and Muldoon—"

"Get out of here, you useless lump of flesh," she said, dismissing him with a wave of her right hand. "And don't forget to fix the hopper in 3C and the ceiling in 2C. In that order. Them peoples been complainin' for days. I'm sick of listening to it already."

"Yeah, yeah," Stevie grumbled, and as he turned to leave, we couldn't help but notice the long piece of toilet paper hanging out from the back of his pants.

Libby shook her head, then looked at us. "My son can't even wipe his lazy ass right. Sorry, girls, that's the best I can do."

"You've been a big help!" Melanie said, rising quickly from the couch. "And someday, when we tell Darla's mother how we found Rebecca, we'll be sure to mention your name."

"That makes me feel real good," Libby said, coughing up another wad of the mystery substance. "And when you do find Rebecca, tell her Libby Ainsworth says 'hey.'"

"Thanks so much," I said, walking behind Melanie to the door. "We really, really appreciate it, Libby, and we'll never forget you."

As the door closed behind us, Melanie whispered, "Omigod, skieve me out! I've never seen anyone cough up so many throat boogers before. Thank God she didn't try to shake our hands! And did you see the way she rubbed them into her dress? Omigod, I'm grossed to the max!"

I nodded in horrified agreement, then we took off running down the hallway toward the sunlight, as if we hadn't seen it in years.

CHAPTER 26

It was ten minutes to five when we got outdoors, and Melanie said that we had plenty of time to walk over to the boutique and still make it back to Brenda's place by six thirty. Fifteen minutes later, true to Skievey Stevie's words, we found a boutique on West Seventy-seventh Street, called Zoey's, and it was indeed right next to a deli.

The moment we walked in and the little overhead bell rang, a well-dressed woman who'd been sitting on a chair behind the counter jumped up and asked if she could help us.

"Hi," I said nervously, intimidated by her obvious attitude and oversized monogrammed eyeglasses. "I hope you can help me."

The woman smiled patronizingly and looked at me as if I were wasting her time.

"Uh, I'm looking for my aunt, Rebecca Connor. I was told she used to work here."

"Well, dear, if she did, she no longer does," she said, pursing her big red lips.

"You don't know her?" I choked.

"You've figured that out," she said sarcastically. "No, I don't."

At that moment, I saw Melanie, who was standing behind the woman, mouth "Bitch," and it was all I could do in my moment of inconsolable disappointment not to burst out laughing.

"Do you think if I came back at another time," I asked bravely, "there might be another employee who knew her?"

"None of my girls would know your aunt. I took over this boutique eight months ago. Changed the name and brought my own staff with me. There are no leftovers." Her eyes tightened as if to warn me that I was pushing my luck.

"Oh. So then nobody would know her, huh?"

"No," she said, looking sternly at me and then at the doorway. "They wouldn't. If that'll be all—"

"I guess it is. Thanks."

She adjusted her glasses and without a word, turned her back and walked away.

I was almost in tears by the time we got out the door. It was all so wrong. Earlier that day, it had never occurred to me to even look for Rebecca during my stay in New York. But then, Mark Brazelton just happened to ask me to find a phone number for a man named Connolly, and that number just happened to be on the page opposite the Connor listings, and right then and there I knew it was fated that I should look for my aunt. I began my search, and within hours, as miraculous as it seems, I had found someone who had actually known her, and she led me to Rebecca's former place of business. Surely, with so much falling right into place, my search could not end now. It would be a cruel cosmic joke to have brought me this far, only to have my hopes dashed by a bitchy boutique owner. There simply had to be something we weren't thinking of and something else we could do, short of hiring a private detective, which I could not afford.

"Dar, I feel so bad for you," Melanie said, draping her arm around my shoulder. "Come on, let's go in the deli and have a soda or something. We'll talk. Maybe there's something we missed."

"Can I help yous?" the large, balding man behind the counter asked as we took a seat.

"We'll both have a diet soda," Melanie told him.

"Coming up," he said to her, placing two napkins in front of us. "Hey, your friend here looks a little sad."

"She's having a bad day," Melanie explained, fiddling with the napkin.

"I have lots o' them bad days too," he said, walking to the soda fountain. "Fifteen years behind the same counter. Doin' the same damn thing. How good can a day get? Last really good day I had was two years ago when I hit the number. Hit it big. Number two-one-seven! Eight months ago, I hit again in combination. Since then, nothin'. Wife's raggin' on me to bring in more bucks, and I tell her, 'Hey, whattya want me to do, rob a bank?' She says, 'Don't be stupid,' and I say, 'Then shut up and stop running your yap. At least I got a goddamn job! If ya wanted a

Rockefeller ya shoulda married one.' "

"Life can be a bitch," Melanie told him, not knowing how to respond.

"Sure can, sweetheart," he said, as he put our drinks in front of us. "Specially when you're married to one."

Melanie laughed, kicking me under the counter to do the same. But I was somewhere else. "Did you say that you've been here for fifteen years?" I asked him.

"Yeah, honey," he said, looking at me curiously. "I did."

"Then maybe you know my aunt, Rebecca Connor. She used to work next door at the boutique—before it was Zoey's."

"Sure! I knew Rebecca," he said, wiping both hands on his stained white apron. "Can't tell you what her last name was, though. Don't remember. Pretty little thing. Tough as nails, but real nice, ya know? Used to come by on her break for a cup of coffee and a smoke. Haven't seen her for a couple of years."

"Do you have any idea where I might find her?" I asked, trying not to get my hopes up.

"Oh, no," he said, apologetically. "I'm friendly with the customers and all, but I don't keep tabs on their whereabouts or nothin.'"

"I'm desperately trying to find her," I said, clutching my drink for moral support.

"Well, I know she used to sing a couple of nights. Little pub called Cabernet's. On one of them little side streets between Columbus and Central Park West. Only reason I know that, is 'cause she asked me to hang up a flyer coupla times. Sang blues, jazz—ya know, the sad, mellow stuff that makes old men like me remember when."

I took a sip of my drink. "Do you think the place is still open?"

"Sure it is," he said, grabbing a rag and wiping the counter to the left of us. "Don't think it opens 'til night, though. Ya might wanna wait, and ya might just wanna bring an adult with ya. Yous girls are too young to go alone. They'll never let you in."

"Thanks so much!" I said, as I threw several dollars down on the counter. "And keep the change."

∗ ∗ ∗

"You're gonna owe me big time for this," Dave joked, as the waiter at Cabernet's led the four of us to a table that evening.

"I'm letting you live with my sister!" Melanie teased him, as we took our seats. "I let you tear her out of the bosom of my family and relocate her butt to New York. I'd say you owe me, mister! Big time!"

"Well, Darla," Brenda said, scanning the room uneasily. "I hope to hell someone here knows where your aunt is. I really hate the thought of you guys running all around New York looking for her. I feel very responsible for you. And I told your dad you'd be careful, remember?"

"Duh, we are being careful, Bren," Melanie said, making a face that only a sister could love. "That's why we asked your big, strong man to play Sherlock for us."

"Oh please, Melanie," Brenda said, then laughed.

Dave smiled and turned to Brenda. "Order me a glass of pinot noir, sweetie. I'm going to go talk to the manager and see what he knows." He looked at Melanie and me and winked. "Wish me luck."

For the next fifteen minutes, I watched nervously as Dave had a long, animated talk with the man in the purple shirt at the end of the bar. When he finally came back to the table, I could barely contain my anticipation.

"Well, what did you find out?" I said, bouncing enthusiastically in my chair. "Does he know Rebecca or not?"

"I think he more than knows her, Darla," Dave said, picking up his wine glass. "The two of them used to be lovers."

"You're kidding, Dave," Brenda said, sitting upright in her chair. "Really?"

"Omigod!"

"Oh my God!" I repeated. "Are you serious?"

"I'm very serious," Dave said, then took a sip of his drink. "Good vintage... seems she sang here regularly for a couple of years." He nodded toward the bar. "Then, she and Ray over there broke up, and he hasn't seen her since. Said he heard through the grapevine that she got married. He did say, though, that she'd been going to NYU for years, part time, for a degree in social work. Apparently, she graduated about two, three years ago and left the boutique for a job as a counselor. Now she helps runaway teens get their lives together."

Dave's words brought tears to my eyes. Rebecca had come full circle and was now helping young people who had been just like her. Mom and Aunt Didi would be so proud.

"So where's she working?" I asked, still bouncing. "I want to go there and meet her."

Dave smiled apologetically. "That's just it, Darla. Ray has no idea where she works. All he knows is that it's some place for runaways, sort of a safe haven where these kids can go so they don't get killed or abused on the streets. He did say that the place is on Broadway, but he didn't know if it was Broadway uptown or Broadway downtown. That sure doesn't narrow it down much. I'm sorry."

"Well, I guess Dar and I will just have to check every place in town," Melanie said. "Omigod! I've got the best idea. We'll dress up like runaways, put torn clothes and dirt all over our faces, and then we'll go in pretending to be homeless. Is that a cool idea or what?"

Brenda looked mortified. "Melanie Grace Davenport! You'll do absolutely nothing of the kind! Haven't you learned anything about New York, you numskull? Listen, I'll call my friend Sharon in the morning. She's a social worker with the state. I'll get a list of places from her, and then you can call these places and get your information. I said, call these places. On the phone. Do you hear me?"

"We hear you, Mom," Melanie said sarcastically, as she kicked me under the table. "We hear you."

The following morning around nine-thirty, Brenda called from work to say that her friend Sharon was sending us a list of runaway shelters via messenger and that it would arrive around ten o'clock. She then warned us to be extremely careful and not to do anything stupid like visit the places in person or, more importantly, dress up like homeless teenagers and put ourselves in danger.

Thankfully, Melanie had already admitted that the dress-up scheme was a stupid idea. But we still had every intention of visiting the shelters in person, although it did occur to us that Brenda had made an excellent point. As she had explained, the list of runaway services was long, and in some cases, there was no way of knowing which ones actually housed runaways, which simply did outpatient counseling, and which served as referral organizations. After careful debate, Melanie decided that we should call every center on the list, pretend to be runaways, and thereby find out which places actually took in people. Then, from that list, we would narrow down the addresses near or on Broadway and go in person to find Rebecca. We both agreed that people in New York were paranoid and that the shelters and agencies were unlikely to give out too much information on the phone.

Neither of us, however, realized what a monumental task we'd set for ourselves, and by six o'clock that evening, when Dave came home from work, we still had not finished calling around, nor had we left the apartment once that day.

The next day was Saturday, and Melanie and I were able to get a few more calls in, but there was no way we could begin our physical search yet, not with Brenda and Dave keeping a watchful eye on us. Besides, they had made all kinds of plans for us, including a trip to the South Street Seaport area, Chinatown, and Little Italy, and after all, I did want to see something of New York.

Early Monday morning, after Brenda and Dave had left, Melanie and I began our search. We spent two grueling, depressing days combing the runaway shelters of New York, were leered at by vile men on dangerous streets we shouldn't have walked, and were absolutely panicked when a drug-addicted teen prostitute stopped us outside Washington Square Park, begging for money. I had never seen such hard evidence of the cold, cruel world before, and suddenly, Rebecca's past life, which up to that point was nothing but a bunch of bad memories for my family, came hitting me in the face like a nightmare come true. I suddenly had no trouble picturing the squalor that my mother had described, and I wondered if she had any idea how Rebecca must've felt actually living in it, day after day after day. How could they harbor such anger, still, after all these years, toward this woman who'd lived such a hellish adolescence? I prayed I would soon find out, but with each address came another disappointment, and by the end of the day on Tuesday, there were only three shelters left on the list, and I was doubtful that Rebecca would be at any one of them.

At each place we'd visited, we'd used the cover that we were searching for a runaway friend named Susan, and that Susan had called us one night to say that she was in a shelter and had happened to mention a counselor named Rebecca. We desperately needed to find Susan, because we needed to let her know that all was forgiven and that her parents wanted her home. Most of the people believed our story, although a few seemed suspicious of our motives. But that didn't really matter because the answer was always the same. "Sorry girls, there's nobody here named Rebecca."

CHAPTER 27

The following morning, Wednesday, I woke up in a blue funk. Not only was I feeling disheartened about ever finding Rebecca, but Melanie and Brenda were off to see a hit Broadway show, and that meant I would be spending the day alone. Even though the tickets had been purchased months before anyone knew I'd be accompanying Melanie to New York, that didn't stop the Davenport girls from developing a serious case of the guilts over the matter. Brenda had even called the theater in the hopes of scooping up a last-minute cancellation, but that day's matinee performance was sold out. So, while Brenda and Melanie continued to make profuse apologies to me, I lamented over the eventuality that their day would probably be ruined by worrying about mine.

After several rounds of "I feel worse about this than you do," we all agreed to cease and desist and made dinner plans for that evening. Melanie then gave me her keys and suggested that I spend the day shopping in the neighborhood, with perhaps a trip to Bloomingdales, which was just a few blocks away. She also promised me, when Brenda wasn't listening, that when they got back from the theater, we'd find a good excuse to slip out for a while and go visit another one or two of the shelters left on the list.

When they left the apartment around eleven o'clock, I turned on the TV and began watching some silly game show where grown people were jumping up and down like maniacs and screaming as their partners performed outrageous stunts to win a prize. The TV audience was screaming as well, and so was the overly effervescent host. The noise was unbearable, so, when the phone rang, it was a welcome interruption.

"Darla, honey? Is that you?"

"Mom!" I gasped, wary of her reason for calling. "Hi! How are you?"

Mom jabbered away as if we were sitting at the kitchen table. "Actually, dear, I'm doing just fine. I'm so glad I caught you. I was afraid you and Melanie might have already left for the day. Are you having a good time? How was the newspaper outing? What else have you been doing?"

"Merriman Newspapers was great," I said, trying to conceal the anxiety that her call had created. "The first day we were there, Mr. Withers took Melanie and me to the plant in Jersey and later we had lunch with him in Manhattan. He told me that he'd heard great things about me from Amelia, and that if I go to college in any city where they have a Merriman paper, he'll make sure that I get an internship."

"That makes me so proud," she said cheerfully. "I can't wait to tell your father. I'm sure there's a lot more, but you can tell us both when you get home. Listen, honey, that's why I'm calling..."

Oh, here it comes, I thought. She's going to ruin my life now.

Her lively discourse slowed a bit. "I was wondering if you might come home a few days earlier, like maybe Friday."

"Friday!" I cried, stomping a foot on the floor. "Mom, I was supposed to stay until Monday. Friday! That's only forty-eight hours from now. God, Mom, why?"

"Well, it's good news, actually. Very good news," she said, picking up speed again. "April called me last night. Didi and George, it seems, are getting back together on a trial basis, and April, bless her heart, has insisted that we all get together for a family picnic at the Alexanders on Saturday—as a going-away present to her. Believe it or not, Didi agreed to this, and this morning, she even called to invite me personally, saying that it was about time we tried to work things out."

"Wow! I can't believe it," I said, relieved that Mom hadn't witnessed my tantrum. "That's incredible."

"So you see, Darla, it's really important that you come home. I wouldn't ask you to cut your time short if it weren't."

My chances of finding Rebecca were dwindling by the second. Despite Mom's good news, the clock was ticking away, and I was practically on the train home.

"I'll be there, Mom," I said, as I longingly looked out the window at the busy street below. "And I'm really happy about Aunt Didi calling and stuff. I just wish I could stay till Monday, that's all."

"I know, Darla," Mom said sympathetically. "And I appreciate your being such a good sport about everything. But you'll be visiting New York again once April moves there. I'm sure of that. I'll let you go now; just call me back and let me know what train you're taking. Either your father or I will pick you up. Oh! I almost forgot. More good news! Two days ago Paul Hatchford was arrested in Chicago on drug trafficking charges. He's in jail pending a hearing. There's a lot more to it, but I don't really understand all that legal mumbo jumbo, so you'll have to wait until Uncle George can explain it to you on Saturday."

"That's great, Mom," I said, wishing her good news could've waited. "You take care. I'll call you back tomorrow."

I turned off the TV. If I only had two days left in New York, I wasn't going to waste time watching people covered in pea-green slime compete for trips to Disneyland. I decided to take Melanie's advice and go to Bloomingdales. I put on my sneakers, fixed my makeup, shoved the list of remaining shelters in my pocket, and headed out the door.

I stayed inside Bloomingdales for about forty-five minutes looking at a lot of things I could never afford. After I left the store, I bought a hotdog and soda from a street vendor and, without really planning to, continued to walk crosstown toward Broadway. Experienced New Yorker that I was not, I ran into a major obstacle on Fifth Avenue called Central Park and could not figure out how in the world to get around it and back over to the West Side where Melanie and I had been several days before. I wasn't in the mood to ask strangers, so I did the next best thing: I hailed a cab and gave the driver an address.

The next shelter on my list was right on Broadway, in the West Sixties, a couple of blocks north of Lincoln Center and about fourteen blocks south of Zoey's boutique. There was no name on the dirty glass door, only a number, and inside was a flight of stairs that led God-knows-where. I stood there on the street, staring at the door and wishing that Melanie were there with me, until it dawned on me that I was a lot safer going inside than standing idly on the street.

The moment I got inside, I could hear the sound of young people talking upstairs, and instantly a surge of relief came over me. As I approached the upstairs landing, a handful of sad-looking teenagers sized me up, then quickly dispersed down the hallway. Immediately, a woman in her late thirties came over to me, smiled, and asked me if I needed some help.

I couldn't help but stare at her. She was about five feet two, with Aunt Didi's petite build, but there was something in her eyes that reminded me of Mom. She had short dark blond hair, lightly frosted at the temples, and was quite beautiful, although not the kind of beautiful that most people would notice right away. She looked tired, as if she were years overdue for a long bubble bath and massage, but she didn't seem to be the kind of person who would ever indulge in such luxuries. She moved with worn confidence, as if to say to her teenage charges: "Don't mess with me; I was once you." I prayed that she might be Rebecca, but when I saw her name tag, "B. Davidson," I knew that once again I was going to be disappointed.

"Can I help you?" she repeated, well aware that I was staring at her.

"Uh, yeah. I'm looking for someone," I said, scanning the room for possibilities.

"Friend, relative? Who?"

"Relative," I told her nervously.

"Boy, girl? How old?"

"A woman. In her mid-thirties."

She laughed. "Sorry. We only take kids here. There's no one here that fits your description."

"No. She wouldn't be a runaway," I corrected her. "She'd be someone who works here. Like you."

"What's her name?" she asked curiously.

"Rebecca Connor," I said quickly, grateful that she hadn't tossed me out yet. "Do you know her?"

She looked at me and went pale. "Follow me. I'll see if I can find out where she might be."

She turned and led me to a small room at the end of the corridor, shutting the door behind us. "Sit down," she said, pointing to an old office chair on casters, as she walked around to the other side of the cluttered steel desk. "Now, tell me again who you're looking for."

"Rebecca Connor."

"Rebecca Connor," she repeated. "And how are the two of you related?"

"She's my aunt. My mother's sister."

"And who are you?"

"Darla McKendrick."

She turned her chair around so that I could not see her face and put her hand to her mouth. Finally, after a minute, she swiveled back, looking at me as if she'd been hypnotized by the sound of my name.

"Who sent you here?" she said, her voice barely above a whisper.

At that moment, a coworker peered through the glass window on the door, knocked lightly, then came in. "Are you okay, Davidson? You look upset."

She shook her head and shooed the coworker away with her right hand. "Please, I'm fine," she said softly.

"You sure don't look fine; you work too damn hard. Your shift was over two hours ago. Why don't quit for the day? I'll talk to this kid for you. Really, Becky, you need to conserve some of that superhuman strength for yourself. Go home, will you?"

B. Davidson, I thought. Becky. Why didn't I think of that?

"This is a personal matter, Kit. I'm fine."

"Yeah, you're fine all right. I'm the Queen of England, my old man doesn't run around, and the Mets are the best team in baseball." She sighed and walked out of the office without waiting for a response.

I looked intently at the woman who sat in front of me. I wondered what, if anything, she would say to me now.

"Darla. That's a very pretty name."

"Thank you," I said.

"One of the Little Rascals was named Darla, she said, as if she were picturing the character in her head. "Did you ever see that show? It was way before your time, of course—mine, too, but I used to watch the reruns with my sisters when I was a kid. My one sister loved the name Darla."

"Your sister Maggie?"

"Yeah," she said, looking into my eyes with an unreadable expression. "She'd be the one."

We sat there and stared at each other. I couldn't quite believe that I had finally come face to face with Aunt Rebecca, while she, of course, had no idea why I was there or what I wanted.

"How old are you, Darla?"

"Seventeen."

"What are you doing in New York? Who's chaperoning your visit? And what do you want with me?" she said a bit uneasily.

"I'm in New York with my best friend, Melanie," I explained nervously. "We're staying at her sister Brenda's apartment. They're off seeing a Broadway show, so I took a cab over here."

She looked at me incredulously. Then she said: "You don't smoke, do you?"

"No," I said, trying to follow her train of thought.

"That's too bad. I mean, that's great. I'm glad you don't smoke. I was just hopin' to bum a cigarette from you. I quit a couple of years ago, when I had my kid."

"You have a child?"

"James Henry Davidson. My son."

So I had a boy cousin after all. I looked at Rebecca. I was still having trouble reading her.

"That's really great," I said. "I'll bet he's adorable."

"He is," she said matter-of-factly. "Now let's cut to the chase. I'd like you to tell me why you're here, Darla."

"It's a really long—"

"I want to know how you found me. And why. Your presence has kind of thrown me," she said with an edge to her voice. "In my life, I've learned to expect the unexpected, but somehow, I never thought I'd ever see—"

"Yeah, I know," I said. "I know how you feel."

"You do, huh?" she asked, challenging me. "You think you know what I'm feeling right now? You couldn't possibly know."

For the first time, she looked away from me and started straightening the clutter on her desk. She picked up a file folder, stood, and quickly filed it in the large black cabinet to the right of her desk. She sat down again and began rummaging through a stack of papers, ignoring me completely, as if I had vanished in a puff of smoke. I watched intently as she stood again to tack something onto the bulletin board behind her, then sat down and continued to shuffle papers. I considered the fact that this might be her way of telling me that the visit was over, but I had no intention of leaving.

Finally, she looked up and blurted out, "Somebody has to do this shit, you know. We don't have secretaries here. Not in the budget."

I didn't know how to respond. I knew she was purposely trying to intimidate me.

"Cat got your tongue, Darla?"

"No, not really," I said. "It's just that—"

"It's just what? You found me, remember. Not vice versa. I'll say it just one more time: I want to know how you found me and more importantly, why you found me. I'm not some damn museum piece to be stared at. If you want to look at dinosaurs or worn-out relics and shit like that, hit the Museum of Natural History on your way out. As for me, I'm tired of being stared at. I got kids checking me out all day long. The minute they walk into this joint, they eyeball me up and down, trying to decide whether to trust me or not. I'm getting the idea that you're doin' the same thing. So, what's it going to be? Placate or vacate, Darla. Your choice."

"I'm ready to talk," I said, as I tried to keep my legs from shaking.

Rebecca stopped what she was doing and picked up the telephone. She made a quick call to someone she called "Mom," and asked if she could keep James Henry for dinner. Then, she leaned back in her chair and gestured with her right hand, as if to say "The floor is yours."

I began by giving her a detailed account of how I'd come to locate her. She appeared to be quite surprised by it all but didn't react strongly

395

until I got to the part about Melanie and me visiting some of the shelters in person.

"That was very dangerous—what you did. You know that, don't you?"

"Yeah, I know."

"You and your friend really put yourselves at risk. Are you aware of that?"

"I know. But I had to find you."

"That fact is becoming increasingly clear. But you don't seem to realize the kind of danger that's out there. Maybe I should introduce you to some of the kids in this joint. They're a lot more street smart than you'll ever be, but that didn't stop them from getting hurt. The world isn't always a nice place. Are you hearing me?"

"Yes," I said, looking down at the floor.

"Speaking of dangerous situations, entering Stevie Ain't Worth Shit's apartment wasn't exactly a cool thing to do, either. I don't care how harmless Libby looked to you. And the fact that someone's a building superintendent doesn't guarantee they're on the level. Are you aware of that?"

"Yeah, I guess."

"Don't guess, Darla. Guessing can get you killed. When in doubt, do without. Am I getting through to you?" Rebecca paused and bit her bottom lip. "All right, screw the how part for now, as ingenious and interesting as your story is, I want to know the why part. Why in the world was it so important to find me?"

"It's really a long story," I warned her.

"For this, I've got all the time in the world," Rebecca said, softening a bit. "Enlighten me, kid."

For the hour and a half, I did most of the talking. I began by telling her about the day when I'd first heard her name, and explained how Aunt Didi had lied by telling me that Squalor was a town in New Mexico, and how years later, in the seventh grade, I'd humiliated myself in Miss Todd's history class.

Rebecca laughed and shook her head. "My sister Didi. She'd yell

'Fire' in a crowded theater if it suited her damn purposes."

I didn't know how to respond to Rebecca's very accurate assessment of her oldest sister, so I continued by sharing my recollection of the day I'd come home from school in tears. As uncomfortable as it was to do, I repeated everything that Mom had revealed to me about Rebecca's life—how she took drugs, ran away to New York, claimed to be pregnant, and on and on.

Rebecca stared at me with keen interest as I recounted Mom's version of her adolescent and teen years. She diverted her attention only momentarily, when her coworker, Kit, peeked through the glass for the third time, to tell her, by means of twisting her face unnaturally, to go home. Rebecca rolled her eyes and once again, shooed Kit away.

"Don't mind her. She thinks I have some morbid desire to live here, which is about as far from the truth as you can get. Go on, Darla. What else did Maggie tell you about my pregnancy?"

"Nothing really. She just said you'd probably gotten pregnant by some 'shady' college boy, or by some horrible man who you were with here in New York."

" 'Shady college boy'? Tony? Maggie, Maggie, Maggie!" Rebecca laughed and shook her head.

"Were you pregnant?" I asked reluctantly.

Rebecca nodded. "I lost the child. When you abuse your body with drugs and alcohol, things like that can happen. Sometimes they don't. And then it can be even worse...for the child. I was a bad kid, Darla. It was just like your mother told you. I'm just still not clear on why you came to find me."

I went on with my story, explaining to Rebecca how her presence had lingered in the wake of her absence, and how for years her name had lurked in the dark corners of conversation, making odd appearances and disappearing just as quickly. I told her about Uncle Martin's visit, and how Aunt Didi went ballistic when he spoke of her like a piece of fruit that had gone rotten.

Rebecca chewed nervously on her cuticles, then, realizing what she was doing, put her hands in her lap. "Didi stood up for me, huh?"

397

"Well yeah, Aunt Rebecca, Martin and his wife, Maudie, were so disgusting. The only reason they even came to visit was because they wanted money from Dad and Uncle George for some land development scheme in Florida."

"Once a pig, always a pig, Darla," she said vehemently.

"You're not kidding," I said, happy for the confirmation.

Next, I told Rebecca about meeting Ryan, and explained how my relationship with Dad began to suffer after that point, and how I'd always felt as if he were expecting me to follow in her rebellious footsteps. It wasn't easy to tell Rebecca that my parents lived in mortal fear that I'd turn out just like her, but she kept encouraging me to "spill my guts" and seemed to desperately crave the information I was giving her. When I told her about the Halloween party and how Dad's accusations of my drinking only furthered the tension between us, she put her head in the palms of her hands, and I was certain that I'd gone too far.

"Are you all right? I asked her. "Do you want me to stop?"

"No, kid. I don't want you to stop," she said lifting her head. "Believe me, whatever pain your family has suffered all of these years, trust me, it's been twice as hard for me. Now go on. I really need to hear what you're saying."

I told her next about the Hoover debacle (which made her laugh and say "Good for you, Darla"), then described the scene in my bedroom afterwards, and told her how Dad had angrily called me by her name.

"Jesus," she said. "Way to go, Ted. Go on."

Rebecca listened in horror as I told her all about New Year's Eve, elucidating on the events leading up to the crash and expressing my surprise at the incidents that followed my homecoming: Dad's running out on Mom; Dad's taking his first drink in many, many years; Mom's conversation with Aunt Didi the next morning about Rebecca; and her subsequent explanation to me about how my near-fatal experience brought back painful memories of Rebecca's wild teenage years.

"I need a damn drink. I need a drink and a cigarette," Rebecca muttered, almost to herself. "But I'm not going to have either one. I'll just chew on my nails. Keep talking, kid."

398

I rambled on and on to my willing listener, telling her how her name had lived in infamy over the years, but even more so in my mother's heart.

"Maggie ever say why she didn't look for me? Why she never tried to find me in all these years? Not once!" Rebecca sounded angry and hurt. "Was it too much for her? Afraid of what she might find? Does she still grab her damn throat every time something surprises her?"

I wanted to laugh. "Yeah, she does that all the time."

"Someday that mother of yours is gonna choke herself to death." She paused, then said, "So tell me, Darla. Do you know why they never tried to find me?"

"Mom told me once that if you wanted to see them again that you knew exactly where to find them, and that you probably hadn't found them because you wanted it that way."

"She did, huh? What else did she say?"

"Well, on New Year's Eve, after I went upstairs, I heard them talking about the past, which I figured might've had something to do with you, and Dad said that even if he faced old demons and stuff, life could still come crashing down on them. He sounded real scared. Do you know what he was talking about?"

Rebecca didn't answer, but I had the distinct impression that she knew exactly what Dad had meant.

"Mom loves you," I told her. "I know that. She loves you a whole lot. That's one of the reasons I came to find you. I know Mom would love to see you...Aunt Didi too."

"I don't think so, Darla. Besides, I'm not ready for any family reunions. Not now," Rebecca said sadly. She looked away for a moment, as if she were trying to restore her hardened façade, then said, almost indifferently: "So tell me, how do your mother and your aunt get along? Best of friends, or are they still fighting?"

Rebecca had asked a loaded question, so I went on with my history lesson, explaining how Mom's forged letter and Aunt Didi's stage mothering had led May and me to Pier 23 that June night, over a year ago. I then told her how the aftermath of that evening had led to a parting of the ways, and how once again, her name had come up in the argument. Rebecca begged me to elaborate, so I explained that Mom and Aunt Didi had argued viciously about how the other one was to blame for Rebecca's fate—Mom blaming Didi for teaching Rebecca how to flaunt her body; Didi blaming Mom for taking something away that Rebecca loved, thereby leaving her with nothing to do but lead the life she led.

Rebecca looked absolutely amazed by my story. For the first time, I saw that she was as much in the dark as I was.

"Do you know what I'm talking about?" I asked curiously.

"Well, Darla," she said, leaning lazily back in her chair, "I remember that Didi and I used to put on these little shows, you know, song-and-dance kinda things. And I remember Mom, your grandma Adelaide, telling her to stop because I wasn't getting much schoolwork done. But Didi's kind of stubborn, and she continued to put on the shows behind Mom's back. At some point, Maggie squealed to Mom about it and the shows stopped for good. But that's all I remember; it was no big deal. I was getting sick of the dodo bird bossing me around, anyway."

I couldn't help but giggle at Rebecca's nickname for my aunt. "That's funny," I said, "Mom and Aunt Didi sounded like it had everything to do with how your life turned out."

"They're so wrong, Darla," she said, as her eyes flickered with anger. "They're just so wrong. Is that the last time you heard my name mentioned?"

"My cousins heard your name on Christmas Day, right after Uncle George told Aunt Didi he wanted a divorce. He said he was tired of soaking up Aunt Didi's family dysfunctions like a wet sponge. And then he told Aunt Didi he was tired of being blamed for one mistake his whole life and that she should have it out with you for a change."

"It's still going on," Rebecca moaned. Why don't these people let it go? Why do they continue to torture themselves?" She paused, then said under her breath, "No wonder Georgie wanted to take a hike."

I didn't have any idea what she meant by that, but I inferred from the way she turned her head that she didn't want to comment any further. I didn't know what else to say at that point so I just looked at her, wondering if she was going to reveal anything about her life over the past eighteen years.

"This is all so incredible, you coming here today and everything. I'm just blown away."

"Aren't you going to tell me about your life?" I asked. "Just a little."

Rebecca heaved a big sigh and looked at me. "I guess you deserve that, don't you?"

"I guess I do. But before you start, is there a bathroom around here?"

She laughed. "You can use the staff bathroom. Go out the door and hang a left. You'll see it. I'm going to get a cup of coffee. You want something? Pepsi? Diet Pepsi? Sprite? Something from the vending machines?"

"Just a Diet Pepsi. Thanks."

I chuckled loudly when I came back to Rebecca's office and found that she had blocked the glass window on the door with a large piece of paper that said, "I'm fine, Kit. Leave me alone." As I entered the office, I found Rebecca staring pensively at the wall. I wondered which of the myriad things I had told her she might be thinking about. There was an open can of Diet Pepsi on her desk, close to where I had been sitting.

"Thanks," I said taking my seat.

She looked at me and smiled warmly. "I guess it's my turn, huh?"

"Yeah, I guess," I said.

"Jesus, Darla, she said, picking up a blue Bic pen and playing with the cap. "What in the world would your mom and aunt think if they knew where you were right now?"

"They'd go nuts!" I said exuberantly, as if I were an appliance someone had just plugged in. "It'd be freak-out city!"

Rebecca laughed. "You're right, Darla. And Maggie would probably have deep red welts on her neck by now, and Didi, well, damn, she'd be bouncing off the walls."

I was wondering if Rebecca cared to wager on what the men in my family might be doing, but she didn't say a word about my father or Uncle George.

"I'm stalling, aren't I?" she said, pushing the cap of the pen with her thumb. "You want to hear my story—now. Well, I can tell you this, Darla, and excuse me if this sounds like something out of a bad teen movie, but my adolescence was not a pretty sight. I wouldn't wish it on my worst enemy." Just at that moment, the cap shot off the pen, went flying in the air, hit me on the nose, and landed in my lap. We both burst out laughing.

"Sorry about that," she said, as I handed the cap back to her. "I'll try to be more careful with my toys. Is your nose okay?"

I laughed again. "It's just fine, Aunt Rebecca. But please, I've waited so long to know the real story."

"Can't fool you with a little diversion, can I?" she said cheerfully. "Well, my early years were pretty much like Maggie told you. I started fucking up my life when I was about eleven, and I didn't stop for a very long time. I smoked cigarettes, got high on weed, drank. By the ripe old age of sixteen, I was doing anything and everything I could get my grubby hands on. Charming, huh? Probably drove my parents to an early grave."

Rebecca put her right hand to her forehead. She looked as if she wanted to cry, but she didn't. "Darla, you'll never know how guilty I feel about hurting my parents. They were such good people. They didn't deserve any of it. I never even got to say goodbye to my father. My friend Tony, that 'shady college boy' your Mom spoke about, he called me when Dad died so I came home for the funeral. I hid in the back of the church in this stupid disguise and left right before the service was over."

"Did you go to Aunt Didi's house, maybe that day or the next, and talk to my two cousins who were playing in the sandbox?"

"How in the world do you know that?" she asked, leaning forward.

"They remember you, April and May, but they didn't figure out until years later that you were you. How come you ran away?"

"I got scared," she said, settling back in her chair. "When the dodo bird saw me from the window, she looked so out of control and so angry that I ran for my life. I was too afraid to face her, knowing that she was still angry with me. Then, I just figured that Maggie had to be equally as angry, and that Mom probably hated me as well—for what I put her through…so I just left town, that same day."

"Why would Aunt Didi, or anyone, have been mad at you, or hated you? I mean, hadn't it been almost seven years since they'd seen you? Why would they have still been angry?"

Rebecca looked uncomfortable with the question. "Trust me, kid, they were pissed. When you've got a fuck-up like me in the family, life is one miserable mess."

"And that's the last time you ever came back? When Grandpa Henry died?"

"No, it wasn't. Tony called me about a year later, to tell me that Mom was sick. His aunt was a very close friend of Mom's. That's how he knew. Anyway, I came home to see her. Tony brought me. We sat in the car outside of her house for an hour and waited for the bird to leave. When I finally got the courage to go inside, well, it turned out to be the best thing I ever did. Mom was so happy to see me, and she kept weeping for joy. I stayed there for hours but made her swear not to tell anyone I'd been there. I don't think she ever did, either. After that, I used to call her on the phone quite a bit, but I never saw her again because she died before I could get to her. Thank God, at least we had made our peace with one another. After Mom was gone, I tried to call Didi and your mom a couple of times, but I could never bring myself to say anything. I just hung up on them when they answered the phone."

"Go back to when you were my age. What happened to you, after you arrived in New York?"

"Well, I met this filthy degenerate, Hector, in the Village one day who said he'd give me a place to live and protect me from—well, you know, the kind of evils that lurked in the hearts of men. Only he had more evil in his heart than anyone I'd ever met. He's the slime who took me to live in that foul, squalid rat condo that your mother spoke about. He had another apartment, one fit for human beings, which was in Greenwich Village, but he used that for business."

"What kind of business?"

Rebecca sighed wearily. "Prostitution business, honey."

"Oh God!"

403

"I was a teenage drug addict, and teenage drug addicts mean dollar signs to slime like that. He called himself my protector, but he was nothing but a lousy pimp who raped me and let other men do the same. I was just a child! A damn child!"

That was all I needed to hear. I burst into uncontrollable tears, despite every intention to stay calm. Rebecca jumped up out of her chair and ran around to console me. I stood up and she put her arms around me, hugging me tightly. It was the first time we had touched each other.

"It's okay, Darla," she said softly. "I'm sorry to tell you all of this. But you really did want to know, didn't you?"

I shook my head yes and continued to sob. She held me tighter and stroked my hair. "You're such a sweet kid, you really are. I feel terrible that I never knew you before today. I really do. I saw your picture at Mom's house, that time I went home, but I never even knew your name. At least, I don't think I did."

I finally managed to stop crying, and Rebecca helped me back into the chair, then resumed her seat.

"You okay now?" she asked, handing me some tissues from her desk drawer.

I nodded and blew my nose.

"Anyway, kid, it does get better. I was only in that horrible place for about six months. That's when I met Emma. She was a retired schoolteacher who lived in the same apartment house where that slime had his business. She'd been suspicious of him for a long time, but one day she asked me to come in her apartment for a visit, and then she coaxed and prodded me until I told her everything that was going on."

"How come she had to coax the truth out of you?"

"I was scared for my life, Darla, that's why. Hector had threatened to kill me if I ever opened my mouth." She paused momentarily, as if she were summoning the courage to continue this unscheduled rerun of her life story. "Anyway, Emma called the police, and shortly afterwards the scum was arrested and the place shut down. But that very same day, she took me uptown to meet her daughter, Suzanne, who was a social worker. Suzanne cleaned me up, gave me some better threads to wear, took me to a doctor, then signed me into a rehab program. Unlike the time your grandpa Henry signed me in, this time I was ready to change my life. So, when I had finished ridding the toxic waste from my body, and when the people at the rehab clinic felt reasonably sure I would stay clean, Suzanne let me crash on the couch at her place."

"Wow, that's incredible. You were so lucky to have met Emma and her daughter."

"They both saved my life. I really believe the guardian angel of lost teenagers sent them to me. Emma, God rest her soul, was an incredible woman, a guardian angel herself. And Suzanne, well, I never had a better friend."

Hearing about Emma reminded me of Victoria, and I couldn't wait until I could call and tell her I'd found Rebecca. She would be so happy.

"So that's where I was when I got out of rehab, some two and a half years after moving to New York. Living in Suzanne's apartment on Amsterdam Avenue. The 'Ain't Worth Shit' building. As it turned out, Suzanne got eventually got married and moved to Seattle, but she let me sublet her place for several years. I'll tell you, I was very, very lucky. God only knows where I would've lived had it not been for Suzanne and her apartment."

"So what did you do with yourself after that?"

"Eventually I got my GED and worked like a dog to keep my head above water. Often I was doing several jobs at a time. Let's see: I've waited tables, served cocktails, worked in the Garment District, sold lingerie, walked dogs, answered telephones, baked Mrs. Chips cookies in a storefront window, and then for years, sold women's clothing in that boutique on Broadway. You name it."

"How did you start singing?" I asked, trying to put the pieces together.

"Well, seven years ago, Suzanne had to give up the apartment. So I moved to a much smaller building, farther uptown, and one of my new neighbors was a voice teacher, who for only a few bucks, helped me work on my singing until I was ready to do small club gigs. Wouldn't Didi be proud, huh?" Rebecca began nervously shuffling papers on her desk

405

again.

"I know," I said, watching her. "These days, Aunt Didi's name has the same effect on me, too."

We both laughed.

"Moving right along," Rebecca said, pushing the papers aside, "I then started singing in little pubs and piano bars in the area, and eventually fell in love with a club owner, Ray Mirotti, from Cabernet's."

"How come you guys broke up?"

"Because after a while, we grew apart. Ray just wasn't what I wanted, and I suppose I didn't exactly float his boat any longer either. Besides, with the late hours he kept, we barely saw each other. Believe me, kid, I'd had enough of boozing it up until the wee hours of the morning. Plus, I'd been going to school for years, to get my degree in social work, and there was no way I could study and do all that mess too. Ray loved the nightlife—it was his heart—and he really couldn't share in the joy that I got out of my educational pursuits, nor was he the least bit interested in doing so. So we broke up and that was that. C'est la vie! About three years ago, I started dating a good friend of mine from school, Randall Davidson, and before you could say, uh, 'shady college boy,' we got hitched. Eleven months later, we had a kid. The sunshine of my life. My James Henry."

"What does Randall do?" I asked eagerly, anxious to know everything about her life.

"He works for the New York City Board of Education, and he's getting his doctorate at NYU. Oh, and by the way, if everything works out, I'll be going for my master's degree next spring."

"That's so great. Mom would be so happy to know how well you've done," I said.

She hesitated. "Maybe. Who knows? So you see, my life hasn't been as exciting as it started out, but its been a lot healthier, and a lot safer. Sheesh, Darla, look at the time. I really do have to leave."

I felt as if I'd been shot from a cannon back into reality. I realized that I had lost all sense of time. "I guess I better get back too," I said reluctantly. "Brenda and Melanie must be freaking by now."

"Why don't you let me escort you back to the East Side? I'd like to meet your friends and know you were safe and sound."

"That would be so cool, Aunt Rebecca."

She smiled.

"Oh no, maybe you don't want me to call you Aunt Rebecca. Would you rather be called Becky? Or Aunt Becky? Or what?"

"Aunt Rebecca is just perfect," she said tenderly. "C'mon kid, let's go."

CHAPTER 28

For as long as I live, I will never forget the look of shock on Melanie's face when I walked into the apartment and introduced her to Rebecca. Her mouth fell wide open, and after several stunned seconds of silence, a string of "Omigods" emerged, followed by the words "I can't believe it. She's real! Omigod, Omigod, Omigod! Nice to meet you."

It was pretty incredible to think that Rebecca was a real person. She was far from the rebellious teenager that had been described to me so often, far from the stranger who dominated every crisis, and not nearly as mysterious as all the half-told truths about her had led me to believe. She was just a woman who had started out pretty miserably, but who had gone on to lead a respectable, honest life. It was still quite difficult, though, to understand how everything could have gone so wrong for Rebecca, yet so right for Mom and Aunt Didi. But I'd been asking myself those questions for far too long, and now that I'd found Rebecca, perhaps the day was near when they'd finally be answered—if indeed I ever saw her again. After all, I had only one more day in New York; then, it was time to go home.

As we sat there in Brenda's apartment, Rebecca, Melanie, Brenda, and I, making light conversation, I mentioned to Melanie that Mom had called and asked me to come home that Friday. Melanie was extremely disappointed that I wouldn't be staying in New York for the weekend, but Rebecca looked positively heartbroken.

"You're leaving already, kid? On Friday?"

"Yeah, I have to go."

"This isn't right...Hell, I can't do it. I just can't let you go like this."

I was so grateful that she cared about me, and that she wasn't ready to say good-bye.

"You know what?" Rebecca said suddenly. "I'm going to give Kit the shock of her life and take Thursday and Friday off and spend them with you. Unless, of course, you've got other plans or don't want me to."

I jumped excitedly out of my chair and plopped down again. "No!

None at all! I'd love to spend the time with you. Are you kidding?"

"This'll work out perfectly," Brenda said. "I'm taking off from work too, so this'll give Melanie and me some time together."

"Okay then," Rebecca said decisively. She stood up. "If everything is settled, I'm gonna run. I need to pick up my kid at his grandma's and do some food shopping. Let's say I see you tomorrow morning at eleven."

"That'll be great," I said, rising to hug her goodbye. And as we put our arms around each other, I felt like the luckiest person in the world.

The minute Rebecca left I picked up the phone to call my cousins. I couldn't wait to tell them the news, and I made them swear that they wouldn't tell anyone what had happened. All three of them were shocked and thrilled simultaneously, especially April, who suggested that I ask Rebecca to come to the "family reunion" on Saturday. "Think about it, Cuz; wouldn't that be the most incredible thing in the world if Rebecca showed up?"

I agreed that it would be incredible, all right, but told April that I felt a bit reluctant to surprise the family with such a traumatic blast from the past. Who knew if they would be ready to see her? Or she to see them?

"Where's your sense of spirit and adventure, Darla? Did you leave it in the supermarket? Wake up, girl! Mom and Aunt Maggie are as ready to see Rebecca as they'll ever be. And vice versa. It's been eighteen years. How much more prep time do they need? If they wait any longer, they'll be so old they won't recognize each other. And if they wait any longer than that, they'll all be dead! Please, Darla, bring her home now. We're dying to meet her! Please! I swear, it's the right thing to do."

April's sentiments were echoed by June and May, who took turns on the phone begging me to extend the invitation to Rebecca. I thought about Victoria and suddenly remembered that not too long ago, she too had suggested that one day I might find Rebecca and bring her home. But it had never occurred to me that such a day would ever come. Now that it had, I wondered, was it merely a wish come true on Victoria's part, or was my dear friend not only speaking sagaciously, but prophetically as well. I had no time to unearth any more of life's mysteries at that moment, especially during a long-distance call, but my cousins had successfully persuaded me to do the right thing. As I said goodbye to them, I made one last promise to do everything in my power to bring Rebecca home again.

✳ ✳ ✳

I worried needlessly all night long that Rebecca would change her mind, or that I had only dreamed about our encounter, but the next morning, at ten minutes after eleven, she arrived at Brenda's door with a stuffed sock monkey in her hand.

"Here, kid," she said, handing me the toy primate. "I never got to give you anything when you were younger. Hope you like monkeys. You should; you've got plenty of them in your family. Ready to go?"

I hugged the monkey and then Rebecca. I could tell that she was embarrassed and was trying to minimize the sentimentality of the moment, but I knew she was pleased that her gift was so well received.

It was an absolutely glorious day. We must've walked ten miles. Rebecca had insisted on knowing every place of interest that I'd been, so she could take me to all of the places I hadn't yet seen, including St. Patrick's Cathedral, Rockefeller Center, and Central Park. As we walked, I learned more and more about her. She told me about the music she sang and described her joy upon hearing James Henry say "Mommy" for the first time. She told me what kind of foods she liked, and what kinds she didn't like, and said that she often made humble attempts at gourmet cooking, and that it had always been a dream of hers to study at the Cordon Bleu in Paris. I heard all about her friends and her cherished husband, Randall. She even explained to me that he was the one, some four years ago, who started calling her Becky. I, in turn, told her all about April, May, and June, and all about my friends, especially Melanie and Victoria. I even told her about the Lughead and our never-ending rivalry, and Rebecca doubled over with laughter when I told her how Rick Anson Hispants'

410

timely mishap had put an end to the Lughead's incessant gloating.

Around four o'clock, we stopped for a soda at a restaurant on Columbus Avenue. It was then that I asked Rebecca how she felt about not seeing Mom and Aunt Didi all of these years.

Rebecca sighed and shook her head. "It's all been so painful, Darla. It hurts more than I could ever tell you. Until I met Randall, I had no family at all. Do you have any idea how many holidays and birthdays I spent alone? I don't mean to come off like 'poor me' or anything, but it's been so tough, knowing that I had a family and four beautiful nieces, and that they were all gone from me, all strangers to me. I used to pray that my sisters would let go of the hate in their hearts—and come find me again—and forgive me. I couldn't understand how they could let all these years go by and not even try—just one more time. I guess in my heart I knew all the reasons they didn't, but frankly, Darla, that didn't make the void in my life any easier to deal with."

"I'm so sorry you were so alone and sad," I said, reaching across the table to hold her hand.

"Alone—but not forgotten, huh?" Rebecca said poignantly. "From what you've told me, it's amazing my ears haven't been burning all these years."

"My friend Victoria told me that you can't heal in absentia. She said that if you came home again, it would be the key to bringing the family back together."

"That's sweet, Darla," she said, squeezing my hand, "but that's also a lot of responsibility to put on my shoulders. Don't you think?"

"Yeah, I guess. I didn't really mean, though, that it was your responsibility."

"I know, kid. I know what you meant," she said, gently pulling her hand away.

"Listen, Aunt Rebecca, after you left Brenda's yesterday, I called my cousins and told them I'd found you."

Rebecca looked alarmed.

"Don't worry. They swore they wouldn't tell anyone. But all three of them begged me to invite you to the family picnic on Saturday. April

411

really wants to know you. She's moving here to New York in a couple of weeks. To attend Juilliard."

"I'd love to meet April, but that'll have to wait until she gets here. I just can't do it, Darla. I just can't go home with you. I'm not ready."

"June told me to beg if you said no."

"Tell June that was a very sweet thing to say. But I still can't come back with you. Absolutely not. I know it's not what you want to hear, but that's the way it is," Rebecca said adamantly, as if she were trying to convince herself rather than me.

I looked down into my soda and poked at the ice cubes.

"Please don't be angry with me, Darla," Rebecca said. She lifted my chin with her right hand. "Look at me. We have so little time left together, and I still want to buy you breakfast tomorrow morning before you leave for home. Please, tell me you're not angry with me."

"I'm not," I said, dropping my chin and stubbornly poking the ice cubes again.

Rebecca grabbed my soda glass and held it close to her. "Do I have to take this glass away to get you to look at me?"

"You sound like my father," I told her.

"God forbid." She laughed. "Listen, kid, I'm just trying to get you to stop sulking."

"I'm not sulking," I said mournfully. "I just wish you'd said yes. That's all."

"Don't argue with me. I know sulking when I see it," Rebecca said with mock sternness. She stood up and held out her left hand to me. "C'mon, kid," she said with a twinkle in her eye, "we've got some more talking to do."

I rose reluctantly from my seat and took her hand. "There's nothing you can say to make me feel better," I warned her.

Rebecca smiled and put her arm around me. "I know, kid, I've been there. Just humor me. I'm gonna give it one hell of a try."

✳ ✳ ✳

I wasn't much fun to be with that last evening in New York. Melanie, Brenda, and Dave did everything they could to cheer me up, but I was overcome with disappointment at Rebecca's refusal to come home with me. I felt as if I'd just read a very long book, only to find that the last chapter had been torn out and that I would never learn what happened to all the characters I'd invested so much time in getting to know.

I also felt very guilty for being so greedy. Surely, finding Rebecca and getting to know her should've been enough for the time being; but no, not me, I had to have it all. Right now. What I wanted and when I wanted it. I was too selfish and immature to understand that Rebecca was frightened and maybe not ready to face her family after all these years apart. And how could I blame her? I'd witnessed firsthand the anger they still held in their hearts. Why was I so willing to throw her to the angry mob? And who knew what Aunt Dodo Bird and her evil broomstick were capable of doing?

When Rebecca picked me up the next morning, I made a minimal effort to hide my despondency, though looking back, I realize that I wanted her to feel every nuance of my pain and suffering.

We left the apartment and began walking uptown to a coffee shop that Brenda had recommended. I said very little, speaking only when Rebecca would point out something in a store window.

"Well, I see your mood hasn't changed since yesterday afternoon," Rebecca said.

"Yes it has," I said, wearing my recalcitrance proudly. "It's gotten worse."

She laughed. "So it has."

We walked the next two blocks in silence.

"You're a loquacious little thing, aren't you?" Rebecca said, smiling.

"What does that mean?" I asked defensively.

"If you talk to me like a normal person," Rebecca baited me, "maybe I'll tell you."

I gave her a dirty look and kept walking. By the time we reached the restaurant, I had achieved a new level of teenage angst, and not even the

413

embarrassment I felt over my childish behavior could snap me out of it. I avoided Rebecca's eyes as she held the door open for me.

"Cheer up, kid!" she told me, as I followed her to the first available booth. "I'm about to make this a happy day for you."

"You are? How so?" I asked suspiciously as we sat down.

"Well, Darla, I've given a lot of thought to what you asked me yesterday. You know, about coming home and all, and about how you and your cousins really want me to be at that party, and how your friend Victoria thinks it will bring the family together, and all that rot. I even had a long talk with Randall about it last night, and he agrees with you. He thinks that my going home is just what the doctor ordered. You know, the missing link in my rehabilitation or something. I don't know. He's a doctoral candidate, kinda in that mind-set where he analyzes everything. Has to, if he wants to put that Ph.D. after his name. Anyway, when I woke up this morning, Randall asked me if I'd made a decision, if I had decided to go home with you."

"Yeah?"

"And I told him that I wasn't going anywhere. I'd slept on it, just like he'd asked me to, but decided that I just couldn't do it. Then, at ten thirty, just as I was dressing James Henry to go to his grandma's, I heard this voice telling me to go. Begging me to go. It kinda gave me the chills. I know a lot of people hear voices telling them to do all kinds of things, but that's never happened to me before. Never."

"Maybe it was one of those angels you told me about the other day," I said enthusiastically. "You know, when you were telling me how you believed the guardian angel of lost teenagers sent Emma and her daughter Suzanne to you. Well, maybe the voice you heard this morning was the guardian angel of long-lost aunts." Eager for her take on the matter, I looked at her, my eyes filled with childlike wonderment, and waited for her response.

She just laughed. "Maybe, Darla. Anyway, I'm not getting on the train with you now. But I will take a train after dinner tonight, and I'll stay at a hotel until the party tomorrow. You're not going to tell them I'm coming, are you?"

414

"No," I said. "April thinks it should be a surprise. And I agree."

Rebecca laughed again. "It gives a whole new meaning to the word. Listen, I'm glad you're not telling them. Don't want to give them time to get their defenses up and to pull out the ammunition—or more importantly, to give themselves a refresher course on all the crap I pulled."

"Are you sure you're not going to change your mind?"

"No, I'm not sure of anything right now. But I don't think I will. That voice I heard was pretty convincing."

"How will I know where to find you?"

"Call me Saturday morning at the Holiday Inn on Chandler."

"What if there's no vacancy and you can't get a room there? Then where will you be?"

"You're a worrywart. You know that? But just so you know, I've already made a reservation. Okay? Feel better? Does that tell you how serious I am about coming?"

"God, Aunt Rebecca, I'm so happy."

"Hope you stay that way, kid. I really do."

CHAPTER 29

When Mom asked me that night at dinner to tell them "every little thing that we did" and not to "leave anything out," it was then that I first learned the true meaning of willpower. It was all I could do not to share my news, which no doubt, would have blasted Mom and Dad into the far reaches of outer space. It seemed a delightfully tempting idea: my parents reeling from shock as they floated in the cosmos, while Aunt Didi and Uncle George, their heads spinning in stupefaction, orbited around them like little lost planets. I was dying to create a parallel scenario right here on earth, but there was no way I was going to ruin the surprise of a lifetime. So, as I savored Mom's spaghetti and meatballs, I recalled the "lowlights" of my trip to New York.

That night, I could barely sleep. I lay wondering if Rebecca had made it to town, then tried to imagine what would happen the following day if and when she braved entrance to the Alexanders' home.

Early Saturday morning, while my parents were safely downstairs chatting over coffee and croissants, I picked up the phone and dialed the Holiday Inn.

"Rebecca Davidson's room, please."

"Hold on while I ring," came the words I wanted to hear.

But when Rebecca answered the phone, sobbing profusely, my anticipation of a happy day flew right out the window.

"Aunt Rebecca? What's the matter?"

"Darla. I just can't go through with it. I can't see them."

"Why?" I asked, clutching the phone cord as if it were her arm.

"I haven't been completely honest with you. Come over here, Room 418, and I'll tell you everything. Please hurry. I'm going crazy being here."

I raced downstairs and asked Mom if I could borrow her car to pay Rachel a visit.

"Maybe tomorrow, Darla," Mom said, wiping a dollop of jam off the table with her napkin. "The party is in a few hours."

"Mom, please! I just called Rachel and she's really, really upset about something. Please, Mom. She's my second closest friend in the world. I have to be there for her! Please!"

"Why don't I drive you over there?" Dad offered.

I was sunk. "Uh, no Dad. 'Cause after I see Rachel, I need to pick up some kind of going-away gift for April. And I don't think you want to go shopping with me. You know how picky I am. And how much time I take. I take forever! I'm really slow!" I said, overdoing it.

"Might as well give her the keys, Maggs." Dad shot me a stern paternal glance. "You just be at this make-up shindig in plenty of time. There's enough to be worked out without explaining why you're late."

"Thanks, Dad! Thanks, Mom!" I said, as I grabbed the car keys and rushed toward the backdoor. "I'll see you later."

Rebecca was an absolute mess. Her eyes were red and puffy, and she was wearing an old, faded NYU nightshirt.

"Sit down," she told me when I entered the room. "Let me get this over with."

"Get what over with?" I asked, reluctantly taking a seat on the bed.

"I need to tell you the real reason that your parents, Didi, and George all hate me so much," Rebecca said, sitting next to me. "I need to tell you why I don't think it's a good idea that I see them. And it's time that you learned just exactly what your parents were afraid might come crashing down on them. And while we're at it, I'll tell you why your old man really hates booze so much, and what mistake your uncle George was sick of being blamed for. Do you think you can handle all that?"

I wasn't sure how to react. I just knew that after years of wanting to know the real truth, the time had come and I felt sick to my stomach.

"You already told me," I said, hoping against hope that I'd already heard the worst of it. "You were a really bad teenager, and you did drugs and drank and stuff, and you cursed a lot, and everyone had to wait up nights to see if you'd make it home alive. Isn't that it?"

"The tip of the iceberg, kid."

I felt my nausea spread to every fiber of my body. I couldn't imagine what else there could be.

Rebecca stood and began pacing furiously around the room. "Darla, my life was a fucking mess! I was one screwed-up kid who didn't know which way was up. She only knew which way was down and she was heading there fast. Down to the pits of hell. And this screwed-up kid had two 'perfect' sisters, and before they were out of their teens, they were engaged to two 'perfect' men. But you know what really got to this kid? Not only was she being chastised and punished at every turn for being so bad, but these four older 'perfect' people seemed to be lording their superior butts over her, night and day, all the time. Pontificating, suffocating bores they were! My God, I hated them!"

Rebecca stopped pacing to see my reaction. She was frightening me and she knew it.

"Anyway, remember that story your mother told you, the one about your dad and his friend Jim Penney?"

"Yeah?"

"Well, what exactly did she tell you?"

"She said that Dad and Jim had been drinking, and then they went out for food or something and got into a car crash."

"And what else?"

"And that Jim died two days later, and that the lady in the other car was pregnant and lost her baby."

"And what else?"

"I dunno. Just that Dad got so scared over what happened that he never took another drink."

"Lie!" Rebecca shouted. "Big fucking lie!"

By this time, my nausea had escalated. This was not the woman I'd met in New York. This was the fabled Rebecca of family lore: a woman worthy of her notorious reputation.

"Ted continued to drink," Rebecca said scathingly. "He continued to drink big time. True, after that day he never got in the car with so much as a drop of alcohol in his system, but I guarantee you, he was still drinking. Drowning his teddy bear sorrows. Drowning his guilt. What a mess Maggie's perfect guy turned out be."

I thought I was going to throw up. I couldn't bear to hear her talk about my father that way, but still, I'd grown close to Rebecca and was worried about her. In a strange way, I felt responsible for her. After all, I was the one who had sought her out and brought her home. How could I not have expected some ill feeling to emerge, after interrupting the apparent idyll of her life in New York, then coaxing her back to the scene of her alleged crimes. And, just maybe, she was right about my father; after all, I'd often felt the same ire toward him myself. But to hear her talk about him that way, I hated it. How dare she? I held my breath and began picking at the loose threads on the bottom of my cut-off jeans. I'm quite sure that Rebecca sensed my anger toward her: the unabashed expression of disgust on my face left little room for doubt. Unfazed, however, she continued her story.

"Well, one night, about a week after the accident," she said, now pacing dizzily in a U-shaped path around the bed, "I went over to Ted and Maggie's apartment. Know why? I wanted to gloat. I wanted to tell this holier-than-thou brother-in-law of mine that he was as fallible as the rest of them—even me. But when I got there, I found the door to their apartment unlocked and nobody home. Then I remembered: Maggie was off at her job taking care of some invalid woman. But where was Ted, I wondered? Well, Teddy Boy was in the bedroom, passed out from booze. Want to know what I did then, Darla?" She stood there, and with an antagonistic stare, boldly challenged my desire to learn the cold, hard truth.

"What?" I snapped resentfully, glaring back at her, then looking down at the rumpled sheets on the bed. I knew that this was no time to cave in to emotion. Besides, I truly did want, no, I needed to know, everything that had happened to my family, and I sensed that this was my only chance to get at the truth. Rebecca had worked herself into a "tell-all" rage, and if I silenced her now, the opportunity would never come again. That much was clear.

Showing signs of wear, she paused in front of me. I could see the anger in her eyes, cleverly camouflaging her shame. "I took my clothes off—I was a slut, you see—and I jumped into bed with your daddy." She was having trouble looking at me and I knew it. Still, she went on. "Then, ever so slowly, I roused him from his drunken sleep, and when a pregnant Maggie came home a half hour later and opened her bedroom door and turned on the lights, what do you think she found?"

I was numb. I looked at her in sheer bewilderment as I tried to wipe away the horrible picture she had just painted. Somehow, I could see beyond the pain in her eyes, and I knew that despite giving a pretty good imitation of it, that she really didn't want to hurt me at all. Rather, she seemed determined to tell me what a hateful person she'd been because she could not accept my loving her any other way.

"Ted was even more surprised than Maggie," she hissed. "He thought your mom had been in bed the whole time, doing the nasty with him. Do you want to hear the rest of the story?

"I guess," I said, feeling lightheaded and unsure of my desire for her to continue.

Rebecca looked at me as if she wanted to make sure I was still breathing before she continued. Apparently satisfied that my destruction was not imminent, she began pacing again, only this time with even greater fury. "Well, you can imagine how popular I was after that roll in the hay. So, when nobody was looking, I packed my stuff and headed off to New York with my friend Tony—the 'shady' college boy."

I noticed that Rebecca could not talk about Tony without referring to him as "the shady college boy," a sardonic jab of sorts to Mom's puritanical way of thinking.

"Anyway, Tony had school to attend, so he couldn't stay, and I, of course, had no reason to go home. That's when I met up with Hector, the scum I told you about who put me up in that rat condo and turned me into a whore."

I became mesmerized as I watched the pain in Rebecca's eyes.

"Well," she said, stopping briefly to accentuate her point. "I wanted my perfect sisters to see how well I was doing. So I called them with my new address, implying through my tears that I wanted them to come to

New York and rescue me. You should have seen their faces when they found me in that squalid hovel. The bird walked around brushing off her clothes, probably wondering the whole time how to get rat shit off the bottom of her designer shoes. Anyway, I threw their prissy butts outta there, feathers and all."

The pacing resumed. "I was so proud of myself for bringing them to New York. Showing them the filth and horror that had become my life was some sort of sick victory to me, as short-lived as it was. Anyhow, about a week later, I was hanging around the outside of the building, talking to one of my charming new neighbors, when who do I see come walking up the street but Georgie Alexander, young lawyer par excellence, come to save poor lost Rebecca. He almost lost his lunch when he saw the building I lived in, and that made me really angry. I just hated it when any of them looked at me like they were so damn superior. So I told Georgie that I had a new place in Greenwich Village, and if he wanted to talk to me, we'd have to do it there, in private. Then I ran to the nearest phone booth, called Hector, and told him I'd come around to his way of doing business and wanted to bring a john to the apartment. Naturally, the slime agreed and had a key left for me at the door."

By this time, I was in such shock that I couldn't do or say anything.

"The apartment was very well stocked," Rebecca continued, "with the very best of scotches, bourbons, cognacs. Whatever tempted your palate. Georgie loved to drink, and being with me made him uncomfortable enough to get very thirsty. I must admit, getting him drunk was a lot easier than I thought. I went into the bathroom, cleaned myself up, and came out in some whore clothing that Hector kept in the closet. I was determined to seduce this son of a bitch if it was the last thing I ever did."

"Oh my God," I whispered.

"I'll spare you the details of how I got your uncle into bed, but suffice it to say, I used every 'trick' in the book."

This must be it, I thought, turning away from Rebecca. The mistake Uncle George was talking about. The one he said he's been paying for ever since.

421

Everything started to make sense. That strange comment Aunt Didi had made to my mother when she said, "At least I didn't punish my husband by refusing to get pregnant again!" So that's why I didn't have any brothers or sisters. Mom was too traumatized by finding Dad in bed with Rebecca to ever get pregnant again. She could have easily had a miscarriage too. I could've died in her womb and it would've been Dad and Rebecca who killed me. My head was spinning, but I could see that Rebecca was finally winding down, exhausted from her trip down Memory Lane.

"Well!" I said angrily, as tears formed in my eyes. "Is that it?"

"Not quite," she said, heaving. "There's still the grand finale. Can you handle it?"

"Gee, Aunt Rebecca, don't hold back now!" I said, almost sarcastically.

Rebecca took a deep breath and leaned against the wall, as if she were trying desperately to lower her blood pressure. Sweat was pouring down her face. "Shortly after Georgie's visit," she said, looking right at me, "I called my sisters. Just happened to find them together at the bird's nest. Sheer luck on my part." Rebecca averted her glance and walked toward the window. She continued to speak as she watched the cars speed by on Chandler Boulevard. "Anyway, Georgie, it turns out, had never come clean about what happened in New York, so I had the honor and privilege of telling my sisters how I seduced him. Didi flew off into a rage unequaled, I'm sure, by her worst of tempers today, and Maggie just cried her eyes out and kept repeating, 'No, this can't be happening!' like some old broken record."

Rebecca turned to face me again. I had shifted my position on the bed in order to see her. She looked at me sadly. "When Didi finally stopped screaming long enough to let me get in another word, I told her that I was pregnant, and that either Ted or Georgie was the father. I just didn't know. They would have to figure it out between them and hold it in their hearts forever that their younger sister had a kid by one of their husbands."

"Oh God."

"So, that's why they never came looking for me, Darla. That's why they kept my parents from finding me. They were afraid of a child. A child who died because his mother was a whore and a drug addict. Imagine, my illegitimate kid crashing into their perfect suburban lives. Maggie's always had an unnatural fear of scandal. You should know that."

Rebecca walked over to me, sat down on the bed, and took my hands in hers. We looked at each other for what seemed to be a very long time. She looked positively exhausted, defeated, as if all the fight had gone out of her. "I've hurt you terribly, Darla," she finally said. "I'm so sorry. But I like and respect you too much to not have told you the truth. You deserve it." She laughed uneasily. "But you sure didn't deserve the show I just put on. Christ, I've got a real swell way of showing that I care, don't I?" She took her right fist and pounded it into her leg. "Damn it, what the hell is wrong with me?" She pounded her leg again. "You know, Darla, sometimes the old Rebecca just takes over. I don't like her very much, but she's a part of me; she helps me to survive in this world. I don't know whether that's good or bad. It's just the way that it is." She sighed in disgust. "Damn, why did I have to tell you every pathetic, hurtful detail? Why did I have to vent my spleen to you? I could have spared you some of this..."

Her voice trailed off. I looked into her eyes. For a moment, I wondered the same thing. "Maybe it was the only way you could heal," I told her, thinking about Victoria and all that she had taught me. "My pain is nothing compared to yours. So don't worry about me, okay?"

She took my hands in hers again. "Aren't you sweet to say that, after what I just put you through. I don't deserve your kindness. Oh, Darla... you cared enough to come find me. You'll never, ever know how much that means to me. I've been waiting for years to be found. Nobody ever came. Nobody except you. I'll always love you for that. I really will. No matter what you think of me now."

A part of me wanted to hate her for the things that she'd done, but I couldn't. There was suddenly something so tender and fragile about her, like a lost puppy who had been abandoned by its owner and couldn't figure out how to find its way home again, or why it wasn't loved. I just sat there watching her. Then she threw herself face down onto the bed, her muffled cries steeped in self-reproach. I didn't know what to do. I just kept telling her that everything would be all right, in the same soothing way Mom had always tried to calm me when I was feeling bad. Finally, Rebecca sat up and looked at me.

"I don't know whatever possessed me to come back here again. I must've been crazy to think they'd accept me after everything I did. Even if it was eighteen years ago, and even if—"

"Even if what?"

"Nothing; it doesn't matter now. The only thing that matters is that I go back to New York and stay out of everyone's lives. Even yours, Darla."

"No! You can't go! You can't! You told me you'd come to the party. And you told me that when I came back to New York, you'd introduce me to my cousin, and to Randall. You promised, Aunt Rebecca."

She shook her head, as if the world had stopped spinning and it didn't even matter. "It seems that breaking my word is the very least of my faults, don't you think?" she said in self-condemnation.

"Stop it!" I demanded, finally asserting myself. "Stop feeling sorry for yourself. Give them a chance to forgive you. Please, Aunt Rebecca. Don't go like this." I grabbed her arm and yanked on it, in the same childish way I had often yanked my mother's arm when I was a child and she and Dad were leaving me at home with a babysitter.

She gently removed my hand from her arm. "I'm sorry, kid. I never should have come. You go now. I need to be alone."

"But—"

"Don't argue with me. Just get the hell out of here...and remember that I love you."

I stood up and looked at her. I started to say something but realized it was futile. Maybe it would have been better had I never found that last chapter to the book. If this is how it was all going to end, I would have been better off just stumbling through my daydreams and wishing for miracles.

I went out to the parking lot and sat in the car. Dad had told me never to drive when I was upset, and that was one mistake I didn't need to make in order to learn from it. So I sat, for a very long time, trying to calm down, until finally, it was time to go to my happy family reunion.

CHAPTER 30

I arrived at my cousins' house about an hour early and was relieved to find April, May, and June alone in the backyard, setting up the picnic table for the party. Aunt Didi, as it turned out, was still at the beauty parlor, and Uncle George was in his study on the telephone.

May was the first one to notice that I was in a terrible state of mind and that I had been crying. She suggested that we all sit down and talk before our parents descended upon us. I explained that I'd just left Rebecca at the hotel, and that I'd finally learned the painful truth about the past, and that she was not coming to the party after all.

April, May, and June looked as if someone had just sucked the life out of them. As synchronistically as they'd learned to smile together on stage, they frowned in unison, and it wasn't until I saw the disappointment on their faces that I realized how much meeting Rebecca had truly meant to them.

I knew the inevitable question "What did she tell you?" was coming, but I still hadn't figured out how to answer it. How could I hurt them by revealing what their father had done, especially now, when family as we knew it was so tenuously held together? How could I tell them any of it, for that matter?

Suddenly, I had the revolting thought that I was being just like my mother, keeping secrets from people I loved because I wanted to protect them. As much as Rebecca's truths had hurt, they had helped at the same time, for I was finally able to make sense of the mystery that had been so much a part of my life and my identity for far too long. Didn't my cousins deserve the same?

The four of us walked over to the large elm tree in the backyard and sat down in the shade. It was then that I gave them fair warning, explaining that the truth wasn't pretty, and that in fact, it was downright devastating, shocking, and horrifying. None of that seemed to matter. My cousins were my kindred spirits and needed to know the truth every bit as much as I had.

They gasped and gulped as I told them Rebecca's sad story, but no one said a word until I got to the part about their father. Even then, they said little more than "Oh God," and when I had finished, we all sat there like department store mannequins—staring at one another with fixed expressions and dead eyes.

"No way!" June finally said, standing up. "No way! Either you're making this up, she's making this up, or you heard her wrong. But no way in hell Daddy slept with Aunt Rebecca!"

"Do you think I liked hearing how Aunt Rebecca slept with my dad?" I asked her. "Are you crazy, June?"

"Well, according to what you said, at least Uncle Ted thought she was Aunt Maggie! But, of course, my father knew exactly what he was doing."

"Do you think that makes it any easier to take?" I asked incredulously.

"How should I know?" June shouted at me. "This is all too sleazy for me to understand."

May bowed her head and started weeping softly. "Why does everything have to be about sex? I always thought sex was supposed to be a beautiful thing. But it's not. It's an ugly thing and it ruins people's lives forever."

April inched closer to May and put her arms delicately around her. They held each other, while June leaned against the tree, glaring down at me, as if I were somehow responsible for the sins of our fathers.

"Why'd you have to tell us this?" June barked at me. "Real good way to start a family reunion party, or whatever the hell this is supposed to be."

April looked up at June. "Don't be angry with Darla for telling us the truth; she's not responsible for what happened in the past. Besides, she warned us the truth would be ugly. You could have walked away if you didn't want to hear it."

"Yeah, right," June snapped. "Sure. Like I could've done that."

"Then don't yell at Darla," May said. "It's not her fault, June. You know that."

"I know," June said, relenting. "I'm sorry. But hearing about Daddy and Aunt Rebecca really makes me sick."

"It makes us all sick," April said, getting up and walking over to June. "But what good is it going to do any of us to argue with each other?" April stood in front of June and put one hand on each of her shoulders. "C'mon, sit down with us. Let's figure out what to do."

June reluctantly consented, and the two of them joined May and me who were still seated on the ground. June picked up a twig and started digging it into the dirt. "In a million years," she said, pouting, as she twisted the stick, "I never thought this would turn out to be Rebecca's big secret."

"I didn't either," May agreed. "It's too hideous."

"But you know," April said, introspectively, "somehow it all kind of makes sense. I've always had the feeling that Mom had something on Dad, and that there had to be a good reason for Mom getting her own way most of the time. I just never thought that this would be it."

"You know the hardest part about this for me?" May said. "The fact that Rebecca was just about my age when this happened. I mean, how could she—"

"I don't know, Sis," April said shaking her head. "But Rebecca's not the only one responsible. It takes two to tango, you know."

"No it doesn't!" May cried. "Not always! You're wrong!"

"May, please. I wasn't talking about...I wasn't talking about what happened with—"

"Don't mention his name to me! Ever!"

"Okay," April said softly, "I'll never mention it again." She picked up a stone and threw it at the back fence. "I don't know why Rebecca did what she did. But it was a long time ago and she's a different person now. I still would've wanted to meet her."

"I guess I would have too," May admitted. "Having her leave like this just makes everything worse. It's not fair that she's going back to New York. Can't you stop her, Darla?"

"She doesn't want to be stopped."

"She wanted to be found all these years," June interjected. "Isn't

428

that what you said? So why wouldn't she want to be stopped from going home? Maybe this is some kind of setup, you know, to test us and see if we really care."

"It's not a setup, June. And I've done everything I could," I said wearily.

"Until everyone forgives each other," May said, "this family is always going to be sick."

"She's right," April said. "I just really wish Rebecca had stayed."

"Don't you guys know how hard I tried to keep her here? Don't you think I wanted her here every bit as much as you do, if not more?" I said, frustrated by what I perceived as a lack of credit for all of my efforts.

"We know," April said reassuringly. "You've done more than any of us could've done."

Our conversation was cut short when Aunt Didi and her new hairstyle appeared in the backyard. She was acting like her old self, as she stood on the patio and waved to us. As soon as we saw her, we got up and headed toward the house. April, May, and June immediately went back to setting the picnic table, and just as I was going to offer my help, I saw Aunt Didi approaching me with a smile almost too big for her face.

"Come here, Darla," she said invitingly. "Can you forgive your big-mouthed aunt for all the horrible things she's said to you and give her a hug?"

"Sure," I said, wondering if I really could. "I forgive you."

"Well, you really deserve more than just a lame apology. I've been blaming you for my own shortcomings as a mother because I didn't want to see that my family wasn't as happy as I might have liked them to be. Sure, you've made some pretty bad mistakes in the past, but who hasn't? That's part of growing up. You've always been a great kid, and you certainly never did anything any dumber than the rest of us have. It was just a lot easier for me to blame you for being the bad seed, than to blame myself for May's unhappiness. And quite frankly, I'm ashamed at some of the things that I said to you, especially that night when—"

"You don't have to say it, Aunt Didi. It's okay."

"No, Darla, the things I've done are not okay. I practically threw you against the wall and split your head open that night! And chasing your mother with a broom? Smashing her clock? Calling you worthless? Threatening to take out a restraining order against your family? All I can do is plead temporary insanity. There's no excuse for my behavior. None at all. I'm going to tell you something else, because I believe you're old enough to understand it. This may surprise you, but your uncle's affair and subsequent request for a divorce were the best things that ever happened to me."

"Really?" I asked, not quite believing my ears.

"Yes, really! It woke me the hell up! You don't think I would've willingly put myself into therapy before that happened, do you? Hell, no! You know how stubborn I can be."

"Muleheaded," I offered.

Aunt Didi laughed. "Your mother taught you that word. And don't try and tell me any differently. I know she did. Speaking of the devil, here are your parents now."

Mom looked absolutely delighted to find Aunt Didi and me engaged in such pleasant conversation, but she could tell from the look on my face that all was not well.

"Are you sick, Darla?" she asked, putting the back of her hand against my forehead to check for fever. "You look a bit flushed."

"I'm fine, Mom," I said, taking a step back. I was in no mood to be fussed over.

"Is everything okay at the Levinsons'?" she pressed.

"I dunno," I said irritably, moving even farther away from her. "I don't want to talk about it now. I'm gonna go help April with the tablecloth."

As I walked away, from the corner of my eye, I saw Mom and Aunt Didi embrace. I stopped for a moment to look at them and to remember how long this day had been in coming and to mourn the time we'd all lost. I glanced over at Dad and saw the sheer delight in his eyes as he witnessed Mom's long overdue reunion with her sister. A few minutes later, Uncle George emerged from the house, and the four of them just hugged each other while the four of us continued to set up the table, moving in silence, our spirits crushed, and unable to share in their apparent joy.

Aunt Didi was in such a good mood that it was almost sickening. Every couple of minutes she would hold onto Uncle George's arm and smile tenderly at him. Then he would return her affection with a big grin and a loving arm around her shoulders.

"You know who they remind me of?" June asked April pensively.

"No. Who?" April asked, ripping open a package of paper napkins.

"You and Ben when you first got together. Remember the way he drooled on you at Darla's house that Christmas?"

"June, he did not drool on me. He may have slightly drooled over me, but he certainly did not drool on me! Who's the ditz in this family? If you don't watch your step, girl, I'm going to have to relinquish my crown to you." April took the stack of paper napkins she had just set out and bopped June on the head with them.

The four of us laughed for the first time that day, but when the fun was over, our smiles quickly faded and we went back to our chores. We weren't planning to eat for quite a while, so there really was no need to set up the table as extensively as we were doing, but we all needed busy work to dull our aching hearts. About twenty minutes later, after we'd done everything at least five times, we decided to retreat back to the tree and leave our parents alone to revel in their togetherness.

"Why don't I get some sodas to bring back with us?" May suggested.

"Sure, May. That would be great," I said tonelessly.

"Darla," May said turning ashen, "is that who I think it is?"

I turned around to see what she was looking at, and there was Rebecca, standing meekly at the side of the house, behind a bush, still looking like the lost puppy trying to find its way home. The adults all had their backs to her and had not yet noticed. My cousins just stood there, staring at Rebecca. I was dizzy with anticipation; Rebecca was only seconds away from being discovered. The tension was unendurable. I felt as if the world were about to blow up, and that I had absolutely no control. My mother, after what could only have been a few seconds, looked over at us and blanched.

"Darla! What in the world?" she said, clutching her throat.

431

I said nothing. Slowly, Mom turned to see what we were looking at and practically choked herself to death when she saw Rebecca.

Dad and Uncle George looked at each other in utter astonishment, while Aunt Didi put one hand on each side of her head, as if to keep it from popping off her neck like a just-loosened champagne cork, premature in its flight.

My mother, nearly frozen in disbelief, looked cautiously at the others, as if to establish that everyone was seeing the same thing that she was. Convinced that her little sister was not an apparition, Mom ran toward her with open arms. "Rebecca!" she cried. "Oh, honey you've come home to us. You'll never know how I've prayed for this day!"

I was not sure how Rebecca would respond. For a moment, she hesitated and stepped back, but then, not able to resist my mother's outstretched arms and loving words, moved toward her. I had never seen anything so passionate in all my life as the embrace between my mother and Aunt Rebecca. For all the tears through all the years, for all the secrets and all the pain, there was more love there than I could possibly have imagined, or possibly have wished for. For me, it was proof that love was more powerful than the darkness that covered it; stronger than the resentment that refused to see it. That day I saw love in its purest form: Mom and Aunt Rebecca, for those moments—letting go, of every grudge, of every reason to turn away, of every "she said, she did," of every ugliness that divides a family and crushes the human spirit. Mom did not want to let go of Rebecca. Every few moments, she'd pull back slightly, as if to make sure she was real. Then, with small, delicate strokes, Mom would caress her hair, then hug her again. Rebecca, like a sick child who had collapsed in her mother's arms, accepted her sister's love with no hesitation, and with a long, overdue need to be loved.

Slowly, it began to dawn on Aunt Didi, Dad, and Uncle George that Rebecca's appearance was not quite the shock to us that it was to them. After all, from the tears in our eyes it was very obvious that we knew exactly who she was, and never having seen a picture of her, it would have been difficult to recognize her had we not had some involvement with her return.

The three of them kept looking at us, then looking at Mom and Rebecca, who were still a good distance from the others. After several minutes, Mom took Rebecca by the hand and slowly led her over to Aunt Didi.

Aunt Didi and Rebecca stood there, facing each other with tears in their eyes, not moving a muscle, not saying a word. Aunt Didi finally turned to look briefly at Uncle George, then turned back to Rebecca. My heart was pounding. Every second was torture. All eyes were upon them. Mom stood there beaming with joy, begging them with her eyes to embrace one another.

"Oh, what the hell!" Aunt Didi choked out. "Welcome home, little sister. I've missed you. Really."

"I've missed you too, Dodo Bird," I heard Rebecca say softly, and the two of them embraced.

My cousins and I shared a look as we watched the chaos intensify in our fathers' eyes. We had no idea what they were feeling, and much less of an idea of what they might do.

"Good to see you, honey," Dad said with effort, putting his arms around Rebecca and giving her a squeeze. "I mean that; I'm very happy you're here with us."

Rebecca smiled quickly and nervously, then looked briefly at her other brother-in-law.

"I second that," Uncle George said with dubious assurance, fully cognizant that all eyes were upon him. "I'm very glad you've found your way back to us." He nodded pleasantly, then downed a swill of his drink.

"Can we meet her now?" June asked me, breaking the awkward silence that followed.

"Sure," I said, and my cousins followed single file as I walked over to greet Rebecca.

"Oh, Darla!" Rebecca cried as she threw her arms around me, to the absolute shock of the adults. "I just couldn't leave."

"I'm so glad you didn't," I said, squeezing her as hard as I could.

"I was on my way home. I really was," she explained, once our embrace was broken. "But when I got downstairs to the hotel lobby, and the cab driver asked me where I was going, I heard that voice again, and it was telling me to stay. Without even realizing it, I gave him this address."

My only regret at that moment was that I didn't have a camera to record the various looks of incredulity and bewilderment on my family's faces. I suppose it wasn't very nice of me to so thoroughly enjoy the one-upmanship that I had on them at that moment. But after having been tortured by their secrets for so many years, I was actually delighted to let them twist in the wind while Rebecca and I talked as if we were old friends.

"Aunt Rebecca, this is June, April, and that's May."

One by one, my cousins embraced her while our parents took turns looking at each other as if to say, "What the hell is going on here?"

After the introductions had been made to my cousins, Rebecca put her arm around me and smiled. "If the four of you haven't figured it out yet, Darla and I met in New York," she said.

All eyes were focused on me.

"Darla and her friend Melanie turned New York City upside down to find me," Rebecca said, and squeezed my shoulder.

Dad looked at me as if I had three heads and was sprouting a fourth. "Really now?"

"Don't be angry with her, Ted," Rebecca said, making a halting gesture with her right hand. "I've already read her the riot act. I've told her what a stupid thing it was to do." She looked at me. Her voice softened. "But I'd be lying if I told you I wished she hadn't. The day Darla found me was the best day of my life."

"Aunt Rebecca is married and she has a little boy," I blurted out. "He's almost two! James Henry. After Grandpa Henry."

"Is that the only child you have, Rebecca?" Aunt Didi asked her.

Rebecca and I shared a look. Then, one by one, she looked at the four lost souls who had been waiting almost eighteen years to hear her answer that question.

"Yes. James Henry is the only child I have. He's the only child I've ever given birth to."

A collective exhalation of bated breath filled the air.

"The sigh of relief heard 'round the world," April whispered too loudly to June.

Everyone turned to look at April and within seconds, broke up laughing. My parents, as well as Aunt Didi and Uncle George, were so happy to hear Rebecca's news that they failed to realize just what an "informed" joke April had made. Moments later, when the laughter subsided, I could see the question marks return to their faces.

Rebecca looked at me, then at everyone else. Pausing first to collect herself, she said: "I've told Darla everything. I told her this morning. She was quite upset, and I would assume she's since shared the details of my lurid past with her cousins. Am I right, kid?"

I nodded.

Aunt Didi looked at the girls, then turned to me. "You told them every—"

"We know, Mom," June said. "Everything."

Uncle George practically dropped his drink, turning several shades of crimson.

"It's okay, Daddy," April told him. "We'll work it out. I'm not going to tell you that the truth wasn't hard for us to hear, because that would be a lie. But it won't stop us from loving you."

"April's right, Daddy," May said tearfully, as June shook her head affirmatively.

"I wish I could believe that," Uncle George said sadly. "But knowing what I did back then...well, it's got to change things."

"Well, of course it changes things." April turned to look at her mother. "We're more than a stage act. We're human beings with feelings. How could this not affect us deeply?" She looked at her father again. "This was a major blow for us, you know, but we'll work on it...we'll deal with it," April said wisely. "Each in our own way...each in our own time."

Uncle George attempted to smile and Aunt Didi looked embarrassed by April's intentional dig at her. As for me, at that moment, I had never been more proud of my cousin and was so amazed by how much she'd grown up.

"Right now," April continued, still addressing her father, "you just need to know that we'll always love you, no matter what. What you did a long time ago doesn't change the fact that you've been a wonderful father to us."

May and June, still distraught over the news, managed to nod in agreement.

I saw Uncle George swallow the lump in his throat. He put his drink down, embraced April, then June and May. I looked at my own father and wanted to cry as I saw the look of shame spread across his face. I walked over and hugged him, and he held me so tight I could barely breathe, but he could not look at me.

"Maybe we'd better move this party to the living room," Aunt Didi said. "I've already donated my share of grist to the neighborhood rumor mill. C'mon, everyone grab something and we'll set up indoors."

It took little time for the nine of us to transfer the party to more private quarters inside. Once the party fixings had been rearranged, we took our seats in the living room and listened intently as Rebecca updated the family on her life. I observed my parents and my aunt and uncle closely as they reacted to her story. I could sense the "I knew its," the "I told you sos," and the alternating pangs of guilt as Rebecca explained to them how her willful abandon had led her to a cruel life of prostitution. And I cheered silently as word of Rebecca's accomplishments made a mockery of their boundless speculations about her sojourn into squalor.

"I'm so proud of you, honey," Mom said, as Rebecca neared the end of her story. "Just so proud. You've come so far and have done so well. I just thank God for that woman Emma and her daughter Suzanne. I don't even like to think what would've happened to you had she not...oh, you poor thing."

"We never stopped wondering," Aunt Didi said gratuitously.

"But you never wondered enough to look for me, did you?" Rebecca ventured to ask. I could see the resentment in her eyes.

Aunt Didi turned her head and covered her mouth, in almost the exact manner that Rebecca had the first day I met her. She paused for several seconds before speaking.

"What can I say to Rebecca?" Aunt Didi said with lazy compassion. "What do you want to hear? That my cowardice was stronger than my love for you?"

"If that's the truth," Rebecca said stoically.

"I don't know what the truth is," Aunt Didi said, raising her hands, palms up, into the air. "My God, Rebecca, it's not that easy to slap a name on what we were feeling. You must understand fear better than any of us. You know how it snowballs until it becomes larger than life."

"At least you all had each other," Rebecca said, sinking into her pain. "I was so alone for so long."

"I don't know what to say," Aunt Didi finally said. "We may not have looked for you, but we never stopped thinking about you."

I cringed as Aunt Didi spoke. I couldn't help but think how meaningless her words must've sounded to Rebecca.

"From what Darla told me," Rebecca said, baiting her, "you and Maggie thought about me quite a bit. I hear you even fought over me, blaming each other for what happened to me."

"Rebecca," Aunt Didi said inflexibly, "this is truly the first day that Maggie and I have been civil to each other in almost fourteen months. Don't ask us to rehash that stuff now. We've agreed to bury the past."

"Not before one final exhumation, Didi," Rebecca said boldly. "That's the way it's gotta be. I deserve that. So do you, for that matter. Now, tell me: do you still think it's Maggie's fault that I turned out as I did?"

"Well, not exactly her 'fault.' Of course not!" Aunt Didi said with an air of expertise on the matter. "But I do think that she was more than instrumental in getting Mom to put an end to the singing, and, well, I think that loss in your life greatly contributed to your downfall. Singing and putting on shows meant everything to you. When that was taken away, everything fell apart. Your dreams, everything."

Rebecca sat back in her chair, crossed her arms, and looked at Aunt Didi as if she'd just said the most absurd thing in the world. "Just how many dreams do you think I had at eleven years old, Didi? For that matter, how many did you have at that age?"

Suddenly, Aunt Didi wasn't so sure of herself. "Well, I guess I don't really know how to answer your question." She looked down at the bowl of potato chips on the coffee table in front of her, plucked a chip from the bowl, then shoved it into her mouth, as if that would excuse her from having to respond any further.

Rebecca rolled her eyes and turned to face Mom. "And how about you, Maggie? Do you think that Didi's innocent choreography and silly handmade costumes are what corrupted my morals?"

"Well, that is what I've always thought," Mom said weakly. "Didi did teach you how to flaunt your body at a very young and inappropriate age."

I looked at Dad and Uncle George, who hadn't contributed a word to the conversation. They kept looking at each other, then down at their shoes.

"Well, let me tell you something," Rebecca said authoritatively. "You're both dead wrong! Like a couple of dumb dogs, you've been barking up the wrong tree your entire lives, blaming each other for the demise of my soul, for my descent into hell. Really, Didi, I can't believe you could honestly think that the absence of your stagemothering was what destroyed me. Geez, if anything, it gave me room to breathe. It's not that I didn't appreciate your efforts at times, but you were a royal pain in the ass. One thing is for certain, though, I sure didn't sell my body to the lowest bidder because I missed our little song-and-dance routines. Really, get a life!"

"Rebecca!" Aunt Didi shot back. "Don't you understand that when bad things happen, people look for reasons? Little girls don't just turn into foul-mouthed sluts at the age of eleven, especially when they're raised in the kind of home you were raised in. And since 'the demise of your soul,' as you call it, happened shortly after the demise of our 'little song-and-dance routines,' how can you blame me for finding a connection there? Where else was I supposed to look?"

Rebecca looked at her as if she were too frustrated to continue. "Well, there was no connection. That's all."

"Oh, goodness," Mom said, then sighed. "Who can understand any of this?"

"I don't know what to say to you all," Rebecca said wearily. "I've hurt each and every one of you so much. If it makes anyone feel better, I've paid for my mistakes with years of misery."

"That doesn't make us happy," Uncle George said, surprising everyone by joining in. "We never wanted you to be miserable. We just wanted to know why."

"That's right," my father echoed bravely. "We wanted to know why."

All eyes turned to Rebecca, who lowered her head sadly as she was once again compelled to journey back in time. I wanted to go over and comfort her, but I felt as if there was something else she needed to say, and I didn't want to lose the moment.

"They're right, honey," Mom said. "We just wanted to know why."

Rebecca paused at length before answering. Finally, she looked up and turned to face Mom. "Because I was bad, Maggie. What other reason do you want? How can I blame my behavior on anyone else? Nobody forced me to jump into bed with Ted or to seduce George—and to do it when both of you were pregnant, you with Darla and Didi with May. There's no way to sugarcoat it. I was a monster."

"So why did you do it, honey? What made you become that monster?"

Rebecca's eyes filled with rage. I could see something happening in her mind. She began clutching at her head and rocking, in the same intense way that May had after the attack. I felt an eerie and sickening sense of déjà vu. I looked around the room. Everyone else seemed as frightened as I was.

"Somebody hurt you, didn't they, Aunt Rebecca!" May shouted. "I can tell. Someone hurt you real bad, didn't they? Just like Hatch hurt me!"

Rebecca looked at May and burst into tears. May ran over to her and the two of them huddled together as if they were old friends.

"Good Lord, is she right?" Aunt Didi asked Rebecca. "Did somebody...hurt you?"

"I was raped!" Rebecca screamed. "When I was just ten and a half! And he kept raping me, and raping me, and raping me until I was sixteen, and by that time, I was letting everyone else in town do the same!"

"Oh, Lord, no!" Mom screamed. "Tell me this didn't happen. Please!"

"Who was it?" Uncle George scowled. "Tell me the son of a bitch who did it. If he's still alive, I'll kill him!"

Rebecca turned to Uncle George and Dad. "You want to know why I hated my sisters so bad? Because I wanted revenge. When I was fourteen, I asked this rapist why he had chosen me, and not my sisters. And do you know what he said? 'Because Deirdre and Margaret already have their men, Rebecca, and you're all alone. You can't be the only girl in the family without a man. That's why you need me. I'll be good to you, too.'"

Rebecca turned to Mom and Aunt Didi. "I hated you because you were protected and I wasn't. And I hated you because I thought you knew what he was doing, and that you didn't care. That's what he led me to believe, and that's why I did what I did. I wanted to get you back. I wanted you all to pay for what that pig did to me. I didn't know how to hurt him, so I hurt you. I wanted to tell Mom what he was doing. I thought maybe she could tell me why it was happening. But he told me that her heart was weak and she'd die if I ever said a word. He said Dad would die too, and it would be all my fault. I would be a murderer, and I would be locked up forever for killing my parents!"

"This is too unbelievable," Aunt Didi said, dizzy from the revelation. "So why in God's name didn't you tell us later? When you were old enough to understand what had happened to you? Don't you think it would've made all the difference in the world?"

Rebecca shook her head. "I didn't think there was anything I could tell you that would change what I did. I just thought you'd hate me even more and accuse me of trying to pass the blame onto someone else. That pig ruined my life. Do you know that I still have trouble looking at myself in the mirror?"

"It's not your fault, Aunt Rebecca," May sobbed. "You didn't do anything wrong. He did. The child molester! The rapist!"

Aunt Didi looked at May and started crying. "That's right, baby. It's not her fault at all."

"Who did this to you?" Mom pleaded with Rebecca. "Please tell us."

Rebecca was hysterical. "Do you know what that pig used to call me, Maggie?"

"No, honey, what? Tell us. What did he call you?"

"He called me his one-in-a-million girl!" Rebecca screamed. "His goddamn one-in-a-million girl."

There was a deathly silence in the room as it registered with each and every one of us what we'd just heard. The collective scrambling to put the pieces together had ended. There was no doubt whatsoever who had hurt Rebecca.

"Martin?" Mom said softly. "Uncle Martin raped you? For all those years?"

Rebecca nodded and curled up in a ball on the couch as she continued to cry. Mom tried desperately to console her, while April put her arms around May, who was also wrapped in pain. We were all lost. So lost. So baffled. So angry at what one evil man had done to our family. So amazed at how one man's sickness could permeate all of our lives so completely, so thoroughly, and turn one dear little child into her own kind of monster, just to protect herself. It was too awful to imagine, too unspeakable, too terrifying, and oh so dreadfully sad. So many odd and disparate thoughts crossed my mind. What would Melanie say, realizing that she had dressed up like a rapist for Halloween? Had Uncle Martin raped other little girls too? Was he still raping them, and if so, how could we stop him? Could he still be tried for his crimes against Rebecca? Did Maudie know? How could Rebecca have kept such a burden to herself all of these years? What would Uncle George do now? Could my family truly forgive Rebecca? Could Rebecca forgive herself? Could she forgive my family for not trying harder to find her? Would we finally be able to heal, now that we were together, just as Victoria had predicted?

I watched Uncle George as he poured another drink. How ironic, I thought. Just days ago, Uncle George's hard work had helped the police

441

to track down one child molester, Hatch, and now there was another one out there for Uncle George to pursue, his wife's uncle, who had been at large for years, and whom Uncle George himself had sat down to dinner with just a few years ago. I prayed that Uncle George wouldn't let another obsession wear him down, especially now when he and Aunt Didi were finally getting back together, but I hoped that Uncle Martin would pay dearly for what he had done.

We stayed together until almost eleven o'clock that night. It took a long time for the tears to dry, but when they did, somehow, miraculously, the laughter found its way back into our hearts. I don't believe that I can remember a time as wonderful as later that evening, a time when everyone was so at peace, so in tune with one another, and so grateful for the opportunity to be together and to call each other family.

Rebecca decided that she would like to stay the night at our house and suggested, much to my delight, that the next day, before she left for New York, the two of us should go to the nursing home to visit Victoria. Neither of us could think of a more perfect way to give Victoria the good news, and Rebecca wanted to personally thank the woman who had guided me so wisely through my pain, and who, so prophetic in her wisdom, had played such a vital role in bringing her home.

He called during breakfast the next morning, just as the four of us were happily planning another reunion in the not-too-distant future. He said that his name was Geoffrey Ashbury and that he regretted to inform me that his mother had died of a massive heart attack that Friday morning. He said that he was very sorry not to have called me earlier but that he had not known how to reach me, until he went through his mother's papers at the nursing home and found a letter specifically requesting that I be called in the event of her death. He wanted me to know that his mother had bequeathed to me several pieces of her favorite jewelry, then read me a message that she had left for me:

Dearest Darla,

Your friendship is the most precious gift that I have received in a very long time. Please do not cry too many tears for me, but remember me, and see my love for you in everything you do, and feel my hope for your happiness, in times of despair, which I hope are very few. Wherever I go now, I will be thinking of you, and I am sure that someday we will meet again, though that day will be long in coming. In the meantime, dear child, please accept a few of my treasures as a small token of the deep love and affection that I have for you. I am with God now, and I am happy. It is just where I want to be.

All my love, Victoria.

To say that I was devastated would be inadequate. I was sobbing so loudly that I could barely hear or understand what was being said to me. Victoria's death was such a terrible, unexpected shock to me. I had been planning to visit her, just a few hours later that very same day, and now she was gone and I would never see her again. I asked him what time she had died, and he told me that it had been approximately ten thirty Friday morning. He then asked me if I would care to attend her funeral, which would be held on Monday morning, at St. Anne's, and promised he would bring Victoria's note with him so I could have it to keep. He said that he would look forward to meeting me. Then he started to cry and had to hang up the phone.

The four of us sat at the table, holding hands and sobbing. I had never seen Dad cry such big tears, and Rebecca, although she had never met Victoria, was totally crushed by her death. Mom wanted to know everything that Victoria's son had told me, so I repeated his words the best I could.

"Goodness, how very sad," she said, blotting her tears with a paper napkin. "She was such a dear, sweet woman. I'm so glad we had the opportunity to know her."

"When did Mr. Ashbury say that she died?" Dad asked.

"On Friday morning. Around ten thirty," I managed to choke out.

"You were probably packing to come home then," Mom said sadly.

At that moment, a look of complete astonishment came over

Rebecca's face. "Oh Darla, I can't believe it."

"What is it, Aunt Rebecca?" I asked, grabbing her wrist.

"Don't you remember what I told you the other day? About hearing that voice? The one that told me to go home? It was right around ten thirty on Friday; I know it was. I was dressing James Henry to go to his grandma's, and I looked at the clock because I was afraid I'd be late to meet you. It was just around ten thirty, and I remember thinking, Oh, good, I have plenty of time to make it to Brenda's. And yesterday, just as I was about to tell the cab driver to take me to the train, I heard that same voice again. It told me to stay and work things out, and that if I didn't, I would never be free, nor would my family. It was so powerful, and so convincing, yet so gentle as it touched my heart. I should've been afraid, 'cause I've never really believed in those things, but I wasn't. Do you think that Victoria could have been the guardian angel we spoke of?"

"You mean the guardian angel of long-lost aunts?" I asked incredulously.

"Yeah, kid, that one. What do you think?"

Mom clutched her throat in slow motion. Rebecca and I shared a look, not knowing if we should laugh or cry.

"I really believe it was Victoria who sent me home to heal," Rebecca said. "It was her last gift to you, Darla. To all of us."

Everyone looked at me, but I had no words. I was so overcome with grief, yet so filled with joy in knowing that miracles can happen. I believed with all my heart that Victoria had sent Rebecca home, and I realized, at that moment, that we should never be afraid of pushing our imaginations to the limit, for it is precisely there that the truth may lie, and only with the truth can we heal our pain and feel our spirits soar again, just as mine was soaring in that terrible moment of pain.

Rebecca decided to stay until Monday afternoon so that she could attend Victoria's funeral. As I sat in the church with my parents, Rebecca, and May, I paid a silent tribute to Victoria and recalled, one by one, all the lessons that she had taught me. Lessons about love. Lessons about forgiveness. And lessons about joining together to heal the pain that touches us all.

I decided then that I would find a place to send my pain and suffering. It would be a place where denial would live and where untold secrets couldn't hurt anyone, even if they grew uglier and meaner with the passage of time. It would be a home for the hatred in our hearts that thrives without reason; for grudges born from incidents no one can remember. It would be a place to keep the lies and half-truths and a place to discard the regrets, the self-incrimination and the self-deprecation that we so often torture ourselves with. It would be a land of make-believe, and I would call it Squalor, New Mexico.

The End